"Victoria Th[...]
Anne Perry and C[...]
—Tamar Myers, auth[...]

Praise for the Edgar® Award–nominated
Gaslight Mystery series

MURDER ON MARBLE ROW

"Victoria Thompson has crafted another Victorian page-turner." —Robin Paige, author of *Death in Hyde Park*

"Cleverly plotted . . . provides abundant fair play and plenty of convincing period detail. This light, quick read engages the readers' emotions." —*Publishers Weekly*

"Engaging characters . . . an enjoyable read."
—Margaret Frazer, author of *The Hunter's Tale*

"Victoria Thompson has a knack for putting the reader inside her character's heads, and her detailed descriptions of New York at the turn of the century bring the setting vividly to life." —Kate Kingsbury, author of *Paint by Number*

"Each novel in the Gaslight Mystery series just keeps getting better . . . [*Murder on Marble Row*] is well executed and the ending will come as a complete surprise."
—*Midwest Book Review*

MURDER ON MULBERRY BEND

"An exciting intrigue of murder, deception, and bigotry. *Gangs of New York* eat your heart out—this book is the real thing." —*Mystery Scene*

"A thrilling, informative, challenging mystery."
—*The Drood Review*

continued . . .

"There are few mysteries set back in history that I enjoy reading. This mystery series is one of those. The characters and settings are so real . . . I highly recommend this book and series."
—*The Best Reviews*

MURDER ON ASTOR PLACE
Nominated for the Best First Mystery Award
by *Romantic Times* Magazine

"Victoria Thompson is off to a blazing start with Sarah Brandt and Frank Malloy in *Murder on Astor Place*. I do hope she's starting at the beginning of the alphabet. Don't miss her first tantalizing mystery."
—Catherine Coulter,
New York Times bestselling author

"A marvelous debut mystery with compelling characters, a fascinating setting, and a stunning resolution. It's the best mystery I've read in ages."
—Jill Churchill, author of
The Merchant of Menace

MURDER ON ST. MARK'S PLACE
Nominated for the Edgar® Award

"Lovers of history, mystery, and romance won't be disappointed. Exciting . . . will hold the reader in thrall."
—*Romantic Times*

MURDER ON GRAMERCY PARK

"The inclusions of [historical] facts make this novel . . . superior to most of those found in the subgenre . . . The lead protagonists are a winning combination." —*BookBrowser*

MURDER ON WASHINGTON SQUARE

"Victoria Thompson's Gaslight Mysteries are always . . . exciting treats to read."
—*BookBrowser*

MURDER ON
MARBLE ROW

A Gaslight Mystery

Victoria Thompson

BERKLEY PRIME CRIME, NEW YORK

THE BERKLEY PUBLISHING GROUP
Published by the Penguin Group
Penguin Group (USA) Inc.
375 Hudson Street, New York, New York 10014, USA
Penguin Group (Canada), 10 Alcorn Avenue, Toronto, Ontario M4V 3B2, Canada
(a division of Pearson Penguin Canada Inc.)
Penguin Books Ltd., 80 Strand, London WC2R 0RL, England
Penguin Group Ireland, 25 St. Stephen's Green, Dublin 2, Ireland (a division of Penguin Books Ltd.)
Penguin Group (Australia), 250 Camberwell Road, Camberwell, Victoria 3124, Australia
(a division of Pearson Australia Group Pty. Ltd.)
Penguin Books India Pvt. Ltd., 11 Community Centre, Panchsheel Park, New Delhi—110 017, India
Penguin Group (NZ), Cnr. Airborne and Rosedale Roads, Albany, Auckland 1310, New Zealand
(a division of Pearson New Zealand Ltd.)
Penguin Books (South Africa) (Pty.) Ltd., 24 Sturdee Avenue, Rosebank, Johannesburg 2196,
South Africa

Penguin Books Ltd., Registered Offices: 80 Strand, London WC2R 0RL, England

This is a work of fiction. Names, characters, places, and incidents either are the product of the author's imagination or are used fictitiously, and any resemblance to actual persons, living or dead, business establishments, events, or locales is entirely coincidental.

MURDER ON MARBLE ROW

A Berkley Prime Crime Book / published by arrangement with the author

PRINTING HISTORY
Berkley Prime Crime hardcover edition / June 2004
Berkley Prime Crime mass-market edition / June 2005

Copyright © 2004 by Victoria Thompson.
Cover design by Rita Frangie.
The Edgar® name is a registered service mark of the Mystery Writers of America, Inc.

All rights reserved.
No part of this book may be reproduced, scanned, or distributed in any printed or electronic form without permission. Please do not participate in or encourage electronic piracy of copyrighted materials in violation of the author's rights. Purchase only authorized editions.
For information address: The Berkley Publishing Group,
a division of Penguin Group (USA) Inc.,
375 Hudson Street, New York, New York 10014.

ISBN: 0-425-19870-7

Berkley Prime Crime Books are published by The Berkley Publishing Group,
a division of Penguin Group (USA) Inc.,
375 Hudson Street, New York, New York 10014.
The name BERKLEY PRIME CRIME and the BERKLY PRIME CRIME design are trademarks belonging to Penguin Group (USA) Inc.

PRINTED IN THE UNITED STATES OF AMERICA

10 9 8 7 6 5 4 3 2

If you purchased this book without a cover, you should be aware that this book is stolen property. It was reported as "unsold and destroyed" to the publisher, and neither the author nor the publisher has received any payment for this "stripped book."

To my terrific editor, Ginjer Buchanan. This one's for you!

Gaslight Mysteries by Victoria Thompson

I

FRANK DIDN'T ACTUALLY HEAR THE EXPLOSION THAT morning. He was down in the neighborhood known as Hell's Kitchen, collecting a drunk who had murdered the bartender who refused to keep serving him after he'd run out of money. The moment Frank entered Police Headquarters a couple hours later, he knew something had happened, though. The place seemed to hum with tension, and before Frank could even think to wonder at it, the desk sergeant called his name.

"Commissioner Roosevelt hisself wants to see you, laddie," the sergeant said knowingly.

Frank glanced around and noticed that the cluster of cops who had been talking in hushed tones had fallen silent and were all staring at him. Not one was smiling. This wasn't good.

"What's he want to see me for?" he tried.

The sergeant just shrugged. "He don't confide in me. Just said to send you up the minute you come in."

Frank figured the sergeant knew perfectly well what Roosevelt wanted, and so did everyone else in the building. The only way Frank was going to find out was by going upstairs, though.

Trying to appear unconcerned, he walked slowly and purposefully to the stairway and began the climb up to the second floor, where Police Commissioner Theodore Roosevelt had his office. Teddy wasn't the only commissioner, of course. He just liked for people to forget about the other three. He was usually successful at doing so, too, except when the others managed to stymie his attempts at reform and the press gleefully reported it.

Frank had to admit that Roosevelt had managed to make a few real reforms in the department. Teddy and that reporter friend of his, Jacob Riis, enjoyed prowling the streets at night to make sure the police were doing their duty. A lot of worthless beat cops had been fired when the two men found them sleeping on the job. Others had been given the sack for being too blatantly corrupt. Roosevelt had also promoted the men he felt had earned the honor. This was a huge change from the old system, where promotions had been bought and paid for. Frank himself had been saving for years to buy himself the rank of Captain.

He wasn't planning to spend that money on something else yet, though. Roosevelt's changes had made for good newspaper copy, but as soon as he was gone, his reforms would likely go, too. With no one to stop them, the police department would return to business as usual. That day was probably coming sooner rather than later, since Roosevelt had campaigned vigorously for McKinley, who had been elected president four weeks ago. The new president would be handing out political appointments to his supporters the minute he took office next year, and everyone knew Roosevelt would be among them. Frank had already felt the rumblings as everyone on the force tried to figure out what was going to happen to them when Teddy and his progressive ideas left New York for Washington.

Frank had reached Roosevelt's office, and he stepped inside with more boldness than he felt. Roosevelt's secretary, a dark-haired Irish girl named Minnie Kelly, looked up from her type writing.

"Commissioner Roosevelt is expecting you, Detective Sergeant," she informed him before he could say a word. No smile lit her pretty face.

"What's he want?" he tried again.

"Didn't you hear what happened this morning? The explosion?"

"What explosion?"

Miss Kelly frowned. "I don't know much about it. You'd better let the commissioner explain." She got up and hurried to Roosevelt's door to let him know Frank had arrived.

Frank sighed. Nothing good came from hiring women. Miss Kelly was the first and only female secretary in the history of the department, another one of Roosevelt's reforms. Roosevelt was probably satisfied with her work, but Frank couldn't help thinking a *man* would have given him the buzz and not let him go into the boss's office blind.

"Go right in," Miss Kelly instructed him before he could feel any sorrier for himself.

Roosevelt sat behind his impressive desk. He wasn't a large man, but his personality was so big, you hardly noticed his size. He grinned at Frank, revealing teeth too large for his face.

"Dee-lighted to see you, Malloy," he exclaimed. Even though he was sitting perfectly still, energy seemed to radiate from him, electrifying the room. "Close the door, will you? Don't want to bother Miss Kelly, do we?"

Frank wasn't sure whether they did or not, but he closed the door just the same.

"Terrible thing, just terrible," Roosevelt was saying, peering through his pince-nez at what was apparently a report of some kind. "Dreadful way to die."

"The explosion?" Frank said, figuring he should say something and not sure exactly what was expected.

"A bomb, they think," Roosevelt said, looking up at Frank again.

"A *bomb*?" he echoed in amazement. The city was full of factories with machinery that exploded from time to time, killing hapless immigrant workers. He'd assumed that was what Miss Kelly's remark had meant. "Where was it? What happened?" he demanded, forgetting for a moment that he was addressing the Commissioner of Police.

"Didn't anyone tell you?" Roosevelt asked, mildly annoyed. "Sit down, sit down." He motioned to the two chairs facing his desk, and Frank obediently took one. "It happened this morning, around nine o'clock. Mr. Gregory Van Dyke owns some factories here in the city. He'd just arrived at his office uptown, and the place exploded. Blew him to pieces. Nearly killed his secretary, too, poor fellow."

Frank was picturing the scene. Bombs were merciless, and the human body had no defense against them. He had a hundred questions, but he figured Roosevelt wouldn't know any of the answers, at least this early in the investigation. "Do they have any idea who planted the bomb?"

"Anarchists, I'm sure," Roosevelt said, waving the problem away with his hand. "No successful man is safe from them. You know what they did to Henry Frick."

Everyone knew about Henry Clay Frick. When his workers in Pittsburgh had gone on strike, Frick hired Pinkerton detectives to break the strike. The workers had been slaughtered, and in retaliation, some Russian anarchist had shot Frick. In the ass. Not a fatal wound and hardly comparable to a bomb exploding. He decided not to point this out to Roosevelt, though. "Did Mr. Van Dyke have problems with his workers?"

"Every employer has problems with his workers, but nothing out of the ordinary that I know of. Anarchists don't need a reason, though, do they? Killing a wealthy man is enough. Sends a warning to others and all that poppycock."

He was probably right. Frank hadn't given the matter much thought. He didn't particularly want to give it any thought now, either, and he still had no idea why Roosevelt had told him all this. "Was Mr. Van Dyke a friend of yours?" he guessed.

Roosevelt's perpetual grin faded. "An *old* friend. Known him all my life. Families were close."

Of course. *Van Dyke* and *Roosevelt* were names that dated back to the original Dutch settlers, the ones they called Knickerbockers. All those families had known each other for generations.

Decker was another of those names, one Frank tried not to remember.

"I'm sorry," Frank said politely. "That's a hard way to lose a friend."

"And that's why I want you to investigate this, Detective Sergeant."

Frank tried not to react, but he wasn't entirely successful.

"Don't be so surprised, Malloy," Roosevelt said. "You've proven yourself to be a man who can be trusted to handle difficult situations discreetly. You also aren't afraid of the truth, no matter where you must go to find it."

"You're sure anarchists killed Mr. Van Dyke," Frank reminded him. "Solving the case won't need much discretion. Or much courage."

Roosevelt's expression grew grim. "I hope not, Detective Sergeant, but one can never be sure what a police investigation will uncover. Everyone has secrets, and even if those secrets don't have anything to do with why Gregory was murdered, they might come out and cause distress to his family."

Frank could feel the dread forming in his belly like a lead weight. "If you know of something in particular, I'd be grateful if you told me now. I'll have a better chance of keeping it away from the press."

"That's just it," Roosevelt confessed. "I don't. But a man in Gregory's position . . . Well, I'm sure he's made enemies."

"People who might want to kill him?"

Roosevelt didn't actually squirm. Men in his position would never do anything so craven. He did look remarkably uncomfortable, though. "Civilized people don't kill their enemies by blowing them to bits."

Now Frank was pretty sure he understood why he'd been selected for this task. "What if I find out it wasn't anarchists?"

They both knew what he meant. The law was a flexible instrument, and it tended to bend a great deal for those with money and power. If Van Dyke's killer had both, bringing him to justice could be problematic, if not actually impossible.

"I want justice to be done, no matter who the culprit is," Roosevelt assured him, somewhat to Frank's surprise. "When you know, come to me, and I'll deal with it."

Roosevelt handed Frank the papers he'd been examining, two typewritten pages containing the details of the case that were known so far. Frank knew the detectives on the scene had hastily scrawled a report, and Miss Kelly had no doubt typed it for the commissioner to read.

Sensing he had been dismissed, Frank rose. "I'll keep you informed," he promised.

"Give Sarah my regards," Roosevelt replied.

Frank looked up sharply, instantly wary. Was he being tested? Like Roosevelt, Mrs. Sarah Brandt was a Decker and one of the Knickerbockers, a woman whom Frank should, in the normal course of his life, have never even met. "I don't expect to be seeing Mrs. Brandt," he said guardedly. Indeed, he'd sworn to himself never to see her again.

Roosevelt's enormous grin appeared again. "Well, I expect you *will*. Felix Decker was the one who called me about Gregory's death. He asked me to put you on the case."

Frank could not have been more stunned. Felix Decker was Sarah Brandt's father. And Frank already knew him to be a murderer.

SARAH BRANDT HADN'T HEARD THE EXPLOSION, EITHER. She had been delivering a baby on the Lower East Side all night and for most of the morning. As a midwife, she traveled the city at all hours, and now she was returning, bone weary, to her home on Bank Street. She'd taken the Third Avenue Elevated Train to Fourteenth Street, where she hoped to find a Hansom cab to carry her across town. Since it was raining—sleeting really—she doubted her chances.

She'd just reached the bottom of the long flight of stairs that led down from the El station three stories above the street when she heard a newsboy shouting about an explosion.

He was peddling an Extra edition of the paper, a one-sheet version that would report on an event so extraordinary, it couldn't wait for the next day's regular paper, or even the evening edition.

"Rich man gets blowed to pieces!" the boy cried. "Read all about it!"

People were crowding around, eagerly paying their pennies to get the gory details. Sarah approached with a sense of dread. While she hadn't moved in those elite social circles for years, she still knew far too many rich men personally. Her own father was one of them.

"Who is it?" she asked, handing the boy her penny. He was sheltering the sheets of newsprint from the rain beneath his tattered coat. He pulled one out for her.

"Mr. Gregory Van Dyke!" he shouted for all to hear. "Blowed up by anarchists! Read all about it!"

Sarah's relief was only momentary. Her father might be safe, but Gregory Van Dyke was one of his oldest friends. She hurried away from the jostling crowd around the newsboy, stopping beneath an overhang where she could "read all about it" and remain relatively dry. All around her, people were voicing their surprise or their shock or their satisfaction that one so wealthy was not beyond the reach of violent death.

Quickly, she skimmed the story for facts, then reread it more slowly for details. Only three hours had passed since the explosion in his office, so they didn't have much to report yet. Mr. Van Dyke had arrived at his office as usual, shortly before nine o'clock. He had been in there, alone, for only a few minutes when something exploded. The police suspected a bomb, and everyone knew that anarchists used bombs. They also killed wealthy industrialists such as Gregory Van Dyke. Hadn't they tried to kill Henry Clay Frick in Pittsburgh, which was why Mr. Frick and his family had moved to New York City? The sheet was filled with words, but very few of them described known facts. Everything else was conjecture and rumor and innuendo.

Her weariness forgotten, Sarah unfurled her umbrella and looked around for a Hansom. She'd have to go home and change into something more presentable, but instead of taking a well-earned rest, she'd be heading uptown to see what she could do to comfort her parents.

FRANK STILL COULDN'T FIGURE OUT WHAT HE'D DONE TO deserve this. All the way uptown, riding on the Elevated Train, he'd thought of a dozen ways he could have avoided working on this case. Unfortunately, all of them involved resigning from the police force. Since employment opportunities for Irish Catholic men were extremely limited, and none of the others would allow him to provide adequately for his deaf son, he knew he was stuck. The best he could hope for was to come out of this without getting himself fired. Considering how many rich people he was probably going to have to offend, he figured he'd be extremely lucky to escape with his hide intact.

Which was a lot more than Mr. Van Dyke had done, Frank noted as he looked around the dead man's office one last time. The coroner had carried away the larger portions of Mr. Van Dyke. The blast had hit him in the face and chest and literally torn his body apart. Smaller pieces of him were still splattered over much of the room. The pattern told the story. The pattern and the smell.

The blast had come from a credenza that stood at one end of the room. Shattered glass among its remains and the unmistakable smell of spilled whiskey confirmed the information that the cabinet had held the liquor that Mr. Van Dyke served to his visitors. The odor of the alcohol helped cover the stench of gunpowder and death. The rain-wet air coming from the shattered windows would eventually clear all of it.

"That's all we know," Captain O'Connor informed Frank belligerently. The captain of this precinct had taken over the investigation personally until Frank's arrival. He was a short, stocky man with a florid complexion that spoke of many years of close association with a whiskey bottle. Most likely, he'd been promoted before Roosevelt came into power.

Frank nodded politely. He'd read the report Roosevelt had given him, and O'Connor hadn't had much to add. "I'd like to question everyone who was here when it happened."

O'Connor frowned sourly. "Suit yourself, but they don't know nothing." The captain would have risen to his current position by knowing exactly how to avoid offending the wealthy residents of the neighborhood. That, and managing to amass the fourteen thousand dollars necessary to buy the promotion. He wasn't going to jeopardize his livelihood by letting Frank annoy anyone important.

"Would you introduce me to them?" Frank asked, still polite. "You know them, and they respect you." He figured they probably knew the captain only too well and *despised* him, but he needed O'Connor's cooperation if he hoped to solve this case. Flattery was always a good way to win some-one over.

O'Connor grunted his consent, although Frank could see he was a bit mollified.

"I'd appreciate it if you'd sit in on the questioning, too," Frank added. "I'd like to get your impressions when we're done."

The captain only nodded, but Frank could see his attitude

toward Frank was beginning to thaw. With a sigh of relief, he followed O'Connor out of the ruined office. The outer office, where Van Dyke's secretary had been sitting, had also sustained some damage. Van Dyke's door had been closed, and the blast had torn it loose from the hinges and sent it smashing into the secretary's desk along with shrapnel from the bomb. The secretary had been taken to the hospital. Frank would question him later. Meanwhile, Van Dyke's partner and son were waiting down the hall.

The partner's office was a good indication of what Van Dyke's had probably looked like before the blast. An ornate desk polished to a high gloss sat in the center of the room. Several leather armchairs formed a seating area at the far end, by a tall window that looked out onto the street one floor below. A young man sat in one of the chairs, a heavy crystal glass in his hand, while an older man stood beside him, his back to the room, staring out at the traffic going by.

"Excuse us, Mr. Snowberger," O'Connor said with such deference, Frank half-expected him to bow. "Sorry to disturb you, but Mr. Roosevelt has sent a detective, and he's got a few questions for you. Won't keep you long, sir," he added with a warning glance at Frank.

Frank ignored the warning and the glance. "I'm sorry for your partner's death, Mr. Snowberger," he said perfunctorily. "I'm Detective Sergeant Frank Malloy. Commissioner Roosevelt has asked me to help clear this up."

Snowberger slowly turned from his vigil by the window and looked at Frank with little interest. He, too, held a glass half-full of amber liquid, probably an attempt to deal with the shock. "Is this absolutely necessary?" he asked O'Connor.

"It is if you want to find out who killed Mr. Van Dyke," Frank said before O'Connor could reply.

The captain gasped at his bluntness, but Snowberger only looked mildly annoyed. The young man, Frank noticed, drained his glass in one gulp.

"You must be Mr. Van Dyke's son," Frank guessed.

The boy looked up. His eyes were red-rimmed and his face ashen. He looked appropriately grief-stricken. "I found him," he said hoarsely.

"After the explosion, you mean?" Frank asked, instinctively reaching into his coat pocket for his notebook and pencil. No one had invited him to sit down, but he took the chair closest to young Mr. Van Dyke and began to make notes.

"Yes." The boy closed his eyes, as if trying to shut out the horrible vision of his father's mangled body.

"Tell me what happened. Everything you remember," Frank urged.

The boy shuddered. "I heard the explosion—"

"Start earlier. Did you see your father today before the explosion?"

The boy drew a breath, probably glad to be thinking about a time before this had happened. "Just for a moment, this morning, at home. I was finishing my breakfast when he came down."

"How did he seem?"

"Seem?"

"Did he seem nervous or preoccupied or did he seem normal, the way he always did?"

The boy was handsome, with light brown hair and pale blue eyes. Frank guessed him to be no more than twenty-two, if that. His smooth forehead creased with the effort of remembering. "He seemed happy," he reported in surprise.

"Happy?" Frank echoed. "How could you tell?"

"He called me by name. He said, 'Good morning, Tad.'

That's my nickname, short for Thaddeus. He hasn't called me Tad in years," he added with a touch of amazement.

"Did he say anything else?"

"I don't . . . Just something about it being a fine morning or a good day or something like that." The boy's blue eyes were wide.

Frank looked up at where the sleet was making streaks on the window just to make sure he'd remembered the weather correctly. It had been miserable all morning. "Are you sure that's what he said?"

"I know, it doesn't make any sense. But that's what he said," the boy insisted.

"I take it your father wasn't normally so cheerful in the morning?"

"He hardly ever said anything besides good morning, if that."

"Then what happened?" Frank asked.

"I got up and left for the office. I always try to get here before he does."

Frank wondered at that, but he'd find out more later. Right now, he just wanted the facts. "And he stayed behind and ate his breakfast?"

"Really, Detective," Snowberger protested.

"Couldn't this wait . . .?" the captain began, but Frank silenced them both with a look and turned back to the boy.

"Your father stayed behind?" he prodded.

"Yes. I mean, I suppose he did."

"And you traveled to the office. How did you get here?"

"I walked. I like the exercise. Don't get much sitting at a desk."

"You don't mind walking in weather like this?" Frank let his skepticism show.

The boy flushed. "My father uses the carriage himself,

and I don't wait for him. As I said, I like to get to the office early."

"You could take a Hansom."

"They're hard to find in the rain," the boy reminded him irritably.

Frank nodded his agreement, ignoring the irritation. "Did you see your father again?"

"No, not until . . ." He shuddered and tried to take another drink from his glass, but it was empty.

Frank took it from his hand and silently indicated O'Connor should refill it. "You said you heard the explosion. Where were you?"

"I was downstairs. That's where I work, with the other clerks."

"Mr. Van Dyke believed his son should learn the business from the ground up," Snowberger explained defensively. Frank wondered whom he was defending.

"Tell me exactly what you heard," Frank said to the boy.

He tried to remember. "A loud boom. We thought the building was falling down."

"You and the other clerks?" Frank guessed.

He nodded. "But then nothing else happened. I mean, nothing fell on us. Nothing collapsed. We must've stood there for a while, trying to figure out whether to run or crawl under our desks. Then I realized that whatever happened had happened upstairs. I ran up to see what it was."

"And what did you see?"

"Smoke, coming from my father's office. We thought it might be a fire, but when we got there, we didn't see any flames."

"You said 'we,'" Frank pointed out. "Who was with you?"

"Some of the clerks. Dickie, I think, and Sam. We ran into Reed's office. That's my father's secretary. We could hear him moaning. The door to my father's office had fallen on his desk, and he was underneath. We started pulling it off of him. I was calling for my father, but he didn't answer. I kept thinking he must not be there yet. Sometimes he didn't come in until later, and when he didn't answer . . ."

O'Connor thrust the refilled glass into his hand, and the boy took a fortifying sip. Frank couldn't help noticing he didn't choke or even wince at the taste. In spite of his youth, he was an experienced drinker.

"You and the other clerks pulled the door off of Mr. Reed's desk," Frank reminded him.

The boy winced at the memory. "He was covered with blood. I've never seen so much blood . . . at least not until . . ." The color was draining out of his face.

"Mr. Van Dyke," Frank said sharply, pulling the boy's attention back. "You rescued Mr. Reed?"

"Yes." The boy stared into Frank's eyes, as if determined not to see anything else, even in his mind's eye. "He was hurt, but not too badly. The door had knocked him to the floor and he'd cut his head, but he was saying my father's name over and over. That's when I thought . . . dear God." He covered his eyes with his free hand.

"You realized your father must have been in his office," Frank guessed. "So you went to find him."

The boy nodded miserably.

"That's enough," Snowberger declared. "I'm going to send Thaddeus home now. He's been through quite enough today, and he needs his family around him. I'm sure they will need him, too."

As if summoned by a silent command, two young men appeared and assisted young Mr. Van Dyke to his feet. From the looks of them, they'd also been involved in the rescue efforts.

When they were gone with Thaddeus Van Dyke, Frank looked at O'Connor. "Did someone question Mr. Reed, the secretary?"

"They took him straight to the hospital," he replied, a trifle belligerently. "He wasn't in any condition to answer questions."

Frank nodded. He'd get to Reed later. Then he turned to Snowberger. "I have a few questions for you, too, sir," he said, adding the "sir" only because he needed the man's cooperation. "While everything is fresh in your mind. People tend to forget things as soon as they get away from a tragedy. It's human nature not to want to remember."

Snowberger looked put upon, but he surrendered with a long-suffering sigh. "Very well, but I will be of even less help than Thaddeus was. I wasn't even in the building at that time." Without being instructed, he took the chair the boy had vacated.

"Where were you this morning?" Frank asked, opening his notebook again.

"At home. I very seldom come into the office before ten."

"Was that Mr. Van Dyke's habit as well?"

"Yes, as his son pointed out."

"Have you noticed anything unusual in Mr. Van Dyke's behavior lately?" Frank asked.

He frowned. "Not that I can recall, but he was hardly likely to have been worried about some anarchist planting a bomb in his office."

Frank refused to be intimidated. He gazed back at Snowberger unblinkingly. "We don't know that anarchists are responsible."

This annoyed Snowberger. "Who else could it be? No civilized person blows someone up!"

Roosevelt had said the same thing. "Civilized people don't commit murder at all, Mr. Snowberger," Frank said. "Do you believe that anarchists had a reason to kill Mr. Van Dyke?"

The color rose in Snowberger's neck, and it wasn't from anger. He actually looked embarrassed. "People like that don't need reasons!" he insisted.

Frank suspected Snowberger was lying, but he couldn't say so to his face, not if he hoped to keep his job. "You may be right, but just in case, did Mr. Van Dyke have any particular enemies? Someone who might have benefited from his death? Or who might have wanted revenge?"

"Certainly not!" Snowberger informed him, outraged.

"I can't believe a man as successful as Mr. Van Dyke hasn't made enemies, Mr. Snowberger," Frank prodded.

Snowberger wasn't going to budge. "Men don't settle business disagreements with bombs, Detective. If they did, New York would be a pile of rubble."

He was definitely right about that. Frank decided to change the subject. "Do you know of any reason why Mr. Van Dyke was especially cheerful this morning? Did he have some recent business success? Or perhaps a personal one?"

"I'm afraid I would have no idea," Snowberger snapped. "Don't let Thaddeus mislead you, Detective. He's just a boy, and he's had a terrible shock. He may not even be remembering everything clearly. His father may have greeted him cheerfully one day last week and now he's sure it was today, because he wants to have parted on good terms with his father. The mind plays tricks on us, as you pointed out yourself."

"Did the boy get along with his father?" Frank asked, ignoring the provocation.

Snowberger blinked in surprise. "I . . . I'm sure he did. Fathers and sons . . . Gregory expected a lot from his sons, but . . ." He gestured vaguely.

So Tad and his father *didn't* get along. Frank made a mental note. "You said 'sons.' Does Mr. Van Dyke have other sons?"

Now Snowberger was visibly uncomfortable. "There's an older boy, Creighton," he admitted reluctantly.

"Does he work here, too?"

"No."

Frank was certain there was something very intriguing about young Creighton. "Do you know where I could find him?"

"I have no idea. You'll have to consult his family."

Frank had every intention of doing just that. "One more question, Mr. Snowberger. Was Mr. Van Dyke in the habit of drinking liquor first thing upon his arrival at work?"

O'Connor gasped in outrage at the implication, and Snowberger sputtered furiously. "What kind of a question is that?" he demanded.

"A perfectly logical one," Frank said. "The bomb was apparently in the liquor cabinet. I was wondering why Mr. Van Dyke would have been opening it at nine o'clock in the morning."

"I'm afraid I can't help you there, Detective," Snowberger said icily. "You'll have to discover that for yourself."

THE VAN DYKES LIVED ON THE SECTION OF FIFTH Avenue in the 60s called Marble Row because all of the houses were fronted with marble. The Vanderbilt family members had made a contest out of mansion building in this neighborhood, each trying to outdo the other in size and stateliness. Marble Row was less grand than the Vanderbilts' mansions, but no less opulent for all of that. The Van Dykes' home was the kind of place where the servants earned more than Frank did.

A very snooty butler escorted Frank up to the second-floor parlor, where three women sat in varying stages of grief. Frank always found it difficult to judge the ages of wealthy females because they were so well kept, but he guessed the oldest of the women to be nearing fifty while the other two were closer to thirty. The older, blond woman sat on the sofa beside one of the younger women and was comforting her as she wept into a hankie. The third woman sat alone in a chair nearby, her hands folded primly in her lap while she studiously avoided looking at the weeping woman.

The butler announced him. "Detective Sergeant Malloy from the police."

"Mrs. Van Dyke," Frank said, addressing the older woman, who was the only one who looked up. "I'm sorry to disturb you at this time, but I have some questions that must be answered immediately if I have any hope at all of catching your husband's killer."

The woman stared back at him, her gaze steady, her clear blue eyes unreadable. She looked upset, but not as if her whole world had suddenly crumbled around her. For an instant he considered the possibility that she might not be too sorry that her husband was dead. Then he started wondering why she looked so familiar to him. He was certain they'd never met.

The dark-haired woman sitting on the sofa beside her had finally looked up. She had the face of a China doll, as clear as porcelain with large blue eyes and full lips. "I'm sure we know nothing that will be of any assistance to you," she said. "My husband must have been killed by a stranger. No one who knew him could possibly wish him harm."

Frank was startled but not stupid. He needed only a moment to realize the dark-haired woman was the widow, regardless of her age. Rich men seemed to have no trouble at all attracting young, beautiful women, no matter how old and ugly they might be. Of course, he couldn't judge what Van Dyke had looked like before the bomb. Perhaps he had been a match for his attractive bride in looks, at least.

"You're probably right, Mrs. Van Dyke," he agreed, "but we need to investigate all possibilities."

"Of course you do," the other young woman said. She was as plain as Mrs. Van Dyke was lovely. Her hair was the color of straw and scraped back in an unbecoming style. She looked pale and drawn and possibly even ill. "Lilly, don't be rude. At least pretend you want to find out who killed my father."

"How dare you say a thing like that? Your father and I were *devoted* to each other," Mrs. Van Dyke informed her angrily. She turned to Frank. "He was making me a surprise gift for our anniversary. He'd been working on it for weeks, and he was going to give it to me tonight!"

"Your anniversary isn't for another month," Van Dyke's daughter said snidely.

"He said he couldn't wait to see the expression on my face," Mrs. Van Dyke said proudly. "I told you, we were devoted to each other."

The daughter made a rude noise.

Mrs. Van Dyke sniffed haughtily. "It's a pity his own children treated him so shabbily. If I'm not mistaken, *you* were more upset over his secretary getting injured than your father being killed."

"Mr. Reed was an innocent bystander and didn't deserve any of this!" the daughter exclaimed, her homely face mottling with color. "But I most certainly am *not* more up-set about him than about Father!"

Mrs. Van Dyke glared at her, but when she turned back to Frank, she was all feminine charm and vulnerability. "You mustn't pay my stepdaughter any mind. She's understand-ably distraught, and she's been ill."

Miss Van Dyke returned the glare, but her stepmother ignored her.

Frank had now identified two of the three women. The older one was still watching him, as if he interested her more than was normal under the circumstances. He once again acknowledged her with a small nod. "Are you also a member of the family?"

Before she could reply, Mrs. Van Dyke said, "Oh, no. Elizabeth is a friend. She was gracious enough to come the moment she heard what happened."

"That was very kind of you, Mrs. . . .?" Frank said, giv-ing her a chance to identify herself.

"Decker," she replied, watching closely for his reaction. "Mrs. Felix Decker."

2

$\mathbf{F}$RANK STARED BACK AT HER, USING EVERY SKILL HE POS-
sessed to keep his true emotions from showing on his face.
No wonder she looked familiar. Her resemblance to her
daughter, Sarah Brandt, was striking. She knew who he was,
too. He could tell by the way she was watching him, judging his every word and deed. She couldn't know everything
about him, of course, because even Sarah didn't know that
he was in love with her. But Mrs. Decker knew enough.

And Felix Decker had asked for him by name.

Had his selection for this case been an honor or a trap?
Did they want to see the murder solved or to see him fail?
Unfortunately, he wouldn't learn the answers until the case
was over, and by then it would be too late.

"Perhaps you'll want to excuse yourself while I speak
with Mrs. Van Dyke and her stepdaughter, Mrs. Decker," he

said, relieved to hear his voice sounded perfectly normal.

"Oh, no!" Mrs. Van Dyke exclaimed in alarm. "Please stay, Elizabeth!" She turned to Frank in appeal. "I'm sure we can tell you nothing Mrs. Decker wouldn't already know."

"Don't be a fool, Lilly," her stepdaughter said acidly. "The detective is going to want to know all our family secrets, and he's trying to spare you from embarrassment."

"Regrettably, we no longer *have* any family secrets, Alberta," her stepmother replied just as acidly, "thanks to your brother, who has taken up with the lowest creatures in the city and made us a laughingstock."

"Are you speaking of Mr. Van Dyke's older son?" Frank asked, reaching for his notebook and pencil.

"Yes, Creighton," Mrs. Van Dyke reported with satisfaction.

"Creighton had nothing to do with this," Alberta insisted somewhat shrilly. What little color had been in her face now fled. "You just want to see him disinherited!"

"If he killed his father, he most certainly will be!" Mrs. Van Dyke replied smugly.

Alberta sprang from her chair, probably intent on doing her stepmother bodily harm, but she stopped instantly and swayed a bit, clapping her hands to the sides of her head as if trying to hold it in place. Frank instinctively rushed to her, grabbing her arm in case she fainted. He was only one step behind Mrs. Decker, who had followed the same instinct and caught her from the other side.

"You've had a terrible shock, Alberta," Mrs. Decker was saying to the young woman. "Perhaps you should rest a bit. Mr. Malloy can speak with you later." She looked at Frank, silently willing him to agree.

He was only too happy to do so. Besides the possibility of this one fainting, he wasn't going to learn very much if the two women were going to quarrel with everything the other said. "I'd actually *prefer* to speak to you separately, if you wouldn't mind, Miss Van Dyke."

Alberta looked at him, her red-rimmed eyes full of misery. "Creighton didn't do this," she repeated. "No matter what she says, you must believe me."

"If he's innocent, he has nothing to fear," Frank assured her.

Mrs. Decker gave him a look of astonishment that he didn't quite understand, but then she was leading Alberta away.

"Please come back, Elizabeth!" Mrs. Van Dyke cried. "Alberta's maid can take care of her, and I need you with me!"

Frank caught the slightest flicker of impatience on Mrs. Decker's face this time, but she covered it instantly. "I will, my dear," she said and went out with Alberta.

When the door had closed behind them, Mrs. Van Dyke sighed dramatically. "That girl is such a nuisance. I don't know why she won't marry. It's unnatural, if you ask me, for a girl that old to still be at home."

It did seem strange. Frank had guessed her to be the same age as her stepmother, around thirty. She was no beauty, but surely her father could have bought her a husband with a large dowry, even if no eligible man had volunteered. Before this was over, he would probably know exactly why Miss Alberta Van Dyke was a spinster, though, along with a lot of other things that should have been none of his business.

"Do you mind if I sit down, Mrs. Van Dyke?" he asked.

She looked startled, as if the thought had never occurred to her. "I suppose you might as well," she conceded ungraciously, motioning to the chair Alberta had just vacated.

Frank retrieved the notebook he'd dropped when he'd

rushed to rescue Alberta and took the offered chair. "I gather you are Mr. Van Dyke's second wife," he began.

She looked a little mollified. "Yes. His first wife died years ago, long before I met him."

"It must be strange having stepchildren older than you are," he observed. He didn't know if this was true, but he figured she was the type of woman to respond to flattery. He was right.

"Why, yes, it is strange," she replied, quite pleased. "Of course, Tad is younger than I, if only by a few years."

"How is the young man doing? He said he was coming straight home."

Mrs. Van Dyke frowned slightly. "He was quite upset, of course. He went straight up to his room, and I'm afraid he took some liquor with him. He wouldn't even tell us about what happened. I'm sure he'll be fine, though. Men don't feel tragedy the way women do, after all."

Frank wondered where she'd gotten an idea like that, but he didn't challenge it. "Tad said your husband was in an exceptionally good mood this morning. Can you think of any reason why he would have been?"

She looked startled. "Why, no, I can't. I didn't see my husband this morning. I never do, because he leaves so early, you see."

Frank didn't think nine or ten o'clock was particularly early, but he wasn't going to argue. The Van Dykes probably had separate bedrooms—rich people often did—so her not seeing him was understandable. "Then you aren't aware of any recent success he might have had or any particularly good fortune?"

"My husband was always successful," she assured him. "I can't think why that would be a cause for him to be unusually cheerful. What exactly did Tad say?"

"That his father greeted him by his nickname and said it was a fine day or something like that. Since the weather is so bad today, I found that odd. I assume he must have had some other reason than the weather to think it was a fine day."

"I'm sure I couldn't say," she said with a puzzled frown. "Unless he was thinking about the present he was going to give me."

Frank was fairly certain that wasn't it. "What can you tell me about Mr. Van Dyke's son Creighton?"

She glanced toward the door, as if afraid Alberta might come bursting in to stop her. Satisfied that she was safe, at least for the moment, she looked back at Frank with a smug smile. "Creighton is an anarchist."

"An *anarchist*?" Frank repeated incredulously. She couldn't have any idea what the word meant, because if this were true, why hadn't someone at Van Dyke's office mentioned it already?

"I think that's what Gregory called him. I don't know anything about politics, but Creighton got involved with some group of foreigners who don't believe we should have a government. Can you imagine? How would we keep order without a government? Someone must tell people what to do, or they'll run wild!"

Frank had to agree. People ran pretty wild when they *did* have a government to tell them what to do. "How did he get involved with these people?" The step from being a million-aire's son to an anarchist was a pretty big one.

"A girl. Isn't that always the reason young men do foolish things?" she asked sincerely. "He became infatuated with some girl, and suddenly, he was running off to these meetings where people ended up in fist fights and the police had to come. Can you imagine?"

Unfortunately, he could. "Did Creighton get arrested?"

"If he did, I never heard about it, but he kept going to the meetings and saying the most outrageous things. He and Gregory argued about it constantly, but always behind closed doors. I'm sure Gregory wanted to protect me from such unpleasantness."

"I'm sure he did," Frank agreed sympathetically.

"I do know that anarchists use bombs and murder people," she informed him with just a little too much satisfaction. "Gregory never told me anything about it, of course, but when Creighton moved out and went to live with those people . . . Well, some of our acquaintances were only too happy to enlighten me. Wealthy females can be terrible gossips, Detective," she confided.

Frank decided not to comment on that. "You said Creighton went to live with those people. Do you know where I can find him?"

"Certainly not. Alberta might, though. She's still quite devoted to him. I think she even sent him money after Gregory cut off his allowance."

"What about Thaddeus? Would he know where Creighton is?"

Mrs. Van Dyke looked offended. "Absolutely not. Tad and his brother haven't spoken since Creighton left here. Tad is devoted to his father and would never do anything to offend . . . Oh, my," she said, suddenly paling. "I keep forgetting about Gregory . . . that he's gone. It doesn't seem real, like a bad dream, and I'll wake up any moment and . . ."

Her lovely eyes were filling with tears, and Frank knew she'd be dissolving into hysterics in another moment. That's why he was so glad to hear the parlor door opening. Mrs. Decker had come back to rescue him.

But when he looked up, he saw Sarah Brandt instead. His

breath caught at the sight of her, and somehow, he managed not to swear.

SARAH BRANDT WAS JUST AS SHOCKED AS HE. "MALLOY, what are you doing here?" she asked, hardly able to believe her eyes. She hadn't seen him for almost a month, and this was the last place she'd expected to encounter him.

He'd risen to his feet, looking disapproving, as he always did whenever he found her someplace he didn't think she should be. He didn't have time to say anything, though, because Lilly Van Dyke spoke first.

"Sarah! How kind of you to come. I don't know what's going to become of me!" With that, she burst into tears.

Propriety demanded that Sarah should go to comfort Lilly, even though she wanted to talk to Malloy. Helpless, she obeyed her conscience, acutely aware of Malloy watching every move she made. Why hadn't she heard from him in weeks? Was he glad to see her? Was she glad to see him? And did any of that really matter?

She went to the sofa and dutifully sat down beside Lilly, who was sobbing with amazingly feminine grace into a fine, lace handkerchief.

"I was so sorry to hear what happened to Mr. Van Dyke," she said, laying a comforting hand on Lilly's shoulder. "I hope you're not alone."

"Oh, no. Your mother came hours ago," Lilly assured her tearfully. "Of course, Alberta is here, although she's no comfort at all. And poor Tad. He was there when . . . when it happened, but they sent him home."

"How is he?" Sarah asked gently.

"He was naturally upset. He went to his room with a bottle of brandy."

Probably the best solution, under the circumstances. Sarah looked up at Malloy for some clue from him what she could do to assist him. He wasn't very helpful. He was too busy glaring at her. That probably answered her question about whether he was glad to see her.

"Sarah!" her mother exclaimed in surprise as she entered the room. "What on earth . . .?"

"I heard what happened and went straight to your house. Your maid told me where you were," she explained, still patting Lilly's shoulder. "Have you met Detective Sergeant Malloy?"

"Yes, I have," she replied, to Sarah's surprise. "I believe he's investigating what happened." Her tone was odd, as if she were asking a question, but Sarah didn't take the time to figure out what it was. She was looking at Malloy for some kind of explanation.

He didn't supply it. "How is Miss Van Dyke?" he asked her mother instead.

"Not very well, I'm afraid. She's been ill, and now with this . . ." Her voice trailed off as her gaze drifted back to Sarah. "Perhaps you could help, my dear," she realized.

"No," Malloy said, surprising everyone. Even Lilly forgot to cry for a moment. Then, seeing all the women staring at him, he corrected himself. "I mean, maybe you should call a doctor, if she's that sick."

"Sarah is a trained nurse," her mother reminded him sternly, much to Sarah's amazement. "Surely, you knew that."

Sarah wasn't sure which was more shocking, the fact that her mother was apparently bragging about the training to which she had so strenuously objected when Sarah had first suggested it years earlier or the fact that she seemed to know that Sarah and Malloy were well acquainted.

"I'll be happy to look in on Alberta while we're waiting

for a doctor to arrive," Sarah said diplomatically, rising to her feet. She hadn't thought to bring her medical bag with her, but she was sure the household would be well supplied with standard medications if she needed anything.

"Oh, Sarah," Lilly cried, catching Sarah's hand. "I'm feeling faint." Her lovely eyes were pleading with Sarah not to leave her, and Sarah couldn't believe that Lilly was so selfish as to pretend an illness to keep her from paying attention to Alberta.

"It's all right, Sarah," her mother assured her, moving to take her place. "I'll stay with Lilly. I'm sure a glass of sherry is all she needs."

Sarah managed to slip out of Lilly's grasp and head for the door.

"Mrs. Brandt?" Malloy said, stopping her.

She turned expectantly, keeping her expression carefully neutral, even though her stomach was fluttering expectantly.

"I need to speak with you. Privately."

Sarah didn't look to see if her mother was shocked by his abruptness. "Certainly," she replied, not letting him see how glad she was he'd saved her the embarrassment of having to ask for a moment of *his* time.

Sarah could hear Lilly complaining about something as Malloy shut the door behind them.

"What are you doing here?" they said in unison the instant they were alone in the hallway.

"Oh, dear," Sarah said in some amusement. "I'm sure Mrs. Ellsworth would say that's an omen of something." Mrs. Ellsworth was her extremely superstitious neighbor, and Malloy was quite familiar with her odd beliefs.

"It *is* an omen—that you're going to be angry when I tell you not to get involved in this," Malloy replied, his face dark with an anger of his own.

"I'm already involved. Gregory Van Dyke was one of my father's dearest friends."

"Then go comfort your father."

Malloy was right; she was very angry now. "Should I just forget that Alberta is ill and leave without a word?"

He seemed to be grinding his teeth, but he managed not to shout. He was probably afraid her mother would hear him. "You can tend to her, but then go home. Or back to your parents' house or somewhere safe."

Safe? He wanted her to be safe! The novelty of that idea almost distracted her from their argument, but not quite.

"Do you expect a bomb to explode *here*?" she asked, managing not to sound sarcastic.

"I don't know what to expect. I don't know enough about the Van Dykes to make a judgment yet, but I do know their son Creighton is living with a pack of anarchists. If they're responsible for this, God knows what they might do next, but if Creighton was the only Van Dyke left alive, they could have his father's entire fortune to finance their crimes."

"If you think the rest of the family is in danger, shouldn't you warn them?"

"I will, and I'll put a police guard on the house."

"Then there's no danger," Sarah pointed out.

Malloy sighed impatiently. "Not if we were dealing with an ordinary criminal, but these anarchists are crazy. They don't even care if they get killed along with their victims. Nobody can stop a man intent on killing himself to accomplish his goal."

"That doesn't make any sense! If they kill themselves, how will they convince the world that they're right?"

"I think I mentioned that they're crazy, so it doesn't have to make any sense. Which is why I don't want you anywhere near this house or this family."

His concern was touching, even though he expressed it with a slight snarl. She smiled sweetly. "I'll go up and check on Alberta now, if you don't have any more orders for me."

He sighed again, even more impatiently. "I do have one more. Don't bother asking her any questions," he warned, "because you're not going to get involved in this. Just find out what's wrong with her and give her some smelling salts or something and then get out of here."

"I wouldn't even know what questions to ask her," Sarah informed him indignantly. "Besides, if anarchists killed her father, Alberta isn't likely to know anything about it anyway."

He'd opened his mouth to argue before he realized she had agreed with him. "Right," he said instead.

"Will you at least tell me what happened to poor Mr. Van Dyke?" she tried.

"No," he snapped. "Now go upstairs and see what you can do, and then go home."

Sarah wanted to argue with him some more, but it would be a wasted effort. She had never changed Malloy's mind by arguing. She had, however, frequently changed his mind by other means, usually by just doing what she wanted and letting him realize it was the right thing after all. "Good luck with your case, Malloy," she said with another smile. "And if you need my help, don't hesitate to consult me."

She didn't wait to see his expression because she knew what it would be. Instead, she headed for the stairs. After a moment, she heard the parlor door open and close with a loud slam.

Sarah remembered the location of Alberta's room from when they had been children, but the décor had changed a lot since then. Gone were the toys and dolls and frilly pink bedclothes. In their place, Alberta had created a sunny yellow room with watered silk wallpaper and graceful French furniture. One end of the room was a sitting area with a small desk, a settee, and several comfortable chairs, a quiet place where Alberta could retreat with the books she had always loved. Several were scattered around where she had obviously been reading them.

The other end of the room was the sleeping area, where Alberta had retired. She lay upon the large, four-poster bed, looking wan, while her maid gently wiped her face with a soft cloth.

"Who's there?" she called weakly.

"It's Sarah Brandt," Sarah replied. "Sarah Decker," she added, in case Alberta had forgotten her married name.

"Sarah?" Alberta repeated incredulously.

"I heard what happened, and I went to see my parents," Sarah explained, moving closer to the bed. "The servants told me my mother was here, so I came to see if I could help in any way. I'm so sorry about your father."

"Yes, it's . . . awful," she said. Talking seemed to be an effort.

As Sarah came closer, she caught the odor that told her Alberta had been sick. Then she saw the slop pail sitting on the floor beside the bed. The maid quickly picked it up.

"Excuse me, miss," she said with a bob of her head, and hurried out with it.

"I'm sorry . . . I haven't felt well for several days," Alberta explained. "And the shock . . ."

"Of course. There's no need to apologize. My mother asked me to come up and see if I could do anything. I'm a trained nurse, you know."

From her expression, she hadn't known, and the knowledge made her frown. "I'm sure it's nothing serious," she said quickly.

"Your stepmother thinks it's serious enough to call a doctor in," Sarah said, stretching the truth a bit.

Alberta looked truly alarmed. "That's ridiculous. I don't need a doctor," she insisted. She had never been a pretty girl, but she had also never particularly cared about her lack of beauty. While other girls had primped and fussed and spent their days thinking about new dresses to wear to parties, Alberta had been content to read and study.

"I can probably determine how ill you are by asking a few questions. If it isn't serious, I can tell Lilly and no one will bother you. How long have you been ill?"

"Since . . . about a week, I suppose," she said, absently clutching at the neck of her dressing gown, as if afraid Sarah would try to open it. "It's probably something I ate that didn't agree with me," she added quickly. "I'm sure it will pass."

She took Alberta's pulse and checked for fever. Everything seemed normal. Sarah asked about her monthly cycle.

"Heavens, I don't know," Alberta said, obviously embarrassed to be discussing such a delicate subject. "I don't keep track of those things."

After some more delicate questioning, Sarah got her to reluctantly admit that her bowel and bladder functions had been abnormal of late.

Sarah was growing suspicious about the true cause of Alberta's illness, but her friend was hardly going to answer the questions she really needed to ask to confirm those suspicions. She knew of only one other way.

"Alberta, would you mind if I listened to your heartbeat? I don't have my stethoscope, the instrument I use for that, but I could put my ear directly to your chest, if you don't mind." Sarah could see that Alberta was wearing only a dressing gown beneath the coverlet.

"Do you think something is wrong with my heart?" she asked doubtfully.

"I just want to make sure," Sarah said with a reassuring smile. "Would you open your gown?"

Still reluctant, Alberta untied the ribbons at her throat and spread the gown open far enough that Sarah could see what she needed to see. She put her ear to Alberta's modestly endowed chest and listened long enough to convince her patient she was thorough. Just as she had suspected, Alberta's heartbeat was strong and regular.

"Fit as a fiddle," Sarah proclaimed with a smile.

"I told you," Alberta reminded her triumphantly. "It's just a touch of Summer Complaint."

Sarah didn't point out that it was almost December. "I'll give you some suggestions for things to do to help with the sickness." Sarah instructed her to eat some dry toast before rising in the morning; to eat frequent, small meals; and to lie down for a while after eating. "If your stomach starts to feel upset, lie down with a hot flannel on it."

"I'll certainly try all that," Alberta said as she retied her dressing gown. "I never heard any of those cures before."

Sarah managed a smile. "You'd be amazed what I've learned in my years of nursing."

"How on earth did you ever become a nurse?"

"After my sister died, I wanted to do something important with my life," she explained, telling her only a tiny portion of the truth.

Alberta nodded her understanding, even though she couldn't possibly understand. No one except Sarah's immediate family knew how Maggie had died, bleeding to death in a filthy tenement after giving birth to a dead child. All she had done to earn such a fate had been running away to marry the man she loved.

"You wanted to do something more important than marrying a rich man and having his children," Alberta guessed. "I wanted that, too, but I wasn't as brave as you, Sarah. I resisted marrying the rich man, but I didn't quite manage to do anything else with my life."

"I thought I had read recently that you were engaged," Sarah tried, hoping against hope.

Alberta's expression hardened. "You're mistaken. I can't even remember the last time a gentleman called on me."

Oh, dear, things were even worse than Sarah had thought.

"Tell me about your work," Alberta was saying, forcing a cheerful smile. "And how you met your husband. I heard he was a remarkable man."

Sarah pulled a chair closer and told her all about Tom and his work as a doctor in the tenements, all the while acutely aware that she had some vital information Malloy might need. Would he still be downstairs when she was finally able to take her leave of Alberta or would she have to seek him out?

She didn't mind seeking him out, but he did so hate it when she left messages for him at Police Headquarters because of the teasing he had to endure. On the other hand, a little teasing would serve him right for trying so hard to keep her out of this case.

FRANK HAD MANAGED TO GET MRS. VAN DYKE TO GIVE him permission to question her servants. Thank God Mrs. Decker was here. She'd been the one to persuade the grieving widow that it would be a good idea. Mrs. Van Dyke hadn't seen the necessity of "bothering" them. What could they possibly know that would be helpful? They were just servants!

He found Mr. Van Dyke's personal valet in the kitchen, drinking something out of a teacup that Frank suspected wasn't tea. From the expression on his face, Van Dyke's death had been a shock to him. He rose the instant he saw Frank, nearly spilling his drink.

Frank introduced himself. "I'd like to take a look at Mr. Van Dyke's room."

The valet nodded. "Don't see what good it will do, but you're welcome to it." He led Frank up the back staircase, the one the servants used.

The valet's name was Quentin. A slender man with slightly graying brown hair, he looked to be about forty-five. He told Frank he'd been with Mr. Van Dyke for over twenty years.

Van Dyke had a suite of rooms on the third floor. His bedroom was typically masculine, the walls covered in something that looked like leather and the furniture made of dark mahogany. A comfortable, overstuffed chair and ottoman sat by the gas fireplace. His bedclothes were shades of brown, and some kind of striped animal skin had been hung on the wall above the bed.

"It's a tiger skin," Quentin explained, seeing Frank's interest. "Mr. Van Dyke shot it in Africa. He had the head mounted. It's in his study downstairs."

"He must've been quite a hunter," Frank said, impressed.

"Oh, yes," Quentin said proudly. "He loved everything about it. He even cleaned his own guns and loaded his own cartridges. 'Never leave anything to chance' was what he always said. A very careful man."

Frank could see that just from looking around the room. He tried to imagine the delicate and feminine Mrs. Van Dyke in this room and failed. This was strictly a male sanctuary. Adjoining were a dressing room and a bathroom with a commode set in a mahogany chair and a tub large enough for Frank to soak in up to his neck. He looked at it longingly.

Back in the bedroom, Frank knew he should go through the man's drawers and cabinets to see if he could find any clue as to why someone wanted him dead. Before he shocked Quentin with his presumption, however, he'd ask him some questions.

"Thaddeus said his father was in an especially cheerful mood this morning. Did you notice that?"

"As a matter of fact, I did," Quentin said, a little surprised. "He'd been a bit down in the mouth for the past few months, you know. Business troubles, he'd tell me."

"What kind of business troubles?"

Quentin shrugged. "I don't like to talk about the family." Of course he didn't. Servants who told tales about their employers found themselves dismissed without a reference.

"It might help me find out who killed Mr. Van Dyke," Frank prodded. "No one will ever know what you told me."

Quentin glanced at the door that stood open to the hallway. Frank strode over and closed it purposefully. Then he turned back to Quentin.

"Mr. Van Dyke, he didn't say much, but what he did say . . ."

"What kind of trouble was he having?" Frank prodded.

Quentin looked distinctly uncomfortable. "No one will know?"

"No one," Frank assured him.

"He was mad at Mr. Snowberger. That's his partner."

"I've met him. What was he mad about?"

"You have to understand, they never did get along, but this time . . . Well, he thought Mr. Snowberger was cheating him somehow."

"Cheating him? You mean taking money from the business?"

"I don't know. Like I said, Mr. Van Dyke don't talk much. He'd just grumble a bit now and then. He'd say Snowberger thought he was getting away with it, but he was wrong. Mr. Van Dyke knew what was going on, and he'd put a stop to it."

Just as Frank had feared, this case wasn't going to be simple. If Snowberger was stealing from the company, and Van Dyke had found out, Snowberger might have decided to kill him before Van Dyke could expose him. "Did Mr. Snowberger know that Mr. Van Dyke was angry with him?"

"I don't know, but I thought they must've made it up, because Mr. Van Dyke was so cheerful this morning. And he had a present for Mr. Snowberger."

"A present? What kind of a present?"

"He got him a bottle of special brandy. That's why I was sure they must've made up their fight. I never knew him to give Mr. Snowberger a present before. Mr. Snowberger likes his brandy, and Mr. Van Dyke ordered this from France. The bottle had gold on it and everything. He took it with him this morning to give it to him. Saw him carry it out when he left."

"Did he say anything to you about it?"

Quentin tried to remember. "Just that . . . I think he said something about how this would make things right between them."

So maybe Snowberger wasn't a suspect after all. Frank felt a small sense of relief. Prosecuting a man in his position would be extremely difficult, even with irrefutable evidence, and Frank doubted he'd find that kind of evidence.

The brandy did help explain one thing, though—what Van Dyke had been doing at his liquor cabinet so early in the morning. He'd probably been putting the bottle inside for safekeeping, not knowing a bomb had been planted there. Did whoever planted it know about the gift or know that Van Dyke would be opening the cabinet that morning? Not likely. Probably, Van Dyke took a nip in the afternoon or early evening. If it was a habit with him, someone would know, someone close to him. Like his partner.

Or his son.

Frank would have to find out where Creighton Van Dyke was as quickly as possible. That would mean questioning Alberta Van Dyke. Which probably meant dealing with Sarah Brandt, too.

Frank managed not to groan aloud at the thought. He distracted himself by thoroughly searching Gregory Van Dyke's rooms, much to the chagrin of his valet.

SARAH COULD SEE THAT ALBERTA WAS TIRING. "YOU need to get some rest now," she said. "The next few days will be difficult."

Alberta closed her eyes against the thought. "Yes, they will, especially with Lilly in charge of everything."

"Won't that fall to Creighton? He's the oldest son, after all," Sarah remembered.

Alberta looked at her sharply, as if seeking some hidden meaning behind her words. Seeing none, she said, "Creighton isn't here."

"He's not? Where is he?" She was thinking he might have taken a European tour or something.

"He . . . he left home several months ago. He lives with . . . with some friends. He . . . Oh, dear." She raised a hand to her forehead and rubbed it as if to soothe an ache. "I guess I might as well tell you. That policeman already found out, and everyone else will know soon enough."

"What?" Sarah asked in alarm. "Has something happened to Creighton?"

"He's taken up with some very strange people. Anarchists, they call themselves."

Sarah could only gape at her in stunned silence. Anarchists killed people with bombs! Everyone knew that!

"Creighton couldn't have had anything to do with Father's death," Alberta insisted, as if reading her mind. "He and Father had quarreled, but Creighton wouldn't kill him! He's not that kind of person."

Sarah hadn't seen Creighton in many years, so she had no idea whether he was or not. "How on earth did he get involved with people like that?"

Alberta rubbed her forehead again. "He's always been a little rebellious. He and Father were constantly at loggerheads about something. I think . . . I honestly think that if *Father* had been an anarchist, Creighton would have become a conservative businessman, just to spite him."

"My sister Maggie was like that," Sarah remembered sadly. Maggie had left home, too, after quarreling with their father, but the consequences for a rebellious female were much greater than for a male. Maggie was dead.

"I'm not sure why, but Creighton started by going to some of their meetings. He was searching for something, I think. Something he could believe in. Then he met this girl."

"Oh, dear," Sarah said, beginning to understand.

"Yes," Alberta agreed. "She's Russian or maybe German. I'm not sure. Very pretty but just as insane as the rest of them. Full of hatred and ideas that don't make any sense at all to rational people. And of course she believes in free love."

"I see," Sarah said, and she did. The whole picture was clear now. Creighton had been looking for a philosophy of his own that would thoroughly shock his father. Then he'd met a girl who offered him not only new ideas but carnal satisfaction as well. The combination must have been irresistible.

"They live on the Lower East Side in a tenement with a lot of other Russian and German immigrants." She looked at Sarah beseechingly. "Someone should warn him that the police think he killed Father."

"Do you think he's guilty?" Sarah asked. "Do you want him to run away?"

"Of course not, and I don't think he's guilty! But when did that ever stop the police from arresting someone? They're looking for a person who planted a bomb, and everyone knows anarchists plant bombs. They'll blame him and his friends because it's easy, and Lilly will be only too happy to let Creighton be accused."

"Detective Sergeant Malloy isn't that kind of a policeman," Sarah told her. "I know him, and I've seen him work. He won't rest until he finds the truth."

"How on earth do you know a policeman, Sarah?" Alberta asked in amazement.

"It's a long story, but you can take my word. Creighton has nothing to fear from Detective Malloy if he's innocent."

Alberta was unconvinced. "Still, someone should warn him. Sarah, do you know anyone who could take a message to him?"

Sarah almost volunteered herself. She often went into those neighborhoods to deliver babies, but she didn't want to seem too eager. "I think I could find someone. Do you have his address?"

Alberta gave her the address of a building just south of

Houston Street in the German Jewish neighborhood. Sarah knew the area well.

FRANK WAS LOOKING FOR A SERVANT TO SEND UP TO Miss Van Dyke's room to ask if he could question her when he heard footsteps on the stairs. He looked up to see Sarah Brandt descending.

The sight of her always amazed him. She seemed to be lit by some inner fire that gave her a presence or a glow, setting her apart from every other woman he'd ever known. He felt the familiar ache of a longing that could never be fulfilled. He had only a moment to admire her before she saw him looking up.

"Malloy, I'm so glad you're still here," she said. "I need to talk to you."

She probably had some silly idea about who the killer was, and he'd have to convince her it wasn't possible. He didn't have time for that. He had to find out who had killed Van Dyke before Roosevelt got impatient and put somebody else on the case. "I need to speak with Miss Van Dyke," he said, hoping to distract her.

"She can't see you now," she said as she reached the bottom of the stairs. "She's too ill. That's what I need to talk to you about." She looked around to see if they were alone. She noticed the parlor door was closed.

"Mrs. Van Dyke and your mother are in there," he explained. "Some minister is with them."

"Good, come with me."

To his annoyance, she headed off toward the back of the house without waiting to see if he would agree. Having no choice, he followed her down the hall and into a dimly lit room. A glance around told him this must be Van Dyke's study. The huge and snarling head of the pelt he'd seen hanging in Van Dyke's bedroom hung on the wall opposite the door, but it was only one of many exotic animals mounted in various poses of ferocity on every wall. Before he could take in more than that first impression, she closed the door behind them.

"Malloy, Mr. Van Dyke's oldest son is an anarchist," she told him.

Was that all? "I know. His wife told me. That's what I have to see Miss Van Dyke about. Her stepmother said she's the only one likely to know where to find him."

"You aren't going to arrest him, are you?" she asked in alarm.

He bit back the sharp retort that sprang instantly to his lips. Getting into a shouting match with her here would be stupid. "I need to question him," he said as calmly as he could.

"He wouldn't have killed his own father!"

"Maybe not, but his friends might have," he countered.

She couldn't dispute that. "Alberta gave me his address. She wants me to warn him that the police are looking for him."

"*What?*" he cried, remembering at the last second not to shout.

"But that's not all. I don't know whether it has anything to do with the bomb or not, but . . . Alberta Van Dyke is with child."

3

FRANK WASN'T SURE HE'D HEARD HER CORRECTLY. "SHE'S what?"

"She's going to have a baby. Which means she has a lover. But I mentioned that I thought I'd read she was engaged— to give her an opportunity to tell me about the man in her life—and she insisted she hadn't even had a gentleman court her for years."

Frank was still confused. "How did she explain the baby then?"

"She didn't. I didn't tell her I knew."

"If you didn't talk about it, how do you know there's a baby?"

"Because she's been ill, and I asked her questions, and I saw her . . . her body, and I know. I've seen enough women in that condition before. She has all the signs."

Frank scratched his head in bewilderment. "All right, even if it's true, what does this have to do with her father's murder?"

She rolled her eyes, silently telling him she thought he must be a dunderhead. "Alberta is my age, more than old enough to be considered definitely a spinster," she explained patiently. "She said herself she hasn't had a suitor in a very long time. That means there's some mystery about who fathered her child."

"You think she might have been forced?" Frank asked, growing more disturbed by the minute.

"It's possible, but she doesn't act as if she's experienced that kind of an outrage. I've seen enough who have to know how they react."

"Could the father be . . . someone in her family?" he asked reluctantly. They both knew that happened far more often than anyone wanted to believe.

"Dear heaven, I hope not. It seems unlikely because of her age, though."

"If she wasn't forced and it's not a member of her family, then she must have a lover," Frank pointed out.

"And since she denied having any suitors, we have to conclude that it's someone her family wouldn't have considered acceptable enough to call on her."

"A servant?" Frank guessed.

"Entirely possible," she agreed. "But whoever it is, if her father wouldn't allow her to marry him, and then she discovered she's with child . . ."

"Alberta and her lover might have decided to kill him so they could be together," Frank finished. "Of course, this might have nothing at all to do with who killed Van Dyke," he reminded her. "Blowing your own father to kingdom come is an ugly thing to do, no matter what your reason."

"Yes, but we don't know who the lover is. He might be an anarchist, too. If Creighton knows some, Alberta might, too. But even if Alberta and her lover aren't involved at all, we can use the information to frighten Alberta, to get her to tell us everything she knows."

Frank felt a familiar tightening behind his eyes, the first symptom of the headache Sarah Brandt frequently gave him. He rubbed the bridge of his nose with his thumb and forefinger and got hold of his temper before replying. "Mrs. Brandt, you keep using the word 'we,' but I believe I already made it clear that you are not to be involved in this case."

"You told me to stay away from this house because it might explode," she reminded him. "I don't think I'll be in much danger going downtown to see Creighton Van Dyke."

"You are not going into a den of anarchists!" he said, forgetting not to shout this time.

She didn't even blink. "Creighton was my partner in dancing class when we were children, and I'll be bringing him a message from his sister. He has no reason to harm me."

He wanted to shake some sense into her, but he knew that wouldn't do any good. Her head was like a block of marble. "You aren't going, and that's final."

"How will you find him, then?" she asked, pretending concern.

"I'll get his sister to tell me where he is."

She shook her head. "She won't tell you a thing, and if you try to make her, she'll cry and scream and even faint, and Lilly Van Dyke will have you thrown out, and you'll never be able to ask anyone in this house another question. She'll probably even ask Teddy to take you off the case, and you'd be disgraced."

Fury turned his face hot. He hated it when she was right. He hated it even more when she tricked him into getting her way. He said the only thing he could to salvage his pride. "Then you're not going down there *alone*. I'm going with you."

"Of course you are," she said, surprising him all over again.

He had to clear his throat because it was all clogged with the arguments he was going to use to convince her. "We should go right away, before he has a chance to disappear."

"That's just what I was thinking."

Before he could blink, she opened the door to the study and went out into the hall. Once again he was left to follow.

Frank had thought they might get away unnoticed, but the parlor door opened just as they passed, and Sarah's mother stepped out, followed by a tall, distinguished-looking gentleman in a clerical collar.

Mrs. Decker didn't look pleased to see Frank and her daughter together, and Frank couldn't blame her. "Sarah, you remember Reverend Carstens, don't you?" she said, ignoring Frank. He didn't mind. He'd already met the man when he first came in.

Sarah and the minister exchanged greetings and remarked on how terrible the tragedy was. He asked after Alberta Van Dyke, and Sarah told him she was too ill at the moment for visitors. After a few more minutes of meaningless conversation, he took his leave.

The moment he was out of earshot, Mrs. Decker said, "Is Alberta seriously ill? Should we call a doctor in?"

"No, that won't be necessary," Sarah said diplomatically, "but she really isn't up to seeing anyone at the moment. She needs some rest. The next few days will be difficult."

"They certainly will." Mrs. Decker looked at Frank, her eyes dark with concern. "Are you finished here?"

"No, but I have to leave for a while. I'll be back tomorrow to finish questioning the servants."

"I can't imagine why you're wasting your time here when he was killed at his office," she said with a frown.

"Mother, Mr. Malloy knows what he's doing," Sarah said to his surprise. "The explosion may have happened at his office, but the killer probably came from someplace else entirely."

"Do you honestly think someone *here* did it?" Mrs. Decker asked in amazement.

"The people here can probably tell me who might have wanted to see Mr. Van Dyke dead, Mrs. Decker," Frank replied as politely as he could, not willing to let Sarah defend him again.

Mrs. Decker looked at him, still frowning. He tried to read her expression, but she was too well-bred to allow her true emotions to show on her face. "I suppose Mr. Roosevelt wouldn't have sent you if he didn't think you were capable," she allowed, as if she herself were reserving judgment.

"Mr. Malloy is extremely capable, Mother," Sarah assured her. "And we're keeping him from doing his job. He must leave now, and I'm afraid I must go, too."

"Oh, Sarah, I was hoping you'd come home and dine with us tonight," Mrs. Decker said. Did she sound a bit desperate, as if she suspected her daughter was going into danger with a disreputable policeman?

"I can't. I have an appointment. But I'll see you tomorrow, I'm sure. I'll be back to check on Alberta, and if you're not here, I'll go to your house afterward. Mr. Malloy," she added, turning to him with an expression of complete innocence. "May I walk out with you?"

When they were halfway down the stairs to the first floor, Frank said, "Neatly done."

She smiled up at him over her shoulder. "Ironically, my mother taught me that trick."

Outside, the sleet had slowed to a drizzle, so they didn't bother trying to find a Hansom cab and walked down to the Fiftieth Street Station of the Sixth Avenue Elevated Train.

She was wearing a hooded cape against the weather, and Frank turned up his collar and pulled his bowler hat down low. Dodging people with umbrellas and the sprays of water shooting up from passing vehicles, they didn't have much opportunity to talk. A public street wasn't a good place to discuss a murder in any event.

Neither was the train station, but no train was in sight when they reached the top of the long stairway that led up to it from the street, so they were forced to stand and wait. Frank glanced at her, feeling suddenly awkward. What had she thought when he'd disappeared from her life without a word? Probably that he cared nothing about her, which was what he'd wanted her to think. At least she'd never guess the truth, that he'd vowed never to see her again because he loved her too much to trust himself with her.

She drew a breath, and he knew she was going to say something. He braced himself for a rebuke.

"How's Brian doing?" she asked.

"He's . . . fine," he stammered. "Just fine. Walks from the minute he gets up until he falls down asleep." Brian could walk because Sarah Brandt's surgeon friend had fixed his club foot.

"I'm so glad," she said. "I'd love to see him sometime."

Frank wasn't going to reply to that. He was trying to keep her out of his life, not draw her into it. It was for her own good. Knowing Frank had already caused her too much pain. "I . . . I'm sorry about your friend," he said, not quite able to meet her eye. Another loss for which he was responsible.

"The newspapers were very kind," she said. "I know you made sure they didn't find out anything sensational."

"The family called in some favors, too," he said modestly. "How's that little girl at the mission? What's her name . . . Aggie?"

"She seems fine," Sarah said a little wistfully. Frank knew she'd grown very fond of the little orphan girl she'd met at the Prodigal Son Mission. "It's hard to tell, of course, since she doesn't speak. I wish . . ."

Hearing the longing in her voice, Frank looked at her sharply, but the roar of an approaching train distracted them both. They hurried forward to be among the first to board, then rushed to get seats before they filled up. Frank directed her to the seats in the front of the car, where they were less likely to be overheard by someone in front of them.

The car smelled of damp wool and coal smoke and unwashed bodies, odors to which they had both become well accustomed.

Frank figured he'd better start questioning her so they wouldn't talk about anything else so personal . . . and so she wouldn't start asking him things he didn't want to tell her about the case. "What do you know about the Van Dyke family?"

Sarah seemed glad for the change of subject. Most women would have asked him what he wanted to know, but she had been involved in enough murder investigations that she didn't need to ask.

"Mr. Van Dyke's wife died when Tad—that's the youngest boy—was very young. Five or six, I think. He didn't remarry until about five years ago. I don't know much about Lilly Van Dyke. She wasn't in the same social circle as the Van Dykes and my parents before she married."

"So she married for money."

"She probably married for security. Most women do, Malloy, even poor ones. They need someone to provide for them."

Sarah Brandt didn't, but Frank decided not to mention that. "Then why didn't the daughter get married?"

"I don't know. Some women just don't like the thought of marriage, and Alberta wasn't the kind of girl to attract suitors."

"You mean she's homely," Frank said to annoy her. "But her father would've given her a dowry, wouldn't he? That would've attracted suitors, even if Alberta didn't."

She glared at him, but he pretended not to notice. "Considering her condition, someone must have found her attractive," she pointed out.

"Someone she couldn't marry as long as her father was alive."

"And someone she needed to marry very soon to avoid a scandal," she added.

"Would her father be likely to relent and let her marry this man if he found out about the baby?"

She frowned, and too late he remembered her own sister had been in that situation. "They might have just sent her away somewhere to have the child. That's what they were going to do with Maggie before she eloped," she reminded him.

"Alberta could have eloped," Frank said.

"Perhaps she planned to. We don't have any reason to think she or her lover were involved in her father's death."

"Not yet," he said, baiting her.

She glared at him, but she didn't argue. "At least Tad doesn't seem to have a reason to want his father dead."

"That we know of," he reminded her, "What about the grieving widow? Any scandal associated with her?"

"I wouldn't know. You'll have to ask my mother."

He stared at her in astonishment, certain he'd misheard her.

"My mother knows everything about everyone in her social circle," she explained.

"Do you honestly believe she'd tell *me* any gossip about my betters?" he challenged.

She gave him a frown, but she didn't argue because she knew he was right. "She'll tell *me* whatever I want to know."

"Then find out if Mrs. Van Dyke has a lover."

She didn't like that one bit. "Why would it have to be a lover?"

"Because that's usually the reason a wife wants her husband dead, especially if the husband found out about it."

"The slightest breath of scandal would ruin a woman in Lilly's position," she reminded him. "Men may take as many mistresses as they like, but if a woman strays, her husband can throw her out into the street with nothing but the clothes on her back. I can't imagine Lilly would risk everything for some clandestine romance."

"Then if it isn't love, it's usually money. She was a lot younger than her husband, and she didn't seem very upset that he's dead. Maybe she saw a way to keep her life just the way she wanted it only without the bother of a husband."

"That does sound more like Lilly, but she would have to find someone who could make the bomb and set it off. Finding a person like that wouldn't be easy for someone whose social life is limited to balls, the theater, and visiting other rich women. Even if she did find someone who could make the bomb, why would he do it for her?"

"For money. She'll have plenty now that her husband is dead."

"Are you sure? Have you seen his will?" she asked. "Even if Mr. Van Dyke left his wife a lot of money, he isn't likely to have given her control over it. Women can't be trusted to manage money, you know."

He heard the disapproval in her voice, but he could see Van Dyke's point of view. "A woman like Mrs. Van Dyke would probably spend it all on new dresses in a month."

"Maybe," Sarah allowed grudgingly. "In any case, she'd never get the opportunity. A trustee would be appointed to manage her funds and give her an allowance and oversee paying her bills. A trustee probably wouldn't be willing to pay an assassin."

"That still leaves love. Maybe some poor mug worshipped her from afar and was willing to do anything to prove his devotion to her."

"Malloy," she said in wonder. "I had no idea you could be so romantic."

"There's nothing romantic about making a fool of yourself over some female," he replied with a fierce scowl, which only made her smile.

"I'm sure you're right," she agreed, still smiling.

Frank decided it was time to change the subject. "What do you know about Van Dyke's business?"

"Absolutely nothing. My father would know, though."

Frank could feel his blood chilling in his veins at the mention of Felix Decker. Sarah's father was the last person on earth Frank intended to consult about this case or anything else. He didn't trust himself in the same room with the man. "Van Dyke's valet said he thought Snowberger was cheating him somehow," Frank said, forgetting his vow not to tell her anything about the case.

"Good heavens," Sarah said, all thoughts of her father forgotten. "If he was, he would have had a reason to want Mr. Van Dyke dead."

"A bomb would be a good way to throw suspicion on Creighton or at least on some of Creighton's friends, too."

"It's dangerous, though. Suppose someone else had been killed in the explosion?"

"Do you really think a man like Snowberger would care? How many people do you think die in his factories every year?"

This silenced her, but Frank instantly regretted his words. "I didn't mean—"

"No, you're absolutely right," she said gravely. "Human life is held very cheaply if it belongs to someone poor and helpless. Men like Snowberger and Van Dyke and even my father have little regard for people like that, I'm sorry to say." She sighed. "I don't suppose the valet knew how Snowberger was cheating?"

"No, but he did say that Van Dyke was planning to make up their argument today. He was taking Snowberger a bottle of liquor as some kind of peace offering."

"I wonder if Mr. Snowberger knew his partner was going to forgive him," she mused.

"I'll find out the next time I speak to him," Frank said.

The train moved steadily down the elevated tracks that sat on girders three stories above the street. The cars were noisy and often overcrowded, but the speed of travel here above the tangle of wagons and carriages and horses that clogged every intersection in the city more than made up for everything else. Frank and Sarah had only a few minutes to consider all they'd been discussing before the train stopped at Bleeker Street in Greenwich Village.

"We need to get off here," she told him, and they left the train.

"When are you going to tell me Creighton's address?" he asked, trying not to sound impatient as they made their way down the long stairway to the street level.

"As soon as we get there," she replied innocently. "I can't risk having you run off and leave me behind, can I?"

"I'd never think of doing that," he informed her righteously. "You might've given me the wrong address."

She couldn't help grinning at that, and Frank grinned back.

They had to walk two blocks in the light rain before they found a Hansom available to take them up. Then the driver balked at going into the Lower East Side. When Frank heard Sarah give him the address, he didn't blame the man. "Just go down Houston Street and get us as close as you can," Frank said, climbing in beside Sarah.

Still grumbling, the man snapped his whip, sending the scrawny horse into motion before Frank had a chance to get settled properly in the narrow confines of the vehicle designed for one passenger. He ended up sitting on Sarah's skirt, and it took them a few minutes of struggle to get untangled. He spent that time trying desperately not to notice how good she smelled or how close her soft, golden hair was to his face.

Their progress through the rain-wet streets was slow, but at least they were relatively dry in the shelter of the Hansom.

"What are you going to say to Creighton?" he asked her when they'd achieved some level of comfort on the seat.

"I'm going to tell him what happened to his father, and ask him to answer all your questions honestly."

Frank managed not to roll his eyes the way she had to him earlier. They'd be lucky if Creighton Van Dyke didn't flee over the rooftops the instant he saw Malloy's big Irish figure turn the corner onto his street. Everyone in this section of the city would recognize him instantly as a cop, in spite of his ordinary business suit. No one would trust him for a second. Truth to tell, no one in this section of town had a *reason* to trust a copper, either, which didn't help the situation.

After what seemed like an eternity, Frank figured they were close enough to get out and walk the rest of the way. He paid the cabbie and let him go on his way after helping Sarah down. He couldn't help noticing the hem of her dress was wet, even though the cape seemed to be keeping the worst of the rain off her head and shoulders. She should be home where it was warm and dry, he thought angrily, not slogging through the rain looking for anarchists.

"If you've seen enough of my ankles, we should be going," she said with a smirk and started on down the street.

Stung, he hurried to catch up to her, jostling pedestrians who got in his way.

The streets in this part of the city were lined on either side with the carts of peddlers selling everything anyone could need and a lot they probably didn't. No one living in the four- and five-story tenement buildings looming above ever needed to cook a meal or walk more than a few steps to purchase whatever they might require for survival. Money brought home by fathers and husbands quickly disappeared into the hands of the merchants camped at their doorsteps as women bartered for goods. The air smelled of the pungent odors of cooked meats and pastries and vegetables past their prime and the offal of the animals and the refuse of the humans. Shouts from the peddlers, advertising their wares, mingled with the shrieks of mothers calling their children and the squeals of children playing in the puddles below. Neighbors called to neighbors and women laughed, sharing a joke.

Frank was aware of every person, judging each of them for any threat he might pose either to Sarah or himself. People fell silent as they passed, recognizing him for who he was and wondering what trouble he was going to bring to them. The police always brought trouble.

He was so concerned with protecting Sarah that he almost didn't notice she had stopped in front of one of the tenements. He nearly stumbled trying not to knock her over.

"This is where he lives," she said, looking up as if trying to see inside the grimy windows to find the correct flat.

"Do you know which number?"

"No, but I suppose everyone knows him." A dirty little boy in mud-spattered rags stood in the doorway, watching them suspiciously. "Do you know where Creighton Van Dyke lives?" she asked him.

He just stared back blankly.

Frank's instinct was to frighten the boy into telling, but common sense told him the kid might not even speak English.

Sarah Brandt used a much more sensible approach. "A tall man," she said, showing the boy how tall with her hand. "Yellow hair." She pulled a lock of her own golden hair loose and wiggled it to illustrate her meaning.

Frank saw the light of recognition on the boy's grubby face. He produced a penny from his coat pocket. "Where is he?" he asked, holding up the penny for the boy to see.

Greed brought a spark of light to the boy's dull eyes, and he motioned for them to follow. He entered the dark hallway and started up the stairs, his wet feet leaving marks in the dust and dirt. Sarah followed, with Frank right behind. Naturally, the anarchists lived on the fifth floor, where the rent was cheapest. Frank was practically gasping by the time they arrived at the top of the stairs.

The boy reached for his reward, but Frank held it away from him. "Where is he?" he repeated, nodding at the closed doors along the landing. The boy pointed at one of them, and before Frank could move, Sarah was knocking on it, as boldly as you please.

Someone opened the door, and the boy snatched the penny and disappeared down the stairs before Frank could grab him. He heard Sarah asking for Creighton Van Dyke and braced himself to catch a fleeing fugitive.

SARAH LOOKED AT THE YOUNG WOMAN WHO HAD answered the door and knew she must be the one who had captured Creighton's heart. She stared at Sarah through coal black eyes set in a delicate face framed in raven curls. Had she been born in another time and place, a great painter might have had her pose as the Madonna. The Madonna with child, Sarah mentally corrected herself, seeing the small mound beneath the girl's apron.

"Is Creighton Van Dyke here?" she asked. Sarah could see several men sitting and eating at the table in the kitchen behind the girl. They had paused to see who was at the door, but none of them looked familiar.

"Who is it, Katya?" one of the men asked, rising from the table, and then Sarah recognized him, if only by his voice.

The slender young man in evening clothes who had partnered her at her debut had become a different person altogether. His golden hair had darkened a bit, and his shoulders were broader and his body more solid. He'd grown a beard and wore the coarse shirt and pants of a laborer, although she noticed they were too clean to have encountered much actual labor. He stood almost a head taller than the girl, and he looked out at Sarah over her.

"Creighton," Sarah said in amazement.

He frowned, squinting to see her in the dim light of the hallway. "Who . . . ?" he began and then recognition dawned. "Sarah? Sarah Decker?" he replied, even more amazed than Sarah.

"It's Sarah Brandt now," she said with a smile.

His eyes lit with pleasure. "How are you?" he asked as if they'd met on a street corner somewhere. He hadn't forgotten his old training in manners. "And what on earth are you doing here?"

He reached out, and she took his hands, squeezing hard. "I'm looking for you," she said.

Beside them, the girl made a small sound of distress, and when Sarah looked at her, she saw both fear and hatred burning the girl's black eyes.

"It's all right, Kat," he said. "Sarah is an old friend."

"Is *he* old friend, too?" Katya challenged with a slight Russian accent, using her chin to point past Sarah to where Malloy stood in the shadows of the hallway.

"Creighton, this is my friend, Frank Malloy," Sarah said quickly. "He was kind enough to escort me down her to find you."

"Do not trust them, Petya," the girl said. "He is police."

Creighton stiffened instantly and dropped Sarah's hands. He was staring warily at Malloy, who stared back with that look he used to intimidate people. She wanted to smack him for frightening Creighton. "Mr. Malloy is a detective sergeant with the police," she admitted. "He accompanied me down here because we have some bad news for you."

The two other men who had been eating with Creighton had come to stand behind him, ready to offer whatever help he might need. Unlike Creighton, they looked as if they were no strangers to work and even violence. Their eyes were hard and their expressions threatening. Sarah held her breath while she waited for Creighton to decide whether to trust her or to turn his friends loose on them.

"What kind of bad news?" he asked, still keeping his gaze fixed on Malloy.

"About your father," Sarah said.

His gaze shifted instantly to her. "Did he send you here? I can't believe it! Well, you can tell him he's wasting his time and yours. I'm not going back there. I could never live like that again."

"He didn't send me, Creighton. He can't. He's dead." She hated breaking it to him like that, but she was afraid to be subtle any longer.

He stared at her for a long moment, uncomprehending. "Dead?" he echoed, as if he'd never heard the word before.

"Yes," Sarah confirmed. "Someone planted a bomb in his office."

Then, to her surprise, he turned accusingly to the girl. "A *bomb*?" he demanded of her.

"Petya, no," she pleaded, shaking her head frantically.

He whirled to face the other two men and said something to them in Russian. They replied angrily, and Creighton started slapping at them. Malloy shoved Sarah roughly aside and grabbed Creighton's arm, twisting it up behind his back until he cried out in pain. The girl screamed and started beating on Malloy while the two men dashed into the front room of the flat. They could hear the sounds of a window opening and the men scrambling out onto the fire escape.

Sarah caught the girl's wrists and struggled with her a moment while Malloy shoved Creighton into the nearest chair. The girl stopped fighting and wrenched free, throwing herself down to her knees beside Creighton's chair. She was babbling in Russian, trying to get hold of his arm, but he jerked it away and turned toward the table, resting his elbows on it among the plates of food and burying his face in his hands.

"Katya!" Malloy said sharply, making the girl jump. She looked up at him with wide, terrified eyes. "Get him something to drink. Do you have any whiskey?"

"Vodka," Creighton muttered.

The girl pushed herself up, using the edge of the table for support. She wasn't more than about six months along, but the baby was already a burden. She stumbled to where several crates had been nailed to the wall to provide cabinet space, and she pulled down a bottle of clear liquid. The bottle was scratched and stained from much use, the mouth stuffed with a scrap of rag. Obviously, the contents were home-brewed. She poured a generous amount into a tin cup and carried it back to the table.

Creighton didn't even look at it when she set it down in front of him. "What happened?" he finally asked Malloy.

"He went to his office this morning, opened a cabinet, and a bomb exploded. He died instantly."

He closed his eyes. "My God."

Malloy gave him a moment to absorb the news. "I don't suppose you know anything about it?"

Creighton looked up, his shock replaced by anger. "That's why you're here, isn't it? You think I killed him!"

"Your family said you'd taken up with a bunch of anarchists," Malloy said. "Anarchists use bombs."

"They use bombs to make a *statement*," he said, still angry. "Not to kill someone for no reason."

"Killing one of the richest men in the city would make a statement. It would say you and your friends are the stupidest men alive."

"Malloy," Sarah tried, but neither man paid her any mind.

"Do you think we're stupid because we want to change the way men like my father oppress other human beings?" Creighton demanded. "Because we think men should be free of tyranny?"

"Do you think killing your father is going to free anybody from tyranny?" Malloy challenged.

"Yes, my sister for one."

"Is that why you killed him? To help your sister?" Malloy asked mildly.

But Creighton wouldn't be tricked so easily. "I didn't kill him. I didn't know anything about it until you walked in here."

"Your friends did, though, or at least you thought they did. What did they say to make you so angry, Van Dyke?"

Creighton glared at him. "They said my father was a"— he glanced at Sarah and then continued more mildly—"an evil man and that he deserved to die."

"So you were defending your father's honor," Malloy said with deceptive calm. "Or were you mad because they hadn't told you about the plot?"

"They have no plot!" the girl insisted. "We know nothing about bombs."

Sarah noticed she was trembling. "Why don't you sit down, Katya," she suggested gently, going to the girl to help her.

Katya shook off Sarah's hand and pulled out a chair with a jerk. She lowered herself into it cautiously, as if afraid this whole thing was some kind of a trick and she might have to flee at any moment.

"Are you all right?" Sarah asked her. "Can I get you something to drink? How long has it been since you've eaten?"

"Leave her alone," Creighton snapped.

"I'm a nurse, Creighton. And a midwife," she added meaningfully.

Creighton looked up at her in surprise, then he looked away just as quickly.

"What's the matter, Van Dyke?" Malloy taunted. "Ashamed of something?"

"I'm not ashamed of anything. Katya is my wife."

"You're legally married then? With a license and everything?" Malloy asked skeptically.

The color rose in Creighton's face. "We don't need the government to declare us married."

"Marriage is slavery," Katya insisted angrily. "Make woman slave. Petya and I, we are free."

"What about your little bastard? Is he going to be free, too?" Malloy asked with feigned interest.

"Malloy, that's enough," Sarah chided as the girl laid a protective hand over the mound of her stomach and glared murderously at Malloy. "Creighton, we don't know if you had anything to do with your father's death or not, but everyone else will believe you did. If you're innocent, you need to help Malloy find the real killer as quickly as possible."

"How could I help? I don't know anything about it," he insisted.

"You can find out things I can't," Malloy said. "And you've got a better reason than I do to catch the killer."

"Really? Didn't my stepmother offer a large enough reward?" Creighton said with disdain. Everyone knew the police didn't exert themselves to solve a crime unless they would be well paid for doing so.

"Not yet," Malloy said mildly. "But I'm sure she'll pay handsomely to have you executed for the murder."

Creighton lunged to his feet, and Malloy shoved him right back down again.

"You better get it through that thick skull of yours that you're in a lot of trouble here, you and your *wife*," Malloy said contemptuously.

"She didn't have anything to do with it!" Creighton cried, finally beginning to understand.

'Then you'd better start telling Detective Malloy everything you know," Sarah advised him. "Even if it involves your friends."

"Unless you're willing to be executed to protect them," Malloy said.

"And leave your wife and baby alone and helpless," Sarah added.

"Tell them nothing!" Katya insisted. "I am not afraid!"

Creighton looked at her for a long moment. "You should be, my darling. You should be."

4

SARAH WATCHED AS TEARS FILLED KATYA'S DARK eyes. Whatever her political beliefs, she obviously loved Creighton and was frightened for him. Perhaps she was also frightened for herself and her child. She certainly had good reason.

"I should lock you up," Malloy was saying to Creighton. "Just to make sure you don't disappear."

"Or so you can make me confess to something I didn't do," he replied bitterly. "I know how the police work."

"If you don't help me find the real killer, I won't have anyone else to blame, now will I?" Malloy replied reasonably.

The two men were glaring at each other like dogs ready to start snarling over a bone.

"Stop it, both of you," Sarah snapped. "This isn't accomplishing anything. Creighton, don't you want to find out who killed your father, if only to clear yourself?"

He didn't reply as quickly as Sarah had hoped, but at last he said, "I suppose so, although I don't for a minute expect justice to be done in such a corrupt society."

"There's never any justice in solving a murder," Malloy informed him, "because the victim is still dead."

Creighton looked at him in surprise. He probably hadn't expected philosophy from a lowly cop, and Sarah played on the momentary advantage.

"Malloy, you don't really want to arrest Creighton, do you? Not if he's innocent, I mean."

Malloy frowned blackly, but he said, "No matter what your politics, Van Dyke, you're still the son of a millionaire. It would be almost impossible to get you convicted even if you're guilty. I sure don't want to go to all that trouble if you aren't. And if it's one of your anarchist friends, wouldn't he want to step forward and become a martyr for the cause or something?"

"You mean like Alexander Berkman?" Creighton asked sarcastically, naming the man who had tried to assassinate Henry Clay Frick. "Rotting in a prison doesn't make a very good martyrdom."

"Frick didn't die," Malloy reminded him. "Your father's killer will be executed in the electric chair."

Katya made a sound of distress and quickly covered her mouth.

Malloy studied her for a moment. "Do you know anything about this?" he asked.

She shook her head, her dark eyes wide. "Nothing," she whispered.

"Was it your brother?" Creighton asked with a frown.

"No, Misha would not do this," she insisted, her eyes bright with a new terror.

"Who's your brother and where is he?" Malloy asked sharply.

"He would not do this. I would know!" Katya said frantically.

"Are you sure?" Malloy challenged. "He'd probably try to protect you. Where can we find him?"

"You can't," Creighton said. "Not if he doesn't want to be found, and I doubt he's anxious to talk to the police about anything."

"Then I suppose you're all I've got, Van Dyke. I don't have any choice but to run you in."

Creighton glared at Malloy, his expression one of pure hatred. Sarah could see that arresting him would only make him less likely to cooperate.

"Don't you think you should take him to the Van Dyke home first?" she asked.

Creighton transferred his glare to her. "I'd rather go to jail."

"I know your sister needs to see you. She's very upset," Sarah tried. "And she's been ill."

"Ill?" he asked in alarm. "What's wrong with her?"

"I don't know," she lied without compunction. "It could be something serious, and the shock of your father's death has only made it worse. Your stepmother hasn't been very sympathetic, and Tad's reaction to everything was to get drunk. She needs you, Creighton. She doesn't have anyone else."

He rose to his feet. "Then I must see her," he said to Sarah.

"No, is trick!" Katya cried, pushing herself to her feet also.

"It doesn't matter," Creighton told her. "I need to see Alberta and make sure she's all right. What happens after that . . . Well, I'll deal with it."

"I'll just go with you," Malloy said mildly. "To make sure you arrive safely."

Creighton frowned. "Suit yourself. Then you can arrest me, if you think it will do any good, but not until I've seen my sister."

"Fair enough," Malloy agreed.

Creighton went to where his coat hung on a peg on the wall and began to shrug into it. Malloy looked at Sarah questioningly.

"Go ahead. I need to go to the mission," she told him, referring to the Prodigal Son Mission, where she had been doing volunteer work. It was only a few blocks away. "I didn't get there at all yesterday."

He nodded, but he wasn't happy. He didn't like the thought of her walking around this neighborhood alone, even though he knew she did it all the time in the course of her work.

"Petya, do not trust them," Katya pleaded, going to where Creighton stood by the door.

He took her hands in both of his and pressed them to his chest. "I'll be all right," he assured her tenderly. "And I'll be back. I promise."

She didn't look as if she believed him, but she didn't protest. From the way her shoulders sagged in resignation, Sarah guessed that she was accustomed to accepting the unacceptable.

He reached into his pocket, pulled out a handful of money, and pressed it into her palm. Then he was on his way, out the door without a backward glance.

"Don't get too far ahead of me, Van Dyke, or I'll think you're trying to get away," Malloy called, heading out after him.

Sarah watched the two men disappear down the dark stairwell, then turned back to Katya. All the color had drained from her face, and her dark eyes looked hollow.

"Please, sit down," Sarah said, taking the girl's arm gently and leading her back to the chair Creighton had vacated. This time she didn't resist, as if all her spirit had gone with Creighton. Sarah glanced around and saw a teapot on the table. She found a clean cup and poured some of the dark black liquid for Katya.

"Drink this," she said. "It will make you feel better."

The girl obeyed, taking a long sip of the lukewarm brew. Then she set the cup down on the table and stared into it forlornly.

"Are you hungry?"

The girl looked up, and Sarah was relieved to see some of her spirit had returned. "I do not need help. My friend is midwife. She live downstairs."

"Would you like me to get her? Or someone else? You shouldn't be alone."

The girl tried to maintain her defiance, but her eyes grew moist and her lower lip quivered. "Petya . . . Creighton," she corrected. "He will go to prison?"

"Not if he didn't kill his father. Do you know something that could help?"

Sarah held her breath as the girl considered her options. Finally, she shook her head.

"Are you willing to see the father of your child executed for something he didn't do?"

Katya looked away. She didn't want Sarah to see her pain or her indecision. As much as Sarah hated the thought of seeing Creighton charged with his father's death, that might be what it would take to make Katya betray whomever she was protecting. Since Creighton had mentioned Katya's brother, Sarah had a good idea who it was, too.

Before she could try again to convince the girl to cooperate, the sound of several people running up the stairs distracted her. A woman appeared in the doorway, but she stopped dead when she saw Sarah. She took in Sarah from head to toe in one sharp glance, then turned to where Katya sat and said something to her in Russian.

Katya replied wearily, and the other woman clasped her hands together in distress. By then two men had appeared behind her. Sarah recognized one of them as one of the men who had fled earlier. The other was a stranger. They both hung back, content to allow the woman to deal with the situation.

"Do you speak English?" Sarah asked.

"Of course I speak English," the woman said with just the faintest accent. She was a small woman but not delicate. Her body was compact and solid, as if she contained more energy than she could ever use. She wore her dark hair pulled back into a sensible bun and had wire-rimmed glasses perched on her nose. "Who are you?"

"I'm Sarah Brandt, a friend of Creighton Van Dyke's. And who are you?"

She raised her chin a notch in silent defiance. "I am Emma Goldman, a friend of Katya Ivanovna." She'd said her name as if she expected Sarah to recognize it.

She didn't.

"Good," Sarah said. "Miss Ivanovna is very upset, and she shouldn't be alone in her condition."

Miss Goldman looked at Sarah with contempt. "What do you know about her condition?"

"I'm a midwife," Sarah replied, surprising her. "She looks as if she may not be getting enough to eat. She's very pale and—"

"I am also a midwife," Miss Goldman said contemptuously. "I studied in Vienna."

Sarah was impressed and allowed Miss Goldman to see it.

Vienna had the best medical schools in the world. "Then
I'm sure you know that Miss Ivanovna needs proper nour-
ishment, for her baby." Sarah glanced at the cheap, tin pots
sitting on the stove. "If she had some iron pots to cook with,
that would help." The iron from the utensils got into the
food somehow and helped prevent anemia.

"Her name is *Petrova*," Miss Goldman said. "Katya
Ivanovna Petrova. *Miss Petrova*."

"I'm sorry," Sarah said. "I didn't know. But I'm sure if
you studied in Vienna, you know about the iron pots and
the importance of proper diet."

"These things are not so easy when you are poor," Miss
Goldman pointed out sternly.

"Creighton Van Dyke isn't poor," Sarah replied. "Or at
least he doesn't have to be," she added, glancing around the
sparely furnished flat.

"He renounced his wealth for the corruption that it is,"
Miss Goldman said righteously.

"Miss Goldman, I see far too many women die in childbirth because they were too poor to feed themselves properly. I can't believe it would be a corruption for Creighton to
properly care for Katya and his child. When I see him again,
I will point that out to him. In the meantime, I trust that
you will look after Miss Petrova." She looked down at where
Katya still sat, seemingly oblivious to the drama taking
place around her. "Katya, if you need anything, please let
me know." She reached into her purse and drew out one of
her cards and laid it on the table. "It was a pleasure meeting
you, Miss Goldman," Sarah said and started for the doorway,
in which the three visitors still stood.

They gave way grudgingly, and Sarah passed by them
without a word, managing to exchange glances with the
man who had fled earlier to let him know she recognized

him. Fortunately, no one followed her down the stairs. If she'd managed to get herself into difficulty, getting herself out would have been only half the problem. The other half would be explaining to Malloy why she should still be allowed to help him with the case.

F RANK HAD A LITTLE TROUBLE KEEPING UP WITH VAN Dyke in the congested streets of the Lower East Side. He was tall enough that he couldn't just disappear, though, so Frank was able to keep him in view. To Frank's surprise, Van Dyke stopped at the bottom of the stairs that led up to the Bleeker Street Elevated Train Station and waited for him to catch up.

His expression was defiant, but he refused to meet Frank's eye. "I don't have any money for the train. I gave it all to Katya."

Frank bit back a grin. "Come on. My treat."

Van Dyke followed him reluctantly up the long stairway, and they waited in silence for the next train to come. Finally, Van Dyke said, "Is my sister really ill?"

"She looked like it, and Mrs. Brandt said she was. She took to her bed and couldn't answer any questions about your father's death."

"What could she possibly know about that?" he asked resentfully.

"Enough to be worried you had something to do with it," Frank replied.

"Well, I didn't."

"Then why are you so reluctant to answer my questions?" Frank inquired.

"Why should I trust you?"

"Because I'm the only friend you've got. Your father's widow was only too happy to tell me you're an anarchist.

When word gets out, your father's friends will easily believe you killed the old man for his money. Everybody knows anarchists have no love or loyalty."

"That isn't true!"

"I didn't say it was," Frank said. "I only said everybody believes it. You want to overthrow everything they hold sacred. They'll hate you for turning against your own kind. They'll want you to be guilty so they can get rid of you and feel a little safer."

His young face hardened as he stared off into the distance, refusing to acknowledge what Frank had said.

"Who do you think did it?" Frank asked after a few moments.

Van Dyke pretended he hadn't heard.

"You asked Katya if it was her brother. That's why you don't want to say anything, isn't it? You don't want to hurt her."

"He wouldn't have done it without telling me," Van Dyke said, still refusing to look at Frank.

"Wouldn't he? What if he was afraid you'd be too cowardly—or too honorable—to kill your own father."

"He'd have nothing to gain from it!" Van Dyke said in exasperation.

"What do anarchists have to gain from killing anyone? They do it, though, don't they? They want to frighten rich people and impress poor people. They kill to make a point, not to gain in any way. You know that as well as I do."

Frank saw the muscles of his jaw tighten as he fought against responding to the provocation.

"Of course, if your father was dead, you might inherit some money," Frank observed.

Van Dyke looked at him sharply, his eyes wary. "I doubt it. I'm sure my father disinherited me."

"Are you?" Frank inquired. "But even if he did, would Katya's brother know it?"

"Money means nothing to them," he insisted.

"Doesn't it? Who pays the rent on your flat? Who buys the food?" Frank grabbed Van Dyke's hand and forced his fingers open, revealing a smooth palm. "Doesn't look like you've been doing much manual labor."

Van Dyke jerked his hand free. "We live communally. Everyone contributes what they can."

"If you don't work, what do *you* contribute? Besides fathering bastard children, of course."

Van Dyke turned on him, instantly furious. His face crimson, his eyes fierce, he looked as if he were going to take a swing at Frank, which is what he'd expected and was ready for. But he only said, "You filthy-minded son of a . . . Don't you dare talk about her! You aren't good enough to speak her name!"

Frank stared back as innocently as he could. "Who? Katya?"

This time Van Dyke's whole body jerked, as if his every instinct demanded he attack Frank and pound him into the ground. But some stronger force held him back. Frank was beginning to think there was something to the theory that the rich had all the spirit bred out of them.

"I can't believe they keep you around just because you're so handsome, Van Dyke," Frank said. "You must contribute something. Rich fellow like you must have some money of his own. You pay their rent, don't you? Maybe you even support them completely. That would give them more time to do whatever it is they do. What *is* it they do? Sit around in saloons drinking and talking, making speeches and printing pamphlets? They wouldn't want to give that up to get jobs, would they? What happened, Van Dyke? Did you run out of money? Did your father cut off your allowance?"

Van Dyke looked as if he was going to explode with fury, which was exactly what Frank had been working for, but just then a train pulled up. Almost desperately, Van Dyke rushed toward it, jostling people who got in the way. Frank was close behind him, but by the time they were inside the car, Van Dyke was back in control of himself again. He'd taken a seat next to an elderly woman holding several packages in her lap. There were no other seats nearby, so Frank had to stand in the aisle to make sure Van Dyke didn't decide to get off at the next stop and disappear.

The old lady smiled up at him, and Frank nodded. Van Dyke just stared straight ahead, either pretending Frank wasn't there or too afraid to look at him and risk saying something he'd regret. Frank sighed. This was going to be even harder than he'd feared when Roosevelt first gave him the job that morning.

SARAH HAD DECIDED TO WALK TO THE MISSION, SINCE finding a cab on the Lower East Side wasn't very likely. The rain was still falling, but not heavily. She didn't mind. She'd find a warm fire and a friendly welcome at the mission.

Sarah turned down Mulberry Street and passed Police Headquarters with hardly a glance. The building had no interest to her because she knew Malloy wasn't there. A short distance down the street, she found the old Dutch Colonial house that had been converted into a home for wayward girls. A fresh-faced girl of about thirteen opened the door and greeted her by name.

Before Sarah could take off her cape, she heard the patter of tiny feet racing down the hall and looked up to see a small girl hurtling herself into Sarah's arms.

"Aggie, I'm soaking wet," Sarah protested even as she caught the child in a hug.

Small arms snaked around her neck and clung fiercely.

"Aggie, at least let Mrs. Brandt get her coat off," a plump older woman scolded gently as she came down the hallway toward them. She was wiping her hands on her apron, and she greeted Sarah with a smile.

"I'm sorry I couldn't come yesterday, Mrs. Keller," Sarah said as much for Aggie's benefit as for the woman's. "I had a baby to take care of."

"Aggie missed you," Mrs. Keller said. She was a widow who had been hired several weeks ago to manage the mission and look after the girls living there. The home had fallen on hard times lately, but those who supported it wanted to see the work continue. Too many poor girls ended up prostituting themselves on the streets because they had no place to go when their families turned them out.

"I missed her, too," Sarah said, holding Aggie away so the girl could see her face and know she really meant it.

The little girl frowned, pretending to pout, but Sarah tickled her and slowly she smiled, showing even teeth.

"Let me get my wet cloak off, and we'll go sit in the kitchen where it's warm, and you can tell me what you've been doing," Sarah said, setting the child on the floor again.

Of course, Sarah knew Aggie wouldn't actually tell her anything since the child didn't speak. At first, Sarah had suspected she was deaf, but she quickly realized Aggie heard and understood everything said to or around her. Since Aggie had been found sleeping on the doorstep of the mission one morning, no one knew her history, but Sarah suspected she had experienced a serious trauma of some kind that had rendered her mute. Sarah did know the child was capable of speech, since she'd heard her utter one word in the middle of a crisis. She hadn't spoken since, however.

When Sarah had hung up her cloak, Aggie took her hand and led her back to the kitchen, where several girls were cleaning up from the evening meal. They all greeted Sarah. The lingering heat from the stove felt heavenly, and Sarah held up her chilled hands to warm them.

"Are you hungry?" Mrs. Keller asked.

Sarah couldn't remember when she'd last eaten. "Do you have anything left from supper?"

"For you, we'll find something," Mrs. Keller assured her with a smile.

Sarah sat down at the kitchen table, and Aggie crawled up into her lap. She "told" Sarah about her day by nodding or shaking her head in response to Sarah's questions. Sarah watched her face lovingly, studying every nuance of her expressions. She'd known the child only a little more than a month, but she'd grown to adore her. As she stroked Aggie's silky hair, her heart ached. Common sense told her Aggie had no place here. The mission was a haven for older girls whose lives had been hard and oftentimes ugly.

Mrs. Keller and the ladies who volunteered here tried to give Aggie special attention, but no one had the time or energy to really mother her the way she needed. The older girls had too many needs and made too many demands. Sarah also worried that some of the older girls would be a bad influence on the small child. Mention had been made of an orphanage, but Sarah knew the chances that a mute child would be adopted were small. She couldn't stand the thought of Aggie growing up in an institution.

"She sits by the window, watching for you," Mrs. Keller said as she set a plate of stew on the table in front of Sarah.

Aggie looked up at Sarah with eyes full of longing, and Sarah had to fight an urge to weep. How many times had she longed for a child of her own, a dream that would never be fulfilled? If only she had a way to care for the girl. But her work as a midwife took her out of the house at all hours on a moment's notice. A child so young couldn't be left alone, nor could she go along with Sarah to deliver babies. She couldn't even consider taking on such a responsibility.

"Come sit on a chair, Aggie, and give Mrs. Brandt a chance to eat," Mrs. Keller said, pushing a chair up close beside Sarah's.

Aggie gave Sarah a last, mischievous look, then quickly reached up and kissed her quickly and sweetly on the cheek before scrambling over to the other chair. Sarah had to blink hard to keep herself from crying.

CREIGHTON VAN DYKE WASN'T QUITE AS IMPATIENT ON the final leg of the journey as he had been in the beginning. Frank had no trouble matching him step for step as they walked the few blocks from the Fiftieth Street El Station to his father's house on Fifth Avenue.

After the first block, Van Dyke said, "You said someone had planted a bomb in my father's office?" He didn't look at Frank, as if afraid to trust himself. Or perhaps he didn't want to show any vulnerability.

Frank wasn't offended. "That's right. Someone had hidden it in his liquor cabinet, and when he opened the door, it exploded."

"Was anyone else hurt?" He sounded genuinely concerned.

"His secretary, a Mr. Reed, was injured. I haven't seen him yet, so I don't know how bad."

They walked a minute or two while Van Dyke absorbed the information.

"Wait a minute," Van Dyke said, looking at Frank at

last. "Why would my father have been opening his liquor cabinet at that hour? He rarely drank at all and certainly not before evening."

"His valet said he'd taken a gift for Mr. Snowberger with him this morning, a bottle of very expensive brandy. I'm assuming he was putting it into the cabinet for safekeeping."

Van Dyke's face creased into a frown. "A gift? What for?"

"They'd had a . . . a disagreement of some kind, I think."

Van Dyke shook his head. "They were always having disagreements, as long as they'd known each other. I can't believe he'd settle an argument like that anyway. His word was his bond. If he needed to apologize—and I can't say I've ever known him to apologize for anything!—I can't imagine he'd feel he needed a *gift* to seal the bargain."

"Do you think the valet was lying?" Frank asked.

"No, but . . . It just doesn't make any sense." He reached up and rubbed his forehead. "What a senseless way to die."

"Dying hardly ever makes sense, Mr. Van Dyke," Frank reminded him.

Van Dyke stared at him for a moment as they walked, as if trying to decide something. "Does *murder* make sense, Detective?"

"Only to the killer."

Frank didn't like the way things were going. He was pretty sure now that Van Dyke was innocent, but he also couldn't ignore the evidence that pointed to bomb-loving anarchists as the killers. His chances of learning anything about the anarchists depended on how much Van Dyke would help, since that group would hardly cooperate with the police voluntarily. Frank knew how to make reluctant witnesses talk, but he'd never tried to use the third-degree method of persuasion on someone of Van Dyke's social class. Besides, Van Dyke was so mild mannered, it would be like kicking a puppy. He also didn't like the thought of what Sarah Brandt would say if she knew Frank had roughed up her friend.

When they reached the Van Dyke house, Creighton hesitated a moment before climbing the front stairs. Gathering his courage, Frank decided. Having met Lilly Van Dyke, he couldn't blame the young man.

A maid answered Creighton's knock, and her expression said she was just about to order him around to the tradesmen's entrance when she recognized him. "Mr. Creighton!" she exclaimed in surprise.

"May I come in, Ella? I'd like to see my sister."

The girl apologized and admitted him, nodding stiffly and suspiciously at Frank when he followed the young gentleman into the foyer.

"Tell Miss Van Dyke that her brother is here and wants to see her," Frank said. "We'll be waiting for her upstairs, if you'll show us to a room."

Van Dyke glared at Frank. "I need to speak to my sister privately."

"Too bad. You're both suspects in a murder investigation. You either talk to her with me there, or you wait until she can visit you at the Tombs," he said, using the nickname for the city jail.

Once again, Van Dyke looked as if he'd like to punch Frank, but his good breeding prevented him. "Can we use the front parlor, Ella?" he asked the maid.

She looked from Van Dyke to Frank and back again anxiously. "Yes, sir. I'll go fetch Miss Alberta."

The maid scampered away, leaving the men to find their own way to the second-floor parlor.

Frank made himself at home this time, taking a seat in the most comfortable chair in the room while Van Dyke paced restlessly back and forth across the flowered carpet. Frank considered trying to make him angry again, but decided not to, since he didn't know how long he would have until Alberta Van Dyke showed up. He didn't want to use the tactic too many times, because sooner or later Van Dyke would catch on and refuse the bait. So they waited in uneasy silence.

At last the parlor door opened, and Alberta Van Dyke came in. She looked even paler than she had earlier, and her expression was bleak. Frank rose to his feet, and Van Dyke hurried to her.

"Creighton," she said, her voice ragged. "You shouldn't have come here."

"It's all right," her brother assured her. "I brought the police with me, so I can't get in any more trouble than I'm already in."

She glanced at Malloy and then silently dismissed his presence as unimportant. She took both of Creighton's hands in hers and searched his face with red-rimmed eyes. "I knew you didn't have anything to do with Father's death," she said after a moment.

"Of course I didn't. Come and sit down. Sarah said you've been ill." He didn't add that she looked awful, although Frank could tell from his expression he was alarmed by her appearance.

She moved to the sofa and drew her brother down beside her. "Creighton, you must be careful. Lilly is determined to blame you and your friends for Father's death." She looked at Frank again, this time accusingly. "The police believe her, too."

"We're looking for the truth, Miss Van Dyke," Frank said. "If you know something that will help me find it, you need to tell me."

"I know my brother would never do a thing like this."

"Then who would?"

She turned back to Creighton with a pleading expression.

"Katya didn't know anything about it," he told her. "I don't think they're involved."

"How can you be sure?" she asked.

"What reason would they have?" he argued.

"I asked your brother if he was supporting his anarchist friends," Frank said to Miss Van Dyke. "If they thought he'd have more to share with them if his father was dead, they might have taken matters into their own hands."

She looked at Creighton in alarm. "If you needed more money, you should have asked me!"

Creighton only stared back at her in dismay.

"Why would he have needed money, Miss Van Dyke?" Frank asked.

Her eyes widened in alarm as she realized she had revealed something damaging to her brother.

Creighton sighed in defeat. "My father had cut off my allowance," he admitted. "Two months ago."

"Before that you were supporting Katya and her brother and how many others?" Frank asked.

"About ten. Sometimes more, sometimes less. Whoever needed a place to stay. It's amazing how cheaply people can live in the tenements," he told his sister.

"Did you know your father had cut off his allowance, Miss Van Dyke?"

"Yes, but . . ." She looked away, unwilling to say anything for fear it would hurt her brother.

"And you were giving him money?"

"I had no idea he was supporting so many people," she exclaimed. "I would have sent more!"

"It's all right," Creighton assured her, taking her hand in his. "You couldn't have known."

"But your friends *did* know," Frank guessed. "They knew

your father had cut you off and your sister wasn't sending you enough for all of them."

Creighton rubbed his forehead. "I can't believe—"

"They knew, didn't they?" Frank insisted.

He nodded. "I had to tell them. I had to explain why I couldn't . . . Their work is so important! I was glad to share whatever I had with them. You understand, don't you?" he begged his sister.

She gave him a pitying look. "I just wanted you and Katya to be all right. I couldn't let you starve, especially with the baby . . ." Her voice broke, and Frank immediately remembered that she was also with child.

"Mr. Van Dyke, you've given me a very good reason why your friends might have killed your father. They could reasonably assume you'd inherit at least part of his fortune if he died. You'd have enough money to support all of them and their cause for the rest of your life."

"Oh, Creighton," Miss Van Dyke said in anguish. "I'm so sorry!"

"They didn't do it!" Creighton insisted, just as anguished. "I can't believe it. I *won't* believe it."

"Then who else might have wanted your father dead?" Frank asked, leaning forward and resting his elbows on his knees to show he was truly interested in their opinions.

Creighton looked at his sister, and she stared back at him for a long moment. Then she turned to Frank. "Lilly probably did."

"Your stepmother?" he asked in surprise. "Why?"

"She hated him," Miss Van Dyke said. "She never wanted to marry him in the first place. I've heard her say it dozens of times."

"Why did she, then?"

"Her father made her. He owed our father money, and he

couldn't pay. Father had seen Lilly and admired her, and her father offered her to him. I didn't think Father was interested in remarrying, but the idea of having such a lovely young woman must have . . . intrigued him."

Frank thought *intrigued* was probably the wrong word, but he didn't contradict her. "Many women are unhappy in their marriages, Miss Van Dyke. Very few of them kill their husbands," Frank observed.

"Lilly was more than unhappy," Creighton said gravely. "She resented Father for not buying her all the things she wanted."

"She thought she should at least have pretty things if she was married to a wealthy man," Miss Van Dyke explained. "But Father was . . . frugal. He couldn't see any reason why she needed so many gowns. He didn't like going to parties and balls, either, so Lilly went alone."

"And made a scandal of herself," Creighton said.

"Did she take lovers?" Frank asked with interest. Maybe Sarah Brandt was wrong. Maybe Lilly had ignored the risks and flaunted all conventions, and her lover had helped her get rid of her husband.

Brother and sister both looked embarrassed. Miss Van Dyke's pale face colored unbecomingly at the bold question.

"Don't get the wrong idea. Even Lilly wouldn't be *that* foolish," Creighton said quickly. "But people still gossiped about her. She doesn't seem to know how to be discreet."

"She's a shameless flirt, though," Miss Van Dyke said. "Other women hated her."

"So you think your stepmother made a bomb and put it in your father's office so she could be free of him?" Frank asked skeptically.

"Someone could have done it for her," Miss Van Dyke insisted.

"Someone she flirted with?" Frank asked, not bothering to hide his doubt. No lover meant no one with a motive to kill.

"Perhaps she hired someone," Miss Van Dyke tried. She looked to her brother for support.

Creighton shook his head in despair. "Where would she meet someone who could make a bomb, Bertie?"

"Miss Van Dyke, I don't want to arrest your brother if he's innocent, but I need his help to find out who really committed this crime."

He waited for a few minutes while the brother and sister engaged in a silent debate. Finally, she said, "Creighton, you must tell him who those people are."

Van Dyke's shoulders sagged, and Frank knew he had won.

5

SARAH WOKE THE NEXT MORNING WITH THE STRANGE sense that something terrible had happened. She needed a moment to remember the bomb and all that had followed, and then she groaned. She'd come straight home from the mission last evening and gone immediately to bed, where she'd slept like the dead. In all the excitement yesterday, she'd forgotten she'd missed a night's sleep the day before. What had Malloy been up to since he'd left Katya's flat yesterday with Creighton? For all she knew, he'd already solved the case. She certainly hoped so, but the only way she'd find out was if she got up and dressed and went to the Van Dyke house.

With another groan, she forced herself to throw back the covers to the morning chill. The first day of December had dawned cloudy and cold. An hour later, she stepped into the Van Dykes' foyer. The maid led her upstairs, but when they reached the second floor, they could hear the sounds of raised voices coming from the parlor.

The maid glanced toward the closed door and winced. "I'll announce you, Mrs. Brandt," she said and reluctantly went to do so.

The voices ceased the moment the girl knocked, and Sarah didn't wait to be summoned. She'd learned from Malloy that angry people often said things they later regretted, and she didn't want to give any of them a chance to regain their composure.

"Good morning," she said cheerfully, pushing past the startled maid and stepping into the room. She found various members of the Van Dyke family staring back at her stupidly. Lilly Van Dyke stood in the center of the room. She had already donned her mourning dress of black bombazine in the latest fashion, but her face was an unbecoming shade of scarlet. Alberta also wore black, but much less stylishly, and the color only made her already pale face look ghastly. She also looked angry, although a silent determination held it in check. At the far end of the room sat Tad Van Dyke, holding his head and looking as if he might be sick at any moment. Sarah remembered the bottle of brandy he'd taken to his room and bit back a smile. "I hope I'm not interrupting," she lied.

"Sarah, I'm so glad you're here," Lilly said to her surprise. "Maybe you can talk some sense into that policeman!"

"What policeman is that?" Sarah asked, even though she was certain she knew.

"Mr. Malloy," Alberta said much more calmly. "Although I don't think that will be necessary."

"Not necessary!" Lilly cried in outrage. "He brought

that . . . that *criminal* right into our home! What's to stop him from murdering the rest of us in our own beds?"

"Criminal?" Sarah echoed in confusion.

"Creighton," Tad explained wearily, "Lilly, this is his home as much as ours, and he has a policeman guarding his room. He's practically a prisoner."

"And even if he wasn't a prisoner," Alberta added, "he has no reason to harm any of *us*."

"No *reason*?" Lilly practically screamed. "He killed his own father!"

"He most certainly did not," Alberta cried, jumping to her feet. "And if you ever say that again, I'll slap you!"

Lilly stared at her incredulously. She could not have been more surprised if a chair had threatened her. Sarah hurried to defuse the situation.

"Lilly, please sit down and tell me exactly what happened," she urged, taking the woman's arm and leading her over to the sofa. She sat down obediently, although she was still staring at Alberta as if she'd grown a second head. "I gather Mr. Malloy brought Creighton back here yesterday," Sarah said, trying to draw her attention away from the stepdaughter.

"Yes," Alberta replied when Lilly simply frowned with distaste. "Creighton wanted to see me, so Mr. Malloy brought him here. Then Mr. Malloy got him to agree to help him find the person who . . . who killed Father."

"Did he use a mirror?" Lilly sniped.

Alberta ignored her and sat back down again. "He was going to take Creighton to jail, to make sure he didn't run away or try to warn anyone. I couldn't bear the thought of Creighton in a place like that—"

"I'm sure it's no worse than the hovel where he lives with that . . . that *woman*!" Lilly insisted.

"Please, Lilly," Sarah said sweetly, "I need to hear the entire story."

Lilly sighed dramatically, but she kept her silence.

Alberta cast her a venomous look, but she continued. "We discussed some alternatives, and we finally were able to convince Mr. Malloy that Creighton would be perfectly safe here, under a police guard."

"Why should we care whether *he's* safe?" Lilly wanted to know. "*We're* the ones in danger!"

"Lilly," Tad said as reasonably as a man with a hangover could manage, "as Alberta pointed out, Creighton has no reason to wish any of us harm."

"He most certainly does! We're all heirs along with him. With us dead, he would have your father's entire fortune!"

"Not if *he* killed all of you," Sarah was happy to inform her. "Murderers can't inherit."

"She's absolutely right," Alberta said with an odd little grin. "He'd most certainly hire an assassin to do it."

Lilly made an unladylike sound of outrage and lunged to her feet. "You unnatural creature! No wonder no man ever wanted you!"

The look Alberta gave her should have struck her dead on the spot, but Lilly was too angry herself to notice or care. Fortunately, Tad chose that moment to intervene. He pushed himself out of his chair and reached Lilly in two long strides.

"Stop it, Lilly," he said sternly, taking her by both her arms and turning her to face him. "You're hysterical."

She stared up at him in surprise, and her anger seemed to melt away into an expression unlike any Sarah had ever seen a mother give a son. Then, just as suddenly, she burst into tears and collapsed into his arms.

Sarah stepped back, wanting to distance herself from

what she thought she might have seen. From the corner of her eye, she saw Alberta turn away and walk to the window, her back unnaturally stiff and her shoulders hunched as if expecting a blow.

"Oh, Tad, I don't know what I'd do without you," Lilly was saying brokenly as she wept against Tad's chest.

He murmured words of comfort to her, caressing her back and shoulders warmly. Too warmly.

"I'm going to check on Creighton," Alberta announced to no one in particular. "I doubt anyone even thought to send him up any breakfast."

She walked out, leaving the door standing open. Sarah watched her, torn between staying to see what else she could learn about Tad and his relationship with his stepmother and going with Alberta to speak with Creighton. She finally decided she knew as much as she wanted to about Tad and Lilly's relationship, and she followed Alberta.

When she caught up with her friend in the third-floor hallway, Alberta was staring down in disgust at the policeman sitting outside Creighton's room. He'd been provided a chair, and he was leaning back on two legs, head and shoulders resting against the wall, sound asleep and snoring softly.

Alberta made a fist and wrapped loudly on the wall beside the patrolman's head. He awoke with a start that almost sent him sprawling onto the floor. He caught himself just in time, at the cost of most of his dignity, and managed to scramble to his feet, losing his hat in the process.

"Oh, sorry, miss," he was saying in acute embarrassment. "Must've dozed off."

"I don't suppose anyone brought my brother anything to eat this morning," Alberta snapped.

The cop rubbed his face as if trying to clear his head. "Not that I remember," he admitted.

She dismissed him with a contemptuous glance and went to the door. "Creighton, it's me," she said, knocking. "May I come in?"

She waited a moment, but apparently received no response, "Creighton, are you awake?" she asked more loudly, pounding harder on the door to rouse him.

"Sound sleeper, is he, miss?" the policeman asked, earning a black look from Alberta. The look she gave Sarah was different, though, and Sarah hurried over to the door.

"Is it locked?" she asked.

"No need, with me sitting right here," the cop was saying as Alberta turned the knob and pushed the door open.

"Creighton?" she called, her voice tinged with alarm. "Creighton, where are you?"

The room was ice cold, and one of the windows stood wide open, the curtains stirring in the breeze.

"No!" Alberta cried, and finally the officer realized something wrong.

He pushed past the two women and, seeing the open window, ran to it. The bedroom was on the third floor. If he'd gone out . . .

"Dear heaven," Alberta whispered in horror.

"Is he . . . ?" Sarah asked, not wanting to say the words but picturing Creighton's broken body in the yard below.

"Don't see nothing," the officer reported. "You sure he ain't here someplace?"

Quickly, he checked the bath and under the bed and the clothes press, every place where a grown man might be concealed. The room was empty.

"He . . . he didn't jump?" Alberta asked incredulously.

Sarah went to the window this time and looked out. The yard below was a small garden, neatly trimmed and readied for winter. Only a few dead leaves lay on the brown grass. Could Creighton have sneaked out the door past the officer? No, surely that would've awakened him. And if he'd gone out the door, why was the window open?

Sarah looked down again. No one could have jumped three stories and not been seriously injured. She leaned out, looking for something, anything, that could explain where he'd gone. Then she saw it. A drain pipe ran up the outside wall between this window and the one in the bath.

When she pulled her head back inside, Alberta was beside her, peering out over her shoulder. "I'd forgotten. He used to climb down there when he wanted to get away."

Sarah turned to the officer, who had finally realized the magnitude of his problem. "You'd better tell Detective Sergeant Malloy that his prisoner has escaped."

FRANK HAD RETURNED TO VAN DYKE'S OFFICE THIS morning. Snowberger was anxious to get the mess cleared away, and no one could blame him for that. With Creighton Van Dyke safely under guard, Frank figured he could finish things up here and make Snowberger happy.

Captain O'Connor had put two of his own men to work going through the rubble to find what they could. O'Connor had probably chosen his best detectives, but Frank could tell from looking at them that they'd likely spent most of their careers investigating the inside of saloons, venturing out on a case only when someone greased their palms with a fat reward. Frank found them standing around in the reception area talking with a third man he didn't know.

The detectives greeted Frank with suspicion. They knew he'd been assigned by Commissioner Roosevelt himself, and they resented him for that. The crime had happened in their precinct, and they'd want the glory—and the reward—for themselves if the case was solved.

"Detective Sergeant Frank Malloy," Frank introduced himself to the stranger and offered his hand, when the others gave no indication they would do the honors.

"John Peterson," the man said. He was in his forties, lean and fit looking with an intelligent face, unlike the paunchy detectives. "I'm an electrician. Captain O'Connor asked me to take a look at what you found and see what I could make of it. I was just explaining it to these gentlemen."

Frank hadn't heard about them finding anything in particular, and neither of the other men would meet his eye. "Why don't you show me and explain it to me at the same time?" Frank suggested. "These *gentlemen* can wait here and make sure no one disturbs anything," he added with satisfaction.

The two detectives glared at him, but he ignored them as John Peterson led him toward the stairs.

"Some of the clerks have their offices down here," Peterson was saying as they descended. "But the part of the building under Mr. Van Dyke's office is used for storage. The furnace is also down there."

Frank followed him through a large room where about a dozen desks sat in neat rows. Only three young men were working there today. Tad Van Dyke wasn't one of them. A door in the back opened into the room Peterson had described. The floor here was packed dirt, the walls rough. Two small windows seemed to be the only source of light until Peterson threw a switch and an electric lightbulb hanging from the ceiling illuminated. Now Frank could see that above them ran pipes carrying the steam heat to the rest of the building from the boiler.

"I found the end of a wire in what was left of the cabinet

that exploded upstairs," Peterson explained. "I'll show you when we go back up there. I followed where it had been threaded into the room from down here through the same hole the pipes go through." He pointed to a spot on the ceiling where one of the many pipes entered the floor above.

Frank could see a couple of wires had been inserted into the hole and where they followed the pipe along the ceiling. "Where do they go?"

"Over here." Peterson moved to the corner of the room where the shadows weren't completely dispelled by the electric light. Still he could see what Peterson had found. On a ledge near the ceiling sat a four-cell electric battery, which was connected to the wires.

"Was this hooked to the bomb somehow?" Frank asked.

"Yes, the battery would have made the electrical charge that ignited the bomb."

"Was it hooked up to the cabinet door somehow so when he opened it, the thing exploded?"

"That's what I thought at first, but I was wrong. Look here." Peterson showed him more wires leading away from the battery and attached to a series of hooks. The wires disappeared through a carefully drilled hole in the outside wall.

"Where does it go?"

"Into the alley." Peterson led Frank to the door on that side of the room. He threw the bolt and opened it. They stepped out into the alley and looked around. The building behind this one faced the next street, and the back wall of it had only a few windows on the upper floors that overlooked the alley. Even Van Dyke's office had no windows on this side. He supposed millionaires didn't like looking at alleys.

Peterson pointed to where one of the wires came out through the wall. It ended in a loop.

"Someone would have had to pull the loop here to set the bomb off." He reached down to demonstrate.

"No!" Frank cried in alarm, but Peterson only grinned.

"It's perfectly safe. The bomb already exploded," he reminded Frank.

Feeling stupid, Frank nodded.

"Go back inside and watch how it works," Peterson suggested.

Frank went back in and let him pull the wire to show how it worked. When the loop was pulled, a bare part of the wire came in contact with a bare portion of the other wire inside making the necessary electrical connection. Even Frank could see the ingenuity of it. In spite of the explosion upstairs, the system still worked.

Peterson came back inside. "Clever, isn't it?"

Frank frowned. "So the killer stood out there to set it off, but how would he know when Van Dyke was opening the cabinet?"

Peterson shrugged. "I'm an electrician, not a detective," he said with another grin. "I think you'll have to figure that out for yourself."

Frank started doing just that. "Was the outside door locked when you came down?" he asked Peterson.

"Yes."

It couldn't be locked or unlocked from the outside. The person who set the bomb would've had to get into the basement and spend a lot of time there. Frank remembered that Tad worked just a few feet away from this room. He'd have easy access to it. So would others.

Not yet convinced the killer hadn't been an anarchist, however, Frank checked the windows. The first one was securely locked, but the second one had a broken latch. At first glance, it seemed secure, but closer inspection showed it wasn't. A man could easily slip in that way.

"Show me the wire you found upstairs," Frank said.

They passed the other two detectives still standing in the reception area. Frank resented the fact that they were just wasting time when there was so much to do. "What about Van Dyke's secretary? What's his name . . . Reed?" he snapped.

"He's all right," one of them said dismissively, "They sent him home from the hospital."

"Get me his address, then. Somebody needs to talk to him."

Neither of them acknowledged the request, but Frank knew they'd be afraid to ignore it, no matter how much they might resent him. Frank and Peterson went on to Van Dyke's office, and they must have realized they needed to hear whatever Peterson had to say, so they hurried after them, stopping short in the doorway.

Even over the odor of the spilled whiskey, the smell of death was still strong here, and Frank didn't blame them for not wanting to go in. Peterson didn't hesitate, though. He went right over to the cabinet.

"A waste of good liquor," Peterson lamented, moving carefully through the shards of broken glass and amber puddles on the floor. He showed Frank where the bare wire stuck out from the remains of the cabinet.

"There were two wires downstairs. Where does the other one go?" Frank asked.

"They both came into the cabinet here. See?" He showed Frank where the second wire came up with the pipe and had been laid along the floor right next to the wall, then started up the wall behind the leg of the cabinet and had been stuffed inside through a tiny crack. Shortly after it entered the cabinet, one of the wires appeared to have been broken off.

"Where's the other piece?" Frank asked.

"Probably around here somewhere," Peterson said. "Funny things happen when something explodes."

"You know anything about bombs?"

"A little. I figure this one was made out of a pipe. There's part of it."

Sure enough, among the rubble lay a short section of pipe. One end appeared to be sealed with a cap. The other was ragged and blackened. Frank picked it up. "A *pipe*?" he asked incredulously. "You can make a bomb out of that?"

"You can make a bomb out of just about anything if you fill it with enough gunpowder," Peterson said. "Looks like they used nails, too. You can see them all over the room."

Frank looked around again. He hadn't paid too much attention before. He didn't know a lot about bombs, and figured the small pieces of metal he'd observed were just parts of it. He found one halfway imbedded into Van Dyke's solid mahogany desk.

"When the bomb explodes, the nails fly like bullets, and they do a lot more damage. Van Dyke would've been standing right in front of it, so he got most of the blast."

"Tore his face clean off," one of the other detectives offered.

"How did the wires make it explode?" Frank asked, not wanting to think about Van Dyke's last moments.

"The battery would've sent a current of electricity along the wires when the killer pulled the loop downstairs, and the wires would've been hooked up to the bomb. That current would've ignited the gunpowder, the way a pistol uses a spark to make it fire."

"How clever do you have to be to make a bomb like this?" Frank asked.

Peterson shrugged. "Even though it seems ingenious, it isn't very complicated. You'd just need a basic understanding of the principles. Anybody could get the pipe and the gunpowder and the nails."

"What about the battery?"

"Every electrical store in the city sells them."

"No sane person would kill a man like this," one of the detectives said from the doorway. "It's got to be them crazy anarchists."

"Trick is to find 'em," the other said with more than a hint of satisfaction, obviously glad that wouldn't be his job—and his failure when the anarchists in question disappeared without a trace into the teaming slums of the city.

At least Frank had Creighton Van Dyke to help him run them to ground. The son might well be his only salvation.

SARAH HAD NEVER BEEN SO HAPPY TO SEE HER MOTHER. Elizabeth Decker arrived only a few minutes after they discovered Creighton had escaped. The officer had immediately gone to search the surrounding streets while Sarah used the Van Dykes' telephone to call Police Headquarters. She pretended to be Alberta Van Dyke because too many people at Headquarters knew of her relationship with Malloy and would tease him mercilessly if they knew she was sending for him. They promised to find Malloy and deliver the message. Meanwhile, they would send some other patrolmen to help with the search.

A useless effort, Sarah knew. If Creighton had been gone even an hour, he would be miles away by now, and he'd most certainly left the house long before daylight. He could vanish into the Lower East Side and never be seen again.

"Sarah," her mother demanded as she entered the parlor. "What on earth is going on? The maid who let me in was crying!"

Before Sarah could explain, Mrs. Decker glanced around the room to find Tad drinking hard liquor even though it wasn't near noon yet. Lilly Van Dyke was having hysterics on the sofa, and Alberta sat in a chair nearby, quietly weeping into her handkerchief.

Sarah quickly explained about Creighton's presence in the house and his nocturnal escape.

"He's going to kill us all!" Lilly wailed, but no one paid her any mind.

"Tad, really," Mrs. Decker said in disapproval at his choice of beverage.

"Hair of the dog, Mrs. Decker," he explained sheepishly, holding up his glass in a salute to her. "I'm afraid I over-indulged last night, and my head's going to split open from all this caterwauling if I don't."

To prove his point, Lilly moaned pitifully, and Tad drained his glass.

Mrs. Decker went straight to Lilly. "Stop that at once," she commanded. "You're not helping anything."

Lilly stopped in mid-moan and stared at Mrs. Decker dumbfounded.

"Good," Mrs. Decker said in approval. "If you feel the need to make a spectacle of yourself again, please retire to the privacy of your rooms." She turned to Alberta, who was also staring at her, her face wet with tears. "You aren't helping either," she informed the young woman. "Get control of yourself."

Without waiting for a reply, she turned back to Tad. "You can't be much support to your family if you're drunk, young man. Put that glass down. Sarah, ring for some coffee, will you?"

Sarah was only too happy to obey. By the time it came, Sarah had been able to explain once again and in greater detail exactly what had happened since yesterday.

"He's gone back to that woman," Lilly informed them all. "He's going to gather up all his anarchist friends and kill the rest of us. We'll be blown to pieces!"

"Don't be ridiculous, Lilly," Mrs. Decker said as Sarah poured coffee for everyone. "Even if he did kill his father—which I don't believe for a moment—he's intelligent enough to know he'd be the first one blamed if anything happened to any of you."

Sarah looked at her mother in surprise. Since when had she developed such fine detecting skills? "Mother's right," Sarah said quickly. "And Mr. Malloy posted a guard on the house, in case anyone does try to harm you."

"A lot of good that did," Tad pointed out. "He couldn't even keep Creighton in a third-story bedroom."

"I should have known he'd try to escape," Alberta said. Her voice was hoarse from weeping, and she looked infinitely weary. "He was much too eager to be confined to his old room, but I thought it was just that he didn't want to go to jail."

"Of course you did," Sarah soothed her.

"There's no use in blaming ourselves, in any case," Mrs. Decker said. "What's done is done."

"That's right," Sarah agreed. "Now we've got to concentrate on what we can do to help. Alberta, do you have any idea where Creighton may have gone?"

"Back to that woman, I'd expect," Lilly offered with a sniff. "If it wasn't for her—"

"Stop it, Lilly," Alberta snapped, a little of her former

spirit returning. "Of course he'd go to her first, but that would have been hours ago. He probably wanted to warn his friends and then find a safe place to hide."

"Would Katya go with him?" Sarah asked.

"Is Katya his . . . *paramour*?" Mrs. Decker asked, having to search for the correct description.

"Yes," Sarah said, still looking at Alberta. "Does he have friends who would take him in?"

Alberta's pale eyes were bleak with despair. "No one I'd know, I'm sure. Katya would know, but if she's with him . . ."

"How can we find this Katya?" Mrs. Decker asked.

Everyone looked at her in amazement, including Sarah.

"Why would we want to?" Lilly asked.

Mrs. Decker gave her a withering glance. "Because it seems the only way of locating Creighton. If you're as frightened of him as you seem to be, I'd think you'd want him found and locked safely away."

Properly chastened, Lilly had no answer for that. Cheeks red, she turned away from Mrs. Decker's glare.

"I know where they live," Alberta said. "Or at least where they *did* live, but . . ."

"I went there yesterday," Sarah said, forgetting her mother probably wouldn't approve of such conduct. "With Detective Malloy. If they aren't there, they have friends in the building who may know. I met one of them. She's also a midwife."

Mrs. Decker brightened at that news. Apparently, she wasn't too shocked to hear Sarah had assisted Malloy in locating anarchists yesterday. "Do you think she'll help you find them?"

"Probably not willingly," Sarah admitted. "She's apparently an anarchist, too, but perhaps she can deliver a message to them, at least. I should probably go right away. The longer we wait, the longer they'll have to escape." This was true, but another motivating factor was that she didn't want to stay another moment in this house with its oppressive inhabitants.

"Shouldn't you wait for that detective fellow?" Tad asked in concern. "You can't go to that part of the city alone."

"I go to that part of the city quite often," Sarah said, rising from her chair. "Besides, these people are hardly likely to confide Creighton's whereabouts to a policeman. I'll have a better chance without him."

"I'll go with you, my dear," Mrs. Decker said to her surprise.

"Elizabeth!" Lilly cried in shock.

"Mother, I don't think that's a good idea," Sarah said, equally shocked.

"Why not?" her mother replied. "You said yourself, you go there often."

"And I'm used to it." Sarah tried to envision her mother in the tenement where Creighton and Katya lived. "I'm afraid . . . well, you'll see things that might . . . disturb you,"

"You underestimate me, Sarah."

Perhaps she did, but she wasn't anxious to find out for sure. "We'll have to go on the El," Sarah tried. "Have you ever ridden on it?"

"I've been thinking for a long time that I should try it," she said.

Sarah doubted this, but she said, "And then we'll have to walk several blocks through the tenements. Hansom cabs don't operate in that part of the city."

She feigned outrage. "Do you think I'm too old and feeble to walk?"

"Mother, please, I'm just trying to—"

"Protect me?" her mother finished for her. "Of course you are, dear, and I appreciate your concern, but I think I'm old enough to make my own decisions." She rose also. "Shouldn't we be going?"

"What will Father say?" Sarah tried in desperation.

Mrs. Decker gave her the same withering glare she'd given Lilly a moment ago. "What makes you think he will ever learn about it? Shall we go?"

FRANK HAD BEEN DREADING THIS TRIP TO THE MORGUE, but he knew that sooner or later he would have to examine the remains of Gregory Van Dyke. When the attendant led him to the correct table, he was struck by the odd shape beneath the sheet covering the body.

Seeing Frank's expression, the young man said, "He was torn up pretty bad." When he drew back the sheet, Frank hardly recognized what he saw as a human being.

The attendant said, "Only good thing, he probably didn't know what hit him. All them nails and stuff, they just tore his heart to shreds. There was some glass, too. They said the bomb was in a cabinet with lots of liquor bottles, I guess. He probably never even heard it go off."

Concentrating on breathing more slowly and shallowly— the body smelled of gunpowder and torn bowels and any number of other unpleasant things—Frank studied what he was seeing and tried to make some sense of it.

From what he could tell, Van Dyke had taken the blast full in the chest, smashing the bones and pulverizing the organs beneath them. The lower part of his face was blown away, too. A few back teeth remained to indicate where his jaws had been, and one eye stared up at the ceiling in frozen surprise. His left hand was gone, and the forearm lacerated. The right arm had been severed from the body. Someone had laid it on the lower part of the gurney beside the legs.

Below where his belt would have been, the body was re-markably unscathed. Stray shards of metal—the nails—had been driven into his thighs and abdomen, but the damage there was minimal compared to the chest. From the knees down, he was untouched.

Lastly, Frank examined the right arm. The wound where it had torn away from the shoulder was ragged, giving Frank a clear vision of the force of the explosion. Much of the tissue had been ripped from the bones, and where the hand had been was a mass of mangled flesh and bone. Frank didn't want to look at it too closely, but something odd imbedded in the hand caught his eye.

"What's that?" he asked the attendant.

The fellow peered more closely. "Can't tell. Doc Haynes ain't looked at him yet. Said there was no rush since every-body knows what killed him."

Frank leaned down and looked very closely, much more closely than he wanted to, and he remembered what Peter-son, the electrician, had said about the broken-off piece of wire—*Funny things happen in an explosion. It's around here someplace.*

"That look like wire to you?" Frank asked.

The attendant took a turn peering at the mangled hand. "Yeah, it does. What's it doing in his hand?"

"That," Frank said, "is something we might never know."

6

SARAH GLANCED OVER AT HER MOTHER AS THEY CLIMBED
the steps up to the Elevated Train Station. Mrs. Decker had
dressed conservatively this morning, thank heaven, since
she was paying a condolence call on a family in mourning.
Her dove gray morning gown was free of ornamentation and
almost completely concealed by her heavy, black cape. Still,
no one could miss the quality of her garments or the way she
carried herself. Anyone who saw her would know her instantly for exactly what she was: a lady born to old money
who had never known a day of want.

"I don't suppose I realized how high the tracks are above
the street," she said as they finally reached the top of the
stairs.

Sarah pretended not to notice how winded her mother
was. "I suppose it's an attempt to keep some of the noise and

cinders away from the people down below, but it doesn't work very well."

"So I noticed," she said, brushing some ashes from her shoulder.

At least a dozen people were waiting for the next train, a crowd that continued to swell as more people made their way up the stairs behind Sarah and her mother. All of them, it seemed, were looking at Mrs. Decker curiously. If she noticed, she gave no indication.

"Is this how you regularly travel around the city?" she asked Sarah.

"When I can. The trains only go north and south, so sometimes it isn't convenient. In that case, I either take a cab or walk."

"That isn't safe. You should have your own carriage," her mother said.

Sarah refrained from responding to that ridiculous suggestion. The expense of keeping a horse and carriage and someone to take care of both would be horrendous. She heard a train rumbling closer to the station. "It isn't too late to change your mind, Mother," she said.

"Nonsense," she replied, peering warily down the track at the approaching train.

Mrs. Decker was momentarily embarrassed when she realized she had no money with which to pay the fare. Ladies in her social position seldom carried cash. Wherever she shopped, she had an account, so she never needed to worry herself with actual money. Sarah came to her rescue and managed not to smirk at her mother's dismay.

The car was far from clean, and for a moment, Sarah feared her mother would refuse even to sit down. At last she did so, however reluctantly and only after Sarah fearlessly took her own seat. The air inside the car was cool but close, rank with the odors of many bodies crowded in day after day. Sarah discreetly ignored her mother's reaction, and then the car jolted into motion again.

Mrs. Decker was clutching the back of the seat in front of her rather tightly with her kid-gloved hands, which Sarah also ignored until her mother said, "Good heavens!"

Sarah looked at her in surprise to find her staring out the window. The train ran only a few feet from the buildings on both sides of Sixth Avenue, beside the third-floor windows. "You can see right into those people's homes!" she whispered incredulously.

"Yes," Sarah said.

"That's horrible! How can people live like that, with no privacy? Strangers can see everything they do!"

"They also pay less rent than the people on the other floors. For some, that's more important than privacy."

Her mother looked at her in amazement, almost as if she were certain Sarah had to be teasing. After a moment, she said, "You're serious, aren't you?"

"Absolutely. I said you'd see things that would disturb you, Mother. This is probably the least shocking thing you'll see today."

They rode for a few minutes in silence. Mrs. Decker kept staring at the passing windows as if unable to turn away, even though the sight horrified her. At last Sarah took pity and distracted her.

"Mother, do you think Creighton had anything to do with his father's death?"

At first Mrs. Decker seemed startled by the question, and then Sarah could see her purposefully refocusing her attention. "I have no idea. He was a perfectly normal child, but I haven't seen him in years. And he *did* reject everything his family stood for when he took up with those anarchists."

Sarah didn't bother to point out that some people might think the determined accumulation of wealth wasn't a particularly noble philosophy on which to turn one's back. "What do you know about the rest of the family? Could anyone else have had a reason to want Mr. Van Dyke dead?"

Mrs. Decker glanced around, probably afraid someone might overhear, but no one seemed particularly interested in their conversation, even if they could have overheard it above the noise of the train. "Gregory Van Dyke was a difficult man," she said.

"He and Father were friends, weren't they?"

"They'd known each other all their lives," her mother reminded her. "And a man behaves differently with his friends at his club than he does with his family at home."

"In what way?" Sarah asked, fascinated by this bit of information.

"Really, Sarah, this isn't a topic I want to discuss," her mother said, looking cautiously around again.

"But we need to discuss it. If Mr. Van Dyke's family hated him, they'd also have a good reason to want him dead."

"I refuse to speak ill of the dead," her mother said primly.

"Then his murder will never be solved," Sarah informed her. "I'm afraid the only way to solve a mystery like this is to find out all about the dead person. That means searching out the secrets he hid from the world and all the petty and mean things he did during his life."

"That's just gossip!" her mother reminded her.

"Exactly. Gossip is the key to solving any murder."

Mrs. Decker frowned her disapproval. "You have become remarkably knowledgeable about solving murders, Sarah."

"Unfortunately, I've had to, but the fact remains, if we intend to find Mr. Van Dyke's killer, we must know as much as we can about him."

"I thought your friend Mr. Malloy was in charge of finding the killer," her mother said.

She'd put just the slightest emphasis on the word *friend,* but Sarah pretended she hadn't noticed. "He's doing the best he can, but you know as well as I that no one is going to tell Malloy anything unflattering about Mr. Van Dyke's personal life. If he doesn't have the facts, he can't do his job."

"So he's assigned you the distasteful task of uncovering these facts," her mother said with a frown.

"I volunteered, because I knew you'd never gossip with Mr. Malloy," Sarah replied.

"What kind of a man would allow a lady to be involved in something like this?" she asked, thoroughly offended.

"The kind of man who wants to see justice done, Mother."

Her mother gave her a pitying look. "Everyone knows the police don't care anything about justice, Sarah."

"If that's true, and you shouldn't be so quick to judge *everyone* on the police force, it's because they aren't allowed the luxury of doing what's right all the time. People who have money and power can do whatever they want and never have to fear the police because no one wants to offend them—or risk their wrath."

"That's ridiculous! No one would allow someone to commit crimes, whatever their social status!"

"Mother, your memory must be fading. The rich commit crimes every day for which they're never punished, and you know exactly to whom I'm referring."

Sarah could tell from her expression that she remembered the people they both knew who had, for all practical purposes, gotten away with murder. "They did pay for their crimes," Mrs. Decker reminded her.

"Which was just luck," Sarah reminded her in return. "But if a rich man killed Mr. Van Dyke, he might very well have nothing to fear, even if Mr. Malloy manages to find the proof that he did it."

"Teddy would never let that happen," Mrs. Decker insisted. She'd known Commissioner Roosevelt all his life, so she felt justified in using his nickname.

"He might have no choice, Mother. He's not exactly the most powerful man in the city, as we both know. All Malloy can do is give him the opportunity to make the correct decision. But as I said, he needs your help."

Her mother's expression was troubled. "I'm sure I don't know *anything* that would help," she hedged.

"Oh, Mother, don't be so modest," Sarah chided gently. "Remember what I said about gossip? You may not spread any, but I know you hear plenty of it. All we have to do is figure out which bit of that gossip will lead us to the killer."

Van Dyke's secretary, Lewis Reed, lived in a modest rooming house not far from Tompkins Square. Frank lived in the same neighborhood, and he knew it to be respectable but working class.

The landlady, a plump Irishwoman in her fifties, showed him upstairs to Mr. Reed's rooms. Reed's sitting room was furnished comfortably with good-quality but slightly shabby furniture someone wealthy had probably discarded. A small fire burned in the grate to ward off the chill, and Reed sat in an overstuffed chair nearby with a quilt across his legs. He'd propped his feet on an ottoman and his bandaged head rested on a pillow wedged between it and the back of the chair.

He'd apparently been dozing, but he was awake when the landlady ushered Frank into the room. A slight man, probably of average height, Reed had brown, thinning hair, from what Frank could see of it around the bandage. His long, narrow, and very ordinary face was pinched with pain and unusually pale. He wore a dressing gown and slippers.

Frank introduced himself "Sorry to bother you, Reed," he added, taking a seat on the sofa without being invited. "I know you're not feeling well, but I need to ask you a few questions about what happened yesterday."

Reed winced. "I'm afraid I don't remember very much. The doctor said that's because I was hit on the head. They told me the door blew off Mr. Van Dyke's office and . . ."

"Yes, that's what happened," Frank confirmed. "I'm more interested in what happened *before* the explosion. Have you seen anyone unusual around the office building lately?"

"What do you mean by unusual?"

"Someone who didn't belong there. He might have been sneaking around in the alley behind the building or trying to get into the basement."

"Many people walk through the alley," he reminded Frank. "It's a busy neighborhood."

Frank figured if he'd noticed someone who looked like an anarchist carrying a bomb, he would have said so long since. "Did you see Mr. Van Dyke come in that morning?"

Reed started to nod and then caught himself, grabbing his head as if to hold it in place. Frank remembered Alberta Van Dyke making the same gesture but for a much different reason. "Yes," Reed finally said, somewhat raggedly. "I'm always at my desk at seven o'clock."

"How did Mr. Van Dyke seem to you that morning?"

"Seem?" he echoed uncertainly.

"Was he the same as usual or was he worried or happy or sad or what?"

Reed's broad forehead wrinkled with the effort of remembering. "Now that you ask, he did seem oddly cheerful that day."

"Cheerful?"

"Yes, he . . . Well, he didn't usually say very much, especially in the morning. He wasn't a man for idle conversation. That morning, though, he greeted me in a very pleasant manner."

"What did he say?"

"I'm not sure I . . . no, wait. He said it was a fine day," he remembered with a trace of amazement.

"Did you think that was odd?"

Reed looked pained. "It was sleeting."

"Yes, it was," Frank confirmed. "Did he say anything else?"

Reed took a moment to remember. "I . . . I think I asked if he'd been shopping."

"Why did you ask him that?"

"Because he was carrying a package."

"What kind of package?"

"I don't . . . A nice box of some kind, I think. I had the impression it must contain something expensive."

"What did he say when you asked if he'd been shopping?"

"He said yes, that he had a special surprise for Mr. Snowberger. He seemed very pleased with himself."

This would be the bottle of French brandy the valet had described. "Was Mr. Van Dyke in the habit of giving people gifts for no reason?"

"Not at all, especially . . ." He stopped suddenly and looked guiltily away.

"Especially what?" Frank prodded.

"I . . . I really don't know what I was going to say," he said apologetically. "I guess I'm not thinking very clearly since the . . . accident."

"Were you going to say especially since Mr. Van Dyke found out his partner was cheating him?"

Reed looked genuinely surprised. "Cheating him? Whatever gave you that idea?"

"Because that's what he told someone," Frank said, failing to mention the "someone" was his servant. "He thought Snowberger was stealing money from the company."

"That's impossible," Reed insisted. "I would've known something like that."

"Why?"

"Because I examine all the financial statements, and I prepare the reports for Mr. Van Dyke and Mr. Snowberger. If there were any irregularities, I would have seen them at once."

"Isn't the purpose of embezzling to make sure no one finds out?"

Reed seemed offended now. "I keep track of every penny that comes into the company, and I know where every one of them goes. Both Mr. Snowberger and Mr. Van Dyke earn generous salaries, even though they don't really need to work at all. Neither of them would have a reason to cheat the other, and if they tried, I'd know about it."

"But something was wrong," Frank reminded him. "Something that caused bad blood between them."

"I'm sure I don't know what you're talking about," Reed said.

"Of course you do. You said you were surprised Van Dyke was giving Snowberger a gift because they'd been angry with each other for a while."

"I had noticed some . . . some extra strain between them for several months," Reed admitted reluctantly.

"I understand that you don't want to say anything bad about Snowberger now that he's in full charge of the company, but whose fault was the argument they had?"

"Mr. Malloy, neither gentleman confided their personal business to me."

"Ah, but a good secretary knows everything that's going on. Your job depends on it."

Mr. Reed was annoyed. Frank could tell because his neck got blotchy and red. "Mr. Van Dyke was angry with Mr. Snowberger. Mr. Snowberger wasn't . . ."

"Wasn't what?" Frank prodded when he hesitated.

"He didn't seem to be angry, not the way Mr. Van Dyke was. You must understand, they never really liked each other, and neither one of them was what you would call a man of great passion. They conducted themselves with decorum and reserve."

"Cold fish," Frank judged.

Reed shrugged one shoulder in agreement. "For Mr. Van Dyke to allow his anger to show proved he was quite disturbed."

"Could Snowberger have just been better at hiding his feelings?"

"Possibly, but I got the impression . . . I really shouldn't be discussing this," he added suddenly.

"Better if you tell me now than having to testify in court," Frank bluffed. "What was your impression?"

Reed paled again. "Mr. Snowberger seemed a bit . . . smug. As if he'd gotten the better of Mr. Van Dyke somehow."

"In a business deal?"

"Nothing that had to do with their company. I'm sure of that."

"Did they have other business dealings together?"

"I have no idea. That's something you'd have to ask Mr. Snowberger." He put his hand to his head, silently reminding Frank he'd been seriously injured the previous day.

"I may come back with more questions later," Frank warned, rising to his feet.

"I'll help in any way I can," Reed promised. Frank figured he'd be helping in any way that wouldn't get him in trouble with Snowberger.

Frank started for the door, but Reed stopped him. "Mr. Van Dyke's . . . family, how are they?"

Frank looked at him curiously, trying to judge if there was more than an ordinary, professional interest in his question. He seemed merely concerned. "Fine, under the circumstances."

"They'll probably need my help with the arrangements. Clearing up the business details and that sort of thing," he added quickly. "I should call on them."

"I doubt they're expecting you. They know you were injured."

"Do they?" This seemed to disturb him. "I hope they know it's not serious . . . I mean, I hope they know they can depend on me for assistance."

"I'm sure they wouldn't think of troubling you, under the circumstances," Frank said. "Get some rest. That's the best thing you can do right now."

Frank was mentally shaking his head as he left Reed's boardinghouse. Something just wasn't right about Van Dyke's last morning on earth. What in blazes had he been so happy about that day? And why was he bringing Snowberger a gift of expensive brandy when he'd been so angry with him? Snowberger was probably the only person who might be able to explain it, but fortunately, Frank wouldn't have to ask him about it. He had Creighton Van Dyke in custody, and through him, he'd soon have the anarchist who'd planted the bomb. Then this case would be over.

ELIZABETH DECKER WAS STARING AT HER DAUGHTER AS if she'd never seen her before. "You're serious, aren't you? That gossip can solve a crime, I mean."

"Of course. I just need for you to tell me everything you know about the Van Dykes. Something should give us a clue as to who might have wanted Mr. Van Dyke dead."

"Really, Sarah, this is silly, especially because anarchists are most likely responsible."

"Humor me, Mother. What do you know about Lilly Van Dyke?"

"That she's a very tiresome creature," she said with a small smile.

"Where did she come from? How did she meet Mr. Van Dyke?"

Mrs. Decker sighed in resignation. "She came from Albany, I think. Her father was in business there. I heard there was some sort of scandal, and her father's business was ruined. He owed Gregory a lot of money. No one knows for certain what happened, of course, but suddenly, he announced his daughter's engagement to Gregory, and then he retired to the country with all his debts settled."

"It doesn't take much imagination to figure out what must have happened. How did Lilly feel about the bargain?"

"I'm sure no one asked her," Mrs. Decker said without the slightest hint of sarcasm. "To her credit, she made the best of it at first. She even seemed to enjoy her new social status. New York society can be very exciting."

The look she gave Sarah was to remind her of what she had

given up when she'd refused to return to her parents' home after Tom's death. Sarah pretended not to notice. "You said she made the best of it *at first*. Does that mean she changed?"

"Unfortunately, yes. She realized that her husband wasn't interested in buying her everything she wanted or going to every party to which they were invited. She was young and . . . well, I suppose she still had her youthful fantasies about the handsome prince and living happily ever after. All of us have to adjust to reality after we marry, and most women at least have their friends to help them, but Lilly knew no one in the city when she came here."

"Didn't Mr. Van Dyke introduce her to the proper people?"

Mrs. Decker looked uncomfortable. "I'm sorry to say that the wives of her husband's friends considered her too provincial and too . . . ambitious. She tried too hard, I'm afraid, and people aren't very tolerant of outsiders. She had no friends, and she grew bored and . . ." She looked down at her hands, now folded primly in her lap, as if she were ashamed to number herself among those who had snubbed Lilly.

"What did she do, Mother?" Sarah prompted. "Did she take a lover?"

"There were rumors . . . No one knows for certain, of course," her mother stressed. "Unless she confessed, which of course she didn't, or her lover bragged, which I haven't heard, we can only suspect."

"But you did suspect," Sarah guessed.

"She was so . . . indiscreet. More than one woman dragged her husband away from a social event after he'd made a spectacle of himself flirting with her. She seemed determined to disgrace herself, almost as if she enjoyed the attention she attracted."

"Did Mr. Van Dyke know?"

"I have no idea. If he did, he hadn't taken any steps to rein her in. She still went to every party and behaved badly."

"Did you hear anything said about who she might have taken as a lover?"

"No one seemed to know, but if she had—and remember, no one knew for certain—he had to be someone who didn't fear Gregory."

"You mean someone so powerful himself that even a man as important as Mr. Van Dyke couldn't hurt him."

"Or perhaps someone who hated Gregory and wanted to take revenge on him in a particularly humiliating way."

"Would Mr. Van Dyke have been humiliated if Lilly had an affair?"

"Undoubtedly. Lilly would be completely ruined, of course, and he would have turned her out with nothing but the clothes on her back. Even still, he'd be tainted, too. No one respects a man who can't control his wife. His true friends would pity him, and others would despise and even ridicule him."

Sarah sighed. "And if Lilly's hypothetical lover wanted revenge on Mr. Van Dyke, he certainly wouldn't have killed him."

"No," her mother agreed. "That would spoil everything, wouldn't it?"

"Unless . . ."

"Unless what?"

"If someone had begun an affair with Lilly—even to get revenge on Mr. Van Dyke—he could have actually fallen in love with her. That *would* give him a reason for wanting her to be a widow," Sarah said triumphantly.

"Which means he'd have to be unmarried himself if he hoped to marry the widow," her mother observed. "But I'm afraid you give Lilly too much credit. I can't imagine anyone being so obsessed with her that he would do murder to have her. She simply isn't that fascinating."

"But you said many men found her fascinating," Sarah reminded her mother.

"I said they flirted with her. They may even have done more than that. She's the type of woman with whom a man might enjoy a dalliance, but to kill for her? You've been reading too many novels if you think a sane man would do something like that for a trifle like Lilly."

Sarah sighed. "I suppose you're right, but . . . What if she managed to find a man who wasn't quite sane, someone who *would* do murder to have her?"

Her mother looked at her in surprise. "I can't imagine such a man. Who would he be?"

"Maybe someone you don't know," Sarah tried. "Maybe someone no one would suspect."

"You mean someone not from our social class," her mother clarified. "But how would she meet such a man?"

"Use your imagination, Mother," Sarah suggested slyly. "You must encounter men from time to time who aren't exactly one of society's four hundred."

"You mean someone like a . . . a tradesman or . . . or a *servant?*"

"Yes, someone no one would expect her to know, much less have an affair with. Someone who would never expect to be noticed by a woman like Lilly, much less win her affection. Someone who could be convinced to do anything he had to in order to have her for himself."

Mrs. Decker shook her head. "I was only teasing about the novels, Sarah, but this sounds like a very bad one."

Sarah hardly heard her. She'd suddenly remembered how Tad had embraced his stepmother and the spark of suspicion she'd felt when she saw them together. Was Tad naïve enough to fall under Lilly's spell and to imagine that, with his father out of the way, he could take the old man's place in Lilly's bed?

"What is it, Sarah?" her mother asked. "What are you thinking?"

"Nothing," she lied, managing a smile. The accusation was too horrible to make on the basis of such a slender suspicion. She wouldn't even consider it herself until she'd had a chance to test the theory on Malloy. Surely, he'd convince her she was wrong. He was good at that. "I guess I was just disappointed we couldn't figure out a way to blame this on Lilly instead of on Creighton."

"I can't blame you, but you have proven my point, Sarah. Lilly simply couldn't inspire someone to do murder. I'm afraid you'll have to find someone else, no matter how much we might like her to be guilty."

"WHAT DO YOU MEAN HE'S GONE?" FRANK NEARLY BELlowed at the officer he found guarding the front door at the Van Dykes' mansion.

The poor fellow was nearly quaking in terror. He was what they called a Goo-Goo, new on the force and too young to know how to even wipe his own nose. Frank would've felt sorry for him if he hadn't wanted to punch him in the face.

"He . . . he climbed out the window and escaped," the Goo-Goo explained.

Frank was sure this must be a bad dream. "He was on the third floor! He'd kill himself!"

The Goo-Goo's Adam's apple bobbed as he swallowed loudly. "He . . . uh . . . he climbed down some kind of drain pipe, looks like."

Frank managed to get the rest of the story from the fellow without scaring him to death, although it was a near thing. Fortunately, the officer he'd left guarding Creighton Van Dyke was nowhere to be found, or Frank might have had to shed some blood.

He went upstairs and burst into the parlor without bothering to let the maid announce him or even to knock. The room's three occupants looked up in wide-eyed surprise. He mentally dismissed the son and the stepmother and turned to Miss Alberta Van Dyke, the only one likely to give him an intelligent answer. "Where is he?"

Her face was blotched from crying, making her even more unattractive than she usually was, but she stared back at him defiantly. "I have no idea. You can't think he'd confide his plans to *me*."

"You're the one who knew where to find him before," Frank reminded her.

"I knew where he lived because I'd taken him money."

"Alberta!" Mrs. Van Dyke exclaimed in outrage. "How could you? Your father had forbidden us to have any contact with him!"

Alberta cast her stepmother an exasperated glance, but she said to Frank, "Mrs. Brandt and her mother went to look for him."

"*What?*" This time Frank did bellow, frightening the women and making Tad Van Dyke grab his head. Frank remembered the bottle of brandy he'd taken with him when he'd retired last night. With difficulty, Frank checked his temper and moderated his voice. "Did you say Mrs. Brandt went to look for Creighton?"

Alberta nodded, reluctant to speak again for fear of inspiring another outburst.

"Where did she go?"

"Back to Creighton's flat," she admitted, equally reluctantly. "Her mother went with her."

Frank had been *certain* he'd misunderstood this part of it. "*Mrs. Decker* went to the Lower East Side with Sar . . . Mrs. Brandt?"

"Sarah did try to talk her out of it," Tad offered hesitantly.

Frank wanted to punch something. What could have possessed Sarah to drag her mother along with her when she was looking for an escaped anarchist who might also have killed his own father? He didn't bother to ask himself why Sarah would have even gone on such an errand in the first place. He already knew she had a remarkable lack of good sense where her own safety was concerned.

"Miss Van Dyke," Frank said with all the control he could muster, "why did they go to Creighton's flat?"

"Because that's the only place they knew to start looking for him," she said, as if that were the most obvious thing in the world. "Sarah was going to see if Katya was still there, and if she was, of course she might know where Creighton is. If not, Sarah said she'd met a friend of Katya's who's a midwife, and Sarah thought that, well, perhaps she would help."

Frank thought that was highly unlikely, but he didn't bother to say so. It wasn't Alberta Van Dyke's fault that Sarah Brandt was acting like a nitwit. He drew a deep, calming breath and let it out in a sigh. "If I find out any of you helped him escape, I'll have to—"

"Don't bother threatening us, Mr. Malloy," Alberta said indignantly. "We had no idea he intended to escape, and we wouldn't have helped him in any case. He's much safer here than with those horrible people who killed Father."

"On the contrary," Mrs. Van Dyke said, "I can't imagine he's in any danger from those people at all. The fact that he escaped from here proves he's guilty. Even if he didn't plant the bomb himself, I'm sure he planned it."

Frank let his gaze rest expectantly on Tad Van Dyke. Might as well get everyone's opinion while he was here. The boy still looked a little green from his overindulgence, but he met Frank's gaze steadily. "My brother turned his back on everything he ever knew to take up with those people, and no one else stood to gain from my father's death."

"You and your sister and Mrs. Van Dyke stood to gain," Frank reminded him.

The boy shook his head. "We never wanted for anything when Father was alive, but he'd cut off Creighton's allowance. Father would've made sure he never got another penny until he came back home, too. How was he supposed to support that woman and her friends? That's why she seduced him in the first place, you know. They saw him as their golden goose."

"Your brother didn't expect to profit from your father's death because he thought your father had disinherited him," Frank said.

"Did he?" Tad said with a trace of surprise. "Well, I guess he might have been afraid of that, but Father was a patient man. He fully expected his prodigal son would eventually see the error of his ways and return home, begging for forgiveness. And he wasn't one to waste money having a lawyer to change his will if he was certain Creighton would come to his senses."

Frank looked at the women. "Is that true?"

Mrs. Van Dyke seemed bored with the entire conversation. "I have no idea. My husband didn't confide his business to me."

"Miss Van Dyke?" Frank prodded.

"He didn't confide in me, either," she said, not meeting his gaze.

"But you must have a theory on the matter. Was your father the type of man to write one of his children out of his will?"

Alberta didn't want to answer, and Frank sensed that was because her reply would implicate Creighton even more. He was right. "What Tad said is . . . true," she said reluctantly. "Father was certain that cutting off Creighton's allowance would bring him crawling back home again. And of course, he had no expectation of dying before that happened."

"Exactly," Tad said with a trace of smugness at being judged correct by his older sister. "You can check with his attorney to be sure, but Father wasn't the type of man to engage in empty gestures. There would be no point in disinheriting Creighton unless Creighton knew it was going to happen so he could repent from his evil ways and prevent it."

They had a point, and as certain as Frank had been that Creighton was innocent, the evidence was mounting against him. Trouble was, he didn't know where the man was, and Sarah Brandt and her mother had already set out after him. He felt a headache coming on.

"I'll leave some officers here to guard the place, and if Creighton comes back——"

"He won't," Alberta assured him. "You must know that as well as we do."

"Then if he sends you a message of any kind, let me know immediately." Alberta opened her mouth to protest, but Frank raised his hand to stop her. "I know it's unlikely, but you'd be amazed at the stupid things people do in situations like this. Oh, and I'll need the name of Mr. Van Dyke's attorney——to check on his will."

When he had the necessary information, Frank used the Van Dykes' telephone to contact Captain O'Connor and suggest he put one of his detectives to work learning the terms of Gregory Van Dyke's will. If Creighton was disinherited, he wouldn't have much of a motive for killing his father except revenge, but if he stood to inherit a sizable sum of money, it might draw him out of hiding to claim it. With his family name behind him and the money to hire a good attorney, he might just be able to walk away from a murder charge.

If he was guilty at all. But Frank reminded himself that the man *had* escaped from custody. Innocent men seldom did such a foolish thing.

Frank put the officers still at the Van Dyke house on notice that there would be hell to pay if they let anything else untoward happen there. Confident he'd left the family as safe as they could be, he started down the stairs to the front door. If he was very lucky, he might be able to catch up to Sarah Brandt before she got herself—and her mother—into trouble.

Then he heard the maid scream.

7

To her credit, Mrs. Decker refused to be shocked—or at least to show that she was shocked—by anything she saw as they walked through the streets lined with peddlers' carts and strewn with garbage and clogged with people of all ages and descriptions.

"This is the place," Sarah said as they approached one of several identical tenement buildings. Her mother hesitated only a moment before following her inside.

"Why is it so dark in here?" Mrs. Decker asked in alarm as the front door of the building closed behind them, cutting off the only source of light.

"Because there aren't any windows in the stairwell. I suppose they could put in gas, but it would be very dangerous to burn the jets in the hallways with no one to watch them." Sarah couldn't see her mother's expression, but she could imagine her horror at the thought of what a fire could do to a place like this. "Be careful on the stairs."

Sarah took her mother's arm and led her to the stairway. They climbed in silence up to the flat where Creighton and Katya had lived. Not surprisingly, no one answered her knock, but the door opened readily when she turned the knob.

"What are you doing, Sarah?" her mother asked in horror. "You can't just walk into someone's home!"

Sarah paid her no attention. She glanced around the cold kitchen where she had first encountered Creighton and Katya and their friends. Someone had cleared away the remnants of the meal they had been eating, washed the dishes, and put them neatly away on the shelves. She called out, but no one answered. A quick check of the other two rooms proved the place was empty. And deserted. She saw no clothing or personal effects anyplace, and the straw-stuffed pallets that served as beds had been stripped of their bedclothes.

Mrs. Decker was waiting for her in the doorway, looking both apprehensive and outraged at Sarah's behavior.

"They've gone," she reported.

"How can you be sure?"

"They took their clothes."

"They left the dishes," Mrs. Decker pointed out.

"Probably because they were too bulky to carry."

"Then we'll never find them." She sounded a bit relieved, and Sarah had to bite back a smile.

"If you have friends, someone will know where you are," Sarah said confidently. To her mother's dismay, she stepped back out into the hallway and began pounding on the doors of the other flats on that floor until she found someone who spoke enough English to direct her downstairs to Emma Goldman's flat.

By now Sarah was certain her mother deeply regretted accompanying her on this expedition, but she had no choice except to follow as Sarah made her way back down the darkened staircase to Emma Goldman's door.

They didn't have to knock. Miss Goldman was waiting for them in her open doorway, and she didn't look pleased to see them.

"Mother, this is Miss Emma Goldman," Sarah said, overlooking Miss Goldman's scowl. "Miss Goldman, my mother, Mrs. Felix Decker."

Sarah figured her mother had never been introduced to a Russian Jewish midwife before, but she gave no indication she found it strange. "Miss Goldman," she said as if they were in an uptown parlor.

"Felix is a strange name for a woman," Miss Goldman remarked, sizing Mrs. Decker up through her spectacles.

"It's my husband's name," Mrs. Decker said, a bit shocked that Miss Goldman wouldn't know this.

"Why would you give up a perfectly good name—what is your name? Your real one?"

"Elizabeth," Mrs. Decker said, now sounding defensive.

"Why would you give up a perfectly good woman's name to take a man's name?"

"That's the custom here," Mrs. Decker explained carefully, probably thinking Miss Goldman, being from Russia, didn't understand American ways. "A woman takes her husband's name when she marries."

"Is the same everywhere," Miss Goldman informed her. "That does not make it right. A woman who marries gives up her freedom. She is a fool!"

"Miss Goldman," Sarah said quickly, before her mother could respond and turn Miss Goldman's odd opinions into an argument. "We're trying to find Katya and Creighton."

"You should know where *he* is. Your policeman took him away," she reminded Sarah.

"He escaped last night. We think—"

"Escaped!" a voice echoed from within the flat.

Miss Goldman snapped something that sounded like a warning in Russian, but it was too late. Sarah had recognized the voice, and even before she could say so, Katya came running out of the back room.

"What do you mean? Where did he go?" she demanded of Sarah.

"Detective Sergeant Malloy left him at his father's house, locked in his room with a police guard, but he climbed out a window and got away," Sarah explained. "I thought for certain he would have come back here for you."

Katya looked stricken. "He did not come here."

"Do not listen," Miss Goldman said. "It is a trick."

"It isn't a trick," Sarah insisted. "What would I have to gain by making up a story like this? Katya, we have to find him before the police do. Now that he escaped, they're sure he's guilty. Where would he have gone?"

She shook her head in despair. "Here, to me," she said, near tears. Plainly, she thought he had deserted her.

"No, he wouldn't want to bring the police here and put you in danger," Sarah said.

"Perhaps we shouldn't be discussing this in the hallway where anyone might overhear," Mrs. Decker said, surprising them all.

Sarah glanced around and saw several of the other doors on the floor opened a crack so people could hear what was going on. Sarah had caused enough of a disturbance that everyone in the building was probably trying to eavesdrop. "Or I could send for Mr. Malloy, and he could take you down to Police Headquarters to—"

"Come inside," Miss Goldman said in exasperation. She slammed the door behind them with more force than necessary.

This flat was far more comfortably furnished than the one Katya and Creighton shared. Miss Goldman had skirted the sink with brightly colored fabric, and a tablecloth adorned the table. Some framed pictures of unfamiliar landscapes hung on the walls, and the dishes on the shelves were of much better quality than the mismatched ones upstairs.

"She knows nothing," Miss Goldman informed them. "She cannot help you."

"Who would help Creighton?" Sarah asked Katya. "Who would he go to?"

Katya shook her head, looking anxiously at Miss Goldman for guidance.

"Katya, you said something about your brother when I was here before. Would he help Creighton?"

This terrified Katya, who sank down in one of the kitchen chairs as if her legs would no longer hold her. "Misha would not do this thing!"

"Do you mean he wouldn't help Creighton or he wouldn't kill Creighton's father?" Sarah asked. "That's what Creighton thought, wasn't it? That your brother and his friends had planted the bomb."

She was shaking her head again, but Miss Goldman had had enough. "Stop this. She knows nothing. Leave her alone."

"If Creighton finds your brother first, he might not wait for an explanation," Sarah warned her. "And if Creighton is charged with killing his father, his attorney would probably try to blame it on your brother to get him off. Tell me where to find him before it's too late!"

"He might be at the First Street Saloon," Miss Goldman said in disgust before Katya could reply.

Sarah frowned. She didn't trust the woman. "How do you know he'd be there?"

"He is always there," Katya said. "He lives with us, but only to sleep and sometimes to eat. He meets his friends there, and they talk . . . about politics."

"Where is this place?" Sarah asked.

"Fifty-one East First Street, between First and Second Avenues," Miss Goldman said grudgingly.

Sarah looked at Katya. "Don't try to run away," she warned her. "I'm sure Creighton will come back for you when he can."

Katya didn't seem so sure. Her life probably hadn't taught her that hope was often rewarded.

"She will stay here," Miss Goldman assured her. "She cannot run away because of the baby."

"If I find Creighton, I'll tell him where you are," Sarah promised. "Thank you for your help," she added to Miss Goldman, who just glared back at her.

Sarah ushered her flabbergasted mother out of the flat.

"Honestly, Sarah, wherever did you learn to speak to people that way?" she asked as they made their way down the dark stairs.

Sarah decided not to tell the truth, that Frank Malloy had trained her by example. "Good manners wouldn't have helped in that situation, Mother. I got the information I needed and that's the important thing. The saloon isn't far from here. If Misha Petrova isn't there, someone might know where to find him."

"You can't mean you intend to go to a saloon by yourself, Sarah!" her mother gasped in horror.

"Of course not, Mother. You're going with me."

* * *

FRANK RACED DOWN THE REST OF THE STAIRS TO THE
foyer, where he found the maid trying to hold an unsteady
Lewis Reed upright. The man looked ghastly, as if all the
blood had drained out of his body and left him perfectly
white. A small trickle of blood was sliding down the side of
his face from beneath the bandage over which he'd carefully
and awkwardly placed his derby hat.

"What in God's name are you doing here?" Frank nearly
shouted as he went to relieve the maid of her burden. The
instant Frank took Reed's weight, she scampered away,
nearly weeping with fright.

"What's going on here?" a man demanded, and from the
corner of his eye, Frank saw the butler hurrying from a
nearby doorway.

"Help me get him upstairs, will you?" Frank said to the
butler.

"Mr. Reed?" the butler said in amazement when he'd recognized the visitor. He quickly moved to help support Reed.

Frank heard footsteps on the stairs, and a woman's voice
cried, "Lewis!"

Reed's head jerked up, and Frank caught a glimpse of an
emotion he would never have expected to see—naked adoration.

Lilly Van Dyke must have a charm that escaped Frank, he
decided. But when he looked up, to his amazement, he saw
someone else entirely. Returning Reed's adoration was none
other than *Alberta* Van Dyke.

Sarah Brandt would be so impressed that he had solved
the mystery of who had fathered Alberta's baby.

"YOU CAN WAIT OUTSIDE IF YOU WANT TO, MOTHER,"
Sarah said when they found the First Street Saloon. "I don't

think this will take very long, especially if he isn't here."

"I can't allow you to go in there alone," Mrs. Decker insisted, although Sarah could see that only her motherly concern outweighed her natural abhorrence of entering such a place.

Actually, the saloon wasn't unsavory at all. Through the window, Sarah could see several women sitting at a table, unaccompanied, and they didn't appear to be prostitutes.

"Suit yourself, Mother. You really don't need to be worried, though. I'll be fine." Without waiting for a reply, Sarah pushed open the door of the saloon and walked in.

A haze of cigarette smoke hung heavy in the air, competing with the rusty smells of beer and burnt coffee. All eyes turned to see who the new arrival was, telling Sarah the occupants were mostly regulars who expected to know anyone who might enter. She could actually feel the ripple of surprise that went through the room as she strode up to the bar.

"I'm looking for Misha Petrova," she said. "Is he here?"

The man standing behind the bar wore a giant apron covered with a montage of stains, some new, some old, and some ancient. He'd been polishing a glass when she came in, but he stopped in mid-polish to stare at her. Then his rather worn-out face broke into a smile. "*Misha Petrova?*" he echoed, mocking her.

A group of men at a nearby table laughed out loud, and the women she'd noticed earlier stared at her in dismay.

"*Misha* is a good friend of yours, yes?" the bartender asked suggestively in a German accent.

Sarah had no idea what she had said to cause this reaction, but she held on to her dignity tightly and refused to be embarrassed. "I've never met the man," she said, quickly improvising, "but I do know his sister. I'm a midwife, and I need to see him immediately. Is he here or not?"

The man didn't know whether or not to believe her. He looked her up and down, judging her, and then he glanced over at her mother, who had lingered near the door, probably ready to make a hasty exit if necessary and hold the door open for Sarah. Sarah might be a midwife, he judged, but Elizabeth Decker certainly didn't belong anywhere near this neighborhood.

"She's a volunteer at the Prodigal Son Mission," Sarah improvised as a way to explain a rich woman's presence here. "We're trying to help Katya Petrova. If her brother isn't here, can you tell me where I could find him?"

The bartender considered her request for another moment, glancing at the group of men who had laughed, to see if they would make any objection. Apparently, they didn't, because he suddenly bellowed, *"Mikail Ivanovich!"*

Everyone in the room turned expectantly toward a doorway that led to the rear of the saloon. In a few moments, a bear of a man with a full black beard and wearing working men's clothing appeared there, looking annoyed. "What do you want, Justus?" he demanded.

The bartender nodded at Sarah. "She is looking for you, *Misha Petrova.*"

That wasn't the name he'd called, and looking at this fellow, Sarah couldn't imagine him being any relation to the lovely and delicate Katya. "I'm trying to find Katya Petrova's brother," she explained.

"Says she's a midwife," the bartender added helpfully.

The man's annoyance evaporated into concern. "Katya, she is sick? What happened?"

"Are you her brother?" Sarah asked skeptically.

"Yes, yes. Where is she? I must go to her!"

"She's not sick, not yet anyway," she added, not wanting

to lose her advantage. "Is there someplace we can talk privately?"

His concern turned to suspicion, and Sarah instantly regretted requesting a private audience with him.

"Take her in the back, *Misha*," the bartender suggested before she could change her mind. "That lady's with her, too."

Misha looked askance at Elizabeth Decker, who returned his gaze defiantly. Plainly, he didn't know what to think, but finally, he grunted, "Come," ungraciously, and led them back to the rear dining room.

The only occupants of the room were three men who sat at a table in the corner, apparently awaiting Misha's return. He spoke to them in rapid Russian. They stared at Sarah and her mother with unabashed curiosity, but they picked up their beer steins and left for the front room without complaint.

Misha sat down in front of the remaining beer stein, and motioned for them to take seats at the vacated table. Sarah sat down immediately, intent on getting this conversation over quickly. Her mother was more cautious, but Sarah wasted no time worrying about her.

"How do you know Katya?" Misha demanded.

"I'm a friend of Creighton Van Dyke's, Mr. Petrova," she explained.

"Petrov," he corrected her.

"Excuse me?"

"My name is Mikail Ivanovich Petrov."

Now Sarah was really confused. "I thought Katya's name is Petrova." In fact, Miss Goldman had insisted that it was.

"It is. Russian names, men and women, are different."

How interesting, she thought. "And from what the bartender said, I guess *Misha* isn't your name either."

"Is my name from Katya, a child name," he explained impatiently. "Now what do you want to tell me about her?"

"You know that Creighton's father was killed when a bomb exploded in his office, don't you?"

His eyes narrowed suspiciously, and he nodded his big head. "The police, they take Petr away."

"Who's Petr?"

He made an impatient gesture. "Creighton. He is Petr now. Petr Gregorovich Petrov."

"Good heavens," Mrs. Decker exclaimed. "You mean to say he changed his name? To something *Russian*?"

Petrov looked at her as if he thought she was insane.

"She's a new volunteer at the Prodigal Son Mission," Sarah hastily explained, hoping that would excuse her. "Yes, the police took Creighton . . . Petr away, but he escaped. The police think that proves he's guilty."

He simply stared back at her impassively.

"We thought he might have come back for Katya, but he didn't," she continued determinedly. "Do you know where he is?"

"You say you are his friend," he reminded her. "Why did he not tell *you* where he is going?"

"I'm his *old* friend. I haven't seen him since . . . since he came here to live. You are his *new* friend, someone he trusts now."

"If I do know where he is, why would I tell you? How do I know you will not bring police?"

"Because I want to help him prove he's innocent," she said, neglecting to mention she'd do that by turning Creighton over to the police. "Have you seen him?"

He simply stared at her, still skeptical.

"Then do you have any idea who planted the bomb that killed Creighton's father?" she tried.

His dark eyes suddenly lit with understanding. "You think *we* kill him," he said. "Police think so, too. Because of bomb."

"Anarchists often use bombs," Sarah reminded him. "And they're known for killing wealthy and powerful men to draw attention to their cause."

Petrov turned his face away and spat on the floor with contempt, making Elizabeth Decker cry out in alarm, but Sarah simply glared at him. He turned back to her, his face twisted with anger beneath his beard. "We have renounced the *attentat*, the . . ." He stopped, searching for the proper word.

"Assassination?" Sarah offered.

"Yes," he confirmed. "Killing these men changes nothing. Another rises up in his place. They are like cockroaches. We must change the hearts of the people so they can overthrow their oppressors."

"The police may not understand that you've modified your philosophy, Mr. Petrov," Sarah said. "After all, you condemn the wealth of men like Gregory Van Dyke, but you take money from his son."

"Petr supported our *cause*," he said defensively.

"By supporting *you* and your friends, at least until his father cut off his allowance. That left all of you to fend for yourselves," Sarah said mercilessly. "But if his father was dead, Creighton would inherit a lot of money of his own. Then he'd be able to support you for the rest of his life without worrying about his father."

"You are like the police," he accused. "They blame us for everything because they hate us."

"I'm just stating facts—facts the police will know also. If you didn't kill Mr. Van Dyke and don't want to be accused of it, I'd suggest you help find out who did."

"Help the *police*?" he asked incredulously.

"Help *me*," Sarah clarified. "I'll take care of the police!"

Now he thought *she* was insane. He even looked at Mrs. Decker, as if seeking an ally against such madness. To her credit, Mrs. Decker simply stared back at him, giving the distinct impression she thought Sarah's claim was perfectly reasonable.

"Mr. Petrov," Sarah continued, trying to *sound* perfectly reasonable, "the detective sergeant in charge of the investigation is a friend of mine. He will trust me if I give him proof no anarchists were involved in Mr. Van Dyke's death."

"She's telling the truth," her mother said, to her amazement.

Petrov just stared at them, his eyes wide.

"We need to find Creighton," Sarah continued. "We need to make certain none of your friends was responsible for doing this terrible thing. Then we need to find out who else might have wanted Mr. Van Dyke dead."

Amazingly, she had convinced him. Or at least worn away some of his doubts. "I do not know where Petr is. After police took him, Katya went to Emma Goldman's flat to stay. Emma is midwife, too."

"I know. I found her at Miss Goldman's a little while ago. They were the ones who told me where to look for you."

This information didn't please him, but he chose not to press the issue. "The rest of us who live there, we take our things and find other places to stay, so if police come back, they find no one."

"You said you and your friends were innocent," Sarah reminded him.

"Still the police would take us. They do not care, guilty or innocent. They just want someone in jail."

Sarah knew this was true, so she didn't argue. "Would Katya know where to find Creighton?"

"Did you not already ask her?"

"Yes, but I thought perhaps she didn't trust me enough to tell me the truth."

He shrugged. Probably, he wasn't sure himself.

"She'd tell you, though, wouldn't she?" Sarah prodded. "Or maybe the two of you could at least figure out where to look for him."

He shrugged again.

"Oh, for heaven's sake," Mrs. Decker exclaimed impatiently. "Why don't we all just go back there and ask her?"

Sarah stared at her mother as if she'd never seen her before. Certainly, she'd never seen her like this before.

Mrs. Decker rose imperiously to her feet. "Come along, Misha or whatever your name is. The longer we delay, the less chance we'll have of finding Creighton. And I won't even consider calling him by a Russian name," she added. "I've known him since the day he was born, and he'll always be Creighton to me."

To Sarah's surprise, Petrov pushed himself out of his chair, glancing uncertainly at Sarah to see if she would obey as well. She did.

Petrov had apparently never learned the "ladies first" rule. He led them through the doorway into the front room of the saloon. Curious eyes watched their progress, but no one challenged them as they left the place.

Sarah and her mother had to almost run to keep up with his long, lumbering strides, following closely in his wake as he made his way across the traffic-clogged streets. They were only half a block away from Katya's building when Sarah saw Frank Malloy coming out of it.

Oh, dear, he'd seen them, too, and he was heading straight for them.

Before Sarah could think of a way to avert disaster, her mother said, "Oh, look, there's Detective Sergeant Malloy," and waved at him.

He lifted his hand in response. It wasn't exactly a wave. More like a warning signal that he was going to skin them both alive for venturing down to the Lower East Side to interview anarchists. Sarah tried frantically to figure out how to signal him to leave them alone, but before she could summon even the glimmer of an idea, Mikail Petrov stopped in mid-stride and turned on them.

"Police?" he roared in outrage.

"I told you I could handle them!" Sarah cried, but it was too late. He'd already bolted, ducking down an alley into the rabbit warrens of the tenements.

"Who was *that*?" Malloy demanded as he closed on them.

"Katya's brother," Sarah replied with a sigh. "He was going to convince her to tell us where to find Creighton."

He glanced down the alley into which Petrov had disappeared. "Should I go after him?" he asked, his amazement obvious.

"Don't bother. I know where to find him."

"You can't think he'll go back to that saloon," her mother said.

"Of course he will," Sarah said wearily. "But probably not until tomorrow. We'll have to come back then."

Malloy turned to her with such fury, she thought for a moment he might explode. *"You are not coming back here,"* he said very slowly and very deliberately. "You are going to take your mother home, and you are going to stay there, and you are going to forget you ever even *heard* of the Van Dykes and all their anarchist friends!"

Sarah knew better than to argue. Neither one of them

would give an inch, so it would be a waste of valuable time.
"Very well," she said, knowing this would confuse him long
enough for her to speak her peace. "But before we go, I have
some important things to tell you. Remember I said my
mother would know why someone might want to kill
Mr. Van Dyke?"

"Why would you say a thing like that, Sarah?" her mother
asked, affronted.

"Because it's true," Sarah replied without looking at her.
She had to keep an eye on Malloy in case he really did explode. "And she told me some very interesting things that I
think you should know."

"Anarchists killed Van Dyke," Malloy insisted.

"I don't think so," Sarah said. "At least Mr. Petrov didn't
know anything about it."

"Did you expect him to confess to you?" Malloy asked,
not even trying to sound polite.

"Of course not, but I can tell when someone is lying. He
really didn't know anything about it. He ran away from the
flat because he was afraid of being arrested, but he was only
over at the First Street Saloon."

"*You went to the First Street Saloon?*" he croaked.

"It really isn't such a bad place," Mrs. Decker offered.

Malloy just stared at her, speechless.

"We asked Mr. Petrov to talk to Katya," Sarah went on,
taking advantage of his momentary stupefaction. "We suspected she might know more than she was willing to tell
us, and if she didn't really know where Creighton was, we
thought the two of them together might be able to think of
some places to look. But then you frightened him away."

Malloy ran a hand over his face. "Mrs. Brandt," he said
very carefully, "and Mrs. Decker, you can't be wandering

around the Lower East Side looking for anarchists. It isn't safe."

"You're absolutely right, Malloy," Sarah said, knowing this would shock him into silence again. "We don't really have any reason to stay now, anyway. But before we go back uptown, do you suppose we could get something to eat? All I had for breakfast was a piece of buttered bread, and I'm starving. How about you, Mother?"

"Well, I—" she began, but Sarah didn't wait for her answer.

"If we could find a restaurant, I could tell you everything I learned today, and then I'll take Mother home, just as you suggested."

Malloy didn't trust her. She could see it in his eyes, but he also didn't want to jeopardize her apparent cooperation by challenging her. "I think there's a chop suey joint around the corner," he said, with an uncertain glance at her mother.

"A *what*?" Mrs. Decker asked.

"It's Chinese, Mother," Sarah explained. "Which way?" she asked Malloy.

He pointed, and Sarah started walking.

"Chinese?" her mother echoed in horror, hurrying after her.

"It's delicious. You love foreign food, Mother," Sarah reminded her.

"I love *French* food," Mrs. Decker clarified.

Malloy coughed in a very suspicious manner. Sarah managed not to smile.

Sarah set a rapid pace so her mother wouldn't have the breath to argue anymore. They found the restaurant—one of dozens like it in the city run by Chinese immigrants who were pretty much limited in employment to restaurants or laundries—on the ground floor of one of the tenement buildings. The mouth-watering aroma of frying food wafted out into the street.

Sarah's stomach growled. She really was hungry.

Without giving her mother a chance to object, Sarah headed up the steps and into the building. Malloy held the door for her mother and then followed the women inside.

Sarah had eaten at many such places on her trips to this part of the city. The single room was crowded, but she managed to claim one of the small round tables for them. Malloy made a show of pulling out her mother's chair, but since it was a four-legged stool, he couldn't actually seat her. Only when they were all settled at the table did Sarah hazard a glance at her mother.

Mrs. Decker's eyes were enormous as she took in the exotic surroundings. The restaurant was simply the front room of an ordinary flat, but the owners had transformed it into a slice of the Orient. Paper screens painted with brightly colored flowers and Chinese characters lined the walls. Paper lanterns hung from the ceiling and reed mats covered the floor. A small Chinese man dressed in baggy black pants and a black smock and wearing a small black cap on his head hurried over to greet them.

He smiled hugely and bowed rapidly several times. "Welcome, welcome," he said in his singsong accent. "You want eat?"

"Three," Malloy said, holding up three fingers.

"Yes, yes, chop, chop," the man said, "Very good, you see." He turned so quickly that the long pigtail that hung down his back swung out and almost hit Mrs. Decker.

She cried out in alarm, although not as loudly as she had when Mikail Petrov had spit on the floor. Sarah winced.

"That man has a *pigtail*," she whispered, her eyes even wider than they'd been before.

"Chinese custom," Malloy said with amazing kindness.

"His skin is . . ." She gestured helplessly.

"Yellow," Sarah supplied. She felt certain her mother had never been so close to a Chinese man, if she had ever seen one at all.

"I knew they called them the Yellow Race," Mrs. Decker explained, still whispering, "but I thought it was just an expression." She looked around once more, taking in the strange décor. "What did you order three of Mr. Malloy?" she asked when her gaze returned to him.

"Chop suey. That's all they serve here."

"What is it?"

Sarah could see the twinkle in his eye, but his expression remained grave. "No one knows."

Mrs. Decker's jaw actually dropped open, something Sarah had never seen her mother do as long as she'd known her.

"Don't pay any attention to him, Mother. It's just meat and vegetables," she said, and turned to Malloy. "Did you find Katya when you were in the building?"

The twinkle vanished from his eye. "Yeah, I found her. She's staying with that midwife woman."

"That's right, Miss Goldman."

"Miss Goldman lacks some of the finer social graces, but she seems genuinely concerned about that poor young woman," Mrs. Decker offered.

"*Miss Goldman* may lack social graces because of the time she spent in prison," Malloy said grimly.

"*Prison?*" Mrs. Decker exclaimed in surprise.

"That's right. For inciting a riot a couple years ago, when

she made an anarchist speech to a group of people, and they went crazy. But that's not the worst of it."

He wasn't teasing this time. "What's the worst?" Sarah asked with a growing sense of dread.

"Miss Emma Goldman was the mistress of the anarchist who tried to assassinate Henry Clay Frick."

8

ELIZABETH DECKER GASPED IN HORROR, AND EVEN Sarah looked shocked. Frank had begun to think nothing could shock her anymore.

"Are you sure?" Sarah asked.

"Of course I'm sure. I remember when she was on trial. We heard she'd left the country when she got out of prison, but I guess she came back."

"She said she'd studied midwifery in Vienna," Sarah recalled.

"She hasn't been back long, then. The police would've gotten word. Don't you think it's strange that she comes back into the country and another rich man gets blown up?"

"Frick wasn't blown up," Sarah reminded him. "He was shot, and he wasn't even killed."

"The Fricks live here in the city now," Mrs. Decker

reminded them, her voice a little breathless from shock. "They should be warned."

"I'll see to it," Frank said, not wanting to be distracted from his main point. "Do you know what this means? Emma Goldman and her friends are probably the ones behind all this."

"Then why haven't they gone into hiding? Sarah asked.

"Because anarchists like to be martyrs. They want people to know they're responsible for these assassinations."

"Then why haven't they come forward to take responsibility?"

Frank felt his hackles rising, but he remembered Mrs. Decker was witnessing this argument. She wouldn't understand if he said what he really wanted to say to Sarah. "Because they don't want to go to jail," he said reasonably.

"Listen to yourself, Malloy," she replied. "That doesn't make any sense. I always pay attention when you prove my theories are ridiculous, and now it's your turn. If the anarchists killed Mr. Van Dyke, they'd either want recognition for their crime, or they'd try to avoid being blamed. What they're really doing is hiding out and trying not to be falsely arrested and denying responsibility. Does that sound like they're guilty?"

"It doesn't to me," Mrs. Decker said.

Frank gave her a look that should have frightened her into eternal silence, but she didn't even blink. She was as bad as her daughter. He opened his mouth to reply, but Sarah didn't give him a chance.

"I'm certain Creighton and Katya and her brother didn't know anything about a plot to kill Mr. Van Dyke. If Emma Goldman was involved, she certainly wouldn't have taken Katya in. That would lead the police right to her, and I can't imagine she wants to return to prison."

Fortunately, the Chinaman returned at that moment with their food, saving Frank from making a hasty reply he probably would have regretted. Mrs. Decker stared in amazement at her plate of steaming chop suey, while Sarah started pouring tea from the pot he'd left into the small, handle-less cups.

This gave Frank a chance to collect his thoughts and his temper. "All right," he said, proud that he didn't hear a trace of exasperation in his voice. "If the anarchists didn't plant the bomb, who did?"

Sarah glanced at her mother expectantly, but Mrs. Decker was trying to figure out what the chopsticks were for.

"Like this, Mother," Sarah said, demonstrating and helping her mother get the first bite of the meal into her mouth.

"It's quite tasty," she decided in surprise.

Sarah apparently decided not to rely on her to enlighten Frank. "Lilly Van Dyke was probably having an affair," she said.

"How do you know that?" he challenged.

"Everyone knew it," Mrs. Decker supplied between mouthfuls. "I'm surprised the Chinese race didn't starve to death centuries ago, if this is how they eat," she added, struggling with the chopsticks.

"Who was her lover?" Frank asked.

Mrs. Decker looked at him with a small smirk. *"No one knows,"* she replied, mimicking him.

Sarah had the grace to cover her mouth so he wouldn't see her grin. Then she said, "Lilly was unhappy in her marriage. Mr. Van Dyke was stingy and boring, and Lilly was apparently forced to marry him in the first place. She behaved scandalously by flirting with every man she met."

"That doesn't prove she killed her husband, or even that she wanted him dead," Frank said.

"We think she may have influenced someone to do it," Mrs. Decker explained, as if figuring out people's motives for murder was an ordinary task for her.

"How would she have done that?" he asked, not bothering to hide is skepticism.

"The usual way a woman influences a man, Malloy," Sarah said smugly. "But we've decided it probably wasn't a man in her own social circle."

"Heavens, no," Mrs. Decker confirmed. "As I pointed out to Sarah, Lilly isn't interesting enough to inspire a rich or powerful man to murder. We think it must be someone inferior to her, a tradesman or a servant."

"A tradesman or a servant who just happened to know how to make a bomb?" Frank asked sarcastically.

"I'm sure it's possible for anyone to learn how," Sarah said, unfazed. "If the anarchists can do it, other people can, too. And of course, the bomb would immediately cast suspicion on Creighton and his friends."

"Lilly did seem eager to blame Creighton," Mrs. Decker recalled.

"So did Tad," Malloy said without thinking.

Sarah's head snapped up, her eyes wide. "What did he say?"

Frank wanted to bite his tongue. He knew better than to give her information about a case. It only encouraged her. "He just agreed with this stepmother that his brother had good reason to want his father dead."

Sarah glanced speculatively at her mother, then turned back to Frank. "I didn't want to say anything about this, but it might be important."

Frank's grip tightened on his chopsticks. He respected Sarah's powers of observation enough to know she was probably right. He glanced at Mrs. Decker, too. Sarah plainly was hesitant to say anything in front of her, but what could it matter now? The woman already knew far too much about the case. "What is it?"

She looked down at her half-empty plate and carefully framed her reply. "The way Tad treats Lilly," she said, looking up with misery in her eyes. "I think his feelings for her are . . . deeper than would be appropriate for their relationship."

"Sarah, what are you saying?" Mrs. Decker asked in alarm.

She sighed. "Remember we thought Lilly might have influenced someone weaker than herself to murder her husband? Someone who thought getting rid of Mr. Van Dyke would win him Lilly? Someone who would have no other hope of attaining her?" Mrs. Decker nodded reluctantly. "Tad fits that description."

"What makes you think he's in love with her?" Frank challenged.

"The way he took her in his arms when she was crying. There's a subtle difference between comforting someone and embracing them. And the expression on his face . . . He's besotted with her, Malloy. I'm certain of that. I have no idea if she knows, however."

"And even if she does know, would she have used him to kill her husband?" Frank said.

"And what kind of a man would he have to be to murder his own father?" Sarah agreed.

"I think that settles it for Tad," Mrs. Decker said decisively. "Patricide is a heinous crime, no matter how one might profess to hate one's father. A young man might have unnatural desires toward his lovely young stepmother. I'm sure it happens with alarming frequency, since wealthy men often take younger wives when they are widowed. But how many of them end up murdered?"

"On the other hand," Frank said, mulling over the possibilities in his mind, "he did have access to his father's office and the basement storeroom."

"Why would he need access to the storeroom?" Sarah asked.

Once again Frank had let something slip. He was losing his grip. "The killer set up the bomb so it could be triggered by pulling a wire in the basement," he said, surrendering to the inevitable.

"That would have taken a lot of time," Sarah said. "How would someone get into the building who didn't have the right to be there without anyone noticing?"

"There's a window into the storage area that opens into the alley. It has a broken latch. The killer could've gotten in that way during the night, when no one was there."

Mrs. Decker had been paying close attention to their conversation. "Even if the killer was someone with a right to be in the building, he couldn't have set up the bomb during working hours, anyway. Too many people would have seen him going into the storage area and wondered what he was doing there, so the killer could very well have been someone who didn't work there."

Frank hated to admit it, but she was right. She really *was* too much like her daughter.

"I guess we've established that anyone could have managed to plant the bomb without anyone seeing them," Sarah said. "The question is, who had the best reason for killing Mr. Van Dyke?"

"The person with the best reason isn't always the killer," Frank reminded her.

"Why, Mr. Malloy, how very profound," Mrs. Decker said with some surprise. "I'd never thought of it that way.

Although I don't suppose I've given a lot of thought to murder at all, come to that. But I'm sure you're right. Simply having a good reason to kill someone couldn't possibly be enough to make someone actually do the deed. If it were, there'd hardly be a soul left alive on earth!"

Frank's astonishment at her compliment lasted only a moment because her observation reminded him of a conversation he'd had with Allen Snowberger. Van Dyke's partner had remarked that if businessmen settled disagreements with bombs, the city would be rubble.

"You're absolutely right, Mother," Sarah was saying. "We have to figure out who had the most *compelling* reason to want Mr. Van Dyke dead. What are all the reasons we've discovered so far?"

"Creighton still has a good one," Frank pointed out stubbornly.

"So he would inherit a lot of money and be able to support Katya and their anarchist friends," Sarah agreed.

"And if he didn't do it, their anarchist friends could've done it for him," Frank added.

"Lilly probably wanted to be free of her marriage," Mrs. Decker said. "Divorce would have ruined her and left her penniless and disgraced, but if Gregory died, she'd have a comfortable income and no husband to control her anymore."

"I doubt Mrs. Van Dyke built the bomb," Frank said.

"So she would have had to influence someone to do it for her," Mrs. Decker said, undeterred.

"Someone who was in love with her and foolish enough to believe murder would be a reasonable solution to his problems," Sarah said.

"Someone young and impressionable," Mrs. Decker guessed.

"Or naïve," Sarah said. "Or desperately in love."

"Or maybe just stupid," Frank said impatiently.

"We're only trying to help you, Malloy," Sarah reminded him. "What other reason might someone have wanted Mr. Van Dyke dead?"

Frank glared at both women for a long moment, but they didn't seem to notice. They were too busy trying to figure out another motive for Van Dyke's death.

"He must have been standing in someone's way," Mrs. Decker finally said.

"What do you mean, Mother?" Sarah asked.

"The killer wanted something he couldn't have as long as Gregory was alive."

"Lilly," Sarah guessed. "No one else could have her if she was married to him."

"Or his money," Mrs. Decker said. "Lilly wanted to spend far more than he allowed her, and of course, there's Creighton and the anarchists who needed money."

"What other reasons do people kill?" Sarah asked Frank. "For love and money and what else?"

"Revenge," he offered idly, just to see if she could assign that motive to anyone in this case.

"Could he have cheated someone?" Sarah asked. "In a business deal? What about Mr. Snowberger? They were partners. Maybe Mr. Van Dyke did something dishonest to him. Would Father know about it if he had?" she asked her mother.

"Only if one of them told him or it was public knowledge," Mrs. Decker said.

"We've heard a rumor about that," Frank informed them, "but the story was that Snowberger cheated Van Dyke."

"Oh, dear, that doesn't help," said Mrs. Decker.

Frank decided he might as well get their opinions of yet

another possible motive. "Lilly wasn't the only person he controlled."

Sarah looked at him with a frown, but it cleared almost instantly. "Alberta!"

"What about Alberta?" Mrs. Decker asked.

"He refused to allow the man she loved to court her," Sarah said.

But her mother was shaking her head. "Nonsense. Gregory would have been thrilled if *anyone* had courted her. He would have been very generous to her husband, too."

"What if the man she wanted wasn't socially acceptable to him, though?" Sarah asked. "He wouldn't have been generous then. He wouldn't have even allowed her to see him."

Mrs. Decker wasn't impressed. "Thwarted lovers usually elope instead of committing murder."

Frank watched Sarah's expression grow grim. "But if the girl's father is a powerful man, they'd risk his wrath if they eloped."

He saw the memories claim Mrs. Decker, sucking the color from her cheeks and the light from her eyes. Both women were remembering the Deckers' other daughter, Maggie. She'd fallen in love with the wrong man, gotten herself with child, and defied her parents to elope with him. Felix Decker had ruined the man's job prospects, hoping to drive Maggie back home, but instead she had refused to leave her husband—and died in childbirth in a squalid tenement.

"Alberta is nothing like Maggie," Mrs. Decker said, her voice hoarse with emotion.

"She's with child by a man her family knows nothing about," Sarah replied.

Mrs. Decker gasped aloud.

"It's Reed," Frank said to pull them all the way back from their dark past. "Lewis Reed, Van Dyke's secretary."

Sarah turned to him in amazement, the shadows of her sister's memory gone from her blue eyes. "How do you know?"

"I saw them together today. As you said, there's a subtle difference between comforting someone and embracing them. They were definitely embracing."

Frank walked slowly back to Police Headquarters after escorting Sarah and her mother to the El station for the trip back uptown. He didn't believe for a moment that Sarah would really forget all about the Van Dyke murder, but at least he'd gotten her and Mrs. Decker out of the Lower East Side for today.

Remembering what Commissioner Roosevelt had said about finding out the truth made Frank slightly sick to his stomach. Usually when he was working on a murder case, his problem was finding the solution. This case was just the opposite. Here he had too many perfectly logical solutions, but none of them was one the Van Dyke family or Roosevelt would be very happy to hear.

Of course, the anarchists could still be guilty. The fact that Creighton had escaped did cast suspicion on him and the rest of them. Frank just wished his gut wasn't telling him something different or that he didn't have so many other good prospects. He tried to imagine a way he could accuse the Widow Van Dyke or son Tad or partner Snowberger of murder without getting himself fired.

Tom, the doorman at Police Headquarters, greeted him as he held the door for him. Frank mumbled something in reply, but he was still deep in thought, trying to get what he knew about Van Dyke's murder to make sense.

The moment he stepped inside, the desk sergeant called his name, distracting him from his thoughts.

"There's a message for you from Captain O'Connor," the sergeant informed him. "Wants you to telephone him."

Frank trudged upstairs to the detectives' office and placed the telephone call to O'Connor's office uptown, hoping his men had learned something helpful. The captain wasn't very friendly when he finally came on the line.

"Who do you think you are, telling my men what to do, Malloy?" he demanded.

"I thought they were supposed to be helping me with the investigation," Frank replied wearily. The last thing he needed was to get into a power struggle with a captain. "Did they find out anything about Van Dyke's will?"

"The lawyer wouldn't tell them anything. Said it was confidential information. You want to find out, you'll have to talk to him yourself."

O'Connor hung up, before Frank could even reply.

Fine. One more unpleasant thing he had to do today, right after he informed Police Chief Conlin that Emma Goldman was back in the city.

S ARAH AND HER MOTHER SPOKE LITTLE ON THE TRIP back uptown to the Deckers' townhouse. Sarah had accepted an invitation to stay for supper, and she was looking forward to a quiet evening with her parents. She was also hoping her father might have some insight into Mr. Van Dyke's relationship with his partner.

The two women settled comfortably in the back parlor, where the maid had laid a fire and brought them tea to warm them after their long, cold afternoon. Mr. Decker found them there later.

"Sarah, how delightful to see you," he said. He did look pleased, although it was hard to tell if one didn't know him well. He touched her mother lightly on the shoulder by way of greeting, and took a seat in one of the comfortable chairs. "How are the Van Dykes?"

"This is very difficult for them, as you can imagine," her mother said. She briefly told him about Malloy bringing Creighton home and how he escaped.

"I suppose that proves those anarchists were behind this terrible business," her father said. "They're the ones who use bombs, of course."

"Unless someone wanted Creighton and his friends to get the blame," Sarah said, "and used the bomb to cast suspicion on them."

Her father raised his eyebrows in surprise. "Who gave you an idea like that?"

"I got it myself, Father," Sarah said, refusing to be insulted. Her father probably couldn't help his attitudes toward women and their ability to reason. He'd been brought up with an irrational sense of male superiority, and it was rather late to change him. "After I spoke with Creighton and his friends, I don't think they're guilty."

Now her father was alarmed. He looked inquiringly at his wife, but she had picked up some needlework and was concentrating on it, as if completely unaware of the conversation going on around her. "When did you have an opportunity to speak to Creighton's anarchist friends?" he asked sharply.

"When I went to his flat."

Her father's face flushed scarlet with outrage, but before he could speak, her mother said, "Creighton's lady friend is with child, Felix. Sarah went in case the poor woman needed her help." She hadn't even looked up from her needlework.

Completely disarmed, her father had no ready reply to make, so Sarah took advantage of the opportunity.

"Father, there have been rumors that Mr. Van Dyke and

his partner had quarreled about business. The talk is that
Mr. Snowberger had cheated Mr. Van Dyke in some way. Do
you know anything about that?"

Her father stared at her as if he'd never seen her before.
"Sarah, this avid interest in a murder is extremely unseemly
in a female, and asking me to betray confidences about my
friends is unconscionable."

"Even if it helps find out who killed your friend?" Sarah
challenged.

"Sarah, I'm sure your father must feel uncomfortable discussing his friends' foibles with you," her mother said mildly.
"He probably believes it to be disloyal."

"Thank you, my dear," her father said. "That's it exactly.
Not to mention the fact that telling you could serve no
purpose at all," he added to Sarah, "since solving Gregory's
murder is not your concern."

Sarah felt the anger washing over her in a hot wave, but
she checked her temper instantly. Arguing with her father
was a waste of time. Nothing she said would change his attitudes, and if he had any idea how involved she and her
mother had been in the investigation, he'd probably lock
both of them in the cellar. She managed a smile. "I'm sure
Mr. Malloy would appreciate any information Father could
give him, though."

"Oh, yes," her mother agreed. "Mr. Malloy is the detective Teddy assigned to investigate Gregory's death, dear."

Sarah marveled at her mother's ability to pretend they
didn't both know perfectly well who Frank Malloy was. Or
that they both had been dismayed for months that Sarah had
made friends with the police detective.

"Have you met him?" he asked his wife with a frown,
ready to disapprove.

"He came to the Van Dykes' house to speak to the family.

He seems very competent," Mrs. Decker said, her voice still mild, without the slightest indication she was trying to influence her husband. "And very well mannered, for a policeman."

This time Sarah's eyes widened. She hadn't thought her mother's opinion of Malloy's manners would be so high after their conversation over lunch.

"I suppose we'll find out just how competent he is," Mr. Decker observed.

"Whether he is or not, he won't be able to find Gregory's assassin unless he knows everything, Felix. I'm afraid some people might conceal important facts out of a sense of delicacy and unwittingly allow Gregory's murderer to escape without punishment."

"If Mr. Malloy is as competent as you seem to think, I'm sure he'll manage to collect all the facts," Mr. Decker said. "Now I'll leave you ladies to your gossip."

With that, he withdrew from the room, probably to seek refuge in his study. Sarah watched him go with a sigh of frustration.

"Don't worry, dear," her mother said. "If he has any information, he'll make sure Mr. Malloy learns it."

"How do you know that?" Sarah asked in amazement.

"I've been married to him for thirty-five years, dear. I can make him do just about anything."

Sarah smiled. She wondered if she would ever have had such a power over her husband Tom, if he had lived long enough for them to be married for so many years. Memories of Tom always brought a pang of loneliness—for him and for the family they never had—but this time she thought of a child with a real face.

"Mother, I want to tell you about a very special little girl I met at the mission."

* * *

FRANK HAD BEEN TO THE OFFICES OF ATTORNEYS
Smythe, Masterson and Judd before. They weren't any happier to see him this time than they had been before, but after a short wait, he was admitted to the office of Mr. Judd.

Judd was an aristocratic-looking fellow with a thin mus-
tache and even thinner hair and a set of pince-nez perched
on the end of his nose. His expression made him look as if
his bowels had been locked for a while, but maybe he just
didn't like the police. Frank introduced himself, even
though the secretary had already done that, and took a seat
in one of his fancy leather chairs, since he doubted Mr. Judd
would offer it.

"I've been appointed by Police Commissioner Roosevelt
to investigate the death of Gregory Van Dyke, and I need
some information about his estate."

"I can't imagine getting information about Mr. Van Dyke's
estate would help in any way to determine who killed him,"
Mr. Judd said.

"It could if his will gave somebody a reason to want him
dead."

"I have no idea what you mean," Judd lied.

"I guess you never had a client whose relatives were so anxious to get their inheritances that they helped the client along
into the next world, but I can assure you that it happens a lot.
My job is to find out if this is another one of those times."

"I'll tell you what I told those other detectives—"

"No, you won't, because I'm smart enough to know a
man's will is public once he's dead, and Gregory Van Dyke
is very dead. So will you show me the will right now, or do I
have to get a squad of patrolmen in here to go through your
files until they find it?"

Judd's face turned nearly purple, and for a long moment he struggled with his urge to put Frank in his place. A squad of patrolmen would wreck his office, and even if he managed to get Frank fired for ordering such an outrage, his office would still be a wreck. Common sense won out.

With poor grace, Judd jerked open one of the many drawers on his enormous desk and pulled out a large file folder. Slamming the drawer shut, he slapped the folder down on his desk and shoved it across toward where Frank sat.

"Just give me the main points," Frank said, having no intention of trying to wade through a legal document specifically designed to prevent laymen from understanding it "Who inherits?"

"His son Creighton."

Frank blinked in surprise. Creighton was wrong about having been disinherited, which was too bad because it gave him or his friends a perfect motive for killing him. "Who else?"

"No one else."

That couldn't be right. "Didn't Van Dyke make any arrangements for his other children or his wife?"

"He instructs Creighton to give Mrs. Van Dyke an annual allowance, and to provide for his siblings as he sees fit."

Not very generous. "Is this what rich men usually do with their estates, leave everything to the oldest son?"

Mr. Judd resented every word he had to utter to Frank, and his tone showed it. "I can't speak for all 'rich men.'"

"Then what would a typical will say? Wouldn't he have left money to his wife, and their house and furniture, too, at least?"

"Most widows of wealthy men find themselves well provided for," Judd grudgingly allowed.

"How much of an allowance is Mrs. Van Dyke supposed to get?"

Judd looked as if he'd swallowed a lemon. "Five hundred dollars a year."

Frank couldn't believe it. He earned more than twice that in his regular salary alone, and he could never support his mother and Brian on just his salary. He pictured Lilly Van Dyke trying to live for a year on an amount that was probably equal to her monthly pin money. "And the other son and the daughter get *nothing*?"

"Only what their brother wishes them to have," Judd said.

Frank tried to make sense of this. Creighton had rebelled and run off to live with people who despised his father and everything the Van Dykes stood for. Still he'd inherited the entire Van Dyke fortune, while Tad—who had toiled diligently in his father's business—and Alberta—who'd been too afraid of her father to defy him and marry the man she loved—had received nothing. They'd have to make their own way or rely on their brother's goodwill. And Van Dyke had given his wife the biggest insult of all, stripping her of every benefit she'd enjoyed as his wife and reducing her to poverty.

There had to be an explanation. "How long ago did he make this will?"

"He signed it a little more than a month ago."

Frank sank back in the chair. This wasn't the answer he'd expected. An old will, made before Creighton had forsaken his family, might have entrusted him to take care of everyone else, but why would Van Dyke leave his fortune to a professed anarchist? "Are you aware that Creighton Van Dyke had left his father's home?"

"I'm well aware of young Mr. Van Dyke's situation. His father explained everything to me."

"Did he explain why he left his fortune to a man who was fighting against everything his father stood for?"

"I can only assume he felt Creighton would be the best administrator of his estate. Entrusting him with the care of his siblings showed his father had great confidence in him."

Frank didn't believe that for a minute. "What about Mrs. Van Dyke? Sounds like Van Dyke wasn't very happy with her. Or with his other two children, either, for that matter."

"I am legally required only to share the contents of the will with you, not to speculate on the reasons behind it," Judd reminded him.

"If Van Dyke even told you what they were," Malloy said with a shrug. "I guess he considered you just a hired man. He wouldn't have to explain anything."

Judd stiffened at the implication, but Frank continued relentlessly.

"Anyway, it's not hard to figure it all out. He was afraid if he left his daughter money, she'd be a target for every fortune hunter in the country and a lot more from England." Everyone knew that impoverished British noblemen routinely came to the States looking for wealthy brides to support them. "He probably did her a favor. With no money, she might be an old maid, but she wouldn't be taken advantage of. The younger son is a little harder to figure out, but he's not as bright as his brother. Maybe his father thought he'd squander an inheritance. Or maybe . . ." Frank pretended to consider the matter. "Or maybe he did something his father didn't like, so he cut him off without a cent. Now what could a young man do to make his father that mad?"

Judd's face was getting purple again. "This is ridiculous," he tried.

"I wonder if a jury would think so."

"Why on earth would a jury be involved?" Judd asked in alarm.

"In a murder trial, everything becomes evidence. Mr. Van Dyke stopped Creighton's allowance so he couldn't support his anarchist activities anymore, but then he names him as his only heir. This gives Creighton a good reason for wanting his father dead. Van Dyke must've been a fool not to think of that."

"He wasn't a fool," Judd said, his voice nearly strangled.

"What *was* he then?" Frank asked pleasantly.

Judd's narrow shoulders sagged in defeat. "First of all, Mr. Van Dyke had no idea he would die so soon after making the will."

"I figured as much."

"You're right about his daughter. He wanted to protect her from . . . from someone unsuitable."

"Anybody in particular?" Frank asked conversationally. "Somebody who might've wanted him dead, for instance?"

"I believe he mentioned that a man had . . . His daughter isn't someone who naturally attracts admirers," he explained.

"I've met her," Frank said, relieving him of having to say she was homely.

"Someone her father felt was only interested in her possible fortune had expressed an interest in courting her. Mr. Van Dyke wanted to make sure she was always safe from men like that."

"How thoughtful," Frank said without sincerity. "What about Tad, the younger son?"

"Mr. Van Dyke didn't say too much, but I got the impression . . ."

"If you don't tell me," Frank warned when he hesitated, "I'll imagine something much worse."

Judd sighed. "Apparently, Tad had greatly displeased his father."

"When I was a young man, I displeased my father every day," Frank said.

"This was something serious, so serious Mr. Van Dyke felt he could never be reconciled. I tried to convince him to leave the boy some money of his own. A daughter can live with a brother or eventually marry, but a son . . . Tad doesn't strike me as the type of young man who could make his own fortune, and he's been bred from birth to be a rich man."

"What was he mad at Tad about?"

"He wouldn't say. At first I thought perhaps he felt Tad simply wouldn't be able to manage an inheritance, so I suggested a trust. That's a legal vehicle that allows the heir to draw an annual income from the inheritance but never to touch the principle. An arrangement like that would provide for Tad without allowing him to squander his money."

"His father wouldn't do that?" Frank asked in amazement.

"He didn't want Tad to get a penny. Those were his exact words. I finally convinced him to let Creighton decide how to provide for him, but only by pointing out that complete poverty might drive Tad to do something that would bring disgrace on his family."

Frank nodded, beginning to get a clearer picture of Gregory Van Dyke's state of mind before his death. "That leaves his wife. He must've been *really* mad at her."

Judd stared bleakly at Frank. "Mrs. Van Dyke is a careless young woman."

"Careless how? Did she spend too much money or did she take a lover?"

"Even if I knew, I wouldn't say," Judd told him, fury making his voice ragged. "Mr. Van Dyke simply wanted to ensure that no other man received any of his fortune by marrying his widow."

"Did he think Mrs. Van Dyke had already picked out this man?"

Judd looked as if he might have apoplexy, but he kept his voice even. "She may have picked out more than one."

"Why didn't Van Dyke just divorce her, then? He obviously had cause, and that way, he'd never have to worry about her getting any of his money."

"Mr. Van Dyke didn't believe in divorce. Now if you're finished—"

"Not yet," Frank said, leaning forward slightly. "You still haven't told me why he left his anarchist son his entire estate."

Judd drew a deep breath and let it out slowly, as if stalling for time. Finally, he said, "Because he wanted Creighton to know that whatever he might want, he was going to become a wealthy capitalist just like his father. If Creighton wouldn't voluntarily assume his proper place in life, his father would force him to."

Now Frank asked the most important question. "Did Creighton know the terms of his father's will?"

"That," Judd said without bothering to hide his satisfaction, "is a question only Creighton can answer."

9

F<small>RANK</small> WAS CHILLED THROUGH BY THE TIME HE reached the flat he shared with his mother and his son. In the years since his wife Kathleen had died bringing Brian into the world, Frank had dreaded coming home to this place. Far too many nights, he'd slept at the police dormitory down at Headquarters just to avoid the pain of not finding Kathleen here to greet him.

And the pain of seeing Brian, the damaged child she'd left behind.

Tonight, however, he didn't feel that pain. Brian came running to greet him on his own two feet instead of crawling with his club foot dragging behind him. Thanks to Sarah Brandt and her friend the surgeon, his son was no longer a cripple who might end up begging for his living on some street corner.

Frank whooped a greeting and snatched Brian up, lifting him high until his head touched the ceiling. The boy laughed, but it was a harsh, grating sound, and like the other noises that came from this throat, it made no sense at all. For three years, Frank had believed Brian's brain was as damaged as his foot, but now he knew—thanks again to Sarah Brandt—that Brian was only deaf.

Not that being deaf wasn't pretty awful, too, but at least his mind was fine. He could learn to read and write and even communicate with others. He might even learn a trade, in time.

Frank lowered Brian and hugged him fiercely to his chest. The boy wrapped his arms and legs around him as if clinging for dear life. Over the boy's shoulder, Frank saw his mother watching them with a trace of fear in her eyes.

"Hello, Ma," he said.

Mrs. Malloy was a small woman who looked far older than she was. She'd supplemented the family's income by taking in other people's laundry, and the hard work had taken a toll. "Supper's almost ready," she replied, starting for the kitchen. "I'll get it on the table."

"How's Brian doing?" he asked before she could walk away.

Her expression was wary. "Finally got him to take off them shoes to change his socks, but he still sleeps in 'em." Brian had never worn shoes until after his operation.

"Maybe I'll let him see me get ready for bed tonight and show him how I take mine off to sleep."

She didn't look encouraging. "Do what you want, but he's stubborn, just like you were at that age." She started for the kitchen again.

"Ma," he said, stopping her. He'd been dreading this conversation, but he had to give her some warning. "I'm taking Brian out tomorrow after supper. You're welcome to come along."

"Where on earth you taking him at that hour?" she asked, alarmed but pretending to be angry. "The boy needs his rest."

"I won't keep him out late. There's some people I want him to meet."

"Meet? How does a deaf boy *meet* somebody? Or did you teach him to say howdy do when I wasn't watching?"

"It's a deaf family, Ma. I'm going to talk to them about sending Brian to school."

The blood drained out of her face, and she laid a work-roughened hand on her bosom, as if she felt a pain in her heart. "Mother of God, you can't send him away, not after all this." She gestured toward the foot that now worked just like its mate.

"I'm not going to send him anywhere," Frank said, trying not to sound annoyed. "There's deaf schools right here in the city. They'll let him come during the day and go home at night. They'll teach him to talk, Ma."

"He can't *talk*," she insisted. "All he can do is make funny sounds."

"The deaf have a way of talking with their hands. They call it signing. He needs to start learning it before he gets much older, or he won't be able to learn at all. That's what they told me at the school."

"Of course they told you that," his mother said angrily. "They want your money. Brian's deaf and dumb, Francis. There's no operation to fix that."

"The family I want to visit tomorrow, the father's a printer. He earns a good living. They've got two kids, and the mother takes care of them just fine, even though she can't hear, either."

"So I guess you're going to talk to these people with your hands, are you?" she asked skeptically.

"Their children can hear. One of them's thirteen. She's going to translate for me."

"That's fine, then," she snapped, out of patience. "You go and talk to people who can't hear a word you say if you want to, but there's no reason for Brian to go. He can't talk with his hands or anything else."

"They've got a boy, Ma. I want Brian to meet a kid who isn't afraid of him and doesn't make fun of him."

Her face crumpled, and she turned quickly away, but not before he saw the tears glistening in her faded eyes. "I'll get supper," she mumbled and hurried away before he could see her cry.

Brian was squirming to get down. He wanted to show Frank his toys and get him to play a little. Frank let the boy take his hand and lead him to the sofa, where Brian had lined up his tin soldiers in neat little rows. For tonight, at least, he'd forget about Gregory Van Dyke and bombs and anarchists and faithless wives and children.

SARAH'S PARENTS INSISTED ON SENDING HER HOME IN their carriage after supper, and she didn't object. The evening was even colder than the afternoon had been, and she'd already walked a great deal that day. She was thanking the driver for helping her down from the carriage when she heard her next-door neighbor's front door open. Light spilled out of her house and down her front steps, and Sarah could see Mrs. Ellsworth's slender figure silhouetted in the doorway.

"Mrs. Brandt, is that you?" she called.

"Yes," Sarah replied. "I didn't mean to disturb you."

"You didn't disturb me. I've been watching for you.

Someone came by about an hour ago, wanting you to come and deliver a baby. I told him I thought you'd probably be home soon and——"

"Thank you," Sarah said, trying not to feel disappointed at not being able to go in and crawl into her nice warm bed. This was her calling, and she loved her work. She only wished she wasn't so tired. "Did you get the address?"

"Yes, I wrote it down. I'll bring it right over."

Sarah sighed.

"I'll wait and take you, Mrs. Brandt," the coachman said.

"Oh, I couldn't ask you to do that," Sarah said, but he was shaking his head.

"Sure you can. Your mother'd have my hide if she found out I left you to find your own way at this time of night."

He was right, of course. "I'll only be a few minutes," she said and hurried up her own steps to unlock the front door.

She'd hardly gotten inside when she heard Mrs. Ellsworth coming up the stairs behind her. "I would've told him to find someone else, but they wanted you, and from what he said, there's plenty of time," she explained as she stepped into Sarah's house. She handed her a slip of paper with a name and address written on it in Mrs. Ellsworth's neat, spidery hand.

"This is a first baby," Sarah said, recognizing the name. "They usually take their time. Thank you for taking the message."

She turned and went into the front room, which served as her office, and found her medical bag. She began checking to make sure she had all of her supplies.

"Have they found out who killed poor Mr. Van Dyke yet?" Mrs. Ellsworth asked.

"Not yet." Sarah had seen Mrs. Ellsworth yesterday morning when she'd been setting out to visit her parents to comfort them. Mrs. Ellsworth spent a lot of time sweeping her front porch just so she could accidentally encounter her neighbors and find out what they were doing.

"Surely, it was those foreigners who don't believe in government. They're the ones who use bombs and blow poor, innocent people up. Civilized people don't do such things."

Sarah thought of Emma Goldman. She'd looked perfectly civilized. Of course, her lover hadn't used a bomb on Mr. Frick, either. "Mr. Malloy is investigating the case," Sarah informed her. Mrs. Ellsworth held Malloy in high regard.

"Then I'm sure he'll find out who did it. None of us is safe with people like that walking around." She fidgeted as Sarah closed up her bag, not wanting to leave but having no real reason to stay. Sarah knew she was lonely because her only son worked such long hours. "I don't suppose you've had time to visit the mission, have you?" Mrs. Ellsworth asked after a moment.

Sarah smiled at the memory. "As a matter of fact, I was there yesterday."

"How is that dear little girl, Aggie? The one you're so fond of."

Sarah's hands stilled as she pictured the child's sweet face. "She's doing fine, I suppose, but . . ."

"But what?" Mrs. Ellsworth came closer, instinctively wanting to help.

"She really doesn't belong there. She's too young. She should be living with a family, someone who could give her the love she needs."

"Has she started speaking yet?"

Sarah winced. "Just that one time, and not again since. I'm afraid . . ."

"You're afraid no one will want to adopt her if she doesn't speak," Mrs. Ellsworth finished for her. They'd had this discussion before.

"But I'm sure if she was with a loving family, where she felt safe, she *would* start talking again."

"You may just have to take matters into your own hands," Mrs. Ellsworth said.

Sarah looked at her in surprise. "What does that mean?"

"What does your heart say it means?"

Sarah felt the familiar rush of frustration. "I can't take care of a child, Mrs. Ellsworth. Look at me, I'm on my way to deliver a baby, and I won't be home until morning. I couldn't leave a child alone all night."

"I'd be happy to help—"

"You have your own home and your own life, Mrs. Ellsworth. You couldn't always be available at any hour of the day or night, every day of the week. I'd need a nurse-maid, and I can't afford that."

Mrs. Ellsworth smiled sympathetically. "You'll figure something out," she said. "The heart always finds a way."

Sarah didn't want to think about this, not right now. She had too much else to think about at the moment. "I'd better hurry," she said.

"Oh, yes, but do try to get the baby to hold off until morning, won't you? Children born at sunrise are very bright, you know."

Sarah couldn't help but smile. Mrs. Ellsworth's superstitions were always interesting. "Are you certain of that?"

"Of course. I was born at sunrise, you know."

FRANK THOUGHT HIS LIFE COULDN'T GET ANY MORE complicated, but then he arrived at Police Headquarters the next morning and found two messages waiting for him. One was from the coroner, who wanted to tell him his findings on Van Dyke's death. The other was from Felix Decker.

As unappealing as another trip to the morgue was, Frank much preferred it to seeing Felix Decker. Standing there in front of the sergeant's desk and staring at the man's name, all he could think about was the conversation he'd had a few weeks ago with a boy named Danny who lived on the streets. Danny had once earned some pocket change by delivering a message to Sarah Brandt's husband Tom. That message had lured Dr. Tom Brandt to a meeting with the man who'd murdered him. The only thing Danny knew about the man was that he was rich, middle-aged, and that either he or Tom had said the name *Decker* just before he'd killed Tom.

Not too long ago, Frank had entertained the fantasy of repaying Sarah Brandt for all her help by bringing her husband's killer to justice. True, Tom Brandt had been dead more than three years, and his chances of solving the case now were slim, but he'd wanted to try.

That had been his first mistake. His second mistake was in finding a witness who implicated Sarah's father. Felix Decker came from one of the oldest and most powerful families in the city. No one was going to try him for murder, no matter how much evidence Frank managed to accumulate. None of that mattered, though, because Frank had no intention of accumulating any more evidence. If Felix Decker had killed his son-in-law, Sarah Brandt would never know it, at least not from Frank. Sometimes learning the truth could be more painful than the injustice of not learning it.

But Decker had asked for Frank by name to work on the Van Dyke murder, and now the moment of reckoning had come. Decker must know about his friendship with Sarah Brandt, a friendship he could never approve of. If Decker had chosen Frank in the hope that he would fail, Frank was playing right into his hands. He was no closer to finding the truth than he'd been when he'd first walked into Van Dyke's ruined office. On the other hand, if Decker wanted Frank to succeed, he was going to be disappointed. Frank felt the dull weight of dread settling into his stomach.

The doorman Tom let Frank out of the building again. As he walked down the front steps back into the frigid morning, Frank decided he'd go to the morgue first. That would be the more pleasant of the two visits.

THE CORONER GREETED FRANK AS HE STEPPED INTO HIS untidy office. The smell of death seemed to have seeped into this room, or perhaps Doc Haynes had brought it with him.

"What did you find out about Van Dyke?" Frank asked, moving a pile of papers to take a seat on the only chair in the room.

"Pretty much what we thought. Bomb killed him."

Frank gave him a look, and he shrugged.

"Not much else to say, is there? He was standing right over the bomb when it exploded. The thing was packed with nails, and they tore him up pretty good. At first I thought he probably never knew what hit him, but then there's that wire in his hand."

"The engineer said strange things happen when something explodes," Frank said.

"Maybe, but part of the wire doesn't get blown into a person's hand. From what I saw, it looks like he had the wire *in* his hand when the bomb blew up."

"That doesn't make any sense."

"I know. Wasn't the thing rigged to explode when he opened the cabinet?"

"No, it had wires running down to the basement under his office. Somebody had to pull the wire outside the building to make it explode."

"How did pulling the wire make it go off?"

"Something about making two wires touch, and that sent electricity from the battery to set off the fuse."

Dr. Haynes shook his head. Something still didn't make sense. "Then somebody would've been waiting and had to know just when Van Dyke opened the cabinet. How would he know just when to pull the wire?"

"I don't know."

"Why did Van Dyke open the cabinet just then?"

"Near as we can figure, he'd brought a present for his partner and was putting it in there."

Dr. Haynes frowned. "Why didn't he just give it to him? Why put it away?"

"His partner wasn't at work yet. It was a bottle of brandy, and we think he was putting it in his liquor cabinet, maybe for safekeeping or to hide it or something."

"So nobody could've expected him to be opening his liquor cabinet that early in the morning," Haynes said.

"No, which is why I can't figure out why the killer chose that moment to blow him up."

Haynes thought about it, silently acting out the motions a man would make opening a cabinet and putting something in it. "Doesn't work," he decided. "Van Dyke was holding that wire when he died."

"Are you sure?" Frank said in surprise.

"No other way it could've got in his hand like that. He was holding the wire. He must've opened the cabinet and seen the bomb. The killer didn't know he'd be opening the cabinet, so he wasn't ready to blow it up. Van Dyke saw the bomb, though, and maybe he thought he'd pull the wire off so it wouldn't explode."

"But when he touched it, he somehow triggered it," Frank said with growing excitement. This meant that many of the people he knew couldn't have set the bomb off could now be suspects.

"That's the only thing that makes sense," Haynes said.

Frank's excitement faded as quickly as it had blossomed. "Still doesn't tell us who put it there, though."

"No, but that's not my job to figure out," Haynes reminded him with a touch of satisfaction. "You're on your own there, Francis, my lad."

As if he needed a reminder. Frank pushed himself out of his chair. "Thanks for the information, for all the good it did me."

"My pleasure," Haynes said and went back to his paperwork.

FELIX DECKER'S OFFICE WASN'T WHAT FRANK HAD EX-pected. Frank figured he owned the building, but his name wasn't on it. The elevator operator took him to the seventh and top floor, and let him out in a large but plainly furnished room where a middle-aged man sat at a desk, working in a ledger book.

He looked up at Frank from under his green eyeshade and took him in with one swift glance. The man recognized Frank for what he was. People always knew he was a policeman, even though he wore a suit just like half the men in New York.

Using the anger he already felt for Felix Decker, Frank braced himself for the hostility he usually encountered from the clerks and secretaries who wanted to protect their employers from contamination by the lowly police, but the man simply said, "You must be Detective Sergeant Malloy. Mr. Decker is expecting you."

He got up and went to announce him. Before Frank could wonder if he should sit down, the fellow told him to go on into Mr. Decker's office and held the door open for him. Although every instinct rebelled against it, he did.

The office was large but not enormous. High ceilings gave it an airy feel and must have helped in the summer's heat. Tall windows overlooked Fifth Avenue. Decker's desk dominated the room, but only because it sat in the center. Frank thought of all the attorneys he'd visited. None of them would have had a desk so ordinary. Two leather chairs of obvious good quality had been placed in front of the desk for visitors, but they were well worn, as was the rug on the floor. Nothing was exactly shabby, but even Frank could see Decker didn't waste good money on ostentation. He supposed when your social position was as secure as Decker's, you didn't have to impress anyone.

"Mr. Malloy," Decker said by way of greeting. "I see you got my message." He didn't get up or offer to shake hands, which was fine. Frank had no intention of shaking his hand.

"I came as soon as I could," he lied.

"Have a seat. I have some information you might find helpful."

Still wary, Frank sat in one of the chairs. Hundreds of other occupants had broken it in nicely, and he found it quite comfortable. "I thought you'd want to know how the case is progressing," Frank said.

"My daughter informed me that you haven't identified the killer yet," he said. "Unless that's changed since last night."

"No, nothing's changed," Frank admitted, trying to imagine Sarah explaining the case to her father.

"My daughter said you don't believe the anarchists are responsible." It sounded like an accusation.

"I haven't eliminated them as suspects, but I try to keep an open mind. A lot of people might think they should be locked up even if they didn't do it, but that would mean the real killer would go free."

Decker's pale eyebrows rose in surprise. Frank didn't know if that was good or bad, so he didn't allow himself to relax.

"Who do you believe killed Van Dyke?"

"I don't think he was killed to make a political statement," Frank said, not really answering the question.

Decker considered his reply for a moment as if trying to judge him by it. Then he said, "You've heard a rumor that Allen Snowberger had cheated Van Dyke in business."

It wasn't a question. Again, Sarah must have told him that. Frank hadn't missed the fact that he hadn't spoken of her by name to him. It was an interesting omission. "Several people said that Mr. Van Dyke had been angry with Mr. Snowberger. They said he'd accused Mr. Snowberger of cheating him, but there's no evidence of any financial irregularities in the company." At least none that he'd found yet, he silently amended.

"I'm sure you won't find any, either," Decker said as if reading his thoughts. "Both Allen and Gregory were too astute for either of them to cheat the other—at least not in their business."

Frank heard the qualification in his voice. "But they might cheat each other outside of the company," he guessed, wondering why Decker was telling him all this.

"The word *cheat* implies something illegal, Mr. Malloy. Neither of them would stoop to that, either."

In spite of himself, Frank was intrigued. "What *would* they stoop to?"

Decker's aristocratic face pinched with distaste. "You must understand that Gregory and Allen had known each other all their lives. Their fathers were partners, and they inherited that partnership."

"But they weren't exactly friends," Frank said.

"Their families raised them to be, but they were more rivals than friends. And then they met Arabella."

"Arabella?" Frank thought that was a pretty fancy name for the kind of woman he was picturing, a woman who would drive a man to murder his partner.

"She was Allen's wife. Not at first, of course. This was years ago. They both fell in love with her and courted her, but she chose Allen. Gregory never forgave him, even though he eventually married, too. He was always devoted to Arabella, and when she died a little over a year ago, he blamed Allen."

Had Van Dyke suspected murder? "How did she die?"

"They were traveling abroad, and she caught a fever of some kind. She hadn't wanted to take the trip, but Allen had insisted. She came home in a box, and Gregory held Allen responsible."

"So he took revenge?" Frank asked, trying to figure out how all of this tied together to cause Van Dyke's death.

"Not revenge exactly. Gregory found an investment opportunity. He invited several of us to join him in it. The investment did very well for a time, and then Gregory advised us to sell out. Those of us who followed his advice made a lot of money. Those who didn't . . . well, they *lost* a lot of money."

"I guess Snowberger was one who didn't sell out. Why not?"

"Let's just say that Gregory neglected to warn him."

Frank thought this was a rather cold way of avenging the

death of the woman you loved, but he didn't say so. Maybe this was as passionate as rich men got about love. "Snowberger must've been angry." But was he angry enough to blow his partner to pieces with a bomb?

"Naturally. He understood exactly what Gregory had done to him, but he didn't kill Gregory, Mr. Malloy. That would be a hollow victory because Gregory wouldn't ever know about it, and he wouldn't suffer."

Frank remembered the mutilated body he'd seen at the morgue and thought Van Dyke had suffered quite a bit. "What would he have done to make him suffer?"

"I don't know exactly, but I do know Allen took his revenge in an effective way well before Gregory was killed. I know because he told me he had, although he wouldn't tell me what he had done. I also know because Gregory was furious with him. In all the years I've known them, I've never seen him angrier. If Gregory had killed Allen, I could believe that was the reason, but of course he didn't. Gregory is the one dead, and I can assure you, Allen wasn't responsible. As far as Allen was concerned, he was satisfied that he had evened the score once and for all."

If that was true, it would be a great relief to Frank. Snowberger was somebody he definitely wanted to cross off the list. He was too rich and powerful ever to bring to justice. "Do you have any ideas about what Snowberger did to Mr. Van Dyke?"

"No. He was very mysterious, and very smug and pleased with himself, though. He seemed quite sure he'd gotten the ultimate revenge, something that Gregory could never top."

Frank would have to make certain Decker was right, of course, although the thought of asking Snowberger to tell him how he'd taken revenge on his dead partner wasn't appealing. But then, nothing about this case was appealing, least of all Felix Decker.

Decker looked across the desk at him, still sizing him up, so Frank returned his stare. He tried to imagine Decker in a dark alley beating his son-in-law's brains out. "What did you think of Tom Brandt?" he asked before he could stop himself.

Decker stiffened. "I can't see that's any of your business," he said coldly. If he'd been tolerating Frank until now, he had no intention of doing so any longer.

Frank took a calculated risk. "I'm trying to find his killer."

Decker was a hard man to read, but Frank had lots of experience. His expression was surprise and nothing more. "Surely, you can't have any hope of doing so after all this time. The police told us when it happened that it was useless to even try."

"You should've offered a reward," Frank said mildly. "They might've tried harder."

Now Decker's expression grew shrewd. "Are you asking for a reward now?"

Frank felt his hackles rise, but he refused to take offense. Decker had made a logical assumption. "No, and I don't expect one. I'm just trying to give Mrs. Brandt some peace."

Decker considered Frank's claim for a moment. "Do you think finding her husband's killer will give her peace?"

Frank figured he had nothing to lose. "That depends on who the killer is, I guess."

Decker didn't even blink. "Assuming you can even find him. Where do you propose to begin?"

"I've already begun. I have a witness who saw the killer."

"Good God!" he exclaimed, showing the first trace of actual emotion. "Are you sure?"

Frank looked for any trace of guilt or apprehension, but he saw none. "I'm sure," Frank said with more confidence than he felt.

"Then why don't you arrest him?" he demanded. He didn't sound like he was afraid of being arrested.

"Because the witness would know him if he saw him again, but he doesn't know who he is."

"Who is this witness? Is he someone reliable? Why didn't he come forward before?"

"He saw a swell committing murder. He was too afraid to come forward."

"A *swell*?" Decker repeated, as if he'd never heard the word before. Maybe he hadn't.

"A rich man, or at least somebody who was well dressed."

This disturbed Decker. He frowned. "That's impossible."

"Why?"

"Because Brandt was killed in a robbery by some . . . some derelict."

"He wasn't robbed," Frank said.

"Of course he was. The police said——"

"He wasn't robbed," Frank repeated. "He still had his medical bag. Mrs. Brandt still uses it. His watch was in his pocket and so was his money. Just a few dollars, but a robber would've taken it. He would've taken everything."

"Maybe he was interrupted, frightened away or something," Decker suggested.

"He wasn't."

Decker stared at him, trying to make sense of it. "The police said——"

"They wanted you to offer a reward to make them work harder," Frank repeated impatiently. "When you didn't, they stopped trying. That's what happens. They can't afford to work for free."

"*Free?* The city pays their salaries," Decker reminded him, outraged.

"The city pays us a pittance, Mr. Decker. We need every extra dollar we can get."

"You can't be serious!" Decker insisted.

"I'm perfectly serious. People complain about police corruption, but rewards and . . . *bribes* save the city money and keep their taxes low."

Decker was staring at him in amazement. Frank wasn't sure exactly what he'd said that was so amazing, but he took advantage of the moment.

"I asked you what you thought of your son-in-law, Mr. Decker. I gather you didn't approve of the marriage."

Decker stiffened again, angry but too well bred to show it. "As I said, that's none of your business."

"I guess you weren't too sorry when Dr. Brandt turned up dead."

Well bred or not, Decker slapped his hand down on his desk. "I wanted my daughter to be happy."

"She wasn't happy when he died," Frank said.

"He wasn't the man she thought he was," Decker snapped and instantly regretted his outburst.

Too late. "What kind of a man *was* he?" Frank pressed, leaning forward.

Decker sat back in his chair, his face scarlet with rage and something else. Guilt, perhaps? But over what?

"From all accounts," Frank said, "Dr. Brandt was a saintly man who treated anyone who needed his services, whether they could pay or not. Nobody had anything to say against him."

"Then you didn't talk to *everyone*, Mr. Malloy," Decker said through gritted teeth. "When I thought he'd been killed by a stranger who just wanted to steal his watch, I saw no reason to delve any deeper into the mystery. I knew we could have hired a Pinkerton agent to investigate, but . . . When you start turning over rocks, you never know what might crawl out, do you? No good would come of revealing his true character to Sarah. He'd still be dead, and she'd be hurt."

Now Frank was amazed. He almost forgot to press Decker. An angry man often says things he wouldn't dream of uttering any other time. "But now you know he wasn't killed by a stranger. He knew his killer, and the killer was a well-dressed man who'd tricked him into meeting him in a secluded place. They argued, Mr. Decker. What were they arguing about?"

"I don't know," Decker said. "I have no idea."

"What *do* you know?"

"Not who killed Brandt," Decker insisted. "And even if I did, I wouldn't tell you. As I said, I don't want my daughter hurt."

"I'm never going to hurt her!" Frank said before he could stop himself.

He saw the light of understanding spark in Felix Decker's eyes. The two men stared at each other for a long moment.

Silently cursing himself for losing control, Frank rose from his chair. "Thank you for your time, Mr. Decker," he said. "And the information."

Without waiting to be dismissed, he headed for the door, but Decker stopped him.

"Mr. Malloy?"

Frank stopped and turned slowly, warily, to face him, ready for anything except what came.

"Are you in love with my daughter?"

Frank felt the familiar twist of pain he experienced every time he thought of the futility of his longing for Sarah Brandt. "What possible difference could it make, Mr. Decker? Good day."

10

Sarah certainly hoped Malloy solved the Van Dyke murder soon. She didn't know how much longer she could stand dealing with the Van Dykes, especially on four hours of sleep. Luckily, the baby she'd delivered last night had come much more quickly than expected. Still, she hadn't gotten home until the wee hours of the morning. Her body had demanded more sleep, but she had too many things to do today. Maybe later.

The Van Dykes' maid was quite happy to see her. "Oh, Mrs. Brandt, Miss Alberta will be that glad you've come," she said, ushering her inside and out of the freezing cold and helping her remove her cape with unseemly haste.

"Is something wrong?" Sarah asked, wondering what might have happened in her absence.

"It's Mr. Reed, Mrs. Brandt. Mr. Van Dyke's secretary.

He came yesterday, and he's too sick to go home, but Mrs. Van Dyke won't have him here." Then she covered her mouth with her hand, knowing she'd said too much. Servants who gossiped about their employers found themselves on the street.

This was much more interesting than she could have imagined. "Please take me to see Miss Alberta at once," Sarah said.

The maid led Sarah upstairs and took her to the back parlor, the less formal room that the family would use for themselves. Sarah followed closely on the girl's heels, not hanging back and waiting to be announced, which was why she saw Alberta Van Dyke holding hands with Lewis Reed when the maid opened the door. Alberta dropped Reed's hand and jumped up from where she had been sitting a little too closely beside him on the sofa. Her face splotched red with embarrassment when she saw Sarah over the maid's shoulder. "Ella, you should have knocked!"

"Thank you, Ella." Sarah gently guided the flustered girl out of the room and closed the door behind her before Alberta could chastise her again. "This must be Mr. Reed," she said brightly. "I had no idea you were here, or I would have brought my medical bag."

Taking advantage of Alberta's momentary confusion, Sarah went straight to Reed. If she had ever entertained the suspicion that Alberta's lover was a charming fortune hunter who seduced Alberta in hopes of marrying into wealth, one look at Lewis Reed quashed it. He might possibly be the most ordinary man she'd ever seen, and only love could view him differently. "I'm an old friend of Alberta's, Mr. Reed," Sarah said. "I'm also a trained nurse. How do you feel?"

"I . . . fine," he said uncertainly, glancing up at Alberta with dismay.

"Do you have a headache?"

"Yes, but—"

"Were you knocked unconscious by the explosion? Did the doctor say you have a concussion?"

"I believe so . . . I mean, I don't remember the explosion."

"Your bandage is bloody, Mr. Reed. I think it should be changed. Alberta, would you send for some clean bandages and a bowl of hot water, please?"

"Yes, certainly, I . . . I'll ring for the maid," Alberta said in alarm.

"I'm sure the Van Dykes appreciate your dedication, Mr. Reed, but you really should be at home resting. Didn't your doctor warn you against exerting yourself?"

Reed was staring up at her, his plain face slack with shock at her imperious attitude. "I . . . I had to make sure—"

"Mr. Reed was concerned about the *family*." Alberta said quickly, before he could say anything revealing. "He wanted to offer his assistance in making the arrangements for Father's . . . funeral. The coroner hasn't released his body yet, but when they do, we want to have everything ready."

"That's admirable, Mr. Reed, but also rather foolish. I can't believe anyone in the family would want you to risk your own health." Sarah gave him a stern look that silenced any potential reply. "Were you injured anywhere else besides the wound on your head?"

"Just some . . . bruises. Nothing serious," he said meekly.

Sarah glanced at Alberta, who was hovering nearby, wringing her hands. "How long have you and Mr. Reed been in love, Alberta?" she asked, hoping to catch her friend off guard.

Alberta's eyes widened in alarm and the color drained from her face. "I . . . I don't know what you mean," she stammered.

Sarah looked down at Reed. He returned the look, aghast, his lips moving but no sound emerging. She turned back to Alberta, expectantly. "Your father must have been furious when Mr. Reed asked to court you. He would never have considered his secretary a suitable match for his daughter."

"You're . . . mistaken," Mr. Reed finally managed.

"Are you saying you never even *asked* his permission?" Sarah asked with mock amazement.

"No . . . I mean, yes . . . I mean . . ." He turned to Alberta helplessly.

Her shoulders sagged in defeat. "Lewis, I don't suppose any of it really matters now."

"No, it doesn't," Sarah agreed. "With your father dead, certainly no one will object to your marrying Mr. Reed."

"You're probably right," Alberta agreed with visible relief. "I'm sure Lilly will be more than happy to be rid of me, and my brothers won't object. They'll just be relieved their spinster sister won't be their responsibility anymore."

This time the maid did knock, and Alberta instructed her to bring the things Sarah needed to change Reed's bandage. When she was gone, Sarah said, "Did your father know you've been seeing each other secretly?"

"Miss Brandt, we would never do such a thing," Reed insisted.

"It's *Mrs.* Brandt," Sarah corrected him.

"*Mrs.* Brandt," he tried again. "I won't have you insulting Miss Van Dyke by suggesting that she disobeyed her father or—"

"I know your secret," Sarah said to Alberta, ignoring Reed's defense.

"Wh . . . what secret?" she asked in a hoarse whisper, her face splotching red again.

"I'm a midwife, Alberta," Sarah reminded her gently.

Alberta instinctively laid a hand on her abdomen, as if to protect her unborn child, while Reed struggled to his feet, instinctively wanting to protect the woman he loved. "I must insist you stop upsetting Miss Van Dyke. She's not well, and her father's death has been a terrible shock to her."

"What were you going to do, Alberta? Would your father have allowed you to marry Mr. Reed, or were you planning to elope?"

Alberta was shaking her head wordlessly, and Reed took her arm and eased her down onto the sofa again.

Reed looked up at Sarah, with an angry frown. "He told me he'd ruin me if I ever tried to see Bertie again."

"He would have made me get rid of the baby, if he'd known," Alberta said, tears glistening in her eyes. "He never would've allowed us to marry. Thank God he's dead."

FRANK FOUND THE OFFICES OF VAN DYKE AND SNOW-berger filled with the sounds of the repairs being made to Van Dyke's ruined office. A glance inside that room told him the workmen had removed the worst of the debris of the explosion and were replacing the blown-out windows. He moved on to Snowberger's office. The surviving partner didn't look happy to see him when his secretary showed Frank in.

"I hope you're here to tell me you've arrested some anarchists," he said without bothering with a greeting.

"Not yet," Frank said, taking a seat and making himself comfortable. "I need to ask you a few questions."

"I don't know anything about anarchists," Snowberger said irritably "You'd do better to find Creighton Van Dyke. He's intimately acquainted with them." He smiled at his own pun.

Frank didn't return it. "I'm not so sure anarchists killed Mr. Van Dyke."

"That's absurd. Of course they did. They're the only ones who use bombs."

"Unless somebody knew Creighton was involved with anarchists and wanted to cast suspicion on them," Frank pointed out.

"That's a pretty elaborate theory, Malloy. Someone would have had to do a considerable amount of planning, which means he must have hated Gregory quite a bit. I can't imagine Gregory ever inspired that kind of hatred."

"Can't you?" Frank asked with interest. "I've already managed to find *several* people who hated him that much, and I've just started looking."

Snowberger frowned. He didn't like the way the conversation was going. "That's very interesting, but if you've found people like that, why aren't you out questioning them? You're wasting your time here."

"Not if *you're* one of those people, Mr. Snowberger," Frank said mildly. "I understand Mr. Van Dyke had allowed you to lose a lot of money in a business deal."

"Who told you that?" Snowberger tried, pretending to be puzzled.

"Several people who wouldn't lie about it," Frank said. "People who believed he did it deliberately, too."

Snowberger didn't look worried. "My partner and I have been friends our entire lives, Detective. I can't believe he would do such a thing deliberately."

"I think you can," Frank disagreed, even though he knew he was tempting fate. If Snowberger complained to Roosevelt about his methods, his career could be over. "We both know why your partner bore you a grudge, and we both know he arranged for you to lose a large amount of money on a failed business deal. This would've given you a good reason to want revenge."

"Mr. Malloy," Snowberger said, managing to sound merely annoyed and not furious, "I believe I already told you that businessmen don't resort to murder in order to settle disagreements."

"Yes, you did say that. What I need to know is what you *did* resort to in order to settle this disagreement with Mr. Van Dyke."

"I'm sure I don't know what you're talking about," Snowberger tried. He was good at bluffing.

"That's funny. The people I talked to said you were proud of what you'd done to get even with him. You even bragged that Van Dyke wouldn't be able to retaliate. Mr. Snowberger, if you convince me that you settled the score with Mr. Van Dyke over that business deal, you wouldn't have had a motive for killing him, and I can let you get back to your work."

Snowberger wanted to send Frank to perdition. He hated having a lowly policeman threaten him, especially with something so effective, but he couldn't refuse to cooperate without casting suspicion on himself. That made him even angrier. "You force me to be indiscreet, Mr. Malloy," he said, holding on to his temper with difficulty.

"No one else needs to know what happened, Mr. Snowberger. I'd just like to cross you off my list once and for all."

The request was too reasonable to refuse, even though he hated Frank for making it. "I'm afraid I seduced Mrs. Van Dyke."

As Sarah changed Reed's bandage, she couldn't help thinking it was a good thing she knew the killer had been outside in the alley, pulling the wire, when the bomb exploded. Reed had an excellent reason for wanting his employer dead, but if he was at his desk, getting hit by a door, he couldn't be the killer.

She glanced over at where Alberta sat, watching anxiously as Sarah tended the man she loved "What are you planning to do now?" she asked her friend.

Alberta looked up, her expression determined. "We'll marry as soon as possible," she said. Normally, marriages didn't take place during the one-year mourning period after a family member died. "Everyone will be scandalized, of course, but when the baby comes, they'll have something new to talk about, and they'll forget all about it."

Sarah finished with the bandage and snipped off the loose ends with scissors. "Will you continue to work for the company, Mr. Reed?"

He didn't look as confident as Alberta. "If Mr. Snowberger will have me."

"I've told Lewis we can probably live on my inheritance," Alberta explained, "Father would've left me a small income, at least. He would have considered it pin money, but I'm sure we could support ourselves modestly with it."

"That's your money, Bertie," he scolded her gently. "I'm perfectly capable of supporting you myself."

Yes, Sarah thought, now that Van Dyke wasn't around to make sure he never got another job. "Is there any reason Mr. Snowberger might let you go?"

Reed's expression was troubled, but he only said, "He might want to make some changes . . . And technically, I did work for Mr. Van Dyke."

"Even if he does let you go, you could find another job easily," Alberta assured him. "Anyone would be glad to have someone of your abilities." She turned to Sarah. "Mr. Reed is extremely clever. Father put him in charge of preparing all the financial reports for the company. He trusted Lewis to make sure every dollar was properly accounted for."

"Bertie, Mrs. Brandt isn't interested in my accomplishments," Reed said with a fond smile.

Alberta's cheeks colored becomingly, but she ignored his request. "He's also very progressive and modern. He convinced Father to electrify the office building, and then he oversaw the workers when they installed the wiring. The workers said they thought he knew more about it than they did!"

Sarah nodded approvingly. "If he's clever enough to understand electricity, I doubt you'll ever have to worry about him finding employment, Alberta."

Suddenly, the door flew open, and Lilly Van Dyke stormed into the room. "Why are you still here, Mr. Reed?" she demanded. "I'm sure my husband would never have approved your visiting here, and he most certainly would never have allowed you to remain overnight."

"He was ill," Alberta protested. "He needed medical attention."

"Medical attention?" Lilly mocked. "Since when are you qualified to give medical attention?" Then she glanced at Sarah and down at the tray of supplies the maid had brought for her. "Oh, well, I see Mrs. Brandt has taken good care of you, Mr. Reed. I trust you will instruct him to return to his home now," she added to Sarah. "It's really the best place for him."

Sarah bit back an evil smile. "I'm afraid Alberta was quite right to insist Mr. Reed stay here last night. It was very dangerous for him to come in the first place, of course, but we can't fault him for his dedication to his employer. Since he is here now, we also can't permit him to put his life in danger again by leaving. He needs peace and quiet and rest for at least a week before he can be moved."

"A *week*!" Lilly fairly shrieked.

"Perhaps longer, depending on how quickly he recovers," Sarah said gravely.

Alberta coughed suspiciously into her handkerchief, and Mr. Reed had to cover his mouth.

"What will people think if we keep him here?" Lilly demanded. "He's Gregory's secretary!"

"They'll think you're a kind, Christian woman," Sarah said. "Why, Mr. Reed might've been killed along with your husband, yet his first thought was for Mr. Van Dyke's family. He risked his own health and perhaps his life to be of service to you."

Lilly glanced at Reed, as if trying to reconcile his meek appearance with the hero Sarah was describing. "We could send him home in the carriage," she tried. "I'd instruct them to drive very slowly."

"Even that might cause him to have a brain hemorrhage," Sarah said. "But don't worry, I'll instruct Alberta in how to care for Mr. Reed's wound. You won't have to be bothered at all."

Still unhappy, Lilly could think of no more objections to make, but she turned to Alberta. "Don't make a nuisance of yourself with Mr. Reed, Alberta. I'm sure he only wants peace and quiet while he recovers." With that she swept out of the room, mumbling something about still not knowing what she would say to people.

"A brain hemorrhage?" Reed asked with a frown as Alberta hurried to his side.

"I made that up," Sarah assured him. "And now you can tell everyone that you fell in love while Alberta was nursing you back to health."

"Oh, Sarah, how can we ever thank you?" Alberta asked.

Sarah smiled at the two of them. "Just be happy."

FRANK STARED AT SNOWBERGER INCREDULOUSLY. "YOU seduced *Lilly* Van Dyke?" he asked to clarify. If Snowberger had seduced the first and late Mrs. Van Dyke, that would be something else entirely.

Snowberger nodded reluctantly.

"Did Mr. Van Dyke know?"

"That was the whole point, Mr. Malloy," he said testily. "He had to know that I'd gotten even with him in a way he could never avenge."

Frank considered this for a long moment. "Mr. Snowberger, you have just given yourself an excellent motive for killing your partner."

"What?" he demanded, as if he really didn't know.

"You had an affair with your partner's wife. Whose idea was it to get rid of Van Dyke so the two of you could be together?"

Frank braced himself for the explosion of rage. Snowberger stared at him in shock for a long moment, but when the explosion came, it wasn't rage.

Snowberger burst out laughing.

Frank watched as this man who probably hadn't laughed out loud in years threw back his head and fairly roared with hilarity. His secretary came rushing into the room to see what was wrong, and Snowberger waved him away as he tried to get control of himself again.

"Oh, Malloy, that's a good one. Haven't heard anything so funny in years!" He chuckled for another minute or two, wiping tears from his eyes, before he could catch his breath and regain his composure.

Frank could only stare at him in amazement. When Snowberger was finally calm again, Frank said, "Exactly what did I say that was so funny?"

Snowberger shook his head, still smiling. "That I would kill for Lilly. First of all, we didn't have an *affair.* I said I seduced her, and I did, once, and once was quite enough. A more tedious woman, I've never met. The thought of being forced to spend any more time with her is appalling to me, and I can assure you, if I never see her again, it will be too soon."

"But you made sure her husband knew she'd been unfaithful."

"Yes, in order to infuriate him. Please don't imagine I have tender feelings for her or any feelings at all, for that matter. As for having a reason to kill poor Gregory, I wanted him alive and well for many years to come. He wouldn't dare divorce Lilly because he'd have to accuse her of adultery. That would make him a laughingstock. No man wants the world to know he couldn't hold on to his young, beautiful wife. So he'd have to live with her and treat her as his wife for as long as he lived, but all the time he'd know she'd betrayed him with me."

"You must've hated him a lot."

"Hated him? You can't even imagine," Snowberger said, warming to the subject now that he'd finally admitted the truth. "We'd been rivals all of our lives. Our fathers were best friends. They started this business and raised us to know we'd inherit it. They took joy in comparing us in everything we did, and we spent our childhoods trying to win our fathers' favor by besting each other in school and sports and later in business."

"You even fell in love with the same woman," Frank reminded him.

"I told you, I don't have any feelings at all for Lilly, and I don't think Gregory really did, either."

"I didn't mean Van Dyke's wife. I was talking about *your* wife."

This time Snowberger did get mad. "Don't you dare speak of her. She has nothing to do with this."

"Doesn't she? I thought Van Dyke blamed you for her death."

Snowberger controlled his anger better than he had his amusement. "He blamed me for everything that ever happened to her. She was very fragile, and her health was never good. The doctor recommended she spend the winter in the south of France . . . But why am I explaining myself to you? The truth is that Gregory was jealous of me and had been since we were boys. When Arabella chose me over him, he dedicated himself to making her regret her choice by trying to make me look foolish every chance he got."

"Like the investment he tricked you into making," Frank guessed.

"Only the last in a long line of humiliations. He'd already set that plan in motion before Arabella died, and I think he took special pleasure in causing me embarrassment on top of my grief."

"So you came up with a plan of your own," Frank said.

"He wasn't likely to fall for the kind of trick he'd pulled on me, and the only thing he truly valued anymore was his bride. He'd taken her to prove he was still vital enough to win the affections of a young, beautiful woman, even though everyone knew he'd practically blackmailed her father to force the marriage."

"Didn't you feel the least bit guilty seducing another man's wife?" Frank asked, taunting him to betray himself.

"I wasn't the first, Mr. Malloy," Snowberger said, not the least bit angry now. "Lilly Van Dyke is a trollop. Gregory didn't know, of course. He'd have locked her away in the country if he had. I didn't compromise Lilly's virtue, because she doesn't have any. I merely took a turn, and then made sure Gregory found out. So you see, we were even. More than even, in fact. I expect Gregory was a little afraid of me after that."

"Why would he be afraid?" Frank asked, hoping for any hint Snowberger might be guilty after all.

"Because with Arabella dead, Gregory knew I no longer had anything worth losing."

"You didn't mind losing money?" Frank asked skeptically.

"I can always make more," Snowberger said, dismissing the threat with a wave of his hand. "The only reason the money ever mattered at all was because it gave Gregory a way to make me look foolish in front of Arabella. Without that, he had nothing."

Frank considered everything Snowberger had told him. The story had the ring of truth, and Snowberger had no reason to make up such an unflattering story about himself, in any case. Still, one thing didn't make sense.

"Mr. Van Dyke told people that the two of you had made up your argument, and that you were on good terms again."

Snowberger frowned. "We'd never been on good terms before, so I'm not sure how he'd accomplish that. He hadn't apologized to me, and I doubt he ever would have, especially after finding out about Lilly, and I certainly hadn't made any overtures to him."

"Then why would he have bought you a gift?"

"A gift?" Now Snowberger was really puzzled. "What kind of gift?"

"A very expensive bottle of French brandy," Frank said. "He told everyone it was for you, to settle your argument once and for all."

Snowberger considered this for a moment. "I do have a weakness for French brandy, but I can't imagine . . . Unless he was planning to break it over my head," he said with a hint of a smile. "What happened to it? I'd hate to see good brandy go to waste, and I know no one at Van Dyke's house would appreciate it."

"It blew up in the explosion."

Snowberger winced in genuine pain at the loss. "Pity."

"We think that's why Mr. Van Dyke was opening his liquor cabinet that morning," Frank explained. "He'd brought it to work with him, and he must've been putting it in there for safekeeping."

"Poor bastard," Snowberger said with a sigh. "That's a horrible way to die, no matter how much he might've deserved it."

Frank knew he'd already stretched his luck as far as it would go with Snowberger. After the questions he'd asked, he was fortunate the other man hadn't thrown him bodily out of his office and threatened to get him fired from the police force. He still could, of course, if Frank didn't get out while he was still in a sympathetic frame of mind.

Frank rose from his chair. "Thank you for answering my questions, Mr. Snowberger."

Snowberger allowed himself a satisfied smile. "My pleasure, Mr. Malloy. I enjoyed your speculations. They were quite entertaining."

Frank hadn't meant to entertain him, but he knew enough to be glad Snowberger saw it that way. "If you think of anyone else who might have had a reason to want Mr. Van Dyke dead, please send for me."

Snowberger didn't reply, and Frank figured the chances of that happening were zero.

AS SHE WAITED FOR THE MAID TO FETCH HER CLOAK, Sarah thought how glad she'd be to get home to her own bed, where she could finally catch up on her sleep. She wondered what Malloy had been doing and what he had learned, but she couldn't find out unless she could find him. Short of leaving a message for him at Police Headquarters, which she knew would only make him angry, or simply waiting here until he showed up, which might take days, she couldn't think of any other way to let him know she wanted to see him. She also didn't want to take the chance that he'd ignore her message. Better to wait until she encountered him again—or get the story from Alberta when he finally solved the murder.

The maid returned with her cloak just as someone rang the bell. Sarah took the cloak so the girl could answer the front door. She'd draped it over her shoulders the instant before Frank Malloy stepped into the foyer.

Sarah couldn't help feeling like a child caught with her hand in the cookie jar. She managed a guileless smile of greeting, even though Malloy was staring at her as if he wanted to shake her. "Malloy," she said sweetly.

"Mrs. Brandt, I'm surprised to see you here." He didn't mean *surprised,* of course.

"Mr. Reed needed medical attention, and I was only too happy to help," she said, even though that hadn't been the original reason she'd come.

Fortunately, this distracted him a bit. "Reed is here *again?*"

"He's *still* here, I'm afraid. He was too ill to go home last night, and it's my opinion that he shouldn't be moved for at least a week."

Malloy opened his mouth to give his own opinion on the matter, but then he remembered the maid standing there, wide-eyed and taking in every word to spread to the rest of the servants the instant she got back to the kitchen. "Is there a room where Mrs. Brandt and I might speak in private for a moment?" he asked her.

"What? Oh, yes, sir," the girl stammered. "Right this way, please."

She led them to a small but fashionably furnished room just off the foyer. Malloy looked around curiously as she closed the door behind them.

"It's a waiting room for visitors the servants aren't sure the family wants to receive," Sarah explained. No fire had been laid to ward off the winter chill, and Sarah was glad for her cloak.

Malloy gave her his full attention, and she immediately regretted letting the maid escape. He didn't have to be polite if they were alone. "Talking to you is like talking to a stone," he informed her. "Didn't I warn you it wasn't safe to be here?"

"Yes, you did," she replied, refusing to be defensive. "I considered your warning, and I chose to disregard it. I don't think anyone else in the family is in danger from the killer."

"How very clever of you to figure that out," he said sarcastically.

"It wasn't clever at all. *You* don't think the anarchists were responsible for Van Dyke's death, either."

"That doesn't mean I'm right!"

"Then why aren't *you* afraid to come here?"

"Maybe I am!"

That was so patently ridiculous, Sarah didn't even bother

to respond. "What have you learned about the murder? I assume you haven't solved it yet, or you wouldn't be wasting time yelling at me."

"I'm not yelling!" he yelled.

Sarah gave a long-suffering sigh. "You were right about Mr. Reed being Alberta's lover," she said in an effort to get him on track. "Her father forbade them to see each other, and he threatened to ruin Reed if they eloped. Alberta was even afraid he'd make her get rid of the baby if he found out. I don't know if she meant adoption or abortion, but . . . What is it, Malloy?"

"They needed to get married right away, and Van Dyke had forbidden them to even see each other," he said, as if that were important.

Fortunately, Sarah knew it wasn't. "He can't be the killer, Malloy. He was right outside the office when the bomb went off, so he couldn't have pulled the wire. He might even have been killed himself."

"We think the bomb went off by accident."

"*What?*"

"The killer set it to go off when he pulled the wire outside, but we found a piece of wire in Van Dyke's hand. He must've seen the bomb, figured out what it was, and tried to disarm it by pulling the wires loose himself."

"And instead it went off right in his face," Sarah said with an involuntary shiver. Then she realized what this meant. Lewis Reed could have set the bomb after all, and he certainly had an excellent reason for wanting Van Dyke dead. "But Mr. Reed couldn't have done it," she insisted.

"Why? Because he was in love? That's one of the main reasons people commit murder, Mrs. Brandt," he reminded her. "He and Miss Van Dyke must've been desperate. As long as her father was alive, they didn't have any hope at all."

"Have you met Mr. Reed?" she argued. "He couldn't hurt a fly!"

"It's men like that, the ones who don't know how to stand up for themselves and can't figure out any other solution, who commit murder."

"I don't believe it!" she insisted.

"*You* don't have to, but *I* have to at least consider it," he reminded her.

She wanted to beg him not to, but she knew that would be idiotic. He was right, Lewis Reed and Alberta had the best reason they'd found so far for killing her father. "Haven't you at least found someone else who might have done it?"

"You mean besides the anarchists?" he asked. "I thought you didn't want them to be guilty, either."

"What about Lilly? She didn't like her husband very much. I'll bet she's glad to be rid of him."

"You're probably right, and she had at least one lover, too."

"Who is it?" Sarah demanded in surprise.

He gave her a withering look that reminded her he didn't have to share information with her.

"I told you I suspected Tad was in love with her," she reminded him. "Is he the one?"

"I said *at least* one, and we don't have any proof she and Tad were actually lovers. A lot of young men fall in love with older women they know they can't have. That doesn't mean he did anything more than moon over her, and it doesn't make him a killer, especially of his own father."

"What if Lilly knew Tad loved her? I'm sure she does. A woman like that is always aware of her effect on men. What if she used him to get rid of her husband? She could have convinced him they'd be together if only his father were dead."

Malloy sighed. "I'll be sure and ask her about that, right after I ask her about her other lovers." He looked meaningfully at her cloak. "Weren't you just about to leave?"

Sarah sighed, too. "I was. I delivered a baby last night."

"That explains why you look so awful," he said. "Go home and get some rest and let me do my job."

Stung, Sarah glared at him. "Do you really think I look awful?"

Malloy rubbed a hand over his face. "I meant you look tired. Now go home." He went over and opened the door, holding it for her.

"You look tired, too," she informed him tartly as she breezed past him.

He made a funny noise in his throat.

As they stepped into the foyer, the maid was opening the front door again. This time Creighton Van Dyke came in.

"Mr. Malloy," he exclaimed when he saw him. "You're just the man I need to see."

II

FRANK HAD FIGURED HE'D NEVER SEE CREIGHTON VAN Dyke again, or if he did, it would only be the result of relentless searching or dumb luck. This must qualify as dumb luck. "You have a lot to answer for, Van Dyke," he said angrily.

"I apologize for running out like that," Creighton said, rubbing his hands together to get them warm.

"The police call it *escaping*," Frank pointed out.

"I don't think so," he replied quite cheerfully. "I wasn't under arrest, after all."

"You were in police custody." Frank wasn't in the mood to split hairs.

"The important thing," Sarah pointed out, irritating him even more, "is that he's back now. What have you found out, Creighton?"

Creighton glanced at the maid, who was drinking in every word. "Let's go upstairs, and I'll tell you." He shrugged out of his jacket and handed it to the maid. Then he headed up the stairs to the second floor in his shirtsleeves, leaving them to follow.

Frank caught Sarah's arm when she started up after him. "I thought you were going home."

"I'm not *that* tired," she informed him. "No matter how bad I look."

Frank sighed as she handed the maid her cloak as well and followed Creighton. He'd never hear the end of that "tired" remark. He took off his overcoat and handed it to the maid also.

"Your sister's in the back parlor with Mr. Reed," he heard Sarah telling Creighton when he reached the top of the stairs.

"Reed? What's he doing here?" Creighton said. "I thought he was injured in the explosion."

"He was, but he felt it was his duty to help the family with the arrangements for your father, so he came over yesterday. He overestimated his strength, however, and he had to remain here overnight. Alberta has been tending him."

A pretty story, and Frank wasn't going to contradict it.

"I should tell Bertie that I'm back," Creighton said, "but that can wait." He headed for the front parlor. The door stood open, showing the room to be empty. He led them inside and shut the door behind them.

"All right, Van Dyke, where have you been?" Frank demanded.

"The Lower East Side. I've been questioning everyone who might know anything about my father's death."

Frank felt the fury boiling inside of him, but he knew how to hold it in check. "I thought we'd decided that we'd do that *together*," he reminded him.

"No, *you'd* decided that, Mr. Malloy. I knew perfectly well no one would tell me a thing if you were with me. My friends don't trust the police, you know. Too many of them have been thrown in jail for things they didn't do, just because the police don't like their philosophy."

Sarah had taken a seat on the sofa. "You can't blame them for not trusting the police," she said to no one in particular.

Frank ignored the provocation. "What makes you think they told *you* the truth?"

"I used persuasion. I can be charming when that will work, and when it doesn't . . ." He held up his hands. The knuckles were skinned.

"I don't suppose you found out who killed your father?" Frank asked sarcastically.

"No, but I found out who *didn't*. I'd stake my life that he wasn't killed by an anarchist. The truth is, they're just too afraid to take a chance on a crime so shocking. They've learned from those who've gone before and made grand gestures, only to end up rotting in prison in obscurity."

"Like the man who tried to assassinate Henry Frick," Sarah said.

"Exactly," Creighton agreed. "A friend of ours only missed being with Alexander Beckman in Pittsburgh because they didn't have enough money for her train ticket. Otherwise, she probably would've gone to prison, too."

"Yes, Emma Goldman," Sarah said. "We met her. But she did go to prison herself a few years ago."

"Yes, and she doesn't want to go back. There's too much important work to be done for us to allow any of our people to be locked up. They didn't do this, Mr. Malloy."

"I suppose you think they'd confess to you if they did," Frank said.

"My father's death would be worthless as a political state-ment if no one claimed responsibility for it."

"What if they did it for the money you'd inherit to sup-port them?" Frank challenged.

"We have other patrons, Mr. Malloy. Besides, my father disinherited me."

"No, he didn't," Frank said, watching Creighton's reac-tion carefully.

"What do you mean?"

"I mean that your father did change his will recently, and he did disinherit some family members, but not you. In fact, you'll inherit almost his entire estate."

"*What?*" he asked incredulously. He wasn't faking. This was genuine shock. He truly hadn't expected to profit from his father's death, which meant he didn't have a motive. That was something, at least.

"Your father thought you should be forced to accept your responsibility as a capitalist, so he left everything to you."

"What about Bertie and Tad?" he asked, still shocked. "And Lilly?"

"You can provide for your brother and sister as you see fit, and your stepmother will get an income of five hundred dol-lars a year."

"*Five hundred dollars?*" Sarah echoed in amazement.

"She'll never be able to support herself on that, even if she lived here in the house with me!" Creighton said, equally surprised. "Why would he do a thing like that?"

"He must have been very angry with her," Sarah guessed. "And with Tad, too." She was asking a silent question, but Frank wasn't going to answer it.

"And with Bertie," Creighton added, still trying to make sense of it. "What on earth could *she* have done?"

"I think your father was trying to protect her from fortune hunters," Frank said, hoping to find out if Creighton knew Alberta and Reed were lovers.

"She was never bothered by fortune hunters when he was alive," Creighton said. "Why should he worry about it after he's dead?"

Frank looked at Sarah, silently warning her not to tell, but she didn't need a warning. She simply sat staring up at Creighton with a slightly puzzled look on her face, as if she didn't have any idea.

When no one responded, Creighton said, "Well, I don't care if she does want to marry a fortune hunter. If he makes her happy, she can have all the money she wants. In fact, she can have the whole estate. I don't want a cursed penny of it."

Frank had never expected to hear a man say anything so foolish in his entire life, but before he could think of a response, Sarah beat him to it.

"Don't be so hasty, Creighton," she said reasonably. "What about all the people who work for your father's business? This would be your chance to introduce better working conditions and higher salaries, everything you believe in. You can't change the world all at once, but you could start with one company. If you were able to make money while treating your workers well, others might want to learn from you."

Sarah Brandt never ceased to amaze him. Frank had been disarmed by her logic many times, and it was nice to know he wasn't her only victim.

Creighton was staring at her, uncertain whether her argument supported anarchist philosophy or not, but Frank wasn't going to give him time to decide. "Do you know why your father would have cut your brother and stepmother out of his will?"

Creighton looked uncomfortable, and he finally decided to sit down. "Father was a very difficult man to please," he hedged, not meeting Frank's eye.

"Did your brother have a hard time pleasing him?" Frank pressed.

Plainly, he didn't want to answer. "Tad was the youngest child. He's a bit spoiled, and of course he's still very young."

"Which means he didn't like to work," Frank guessed. "Is that why his desk is in the basement with the other junior clerks?"

"Father wanted him to learn the business the way he had, especially after I . . . left."

"How did Tad feel about that?"

"He didn't have a head for it. He hated working with numbers and sitting at a desk all day. What young man wouldn't?"

"Lots of them," Frank said, thinking of how lucky he would've felt for a job like that, where he could earn a decent wage honestly and work in a clean, safe office. But for jobs like that, no Irish need apply.

"Not Tad," Creighton said wearily. "He was the son of a millionaire, and he didn't see why he had to work. I guess he still doesn't."

"He probably expected to inherit a sizable amount of money when your father died," Frank said mildly.

"I suppose," Creighton said, and then the implication of that statement dawned on him. "He couldn't have done a thing like this," he insisted. "In the first place, he isn't clever enough."

"What do you mean?" Frank asked.

"The killer planned this carefully. Then he made the bomb and set it up. That would've taken a lot of time."

"Your brother could have gone into the building anytime

he wanted and stayed as long as he liked. No one would've questioned him."

"But he'd have to know how to make a bomb and how to wire it. He'd have to study the process and have patience and take great care in building it. Tad couldn't do that. It's not in his nature. He can't even play chess because it takes too long!"

"Your father must've always known what Tad was like. That wouldn't be enough for him to suddenly change his will. Could your brother have done something in particular to make your father angry?"

"I suppose so," Creighton said grudgingly. "I hadn't seen them for months, though."

"How did Tad feel about your stepmother?"

Creighton saw no purpose to this question. "He liked her well enough, I suppose."

"Could his feelings have been deeper than that?"

Creighton stiffened. Now he saw the purpose. "That's ridiculous!"

"Is it? You said yourself Tad is a young man. Mrs. Van Dyke is a young woman and very attractive."

"He's obviously very fond of Lilly," Sarah offered, "and she encourages him, I'm afraid. I think she enjoys the attention."

Creighton didn't like this one bit. He looked as if he'd like to bolt, but good breeding kept him in his seat.

Frank pushed him a little harder. "He wouldn't be the first young man to do something stupid for love."

"Killing your father is more than just stupid, Detective," Creighton said stiffly.

"If your anarchists friends didn't do it, someone else did," Frank reminded him. "Most of the people who could've wanted him dead are relatives."

"Do you think *Bertie* could've killed him?" he asked,

angry now. "I can just see her carrying a bomb to Father's office and wiring it to explode. Or maybe Lilly. She could've gone down there one evening when Father thought she was at a concert or a play and planted the bomb."

"Either one of them could've gotten a man to do it for them," Frank said provocatively.

"Oh, yes," Creighton agreed bitterly. "Bertie is a well-known seductress. I can think of any number of men who would've gladly sacrificed themselves just for a touch of her hand."

"Well, there's at least one," Frank said.

Creighton didn't believe him. "No man has called on her in years!"

"That's because your father wouldn't let him."

"Who is it?" he challenged. Plainly he didn't believe Frank knew.

"Lewis Reed."

"Reed?" he echoed in surprise, and then his head snapped up, and he looked in the direction of the back parlor, where Sarah had told him Alberta and Reed were. "She and *Lewis?*" he asked incredulously.

"Your father forbade them to see each other," Sarah said. "He genuinely loves her, Creighton, but your father would've ruined Mr. Reed before he'd let him marry Alberta."

Frank waited to see if she'd mention the baby, but she didn't. Probably, she was respecting Alberta's secret. He wouldn't have been so honorable if it meant shocking Creighton into a revelation, but he'd let it go for now.

"Reed could've built a bomb, and he had access to the building," Frank pointed out.

"But Lewis was injured in the blast," Creighton said. "If he was the killer, surely he wouldn't have put himself in danger."

"We think it went off by accident, long before the killer intended for it to," Frank said.

Creighton was shaking his head. "I can't . . . This is too horrible to even contemplate. Don't you suspect anyone outside of our family?" he added desperately.

"How about Allen Snowberger?"

Creighton eagerly grasped at this. "You'd asked me about him before. He and my father were arguing or something. But that wasn't unusual. They never got along."

"Until the day your father died," Frank reminded him. "Mr. Van Dyke was taking him a bottle of expensive French brandy."

"You told me that before, and it still doesn't make any sense. Why would he do a thing like that?"

"No one seems to know."

"Didn't you ask Snowberger?"

"He doesn't know either, or so he says."

Creighton was still considering the situation when the parlor door opened and Lilly Van Dyke stormed in.

"Creighton, how dare you show your face here!" She turned to Frank. "I hope you're going to lock him up this time. None of us are safe with him running around loose!"

"I don't have any reason to arrest him, Mrs. Van Dyke," Frank said as respectfully as he could when he really wanted to toss her back out the door.

"What do you mean, no reason? He killed Gregory!"

"Creighton!" Alberta cried from the doorway and rushed to her brother. He rose and caught her hands in his as she reached out to him. "I'm so glad you're safe."

"*Safe?* Why wouldn't he be safe?" Lilly demanded shrilly. "No one wants *him* dead! He's the golden goose for all those foreign revolutionaries!"

Creighton and Alberta ignored her.

"Is Katya all right?" Alberta asked.

"Fine," he said. "I saw her this morning, just before I came here. She's worried, but I told her not to be."

"I can't imagine why you'd say a thing like that," Lilly snapped. She turned to Frank again. "If you aren't going to arrest him, I'm going to have to call Commissioner Roosevelt and insist that he send someone who will."

"If that's what you think is best, Mrs. Van Dyke, go right ahead," Frank said, figuring she was bluffing. Teddy wasn't going to take orders from someone polite society frowned on.

Lilly Van Dyke wasn't used to being dismissed, and she stared at him, open-mouthed for a moment before she remembered herself.

Taking advantage of her temporary silence, Frank said, "I was just explaining the terms of your husband's new will to Mr. Van Dyke."

This caught her attention. "I *knew* my husband was making a new will," she said, contradicting what she'd told Frank a few days ago. "He said he needed to make some changes in light of recent events," she added, giving Creighton a meaningful look.

Creighton released Alberta's hands and met Lilly's gaze unflinchingly. "I think you'll be surprised, Lilly."

"Surprised that he left you nothing?" she scoffed.

"No, surprised that he left me everything."

Shocked and unbelieving, she turned to Frank for confirmation.

"That's right, Mrs. Van Dyke," he said, watching her carefully for her reaction.

She still didn't comprehend. "You mean after he provided for me," she said. "I'm his wife!"

"Of course Father provided for you, Lilly," Creighton said, not bothering to hide his satisfaction. "He left you an annual income of five hundred dollars a year."

She needed a moment for this to register. "I must have misunderstood you," she said, trying to smile, trying to make her charm work.

"You didn't misunderstand," Creighton said, taking a perverse pleasure in explaining. "He left you a pittance. If you're very careful not to offend me, I may allow you to continue to live here, so you won't have the expense of room and board someplace else. That will leave your entire income to use on clothes and whatever else you think you need."

They both knew the "pittance" wouldn't pay for even one custom-made evening gown. Lilly stared at Creighton as if she'd never seen him before. "*No!*" she shrieked. "You're lying! He was going to disinherit you! He knew you'd just give it to those foreigners! He wouldn't have left you a penny!"

She lunged at Creighton, hands clenched into claws, but Creighton caught her wrists before she could attack him. She screamed in frustration as she struggled to get her nails into his face.

Creighton wrestled her down into the chair where he'd been sitting. By then she was sobbing hysterically.

"Bertie?" Reed called from the doorway. "Are you all right?" His face was pale, and he held one hand to his wounded head, but his eyes were bright with concern.

"Lewis," Alberta said, hurrying to his side. "You shouldn't be up. Come and sit down." She took his arm and Sarah jumped up to help. The two women escorted him safely to the sofa and sat down on either side of him. "What's wrong with Mrs. Van Dyke?" he was asking when Tad Van Dyke appeared in the doorway.

"What's going on in here? Lilly, what's wrong?" He glanced

around at everyone else in the room. "What have you done to her?" he demanded of Creighton.

He didn't wait for an answer, but went immediately to Lilly's side.

Frank rubbed a hand over his face. Now if Gregory Van Dyke would just return from the grave, this scene would be a *perfect* disaster.

"Lilly, what is it?" Tad was asking her, his voice soft, his touch caressing as he knelt beside her chair and handed her his handkerchief. "There now, don't cry. I'll take care of everything."

That made her cry even harder as she buried her face in his handkerchief. Frank noted that Creighton was watching them closely and frowning. He'd be remembering what Frank had said about them being lovers and trying to see some evidence to prove him wrong.

"You can't do much to take care of this, Tad," Creighton informed him. "Lilly's crying because Father left his entire estate to me."

Tad's head jerked up, and he stared at his brother in patent disbelief. "He just made a new will," he said. "He was going to cut you out completely!"

"Who told you that?" Frank asked.

Tad glared at him, probably thinking it was none of his business. "Father did!"

"What did he say?"

Tad rose to his feet. "He said no son who betrayed him would ever inherit a penny of his money!"

"That's funny," Frank said, as if he really thought it was. "You're the one who didn't get a penny."

Tad wasn't very good at concealing his emotions. His face registered shock, then guilt. He glanced down at Lilly, who was staring up at him, having forgotten her own misery for a moment. A red flush crawled up his neck and over his young face. "You're lying!" he accused Frank. "I won't believe it until I see the will myself—the *new* will!"

"I'm sure Mr. Judd will be happy to explain everything to you, the way he did to me," Frank said, naming the Van Dykes' attorney.

"Is it true?" Alberta asked Frank. "Did father really leave everything to Creighton?" She was holding Reed's hand and patting it almost absently.

"Yes," Frank said, trying to judge her reaction. Reed seemed only mildly curious, but perhaps his head injury kept him from fully understanding what all this meant to him. Alberta understood every word, though.

She didn't seem very upset, though. She turned to Creighton with pity on her plain face. "Poor Creighton," she said. "I'm so sorry."

Creighton smiled slightly at the irony. "According to Mr. Malloy, I'm supposed to take care of you, Bertie, and I will, so you won't have to worry."

"We don't need anything," she said with a fond glance at Reed. "I'll be content just to be Lewis's wife." Reed returned her glance with a look so tender, Frank had to turn away.

At least he knew Reed and Alberta hadn't killed her father for his money. There was still the matter of them being allowed to marry, though, which was an even better reason, considering Alberta's condition.

"Is that why you're crying, Lilly?" Tad asked her. "Because you think Father didn't leave me anything?"

She glared at him. "Of course not! He didn't leave *me* anything, either!"

"That's impossible," Tad insisted. "You're his wife!"

"Father did provide a small income for her," Creighton explained. "Apparently, she doesn't feel it's adequate, though."

"How small?" Tad asked, still not willing to accept this.

"Five hundred a year," Lilly said through gritted teeth, her hysteria giving way to anger now.

"Send for Judd," Tad said furiously. "Get him over here immediately *with* this so-called will. We'll see once and for all who's telling the truth!"

"Mr. Malloy was just asking me why Father might have changed his will in such a way," Creighton said. "Do any of you have any ideas?"

Frank looked at each of them in turn. Alberta and Reed seemed puzzled but not really concerned. Lilly's face turned red, and Tad turned stiffly and went straight for a cabinet on the far side of the room.

"He was a wicked man," Lilly said. "He took pleasure in making other people miserable. *That's* why he did it."

"He wasn't wicked," Alberta contradicted sadly. "He did have set ideas on how things should be, though, and he didn't tolerate anyone who wouldn't conform to those ideas."

Tad had pulled a bottle of liquor out of the cabinet and was pouring himself a generous drink. *"Tolerate?"* he mocked. "Is that what you call it? I call it *punish*. He was ruthless if you didn't meet his standards."

Shocked by his indictment of his father, everyone else in the room stared at him in stunned silence as he raised the glass to his lips. The instant the liquor hit his tongue, however, he flinched and spit it out and flung the glass on the floor, smashing the crystal into a hundred pieces and making everyone in the room jump.

"Horse piss!" he announced in disgust. He grabbed the bottle by its neck and held it up. "This is a perfect example. He put the cheap stuff down here for his guests, but he only bought the best for himself. He'd hide it in his room so no one else could get it. Bastard!"

"Tad, watch your language!" Creighton said. "There are ladies present."

Tad looked around the room as if to verify Creighton's observation. Then he looked straight at Sarah, dismissing the others, and bowed slightly. "Pardon me, Mrs. Brandt. I forgot you were here."

Lilly gasped in outrage, and Alberta flushed, but Tad ignored them both. Still holding the bottle of "horse piss," he stalked out of the room.

Frank briefly considered going after him, but decided to let him stew a bit. Once he was convinced of the terms of his father's will, he'd be too furious to mind his tongue at all.

"Mr. Van Dyke," Reed said to Creighton, breaking the awkward silence. His voice was weak but determined. "Since you're now the head of the family, I'd like to ask permission to marry your sister."

Taken off guard, Creighton looked to Frank for guidance. He'd be wondering if Reed had killed his father and if he dared give permission for his sister to marry a murderer. Frank shrugged. He had no guidance to give.

"If you don't give permission," Alberta said, "we'll still be married as soon as possible. We'd like your blessing, but it isn't necessary."

"Well, of course, I mean . . ." Creighton stammered, still seeking an ally in the room but finding none. "By all means. You have my blessing."

Lilly sighed in disgust, but no one paid her any mind. Alberta turned to Reed, and he clasped both her hands in his. For a moment, Frank thought she looked almost beautiful as she gazed at her lover's bandaged face. Dear God, he hoped he didn't have to arrest them for murder.

"Now I suppose I should send for Mr. Judd and find out

exactly what Father's will does say," Creighton said, sounding a little overwhelmed.

"You must send for Katya, too," Alberta said. "There's no reason for you to live in a hovel any longer, and she should be here, with you."

"You aren't bringing that trollop into this house!" Lilly exclaimed. "I forbid it!"

Alberta glared at her. "This is Creighton's house now, and you can't forbid anything. You'd best mind your manners, Lilly, or you'll find *yourself* out on the street."

Lilly made an incoherent sound in her throat, lunged to her feet, and hurried out of the room in a swish of skirts.

Frank heard Sarah sigh beside him. "That went well," she observed.

BRIAN WAS ONLY TOO GLAD TO ACCOMPANY HIS FATHER for a walk after supper that night. Frank wished he could explain to the boy where they were going and why, but he was trapped in his silent world, and Frank had no way to break through.

Yet.

As they made their way through the crowded streets, Frank couldn't help recalling the terrible scene at the Van Dyke house that afternoon. If he'd ever entertained the notion that money could buy happiness, the Van Dykes had disabused him of it once and for all. Now that he thought about it, the only person he knew who was truly happy was Brian, who had nothing at all.

Frank glanced down to where the boy was fairly skipping along beside him, holding Frank's hand tightly but thoroughly enjoying being with his father and seeing all the other people. His shoes looked perfectly normal, even though one of them had been specially made to fit his repaired foot. He looked just like any other three-year-old boy out for a walk with his father.

But if Frank let go of his hand, and he wandered off, he wouldn't even be able to tell anyone his name or where he lived.

His heart heavy, Frank led Brian through the streets leading toward Tompkins Square, where the Isenberg family lived. He found the building at the address he'd been given, and Brian didn't even hesitate to go inside with him. The boy trusted his father completely and would probably follow him into the jaws of hell if Frank wanted him to.

The building was cleaner than most and in good repair. The family lived on the second floor, in the front apartment, which meant they paid a premium rent. Those on the upper floors paid progressively less, and those in the back, where little air circulated, paid even less. The second floor, above the street-level noise and dirt but still an easy climb up the stairs, was a prime location.

The door to the flat was already open when they arrived, and a girl of about thirteen stood there. "I was watching for you," she explained happily. "I'm Trude."

Frank returned her smile. "I'm Mr. Malloy. This is Brian."

A tall, well-built man appeared in the doorway behind her. He put a hand on her shoulder, and she looked up at him while he made some strange motions with his hands.

"My father said to introduce him," she said. "His name is Bernard Isenberg."

Isenberg reached out his hand to Frank, who shook it. The hand was rough and ink-stained, reminding Frank that he worked as a printer. He reached down and ruffled Brian's red-gold curls affectionately, making Brian grin.

Isenberg motioned them inside and took their coats. Frank could see at a glance that Isenberg provided well for his family. The furniture was comfortable and of good quality, and everything was neat as a pin. Even his mother would approve.

Trude presented them to her mother and her brother, Leo. Mrs. Isenberg was also deaf, and she made the same kind of motions with her hands that her husband had. She was a small, plump woman with a handsome face, and she wore a stylish dress. She made them welcome and silently invited them to sit down.

Leo was about eight and all boy. His knees were skinned beneath his short pants, and while it was obvious his mother had cleaned him up for the occasion, his hair was already mussed from her careful combing and his shirttail was half out. He marched right up to where Brian was perched in Frank's lap and began to sign to him.

"I told you," Trude said, signing so her parents would know what she was saying. "He doesn't know how. He won't understand."

Leo glared at his sister. "How's he going to learn then, if nobody shows him?" he demanded, signing also to include his parents.

His parents chuckled, and even Frank had to smile.

Leo held out his hand to Brian and jerked his head toward a corner of the room where Leo had laid out some toys. "Come on," he said, and started toward the toys.

Brian looked at Frank questioningly. Plainly, he understood the invitation, although how he could, Frank had no idea, but he was clinging possessively to Frank's lapel. Frank nodded encouragingly. Brian looked back at Leo, who was sitting down on the floor beside the toys. He began to set up a row of wooden soldiers, and again he motioned for Brian to join him.

After another pleading look at Frank, who nodded again, Brian finally scrambled down and hesitatingly made his way over to where Leo sat on the floor. The older boy offered him a soldier, and Brian sank down beside him and began to help.

Bernard made some signs.

"He says, what do you want to ask him?" Trude translated.

Frank had so many questions, he didn't even know where to start. "Everything, I guess," he said. "How did they learn sign language . . . and how did you learn to talk if they can't?" he added to Trude.

She smiled importantly. "That's easy. We just did." Then she turned to her father and asked Frank's questions.

For the next hour, they conversed in this awkward way, with Frank asking and Trude translating both questions and answers with signs and giving the answers verbally back to Frank.

He learned that Bernard had been born deaf, like Brian, even though no one else in his family was deaf. His parents had sent him to school when he was young, and he'd learned sign language and all the other things a child learns in school. When he got old enough, he'd been apprenticed to a printer. Many deaf men became printers because the job required little verbal communication to perform and deaf men weren't bothered by the loud noise of the presses. As a skilled laborer, he earned a good wage.

Mrs. Isenberg had become deaf after having a high fever when she was six. She could speak, although her speech was sometimes difficult to understand, and she lip-read fairly well. Still, she preferred using sign language, and it was a necessity when communicating with her husband. She'd met Bernard at the school they'd both attended. She'd learned all the academic subjects she would have at a regular school, as well as the womanly skills of sewing and cooking and cleaning. She was glad that both of her children could hear. Life was hard even when all your senses worked properly, but she and Bernard had a good life together. Brian could, too, she assured Frank.

"He needs to be in school, though," Trude said with no prompting from her parents. Her mother poked her as a reprimand for presuming to instruct an adult, but she stood firm. "He does!"

Frank had been watching Brian and Leo from the corner of his eye during the conversation with the Isenbergs, and he could see the boys were getting along fine. Leo kept making signs to Brian and coaxing him to imitate them. Brian's small fingers were nimbly mimicking Leo's, although Frank was sure he had no idea what he was doing besides playing a game with a new friend.

Seeing that the adults were watching them, Leo scrambled to his feet. "See what he's learned already." He led Brian over to them, and pointed at himself. Brian made some quick signs with his fingers, and the Isenbergs laughed in delight, making Brian grin.

"What did he say?" Frank asked, intrigued.

"He spelled Leo," Leo said proudly. Then he pointed at Brian, and the boy made different signs. The Isenbergs clapped in approval, and Brian brightened and clapped, too.

"He spelled his own name," Trude told a mystified Frank.

"Watch this," Leo commanded them. He pointed at Frank and made a sign like a salute, with a hand to his forehead and then lowered it, palm up. Brian tried to imitate him, and after a few tries and some additional guidance from Leo, he made the sign correctly. Then Leo pointed at Frank, and Brian happily made the sign.

"What did he say?" Frank asked Leo.

"He said Father. He knows your name now."

Thrilled at being the center of attention, Brian made the sign again, looking up at Frank with his small face aglow with pride. Frank felt the sting of tears and a rush of love so strong it staggered him. He snatched Brian up and hugged him fiercely to his chest.

"I think he'll send him to school now," Trude said.

12

Sarah felt a lot better the next morning. She'd gone straight home and right to bed after that awful scene in the Van Dykes' parlor. Fortunately, she wasn't summoned to deliver any more babies, so she'd spent most of the time since then sound asleep. Now she felt ready to face the Van Dykes again. With any luck at all, they'd figure out who killed Mr. Van Dyke today, and she could forget all about their petty bickering and scandals, at least Sarah hoped so as she set out for Marble Row.

The maid greeted her warmly and took her cloak. "Miss Alberta and Mr. Tad haven't come down yet," she said. "Mr. Creighton went out early and isn't back yet, and Mrs. Van Dyke already has a visitor. You can wait down here if you like, and I'll see if Miss Alberta can receive you."

"Who is Mrs. Van Dyke's visitor, Ella?" Sarah asked,

knowing full well the maid shouldn't reveal such information. "If it's Mr. Malloy, I know he wouldn't mind if I interrupted them," she added, hoping to trick her into telling.

"Oh, no, it's Mr. Snowberger," the girl said gravely. Plainly, she was certain Sarah wouldn't dream of interrupting such an important person.

She was wrong. "Really?" Sarah said brightly. "I've been wanting to see him to express my condolences," she lied, heading for the stairs.

"Wait, Mrs. Brandt," Ella cried in alarm, hurrying after her. "I'll announce you."

"No need," Sarah said, climbing the stairs as quickly as she could so the girl couldn't catch up with her. "Mr. Snowberger is an old friend." Just a slight bending of the truth. She *had* known him all her life, although he'd never been particularly friendly.

"Mrs. Van Dyke don't like it when I don't announce people," the girl was arguing as she tried to catch up to Sarah.

The front parlor door was closed. Sarah figured Allen Snowberger would merit being entertained in the best room, so she headed straight there.

"Please, Mrs. Brandt," Ella begged, but Sarah had already reached the door and threw it open. What she saw stopped her dead in her tracks.

Allen Snowberger was sitting on the sofa with Lilly Van Dyke in his lap. His face was buried in her bosom, and when the sound of the door opening brought his head up, Sarah could plainly see that Lilly's bodice hung open and her breasts were completely exposed.

Lilly jumped up with a shriek, grabbing the edges of her bodice and yanking them together as she stumbled away from Snowberger. As for him, he bolted to his feet, hastily turning his back. He began adjusting the front of his trousers.

"Pardon me," Sarah said insincerely. She'd been hoping to catch Lilly and Snowberger unawares, but not *this* unawares.

"I'm terrible sorry, Mrs. Van Dyke," Ella exclaimed frantically, coming up beside Sarah. Both of the room's occupants had their backs to her, so she was spared the shock Sarah had sustained. "I tried to stop her!"

"Get out," Lilly screeched. "Just get out!"

Looking terrified, Ella did as she was bid. Lilly had probably meant the command for Sarah, too, but she closed the parlor door behind her and stayed right where she was. "Does Mr. Malloy know the two of you are having an affair?" she asked mildly.

They both started and turned sharply to look at her. They obviously had thought she'd left with Ella.

"We aren't having an affair," Snowberger insisted. He'd finished with his trousers and now turned to face her fully, running a hand nervously down his waistcoat, as if checking to make sure everything was in place.

"Oh," Sarah said in surprise. "I suppose you were giving Mrs. Van Dyke a medical examination, then. You were certainly close enough to hear her heart beating."

His face flushed scarlet, but he continued to meet her gaze defiantly. Now that he'd gotten a look at her, he was trying to decide if she was really someone he need worry about. He wouldn't recognize her, of course, since he hadn't seen her in years.

Lilly was still struggling with her bodice, but she whirled on Sarah. "Why can't you mind your own business? No one invited you here!"

"Alberta asked me to come by and check on Mr. Reed," Sarah lied. "I thought Ella said I would find them in here. I certainly didn't intend to find you . . . well, the way I found you." This much was true.

"Who *are* you?" Snowberger demanded.

"Felix Decker's daughter," Sarah replied, giving him the fact most likely to inspire fear in him. "You may call me Mrs. Brandt."

He blanched. He now knew she was dangerous indeed. "Mrs. Brandt," he tried again, more conciliatory this time. "I think you misunderstood what you saw here. Mrs. Van Dyke and I are old friends. I was merely trying to comfort her on the loss of her husband, who also happened to be my friend and partner."

"You have an interesting way of offering comfort, Mr. Snowberger," Sarah said. "I'm sure Mr. Malloy will find your relationship with Mrs. Van Dyke very interesting."

"I've already spoken with Mr. Malloy about it," Snowberger assured her, "so you need not trouble yourself. He understands completely."

Sarah raised her eyebrows, remembering what Malloy had said about knowing Lilly had at least one lover. But if he knew about Snowberger, why hadn't he mentioned him as a possible suspect when they were discussing this yesterday? "What exactly does Mr. Malloy understand?" she asked.

Snowberger smiled in that condescending way some men did when explaining something to a female he considered of inferior intelligence. "He understands that Mrs. Van Dyke and I are merely . . . friends."

"*Friends?*" Lilly shrieked again. "We're more than *friends*, you pudding-headed gasbag, and you'd better not forget what I told you!"

"Lilly, *shut up*," Snowberger said nervously.

Ignoring him, Lilly turned to Sarah, lifted her chin, and said, "Allen and I are going to be married."

Behind her, someone threw the door open again, nearly knocking her over, and Tad Van Dyke burst in, with Lewis Reed and Alberta right behind.

"What did you say, Lilly?" Tad demanded, his young face white to the lips.

"Nothing, Tad," Snowberger assured him hastily. "She's very upset and isn't thinking clearly."

Lilly looked at Snowberger as if she'd like to slit his throat, but Tad distracted her.

"You said you were going to *marry* him!" he repeated, horrified.

Alberta had noticed something else. "Lilly, what happened to your dress?"

Lilly glanced down at her half-buttoned bodice. When she raised her head again, she gazed straight at Snowberger with a triumphant smile. "Allen was simply sampling what is going to be his."

Snowberger was desperate with either embarrassment or fear. "It isn't what you think," he said to no one in particular.

"It's exactly what you think," Lilly insisted.

Tad made a strange sound and took a step toward Lilly, then stopped, staring at her as if he'd never seen her before.

"Mr. Snowberger," Reed said, his voice quivering with outrage. "How could you? Mr. Van Dyke isn't even in his grave yet."

Snowberger stared at Reed in surprise for a moment before giving a bark of mirthless laughter. "Are you presuming to chasten me, you little toad? You wouldn't dare come near this house if Gregory was alive. He told me how you'd tried to get under his unfortunate daughter's skirts just so you could get your hands on his money."

Instinctively, Reed lunged for him, but Alberta and Sarah grabbed him and held him back.

"Don't, Lewis!" Alberta cried.

"Listen to her, Lewis," Snowberger advised. "Lay a hand on me, and I'll have you arrested. In fact, if you so much as show your face at my office again, I'll have you arrested."

"For what?" Reed challenged, surprising Sarah. Apparently, he could show some spirit when aroused.

"Trespassing," Snowberger said smugly. "You are no longer employed at Van Dyke and Snowberger."

Reed was livid, but common sense prevailed. His face was still bright red with rage, but he straightened away from Alberta and Sarah's restraining hands, squaring his shoulders. "Come, Bertie. This is no place for you." He took her arm and led her out of the room.

Tad was still staring at Lilly, his face a mask of misery. "Lilly, I don't believe you," he was saying. "You said we'd always—"

"Go away, Tad," she said quickly, cutting him off. "You're just a boy, and now you're a *poor* boy. Don't be a nuisance. Allen and I have things to discuss."

He looked at Snowberger and back at Lilly again. She was fiddling with her buttons, pretending to fasten them, and didn't even spare him a glance. With a cry of despair, he turned and fled the room.

Finally, Lilly looked up at Sarah. "I'm sure you were just leaving, too," she said coldly.

"And so am I," Snowberger said hastily.

"Allen!" Lilly cried in protest, but he was already moving toward the door.

"I'll . . . We'll talk later," he said over his shoulder.

"You promised!" she called after him, hurrying to the door, but he was gone, clattering across the hall and down the stairs with unseemly haste.

"What did he promise?" Sarah asked.

But Lilly only glared at her and flounced out of the room.

Something important had happened here, and Malloy needed to know about it. Without bothering to ask permission, Sarah went to the small room under the stairs where the Van Dykes kept their telephone. She called Police Headquarters and, after careful consideration, left a message for Malloy to call Mrs. Felix Decker at her home. Waiting here for him to arrive could be awkward, particularly since Lilly was so angry with her at the moment. Besides, Lilly might have her thrown out. She might not really be the mistress of the house anymore, but the servants didn't know it yet. Her mother would welcome her, though, and she could wait there as long as necessary for Malloy to reappear.

FRANK COULDN'T BELIEVE HE WAS GOING TO FELIX Decker's house. The instant he'd gotten the message to telephone Mrs. Decker, he'd known it was from Sarah. She'd been meddling again, in spite of his warnings and threats, and now she claimed to have important information. If only she could've told him over the telephone, but with operators listening and the connection being so poor, he'd had no choice but to meet her at her parents' house to discuss it.

He wondered if he could convince her mother to tie up Sarah and keep her there until he'd solved this case.

To his surprise, the Deckers' townhouse wasn't nearly as grand as the Van Dykes'. Away from the bustle of Fifth Avenue, their street was quiet and the homes comparatively modest. A maid opened the door and welcomed him by name, telling him he was expected. He asked if Mr. Decker was home, and she informed him Mr. Decker was out of town on business. At least he'd be spared having to deal with the old man.

The maid showed him to a distinctly feminine room in the back of the house that overlooked a patch of yard and a tree. Sarah and her mother were there, sitting on a small sofa in front of a crackling fire, and Sarah rose to meet him, smiling the way she always did when she saw him. She didn't look tired this morning. She looked beautiful.

"Malloy," she said by way of greeting. "Come and sit down. We have a lot to tell you."

Frank nodded at Mrs. Decker, who had also risen from her seat. "Good morning, Mrs. Decker."

"Good morning to you, too, Mr. Malloy." Her mother looked well kept, as always. "Sarah has made some exciting discoveries."

"So she said," Frank replied as neutrally as he could. He took the wingback chair opposite the sofa and tried to remember he couldn't yell at Sarah in front of her mother.

"Lilly and Snowberger are having an affair," Sarah announced when they were all settled.

Frank couldn't help but glance at Mrs. Decker to see her reaction to such a bald and shocking statement coming from her daughter. She seemed remarkably undisturbed. Frank wondered how long that would last. "I know," he said. "Snowberger already told me."

"Did Mr. Van Dyke know about it?" Sarah asked.

"Snowberger made a point of telling him, or so he said. They'd been rivals all of their lives, and Van Dyke had recently made him lose money in a business deal. He did it to get revenge on Van Dyke once and for all, not because he had any affection for Mrs. Van Dyke."

"How ungentlemanly," Mrs. Decker said with a frown of disapproval. "Adultery is unforgivable under any circumstances, of course, but to compromise a woman's honor simply for revenge is unconscionable."

"It would be, if it's true," Sarah said. "I suppose he was the one who told you he didn't have any affection for her."

"Yes. He said he only . . ." He glanced at Mrs. Decker while he searched for an acceptable way to say it. "That is, they were only . . . It just happened once."

"That would hardly qualify as an affair," Mrs. Decker pointed out, not the least disturbed. "That would merely be a seduction."

"And he only did it to humiliate his partner. He said he hopes never to see Mrs. Van Dyke again," Frank explained, glad to put an end to this uncomfortable discussion.

"Except he saw her just this morning," Sarah informed him.

"Sarah caught them *in flagrante delicto*," Mrs. Van Dyke added with apparent pride.

"In *what*?" Frank asked, knowing the words couldn't possibly mean what he thought they did, especially not if Mrs. Decker had said them.

"She was sitting in his lap and . . ." Sarah glanced at her mother the same way Frank had.

"Stop looking at me like that, as if you think I'll be shocked," Mrs. Decker protested. "You already told me what they were doing. I'm not going to faint."

"Her bodice was undone and . . ." Sarah glanced at her mother again.

"And he was kissing her bare bosom," Mrs. Decker finished impatiently. "Does that sound to you as if he has no affection for her?"

Frank didn't know what was more shocking, what Sarah had seen Lilly and Snowberger doing or hearing it from Mrs. Felix Decker. He had to swallow before he could reply. "This happened today?" was all he could think to ask.

"I already told you it did," Sarah reminded him sharply.

"When I caught them, right in Lilly's front parlor, Snowberger was embarrassed, but Lilly wasn't. She proudly announced that they were going to be married."

"*Married?* Her husband isn't even in the ground yet!" Frank said.

"I believe it was Mr. Reed who pointed that out to them," Sarah said.

"Reed? What was he doing there?"

"Oh, he and Alberta and Tad all came running when they heard Lilly screaming."

"What was she screaming about?"

"Various things. Getting caught, first of all. Then she objected rather loudly when Snowberger tried to convince me there was nothing between them."

"With her bodice open like that, I don't suppose there was," Mrs. Decker observed wickedly.

Shocked again, Frank looked at her, but she didn't bat an eye. He cleared his throat. "You said Tad was there, too? What did he say about all this?"

"Plainly, he was jealous and devastated by Lilly's announcement. He's certainly in love with her, and I'm sure she led him on, at the very least. He seemed to think she'd turn to him now that his father is dead. I got the impression she'd told him as much at some point."

"She may have assumed he'd inherit a goodly portion of his father's estate," Mrs. Decker said.

"Especially since everyone thought he'd disinherit Creighton," Sarah added.

Frank took a moment to consider this new information in light of what he already knew, but Sarah apparently couldn't stand the silence.

"Was Snowberger the one you were talking about when you said Lilly had at least one lover?"

"Yes," Frank admitted. "But he said he had no further interest in her. He'd only seduced Lilly to get revenge for the business deal. He considered them even."

"Which meant he wouldn't have had any reason for killing Mr. Van Dyke. But now . . ."

"Yes, now," Mrs. Decker offered eagerly, "it appears he's actually in love with Lilly and planning to marry her. That would certainly give him a reason for killing poor Gregory."

Indeed, it did. Snowberger had sounded very convincing when he'd insisted he cared nothing for the widow. What had he called her? Tiresome? Frank felt the same way about her, so he'd readily believed Snowberger did, too. Frank usually had no trouble at all figuring out who was lying and who was telling the truth, but Snowberger might well be one of the few men who could lie well enough to fool him. He rarely dealt with millionaire businessmen as suspects. For all he knew, lying well was one of their major characteristics.

"I need to pay Mr. Snowberger another visit," he said.

From the expression on Sarah's face, he could see she'd give anything to accompany him. She also knew better than to ask. This was official police business.

"If you'll excuse me, ladies," he said, starting to rise.

"I'm sure Mr. Snowberger can wait for an hour or so. Why don't you stay and have luncheon with us, Mr. Malloy?" Mrs. Decker said.

"No, I—" he tried, but she was having none of it.

"You must eat, to keep up your strength," she pointed out. "Everything's ready, and Allen Snowberger isn't going to leave town, even if he did blow up his partner. He'll be right there waiting for you whenever you arrive. Sarah, would you ring for the maid and tell her to set an extra place?"

Now he was going to *eat* at Felix Decker's house. At least

the old man wasn't there. Frank figured he wouldn't have been invited otherwise. Decker might tolerate him in his professional capacity, but sitting down at table with him was asking way too much.

"MR. MALLOY HAS VERY GOOD MANNERS," SARAH'S mother observed later, after they had seen him off on his mission to find Snowberger.

"You sound surprised, Mother. Did you expect him to eat with his fingers and wipe his mouth on the tablecloth?"

"Don't be sarcastic, dear," her mother chided. "It isn't becoming. You know what I meant. He has a certain delicacy of mind I wouldn't have expected, either."

"Mother, you naturally inspire gentlemanly conduct in men," Sarah said with a smile. "I can assure you, Malloy can be extremely indelicate when he wants to be."

"Is he indelicate with you?" she asked with some interest.

Sarah wasn't going to answer that question. "Let's just say he doesn't hesitate to tell me when he finds my conduct unacceptable."

"Which is often, or so I gather. He seemed extremely displeased that you're involved in all this. Doesn't he appreciate your help?"

"Oh, yes, although he'd probably never admit it. In this case, he's concerned for my safety, though."

"Your safety?" her mother said in alarm.

Sarah shrugged. "I suppose there's a chance someone might try to blow up the Van Dyke house, too."

"Why would they bother? Gregory is already dead."

"My point exactly," Sarah said with satisfaction. "Malloy likes to consider all the possibilities, however."

"I suppose he must, if he's going to solve this puzzle.

Now, what shall we do to pass the time until he finds Allen and questions him?"

Sarah considered the possibility of whiling away a long, boring afternoon at her mother's house with dismay. "I really should pay a visit to the mission," she decided. "I haven't been there in days."

Her mother smiled. "You want to see little Aggie, don't you? The child you told me about."

Sarah was afraid to admit how much, even to herself. "She's become very attached to me. I don't want her to feel I'm just one more person who has abandoned her."

"I'd like to meet this little girl myself," she said. "Why don't I go with you?"

Sarah's first instinct was to refuse, and she wasn't sure why. Was she afraid for her mother to meet Aggie? Or was having her mother meet Aggie more of a commitment than she wanted to make right now?

Her mother misunderstood her hesitation. "Don't worry about taking me into the Lower East Side again. I'm sure I'll survive another visit."

Sarah looked at the frilly gown she wore. "May I suggest you dress a bit more conservatively than you did the last time? Do you have anything that's actually *plain*?"

Her mother smiled indulgently. "Maybe I could borrow something from the maid."

FRANK WAS BEGINNING TO WONDER IF MRS. DECKER had been wrong about Allen Snowberger leaving town. He'd gone straight to Snowberger's office after leaving Mrs. Decker's house. Snowberger wasn't there, and no one knew when he might appear. They directed him to Snowberger's home, which turned out to be an apartment in one of the new buildings on Fifth Avenue's Marble Row, just a block from the Van Dykes.

The doorman insisted on escorting him up. Probably he didn't trust a cop in a building like this, full of expensive things. But no one answered the door at Snowberger's flat, even though the doorman had said he was home.

"Doesn't he have any servants?" Frank had asked.

"A girl who comes in to clean, but she doesn't live in. His valet does, but he's been gone all day on some errand."

"What kind of errand?"

"How should I know?" the doorman asked, offended. "I don't pry into the tenants' private business."

"You seem to know pretty much everything else," Frank pointed out. "I thought you said Mr. Snowberger was at home."

"I saw him come in, but . . . Well, he may have gone out when I was busy elsewhere," the man admitted reluctantly. "You might try his gentleman's club."

Frank had banged on the door a few more times, but still got no response. Having no other options, he'd gone to check Snowberger's club with no luck.

Now he was back. The sun was setting and no one had seen Snowberger anywhere since he'd returned to his flat right after he'd left the Van Dyke house. The doorman wasn't happy to see Frank again.

"He hasn't come back yet," he protested.

"Let's check anyway," Frank suggested less than kindly.

The doorman gave in with little grace.

"Why does Snowberger live in an apartment?" Frank asked as they rode up in the fancy elevator. "I figured he'd have one of these mansions along here."

"He did, until his wife passed away. I suppose he didn't see any reason to keep up a big place when he was alone."

"How long has he lived here?"

The man considered. "About six months, I guess."

Frank frowned. That would've been about the time he lost the money in the deal with Van Dyke. Snowberger had sold his big, fancy house and moved to a flat with only one live-in servant. His protests that losing the money hadn't mattered to him seemed less convincing now.

Frank pounded on the door again, and once again, no one answered. Now he was starting to believe Snowberger had fled. He wouldn't have wanted the doorman to see him leaving with luggage, so he'd have sneaked out when the man wasn't looking. He also would've sent his valet away on some phony errand so the man wouldn't know what he was doing. Frank needed to check inside to see if his belongings were gone.

"Open the door," he told the doorman.

"I can't do that!" he protested in alarm.

"Then I'll have to kick it in."

The poor man gasped "Wait, I . . . I'll get the key."

He'd just turned toward the elevator when they heard a cracking noise from inside. "What's that?" Frank asked.

"I don't know. I—"

Before he could complete the thought, they heard a roar of shattering plaster and breaking glass. Without waiting for permission, Frank threw his shoulder against the door, instinctively turning the knob. To his amazement, it gave beneath his hand and his weight carried him staggering into the room. The door hadn't been locked at all!

The small entry hall opened to a larger parlor and beyond it a dining room. The whole area was filled with a cloud of plaster dust, but no smell of gunpowder. He'd expected gunpowder. He could see what looked like two legs on the floor in the dining room beneath a pile of debris.

As the cloud of dust began to settle, Frank identified the hole in the ceiling where a chandelier had recently hung. That chandelier and part of the ceiling comprised the debris now covering the body on the floor. Frank hurried to where it lay and began pulling pieces of bent metal and broken plaster and glass off the body. The instant he uncovered the head, he knew this man hadn't been killed by an explosion. The face was blue and the eyes bulging. A rope had been fashioned out of a sheet and knotted around the neck. The other end was tied to the remains of the chandelier. He must've been hanging there a while before his weight finally pulled the electric light fixture loose.

Frank had never pictured Snowberger as a suicide. The act was too cowardly for such a proud man. Had he done it out of guilt or fear of discovery? Was he ashamed of his crime, consumed with guilt for what he'd done to his partner, or afraid of the public humiliation that would come if he was discovered? Frank looked around for anything that might be a note explaining his act. A confession of murder would be helpful, too. He saw nothing.

"Is he . . . dead?" the doorman called from where he stood in the front hall.

"I'm afraid so. You'd better call the police."

"I thought you *were* the police!" the man said, newly outraged.

"I am," he assured him impatiently. "I just need some help with this. Now hurry up!"

The man disappeared, and Frank stared down at what remained of Allen Snowberger.

SARAH HADN'T EVER EXPECTED TO BE SITTING ACROSS from her mother in the dining room of the Prodigal Son

Mission while they shared a simple meal with the girls who had found refuge there. About a dozen girls, ranging in age from thirteen to sixteen, and their chaperone, Mrs. Keller, were eating at the two tables. Aggie sat beside Sarah on the bench, as close as she could get. Her small body felt good pressed up against her, warm and safe. Sarah had an overwhelming urge to keep her safe forever.

A very dangerous urge for a woman who couldn't possibly manage to actually do it.

Mrs. Decker was thoroughly enjoying her one-sided conversation with the little girl. "What's your favorite thing to do here at the mission?" she asked.

Aggie grinned and pointed to her fork, then lifted a bite of potato into her mouth.

"What's your favorite food?" Mrs. Decker tried again.

Aggie considered a moment, then laid her fork down, tucked her hands into her armpits, and flapped her elbows.

"A bird?" Mrs. Decker guessed, pretending not to understand.

Aggie giggled and shook her head. Then she lowered her head and pretended to peck at her plate while flapping her elbows.

"A flying horse?" Mrs. Decker guessed again.

Aggie gave her an impatient glance and scrambled off the bench before Sarah could stop her. She started strutting down the aisle between the tables, scratching at imaginary dirt with one foot, flapping her elbows, and bobbing her head in an amazingly accurate imitation of a chicken. The other girls stopped eating to watch, laughing at the child's antics.

"A chicken!" Sarah couldn't resist saying, even though she knew perfectly well her mother was trying to trick Aggie into speaking out of frustration at not being able to communicate.

Aggie beamed and proudly climbed back into her seat beside Sarah again.

"You make it too easy, Sarah," her mother scolded.

Sarah knew she was right. Ever since meeting the child, she'd communicated with her by asking questions that could be answered by a simple "yes" or "no." Her mother had instantly understood that Aggie needed to be challenged, or she would never feel the need to speak.

But Sarah was thinking about something more important. "Aggie, when did you ever see a chicken?"

Aggie looked up at her and shrugged before picking up her fork and taking another bite.

Her mother instantly realized the implication of that question. "A child growing up in the city would probably never get to see a live chicken."

"Not one scratching in the dirt, at least," Sarah agreed. "And she wouldn't have eaten chicken here at the mission," she added. It was too expensive.

They both looked at Aggie with new eyes. The child glanced up and grinned smugly, as if she enjoyed being an enigma. Everyone had assumed she was an orphan because she'd shown up on the mission's doorstep one morning, but for the first time Sarah considered the possibility that she might have a family somewhere, perhaps out in the country, someone who loved her and grieved over her loss.

"Who are you, Aggie, and where do you come from?" Sarah asked, stroking the girl's soft hair affectionately.

She looked up at Sarah with sad eyes and then laid her head against Sarah's side. Unable to resist, Sarah slid her arm around the narrow shoulders and hugged her close.

"You can't leave her here," her mother said. "She needs a family."

"She understands what you say," Sarah reminded her. People tended to forget that even though Aggie was dumb, she wasn't deaf.

Mrs. Decker studied Aggie for a moment. "Would you like to go back to your own family?" she asked, violating her own rule about yes and no questions.

Aggie looked back, her brown eyes enormous in her small face. Then, slowly, she shook her head.

"Why not?" Mrs. Decker asked.

But Aggie wasn't going to speak. She just shrugged her shoulders and looked up at Sarah with a silent plea.

"It's all right, Aggie," Sarah assured her. "You don't have to go anywhere. You're safe here."

Her little face crumpled, and her soulful brown eyes filled with tears.

"Aggie, what is it?" Sarah asked in alarm. "What's wrong?"

The girls around them fell silent, and the clatter of forks on plates ceased as they all looked to see what was wrong with Aggie.

"She never cries," one of the girls said in wonder as a crystal tear slid down Aggie's cheek. "Not even when she hurts herself."

Sarah watched helplessly, not knowing what to say or do.

"Don't you want to stay here, Aggie?" her mother asked relentlessly.

Sarah wanted to tell her to leave the child alone, but Aggie was already shaking her head vigorously.

"But you don't want to go home, either," Mrs. Decker guessed.

Sarah felt the little body stiffen beneath her arm, and once again Aggie shook her head.

"Where do you want to go?" Mrs. Decker asked.

Aggie went perfectly still, and then slowly, almost reluctantly, she turned and looked up into Sarah's face with a longing so naked, it almost took her breath.

Sarah tried to take her in her arms, but Aggie wriggled free and scrambled off the bench again. She ran out of the room, her shoes clattering on the bare, wooden floors.

"Maeve," Mrs. Keller said to one of the older girls. "Make sure Aggie's all right, and don't let her leave the house."

Maeve got up and hurried after the child. Mrs. Keller came over to where Sarah and her mother sat. "She'll be fine," she said. "The girls get attached to the ladies who come to help out. You can't blame them, really. Most of them never got any kindness in their lives."

"I wouldn't have any way to take care of a child," Sarah explained, staring longingly at the doorway through which Aggie had disappeared.

"You don't have to feel guilty," Mrs. Keller assured her. "You do what you can, and we're all grateful."

But Sarah couldn't help remembering what Mrs. Ellsworth had said. The heart finds a way.

13

Captain O'Connor wasn't happy with Frank. Having one millionaire die in his precinct was bad enough, but two was inexcusable. He intended to hold Frank personally responsible. "What do you think Commissioner Roosevelt is going to say when he finds out you drove this poor bastard to suicide?" the captain asked angrily when he'd had a chance to survey the scene. He'd brought along his two pet detectives, and they were standing around, trying to look important while not getting in the captain's way.

"He didn't kill himself," Frank told him.

O'Connor gave him a blistering look. "I guess he just stood up on the table and let somebody tie a sheet around his neck and push him off, then."

Someone had shoved the substantial dining room table out from under the chandelier but left it close enough to stand on while attaching the wound sheet to the chandelier and Snowberger's neck. Snowberger would have only had to step off the table to accomplish his purpose. But that wasn't the way it had happened.

"He didn't stand up on the table at all," Frank said. "I figure whoever knocked him unconscious—"

"What?" O'Connor nearly shouted.

"I said, whoever knocked him unconscious managed to lift him up onto the table. He's not a large man, so anyone who's reasonably fit could've done it. It was a simple matter to wind the sheet into a rope, tie one end to the light fixture up there and the other end to Snowberger's neck. I'm guessing he sat Snowberger up for that, so the length would be right. Then all he'd have to do is push him off the table. His feet wouldn't quite touch the ground, and he'd choke in a few minutes."

"A very nice fairy tale, Malloy, but what makes you think Snowberger wasn't conscious when he was hanged?"

The dead man was now lying peacefully on the floor amid the rubble Frank had pulled off him. Frank hunkered down and lifted one of Snowberger's hands. The fingers were dusty but otherwise unmarked. "Even suicides claw at the noose when they start choking. It's a natural reaction. But there's no marks on his hands or his throat."

O'Connor still didn't look impressed.

"Then there's this gash behind his ear," Frank continued, turning Snowberger's head slightly so O'Connor and the detectives could see the hair matted with the blood that had also stained Snowberger's shirt collar.

"He probably got that when the chandelier fell on him," O'Connor snorted.

"By the time it fell, he'd been dead for a while. Dead men don't bleed, Captain." Frank pointed to several other places on Snowberger's face where the skin had been broken in the fall. Not one drop of blood seeped from any of them. "This one happened when he was still alive. I found blood on the fireplace poker." He pointed to where the poker sat in its stand. The killer had carefully replaced it, but he hadn't wiped it completely clean.

O'Connor frowned and crossed his arms over his chest. "I guess you think whoever killed his partner killed him, too."

"I'm not guessing about anything. I've got to *prove* what happened."

"Then have at it, Malloy, and may God help you. Let's get this stiff out of here before it starts to stink." With that he nodded to the orderlies from the morgue to get started. Then he turned on his heel and left, his detectives following.

Once the orderlies had taken the body away, Frank sent for the doorman again. This time he was much more cooperative. Frank made him sit down in the dead man's front parlor, where he could see the rubble left from the falling chandelier.

"So he hanged himself, did he?" the man asked nervously.

"No, somebody killed him," Frank said. "Tried to make it look like a suicide, but it wasn't. Now tell me again when you saw Snowberger come in."

"I didn't notice the time. Around midmorning maybe. I hadn't eaten lunch yet. He said hello, the way he always does, and walked up the stairs, like he usually does. He likes the exercise."

"Did you see anybody else coming in? A visitor maybe?"

He thought about this a moment. "Not coming in, I didn't. I saw somebody leaving, though."

Frank managed not to grab the man by the lapels and shake him. "Why didn't you mention this before?"

"Because you didn't ask me," the doorman reminded him

defensively, as if he sensed Frank's desire to throttle him. "You only asked me if I saw Mr. Snowberger leave, which I didn't. Besides, the visitor didn't leave until after you were here the first time."

Good God, the killer could have still been there when Frank was pounding on the door! Holding his temper with difficulty, Frank continued, "Who was it you saw leaving?"

"I didn't know him. I don't even know if he was visiting Mr. Snowberger. He had his face turned away, and he was in a hurry."

"Could it have been one of the other tenants?"

"No, I know all of them. And they all speak to me."

"How would he have gotten in without you seeing him?"

"I could've been taking somebody up in the elevator. I told you, I was away from the desk a few times, so I thought maybe Mr. Snowberger went out when I didn't see him."

The killer could have taken the stairs up, the way Snowberger had, too.

"What time was it when this stranger left?"

"I don't know. Maybe an hour or so after you left the first time. I wasn't paying much attention. Before supper, at least."

Frank figured the mysterious man was the killer, but he would have to speak to all the other tenants and find out if any of them had had a visitor that afternoon, just to make sure.

"What did this man look like?"

"I told you, I didn't see his face."

"What *did* you see?" Frank asked impatiently.

The man blinked uncertainly. "He was medium height, not fat or thin. He was wearing a black suit of good quality and a hat pulled down low. I . . . that's all I noticed."

He'd just described half the men in the city. Frank sighed wearily and let the man go.

Alone again, he took another turn around the apartment. This time he was looking for anything that might indicate Snowberger had constructed a bomb here. Even if he was now dead, he might've been the one who had set the bomb that killed his partner. In fact, that might be why someone had killed him. But an hour of searching failed to turn up so much as a pair of wire cutters. If Snowberger ever did any kind of manual work, he did it elsewhere. Remembering how soft and well groomed his hands had been, Frank figured the roughest thing he'd ever handled was a sheet of paper.

Frank did find a portrait of a young woman hanging in Snowberger's bedroom. He had to look at it twice before he realized it couldn't possibly be Lilly Van Dyke. The style of her dress was much too old-fashioned, and her hair was lighter. Still the resemblance was noticeable. Could this be Snowberger's wife, the legendary Arabella who had been loved by both her husband and his partner? That would certainly explain why Van Dyke had chosen Lilly. He must've been disappointed when he found out her true character was nothing like the saintly Arabella. Had the resemblance been what attracted Snowberger, too? But surely, he'd known what she was really like long before he became involved with her.

Since both men were dead, Frank would never know the answers to his questions. He'd have to be satisfied with finding the killer or killers. He used Snowberger's telephone to place a call to Commissioner Roosevelt's home. He'd want to know about this before the newspapers came out in the morning.

* * *

Sᴀʀᴀʜ ᴡᴀsɴ'ᴛ sᴜʀᴘʀɪsᴇᴅ ᴛᴏ ʙᴇ ᴀᴡᴀᴋᴇɴᴇᴅ ʙʏ sᴏᴍᴇᴏɴᴇ knocking on her front door the next morning. People pounded on her door at all hours when a baby was coming. But this visitor wasn't one of them. She recognized her mother's coachman. He took off his hat and wished her good morning, his breath frosting in the morning air.

"Mrs. Decker asked me to deliver this message," he explained, handing her a cream-colored envelope scented with her mother's perfume.

Alarmed, Sarah tore it open, heedless of the richness of the paper. Inside was a note written in her mother's elegant hand informing her that Malloy had found Allen Snowberger murdered in his apartment. Teddy Roosevelt had telephoned late last night to notify her father. She'd known Sarah would want to hear the news as soon as possible.

When she looked up, the coachman was smiling. "Mrs. Decker told me to wait for you. She said you'd probably want to go to the Van Dykes' house."

"I'll only be a moment," Sarah told him, hurrying back inside to get her things.

When Sarah came out of the house again, her next-door neighbor hailed her. Mrs. Ellsworth had appeared on her front porch with a broom, ostensibly to sweep but really to be available to find out where Sarah could be going in her parents' carriage. The old woman would have recognized it from previous visits.

"Is anything wrong, Mrs. Brandt?" Mrs. Ellsworth asked with genuine concern.

Sarah hated discussing this on a public street, so she went over to Mrs. Ellsworth's porch, where she wouldn't have to

shout to be heard. "Mr. Snowberger has been found murdered," she explained.

"Oh, dear, poor man," she said. "I knew something had
happened. I sneezed this morning for no reason at all."

Sarah knew better than to ask what she meant. "Perhaps
you're getting a cold."

"Oh, no, I'm perfectly healthy," Mrs. Ellsworth assured
her. "Sneezing for no reason on a Friday means sorrow, you
see. It means something different for each day of the week,
Sneeze on Monday, sneeze for danger; sneeze on Tuesday,
kiss a stranger—"

"Well, if you keep standing out in this weather, you
might very well catch a cold," Sarah warned, hiding a
smile. "I've got to be off, now. I'm needed at the Van Dyke
house."

"Oh, of course, dear," Mrs. Ellsworth said. "I didn't mean
to keep you. I hope everyone is all right."

Sarah hoped so, too.

THE MAID ELLA OPENED THE DOOR TO HER HALF
an hour later, and she all but pulled Sarah inside. "Oh,
Mrs. Brandt, I'm that glad you're here. Everything's at sixes
and sevens!"

Sarah could hear raised voices coming from upstairs. She
hadn't expected such an uproar over Snowberger's death.
"What's going on?"

"That policeman, Mr. Malloy, he came first thing to tell
everyone about Mr. Snowberger. He tried to ask questions,
but Mrs. Van Dyke started screaming something awful, and
we had to put her to bed with some laudanum. Miss Alberta
is near about to faint, but she won't go to her room, and

Mr. Tad is . . . well, he's not himself." Sarah figured he was drunk. "Then there's that Russian woman."

They heard a crash upstairs, and Ella winced. "She's been screaming at Mr. Creighton since he brought her here last night." The poor girl looked near tears.

"I'll see what I can do," Sarah said. "Is Mr. Malloy still here?"

"Oh, yes, ma'am. Should I announce you?"

"Don't bother. I'll find my own way."

This time Ella didn't object. Plainly, she didn't relish another encounter with the family and their hysterical guest.

"Katya, *please*," Creighton was saying when Sarah reached the open doors to the front parlor. The couple were standing in the middle of the room, glaring at each other. "Don't talk so fast. I can't understand you!"

"I will not stay here," Katya replied, speaking very slowly and distinctly in English and with a definite touch of exasperation.

"Good morning, everyone," Sarah said brightly and loudly. Four faces looked up at her in surprise. One of them belonged to Malloy, and for once he looked happy to see her. Or maybe it was just relief she saw on his face. Alberta's was the fourth, and she definitely looked relieved.

"Sarah, how good of you to come," she said, rising from where she'd been sitting on the sofa watching her brother argue with his mistress. "Have you met Miss Petrova?"

Sarah smiled at Katya, who didn't smile back. She was furious and rubbing her side absently.

"How are you feeling, Miss Petrova?" Sarah asked, instantly concerned.

"I am a prisoner here!" she exclaimed in outrage. "He will not let me leave!"

"Your place is with me," Creighton insisted. "Why

would you want to go back to the tenements when you can live in a mansion?"

Katya cried out incoherently in frustration, but the cry strangled in her throat as she doubled over on a stab of pain.

Sarah and Creighton rushed to catch her.

"Katya, what is it?" Creighton asked in alarm, forgetting his anger.

"Sit her down," Sarah instructed, and they eased her into the nearest chair. "Where does it hurt?" she asked Katya.

The girl looked up with eyes filled with fear. "Here," she said, rubbing her side.

"It's probably just false labor," Sarah said reassuringly. "Excitement can bring it on. Probably nothing to worry about, but we shouldn't take any chances. Creighton, can you carry Miss Petrova up to"—she hesitated, wondering where Katya might be staying—"her room," she finished uncertainly.

"Take her to the blue guest room," Alberta said, taking charge of the transfer. "She'll be more comfortable there than in your room."

Creighton lifted Katya effortlessly and carried her out, with Alberta following at his heels. Sarah glanced at where Malloy stood watching helplessly. "I'll be back as soon as I can," she promised. She pointed to the bell rope. "Ring for the maid. She'll be happy to bring you some coffee."

"Do you think something's wrong with her?" he asked, and Sarah really looked at him this time. She saw an expression she'd never expected to see on his face—fear. For a moment, she couldn't imagine what he could be afraid of, and then she remembered. His wife had died in childbirth.

"It's probably what I said," she assured him, even though she wasn't sure herself. "I'll take good care of her."

With that, she hurried out.

She found Creighton in the third-floor hallway, pacing outside a closed door. "We put her in there," Creighton said. "Bertie told me to get out."

"Of course she did," Sarah said brightly. "This is women's business."

"Isn't there anything I can do?"

"Have the cook send up some hot water, vinegar, and compresses. Also some warm milk and weak tea."

Creighton bounded down the stairs to do her bidding, grateful to be able to take some action. Sarah went into the bedroom. It was a pleasant room facing the street and decorated in shades of blue. Katya lay on the bed, and Alberta was helping remove her shoes.

"How do you feel?" Sarah asked, going over to help. "Have you had any more pains?"

"No, I . . . ah!" She grabbed her side again, her face contorting. Alberta's face went white, and she stared at Sarah with terrified eyes.

As soon as the pain passed, Sarah said, "We should get you out of these clothes so you'll be more comfortable. Alberta, would you fetch Katya a nightdress?"

Alberta scurried out, probably as grateful as Creighton for something to do besides watching Katya.

"What is it?" Katya whispered, even more terrified than Alberta.

"False labor, like I said," Sarah said, even though she feared it might be a miscarriage. "You just need to get comfortable and rest and be calm. Lie still and let me unfasten your dress. Do you feel anything wet between your legs?" she asked as casually as she could while she began unbuttoning the girl's bodice.

Katya's eyes widened. She knew the significance of the question. "No, nothing," she said quickly.

Sarah smiled. "That's very good. Now take a few deep breaths and let them out slowly. Yes, that's right."

Sarah laid her hands on the small mound of Katya's stomach and gently began to massage the side where the cramping had started. She also tried to detect some movement from the baby. The child was still very small and might lie motionless for hours, but even so, Sarah experienced a frisson of fear when she felt no movement.

An hour later, she had Katya settled comfortably. She'd drunk a cup of milky tea and had a vinegar compress across her forehead. The contractions had died away, and Katya had drifted off to sleep. Leaving a maid to sit with her, Sarah and Alberta stepped out into the hallway.

Creighton was still pacing outside.

"She's asleep," Sarah told him. "She just needs to rest for a few days, and no excitement."

"I never should've brought her here," he said. "She didn't want to come."

"This is the best place for her," Alberta insisted. "You know that yourself. She doesn't have to worry about anything here, and we can make sure she eats well and gets plenty of rest."

"She doesn't believe me, Sarah," he said brokenly. "I told her what I plan to do with Father's business, how I'm going to treat the workers fairly and show the world that's the best way to be successful. But she doesn't believe it will work. She thinks I've already been corrupted by my father's wealth."

Sarah didn't know what to say. She could understand Katya's skepticism. How many businessmen considered themselves humanitarians and good Christians and still thought nothing of cheating their workers at every turn? Could Creighton's good intentions survive in such an environment? Was he strong enough to go against every tenet of popular wisdom?

"I'm sure you can work all that out later," Sarah said. "Right now it's important that she not get upset about anything. Only talk about pleasant things and distract her if she tries to argue with you."

"I will," he promised.

"Good. Now I need to speak with Mr. Malloy for a few minutes, but you can call me if Katya needs anything."

Sarah started down the stairs, and Alberta went with her.

"How is Mr. Reed doing?" Sarah asked, wondering why he hadn't been present at the family conference.

"I don't know," she said with a worried frown. "He left yesterday, right after you did, and I haven't heard from him since. I tried to convince him to stay, but he said he had something important to do."

Sarah was surprised. What could he have had to do that was more important than being with Alberta? But she didn't want to worry her friend. "I'm sure he's fine. He really didn't need to stay here, you know. I only said that so Lilly wouldn't send him away and the two of you could be together."

"I know, but I can't help worrying. I thought he'd come back here when he was finished with his business, or at least telephone, but he didn't."

"Alberta," Sarah chided playfully, "I already have one upset expectant mother to worry about. I don't want another."

Alberta tried to smile. "I'll try not to become a burden to you."

"See that you do!" she teased back.

They'd reached the second-floor hallway.

"I need to speak with Mr. Malloy alone," Sarah said.

"Yes, of course. I'll be in the back parlor if you need me.

I think I'll send one of the servants to Lewis's flat to make sure he's all right."

"Good idea." Sarah opened the parlor door and stepped inside.

Malloy rose to his feet politely. He'd been drinking coffee from a silver service that had been carried in. "Good morning, Mrs. Brandt," he said neutrally.

"Don't bother pretending you're angry that I'm here," she warned him. "I saw your expression when I walked in."

"I won't deny that I was glad to be rescued from the arguing anarchists," he admitted. "How is Miss Petrova doing?"

"She's resting, but I'm afraid she's still in danger of losing the baby."

He nodded grimly and looked away. "Would you like some coffee?" he asked to change the subject as she took a seat opposite him. "It's very good."

The maid had brought several extra cups, and Sarah helped herself.

"Tell me what happened to Snowberger," she said as she raised the cup to her lips.

Briefly, he explained how he'd happened to find the body and how the killer had tried to make it look like suicide.

"The killer was clever," she said.

"Reasonably. Snowberger did die by hanging, so everything looked right. He didn't know much about police work, though, or he would've realized somebody would notice the gash on the back of Snowberger's head."

"Maybe he just didn't have any *respect* for police work," she pointed out. "How many detectives would bother to look beyond the obvious, especially if it meant more work for them?

Finding a murder suspect who committed suicide would be an easy solution to a difficult problem."

He didn't like what she'd said, but he knew she was right. "Well, he didn't commit suicide, so now I've got two murders to solve."

"But only one killer to find," she pointed out. "This second murder should make the job easier, too."

"If the same person killed them both," Malloy said.

Sarah frowned. "Two killers wouldn't make any sense."

"It would if they were killed for different reasons, and they probably were, whoever killed them."

"That would certainly complicate matters," Sarah agreed. "Why don't we try the obvious solution first? Who wanted *both* men dead?"

Malloy considered. "I think we can eliminate the anarchists on Snowberger's death, too. Not their style at all."

"Creighton had nothing to gain, either. He's already got his father's money and his half of the business, although . . ."

"Although what?" Malloy prompted.

"Although he does have some grand ideas about changing the way the company treats its workers, sort of putting the anarchists' theories into practice. I doubt Snowberger would've gone along with his plans."

"Killing him seems like a drastic solution, though," Malloy pointed out. "Especially since he probably hasn't even had a chance to talk to him about it yet."

"That's true," Sarah agreed, glad Creighton could be eliminated.

"That leaves Lilly and Tad and Reed."

"Lilly wanted to marry Snowberger," Sarah said. "She was probably feeling desperate because her husband didn't leave her any money, so she picked a man who was equally wealthy."

"Didn't Snowberger have any choice about it?" Malloy asked skeptically.

"I got the impression Lilly had extracted a promise from him somehow, but he was still reluctant. I can't imagine she'd kill him if he was going to rescue her, though. How did she react when she found out he was dead?"

"She got hysterical. Started screaming and throwing things."

"I'm guessing killers don't usually act like that," Sarah said with a small smile.

"She couldn't have lifted Snowberger onto the table anyway," he allowed, returning her smile. "That leaves only the men."

"Tad and Reed," Sarah guessed. "Oh, dear!"

"What now?" Malloy asked with another frown.

"I just remembered. Snowberger told Reed he was fired from his job."

"When did he do that?"

"Yesterday. With everything else that happened, I'd forgotten they'd argued, too. Snowberger said something insulting about him and Alberta. Reed tried to . . . uh, lay hands on him, but we held him back."

"*We?*" Malloy asked, intrigued.

"Alberta and I," she replied. "He's weak, from his injury," she added so Reed wouldn't sound like too much of a sissy.

Malloy raised his eyebrows, but he didn't comment. He just said, "So Snowberger fired him."

"Yes, he said he'd have Reed arrested for trespassing if he showed his face at Van Dyke and Snowberger again."

"Then he's lucky you arranged for him to stay here so he's got an alibi," Malloy said.

Sarah winced, wishing she didn't have to admit this.

"Alberta just told me he left the house right after Snowberger did yesterday, and he hasn't been back."

"Where did he go?"

"Alberta doesn't know. He just said he had some business to take care of."

Malloy sat back in his chair and considered this. "We already know he had a good reason to want Van Dyke dead. Then he finds out Alberta didn't inherit any money, so he'll need a job to support her and the baby."

"Creighton said he'd take care of her, though," Sarah reminded him.

Malloy wasn't impressed "Not many men would enjoy living on charity like that, or having to constantly please Creighton so he didn't change his mind and cut off their allowance."

"Reed wouldn't care," Sarah insisted. "He loves Alberta."

"All the more reason why he'd want to support her himself," Malloy said. "A man wants the woman he loves to respect him. With Snowberger gone, Creighton would be in charge. He'd probably give Reed his job back and might even promote him. From what I've heard, he practically runs the place already."

Sarah rubbed her forehead. "I can't believe he'd kill two men. He's so . . . meek!"

"Like I said, they're the most dangerous kind. Reed is also clever enough to try to make Snowberger's death look like a suicide. He even knows enough about electricity to have figured out the wiring for the bomb."

Sarah thought of how devastated Alberta would be if Reed was the killer. "Surely, someone else must've wanted both of them dead!" she tried.

"Tad's our only other suspect for both murders."

Sarah wasn't thrilled about seeing Tad accused, either. "He's so young," she said.

"He's in love with Lilly. Being young just means he might be stupid enough to kill off his rivals."

"But to murder his own father," Sarah protested.

"He didn't exactly shoot him in the head," Malloy reminded her. "Whoever killed Van Dyke did it in a way that meant he wouldn't even have to see it happen."

"And a way that would cast blame on the anarchists. Finding the anarchist who did it would be almost impossible."

"Especially since it wasn't an anarchist. The killer probably figured the police would waste all their time down in the Lower East Side and never solve the case."

"If you weren't the detective in charge, that's probably what would've happened," Sarah said.

She hadn't intended to flatter him. She was just stating a fact, but he looked uncomfortable, almost embarrassed.

"Why would Tad have wanted Snowberger dead?" he asked gruffly.

Sarah recognized the effort to get her back to the subject. "Same reason he might've wanted his father dead," she admitted. "He was distraught when Lilly said she was going to marry Snowberger."

"Where was Tad yesterday afternoon?"

"I don't know, but I'm sure we can find out." Sarah got up and went to the bell rope. She sent the maid to fetch the younger Van Dyke son.

Alberta came in first. "I heard you sending for Tad. Is something wrong?"

"We just want to ask him a few questions," Malloy said.

"About what?"

"Mr. Malloy is investigating Mr. Snowberger's death, too," Sarah explained.

"What would Tad know about that?" Alberta asked.

"He was very angry with Mr. Snowberger yesterday," Malloy said.

Alberta's eyes widened. "That's ridiculous. We were *all* upset with Mr. Snowberger yesterday. Why don't you want to question me? Or Lewis?"

"I don't think you're capable of killing Mr. Snowberger, Miss Van Dyke."

"Why not?" she challenged, angry now. "Because I'm a woman? Women are capable of killing, too."

"You're right about that, but I don't think you're capable of lifting Mr. Snowberger onto the dining room table and hanging him by the neck from his chandelier."

Alberta gasped, covering her mouth with a trembling hand. "Is that . . . how he died?" she asked, horrified.

Tad appeared in the doorway behind her. He looked awful. His face was ashen, his eyes bloodshot. Although he'd made an effort to dress appropriately, his vest was buttoned crookedly and his shirt collar wasn't properly attached. "Still here, Detective?" he asked with a effort at his usual cockiness. "I thought you'd be off trying to find out who killed poor Snowberger."

"I just wanted to ask you where you were yesterday afternoon," Malloy said amiably.

Tad stiffened slightly, as if offended at being asked. "I was right here in this house, where I've been since my father died."

"That's true," Alberta confirmed eagerly. "You can ask any of the servants. Tad went up to his room, and he didn't come down again until you insisted on seeing the entire family this morning."

"Didn't you even have any supper?" Malloy asked.

"I drank my supper, Detective," Tad informed him with a sickly smile. "I'm still trying to finish off my father's liquor supply."

"I brought him a tray after the rest of us ate," Alberta said. She glanced lovingly at her brother. "He didn't eat, but at least he took it."

"I don't suppose you have a drainpipe outside your bedroom window, do you, Mr. Van Dyke?" Malloy asked, reminding them all of how Creighton had managed to escape the house unseen.

"No, I do not," he said with some satisfaction. "You're welcome to check, if you like, but I'm not as adventurous as my older brother. The thought of sliding down the outside of a house isn't very appealing to me, not to mention the difficulty of climbing back up again."

Sarah watched Malloy's expression. He concealed his emotions well, but she saw just the slightest flinch. Now he had only one suspect left, and he was no happier about it than Sarah was.

"Do you know where Mr. Reed is, Miss Van Dyke?" he asked Alberta.

"No, I . . . I'm sure he's at his home," she said uncertainly. "I sent one of the servants to check on him, though he's not back yet. But Lewis doesn't know any more about this than Tad and I do."

"I don't suppose he was here all day yesterday, too," Malloy said.

"No, he—" Alberta caught herself, finally realizing the implication. "No! He had nothing to do with this!" she insisted, alarmed now.

"Then he doesn't have anything to worry about, does he?" He turned to Sarah. "If he comes back here, call Headquarters and get them to send someone to guard him."

"Lewis didn't kill anyone!" Alberta cried, grabbing Malloy's arm as if she could keep him from his duty.

He stopped and looked meaningfully at her hand grasping his coat sleeve. She released him reluctantly, the tears already streaming down her face. "Please, don't hurt him," she whispered.

Malloy made no promise.

14

Frank didn't trouble Reed's landlady to show him upstairs this time. Reed answered his knock after only a few minutes' delay. He'd obviously been dressing to go out. His wounded head was freshly bandaged, and he seemed to be ready except for his suit coat.

"Mr. Malloy, what brings you here?" he asked, apparently surprised to see him.

"I've got a few questions for you, Mr. Reed. Do you mind if I come in?"

"No, not at all," he said uncertainly, stepping back to allow Frank inside. "I was just getting ready to call on the Van Dykes again, but I can spare a few minutes."

The room was exactly as Frank had remembered. He saw no signs that Reed was preparing to flee. "Have you heard the news about Mr. Snowberger?"

Frank caught the slightest flinch, but Reed said, "What news is that?"

"That he was murdered yesterday."

"Murdered?" He said the word as if he'd never heard it before. Had he expected to hear the word *suicide* instead? "What . . . what on earth happened?"

"I was hoping you could tell me," Frank said mildly.

"Me? I . . . I don't know what you mean." He had to sit down. He seemed unusually upset over the death of a man he didn't even like.

Frank took the other chair. "You had an argument with Snowberger yesterday, didn't you? He fired you, I understand."

"He . . . he was just upset," Reed insisted. "I knew when he calmed down, he'd change his mind. I'm the only one who really knows what's going on at the company. He wouldn't be able to run it without me."

"So you went to him yesterday to remind him of how important you are to him," Frank said.

"No! I mean, I was going to, but . . . I decided to wait a few days, until he'd calmed down."

"Don't bother lying, Reed," he said. "The doorman saw you."

"Saw me?" he echoed in alarm.

"Tell me how it happened, Reed. You probably didn't plan to kill him, did you?"

"Of course not!" Reed exclaimed, his face flushed.

"You just wanted to talk him into giving you your job back. With Miss Van Dyke in a family way, you needed to support her and the baby."

"How dare you suggest such a thing about Miss Van Dyke?" he cried in outrage.

"Because it's true, and we both know it. You thought Snowberger would see reason, but he didn't, did he?"

"He would have!" Reed insisted. "The first time he needed a report and there was no one to prepare it, he'd realize how much he needed me!"

"But you didn't think of that until later, did you? All you could think of then was how much you hated Snowberger and how angry you were that he didn't appreciate you."

"He's despicable! He had no right to speak that way about Miss Van Dyke!"

"You didn't mean to kill him, did you?" Frank asked.

"No!" Reed exclaimed, his eyes wide in terror. "I mean, I *didn't* kill him!"

"But you were so angry, and you saw the fireplace poker sitting right there, and you just wanted to hurt him the way he was hurting you—"

"No!"

"So you picked it up. You wanted to teach him a lesson, and you picked it up and hit him—"

"No, I didn't!"

"And when you saw him lying there, you knew he'd never give you your job now. In fact, you knew he'd make sure you went to jail for attacking him. You'd be ruined, and you wouldn't be able to marry Miss Van Dyke because you'd be in jail."

Reed was shaking his head silently, his face ashen.

"You had to make sure no one ever found out what you'd done. You didn't have any choice but to kill him and try to make it look like suicide."

"I didn't kill him! I didn't do anything!" Reed cried. "He was alive when I left him!"

"You mean he was still choking, hanging from his chandelier."

"*Choking?*" he echoed in horror as the color leached from his face.

"Of course, that was nothing compared to how you blew Mr. Van Dyke to bits. Were you surprised when the bomb went off by itself?"

"No, I . . . I don't know what you're talking about!"

"Of course you do, Reed," Frank said relentlessly. "You were so careful to place the bomb so you could be outside when it went off. I have to admit you were clever. Everybody thought Creighton's friends had set it. No one would've even considered you a suspect if I hadn't found out about you and Miss Van Dyke. Did she know how you planned to kill her father so you could marry her?"

Reed gaped at him, horrified. "Dear God, I'm going to be sick!"

He bolted from his chair and dashed into the bedroom, finding the chamber pot just in time. Frank waited patiently until Reed finished and returned, his face pale and his eyes red-rimmed.

"I didn't kill anyone, Detective," he said hoarsely. "You must believe me."

Frank wanted to, but Reed had all but admitted his guilt. He'd had motive and opportunity. Sure he'd tried to deny it, but most killers did. Some were so convincing, Frank had often wondered if they somehow managed to convince themselves they were innocent. But Reed wasn't even very convincing.

"You admit you were in Snowberger's apartment yesterday, and you had a good reason to want him dead. I'm going to have to arrest you, Reed."

Frank had expected a roar of outrage, or at least some

emotional plea for mercy. Instead, Reed simply closed his eyes for a moment and swayed slightly. Frank instinctively took a step toward him, to catch him if he fainted. But he steadied himself, and when he opened his eyes, he'd overcome whatever terrors had tried to claim him.

"Could I . . . would you allow me to write a note to Miss Van Dyke before you take me?" he asked.

"Go ahead," Frank said, sympathetic in spite of himself. "I'll have to call for a Black Maria to take you, so you'll have plenty of time. I'm sending you to The Tombs," he added, naming the city jail. "It's a lot better than the precinct cells."

Reed was beyond caring where he went. He started looking for a pen and paper while Frank went to summon the police wagon.

"LEWIS WOULDN'T HURT A FLY," ALBERTA INSISTED FOR at least the tenth time in an hour. "How could anyone even think such a thing?"

Sarah was tired of watching her pace back and forth in the back parlor, but she had no comfort to offer. "Mr. Malloy is only trying to find the truth."

"Is he?" Alberta asked skeptically. "He must feel a lot of pressure to solve my father's murder, especially now that Mr. Snowberger is dead, too. Lewis is an easy victim. He has no friends to defend him, and no one but I will care if he hangs."

Her voice broke on the last word. She put both hands over her face and began to weep piteously. Sarah hurried to her side and led her to the sofa. "There's no use in getting upset," she tried. "Mr. Malloy isn't like that. He would never arrest an innocent man just to solve a case."

"How can you be sure?" Alberta wailed, finding her handkerchief tucked in her sleeve. "The police do whatever they wish to people who have no money or influence."

Sarah knew it was pointless to argue. Alberta was right, and no one could convince her Malloy wasn't a typical police officer, at least not while she was so upset. "You should at least wait until you've had bad news before working yourself up into a state," Sarah tried.

"I don't need to hear any more," Alberta told her bitterly. "I saw Mr. Malloy's face when he was talking about Lewis. He knows Lewis and I would benefit from my father's death because we'd be able to marry, and he knows Mr. Snowberger fired Lewis yesterday. Even I can see how bad it looks for him. But don't they need proof to arrest someone for murder?"

"Proof or a confession," Sarah said, trying to make Alberta feel more hopeful.

She had the opposite effect. "A confession!" she cried. "How long do you think it would take to beat a confession out of him? He isn't a strong person, Sarah. He never stood up for himself with Father, and he's weaker now that he's injured. They'll be able to get him to say anything!"

Sarah was almost relieved when someone knocked on the parlor door. "Come in," she called.

A maid opened the door hesitantly. Probably, she'd heard Alberta crying and didn't want to interrupt. "Miss Pet . . . The Russian lady, she's awake," she said, unable to remember Katya's name.

"Is she in pain?" Sarah asked, rising to her feet.

"No, ma'am. You just said to tell you when she woke up."

"Yes, thank you," Sarah said. She turned back to Alberta. "I should check on her."

"Go ahead," she said wearily. "I'll be fine."

She looked far from fine, but Sarah had no further comfort to offer. She was very much afraid Lewis Reed had indeed killed two men for the woman he loved. If he had, no one would be able to comfort Alberta.

Sarah climbed the stairs and started down the hallway toward the guest room where Katya lay, but she heard the sound of raised voices in the room directly across from Katya's door.

"That's not what you said when you were naked in my arms!" a man's voice shouted.

Without the slightest hesitation, Sarah swerved straight for the door and put her ear against it.

"Do you know what I did for you?" he was shouting again.

"Stop it, Tad! You're acting like a child!"

"You didn't think I was a child when you crawled into my bed!"

"How ungentlemanly of you to remind me," she snapped. Sarah recognized Lilly's voice now. "Don't you understand? That was all very amusing, but nothing can ever come of it now."

"Why not?" he demanded desperately. "You're a widow. You can marry anybody you want!"

"But I don't want to marry *you*!" she informed him. "Now run along like a good boy and stop bothering me. I've got a frightful headache."

Sarah darted away from the door, figuring Tad would come storming out of the room any second, and she didn't want to be caught eavesdropping. Her hand was on the knob of Katya's door when she heard Lilly scream.

Forgetting discretion, she turned right around, darted across the hallway, and threw open the door. What she saw made her cry out in protest. Tad had thrown Lilly on the bed, and the two were struggling. Her dressing gown had been torn half off her body, and she was attempting to fight him off.

"Tad, stop it!" Sarah shouted.

He turned to her, his face contorted with rage as he held Lilly's wrists above her head, but the instant he recognized her, the anger evaporated into shame. He released Lilly at once and pushed himself upright. "Sarah," he said, as if to confirm the awful fact that she had seen what he'd been doing.

"What's going on in here?" Sarah demanded, as if she didn't know.

"He tried to attack me," Lilly said quickly, struggling to pull the dressing gown closed again. "He came in here and started saying horrible things to me, and——"

"I heard what he said," Sarah informed her. "And I heard what you said, too. Just be grateful no servants were in the hall."

Tad was looking at Lilly now, an expression of loathing on his young face. "You're nothing but a whore," he spat. "When I think of what I did for you——"

"Get out!" Lilly cried. "I'm going to tell Creighton what you tried to do. I'll tell everyone what you tried to do!"

Tad smiled bitterly. "And I'll tell everyone what you *did* do, with me and with Snowberger and God knows how many others."

She started calling him names, but he paid her no attention. He strode away from the bed, past Sarah and out into the hall. A moment later she heard the door to his bedroom slam shut.

"What is the shouting?"

Sarah looked over to find Katya standing in her doorway, looking frightened. "It's nothing," Sarah assured her hastily, going out into the hall to help her back to bed. "You shouldn't be up."

They both jumped as Lilly slammed her door shut, too.

"What is wrong?" Katya asked. "Where is Petya?"

Sarah needed a moment to remember that was Creighton. He'd given up his pacing, and she hadn't seen him in a while. "I'll send someone for him," she promised. He couldn't have been nearby or all the shouting and screaming would have brought him running.

Sarah was helping Katya back into bed and inquiring about how she felt when Alberta came to the open doorway. "Who's slamming all those doors?" she asked. "I could hear it all the way downstairs."

"Tad and Lilly had a disagreement," Sarah said in a masterly piece of understatement. "Do you know where Creighton is? Katya would like to see him."

"He said something about needing some fresh air," Alberta said. "He may have gone up on the roof."

"The roof?" Sarah echoed in surprise. Tenement dwellers regularly used their roofs for sleeping in hot weather and socializing in any weather, but she wouldn't have expected the Van Dykes to do so.

"Don't you remember?" Alberta asked. "Mother had the garden put in up there when the house was built."

"Oh, yes," Sarah recalled. "We used to play up there." Potted trees had provided shade and flower boxes overflowed with color. A gazebo had made a wonderful playhouse or a place for grown-ups to visit. She also recalled the "secret" staircase that led from this floor, past the servants' quarters on the fourth floor, and up to that special place.

"I'll see if he's there," Alberta offered and disappeared, closing the door behind her.

When Sarah looked back at Katya, the young woman was caressing her swollen stomach. "He does not move," she said, terror a darkness in her voice.

"They never move when you want them to," Sarah said

with forced cheerfulness. "Just wait until tonight when you're trying to sleep."

"Two days, he does not move." She closed her eyes, squeezing out a single tear.

Sarah felt the pain in her own heart. She couldn't imagine what Katya must be feeling. Was it cruel to offer her hope or not to offer it? The child might still be alive, of course, but if he wasn't . . .

Where was Creighton? Silently, Sarah stepped to the door, opened it, and looked out. She saw Alberta and Creighton emerging from the "secret" staircase. It wasn't really secret, of course, just inconspicuous, located behind an ordinary-looking door next to Tad's room that might have been a linen closet.

Seeing her, Creighton hurried toward her. "How is she?" he asked, his own fear naked in his voice.

"She's not in any discomfort," Sarah said quite truthfully. "She just wants to see you."

Creighton went in. He hesitated when he saw her lying so still, eyes closed and her hands still lying protectively on her belly. But then she opened her eyes, and he went to her instantly.

Sarah turned away, not wanting to intrude on their private moment, but Katya's voice stopped her. "Tell him," she said.

Sarah turned back. "Tell him what?"

"The baby. Tell him."

"What?" Creighton asked in alarm. "What is it?"

Sarah drew a deep breath. "Katya hasn't felt the baby move for two days. She's afraid . . . something is wrong."

"Is that normal?" he asked. "Tell her it's normal and nothing to be worried about."

"It's really too soon to know," she said quite truthfully. "The baby could be fine."

Creighton took Katya's hand and raised it to his lips. "Don't worry," he said. "Everything will be all right. We'll get married, and we'll have lots of babies. You'll never want for anything again."

Pain flickered across Katya's face, but Sarah knew it wasn't physical. She'd never wanted to be married. She'd never wanted material things. How could he have forgotten that so quickly? This time Sarah did manage to escape, and she really did feel the need to get away. She didn't want to see another person seeking comfort. Too many people in this house needed too much. Remembering the secret staircase and the garden above, Sarah stole quietly down the hall.

The stairway wasn't as dark or frightening as she'd recalled. In fact, it wasn't particularly narrow or steep, either. Two flights up, the door opened onto the roof. The air up here was brisk, but warmer than it had been the past few days. The sun shone brightly, taking away the chill. Sarah wrapped her arms around herself, wishing she'd brought her cape, but not wanting to go back for it. Looking out over the surrounding rooftops, she thought of the tenements that were so physically nearby and yet a world away.

Here on Fifth Avenue, a roof could be a garden hideaway. Others, she noticed, had also transformed their rooftops with plants and trees. In the neighborhood where Katya had lived with Creighton, the rooftops of the buildings, built so close together they actually touched, formed an alternate system of roads. When the streets were clogged with people and vehicles, you could climb up to a rooftop and make your way for an entire block if you didn't mind stepping over the occasional low wall.

"What are you doing up here?"

Startled, Sarah turned to find Tad in the doorway. She sighed. So much for her escape. "I'm enjoying the view," she said.

He wasn't amused. "How did you know about this place?"

"I used to play up here with Alberta when we were children."

He seemed to relax slightly, although he was still wary. "About what happened with Lilly down there . . ."

Sarah waited, curious as to how he would explain himself. Finally, he said, "She was the one who seduced me in the beginning."

From what she'd heard, Sarah thought this was likely. "She must've noticed you found her attractive."

"I was in love with her from the minute she came here," he confessed, his disgust evident. "She didn't love my father. He'd forced her to marry him, to settle a debt. She said I was the only thing that made her life worth living."

Sarah winced at the cruelty of the lie. "At least you found out the truth about her before anything worse happened," she offered, thinking how horrible it would have been if he'd actually married his stepmother.

"Something worse already happened," he said, his young face looking terribly old.

Before she could ask what he meant, he turned and fled back down the stairs.

Sarah rubbed the bridge of her nose to ward off a headache. Something about the Van Dyke household seemed to bring them on. She'd just taken a seat in the gazebo when she heard someone calling her name.

"Sarah, come quick!" Creighton cried desperately as he raced up the stairs. "Katya's bleeding!"

* * *

SOMETIMES SOLVING A CASE WAS WORSE THAN NOT SOLV-
ing it, Frank had decided. From what he knew about the
two dead men, the world was probably a better place without them. Lewis Reed, on the other hand, would most likely
have been a good husband and father, a faithful employee
and a good provider if he'd fallen in love with an ordinary
woman instead of Alberta Van Dyke.

As much as he hated having to tell a murder victim's
family about the death, he hated telling Alberta her lover
was a killer even more. Reed had tried so hard to clear the
way for them, and he'd managed only to ruin both their
lives.

The maid admitted him, and he couldn't help noticing
she looked very grave. In fact, the house itself seemed unusually still. "Is Miss Van Dyke at home?" he asked.

"Yes, sir, she's upstairs in the parlor with the rest of the
family. Would you like me to show you up?"

"Is Mrs. Brandt still here?"

"Yes, sir, she is."

Good, Frank thought. Alberta would probably need her
care. "Yes, please take me up."

The maid announced him and then held the parlor door.
The Van Dyke sons didn't seemed particularly interested
that he'd arrived. Creighton was sitting in a chair, staring at
nothing, his expression grim. Tad sat on the far side of the
room, away from the others, a drink in his hand, as usual.
Alberta looked up at him with terror-filled eyes, though.
Sarah looked up, too, but she was simply resigned.

"Where's Lewis?" Alberta asked in a voice as fragile as
glass.

Frank had to clear his throat. "He's at the city jail."

She cried out in anguish, and Sarah rushed to her side. "I told you!" she said to Sarah, tears glistening in her eyes. "It won't matter that he's innocent! They'll hang him just because he isn't important and won't speak up for himself."

Frank could have reminded her that murderers didn't hang anymore, now that they had the new electric chair, but that wouldn't be much comfort. "He wrote you a letter and asked me to deliver it," he said, reaching into his coat pocket to pull it out.

Alberta snatched it from his fingers. "It's been opened!" she exclaimed in outrage.

"Of course," Frank replied. "I had to see if he'd admitted his guilt." Such a confession would have been invaluable, but Lewis had only maintained his innocence and declared his undying love for Alberta.

She turned away in disgust, unfolded the letter, and began to read.

Frank glanced at Sarah, but she wouldn't meet his eye. Creighton Van Dyke had finally roused himself, though. He got up and came to where Frank still stood by the door.

"What is this all about?" he asked with a puzzled frown. "Why have you arrested Lewis Reed?"

"Because he killed your father and Allen Snowberger," Frank explained.

"That's insane," Creighton exclaimed at the same time his sister cried, "No, he didn't! If you read this letter, you must know that! He swears he's innocent!"

"Why would he have killed my father?" Creighton asked astonished. "Or Allen, either? What reason could he possibly have had?"

Frank looked at Alberta. "Because of your sister."

Alberta glared at him with pure loathing, but Creighton

distracted her. "That's ridiculous. Lewis isn't the kind of man who'd commit murder for some romantic notion."

"*Romantic notion!*" Alberta cried in outrage. "You're the one who turned his back on everything you've ever known just to be with Katya!"

"That's different," Creighton argued, but his sister was having none of it.

"It's exactly the same! Lewis and I love each other just as much as you love Katya, but I'm not a man like you, Creighton. I can't just run away and do whatever I want. Father said he'd ruin Lewis if we eloped, and he'd never be able to find a job. How would we live? And then I found out I was going to have a baby."

Creighton gasped. "A *baby?* Oh, Bertie . . ." Now everything was clear to him. He turned to Frank. "So Lewis did kill Father!"

"No, he *didn't!*" Alberta insisted furiously. "Why won't anyone listen to me?"

Creighton wasn't listening to her. He was looking at Frank. "But why did he kill Allen?"

"Because Snowberger fired him yesterday," Frank explained. "Told him he'd be arrested for trespassing if he tried to come back to work."

"He didn't need a job!" Alberta reminded her brother. "You said you'd take care of me, that I'd never want for anything!"

Creighton gave her a look full of pity. "Poor Bertie."

"*Don't feel sorry for me!*" she practically shouted. "You've got to help Lewis! He didn't do this terrible thing." She whirled to where her younger brother still sat, his eyes glassy from drink. "You're Lewis's friend, Tad. You must know he couldn't possibly kill anyone. Tell him!" She gestured wildly at Frank.

To everyone's surprise, Tad pushed himself purposefully, if a little unsteadily, to his feet. "Bertie's right," he said very clearly. "Lewis Reed didn't kill Allen Snowberger."

No one had a chance to react because the parlor door swung open and Lilly Van Dyke stepped in. She'd done something to herself, Frank noticed at once. She looked almost matronly, with her hair pulled straight back into the kind of bun his mother wore. Her dress was dead black, without a ruffle or a frill to be seen, and she had clasped her hands in front of her modestly. Her chin high and her expression righteous, she looked straight at Frank.

"Mr. Malloy, I want you to arrest Tad Van Dyke. He tried to rape me."

Everyone except Tad gasped in shock.

"You bitch," he said between gritted teeth.

"What a horrible thing to say, Lilly, even for you!" Alberta said.

"It's true!" Lilly insisted. "Mrs. Brandt saw it, didn't you?"

Everyone looked at Sarah, and for the first time since Frank had known her, she actually looked embarrassed. She met his gaze for just a moment before she nodded slightly.

"You see!" Lilly exclaimed in triumph.

Tad lunged for her. "I should've killed you instead!" he cried before Creighton and Frank caught him. He put up a slight struggle, but he was too drunk to resist very much.

"Get him out of here while I talk to Mrs. Van Dyke," Frank told Creighton when Tad had finally stilled.

"Come on, kid," Creighton said, putting his arm around his brother as much for support as to restrain him. He led the boy from the room.

Sarah closed the door behind them, and when she turned back, she glared at Lilly. "I don't think you'll want to press charges, Lilly."

"Why not?" Lilly asked virtuously. "You saw what he did."

"I also know *why* he did it." She turned to Frank. "Lilly seduced Tad. She crawled into his bed one night and had her way with him."

"You . . . you *harlot*!" Alberta exclaimed in horror, using probably the worst word she could think of. "I hope you do go to court! I want Tad to get up on the stand and tell everyone what kind of woman you are!"

Lilly's cheeks turned scarlet, but she refused to be cowed. "It would be his word against mine."

"And you would be ruined by the scandal, but Tad would be excused as a naughty boy," Sarah said reasonably.

"Not after you tell what you saw," she reminded her.

Sarah simply shrugged. She hated the crime of rape, and she hated even more the men who claimed the woman had asked for it. But this time . . . "Now that I think about it, I'm not sure what I did see," she mused. "In fact, you might have fainted, and Tad was merely trying to help you."

"You liar! You know what he was trying to do!"

"You won't get any sympathy in this house," Alberta informed her. "But since you think Tad is dangerous, you should move out immediately to someplace where you'll be safe. I'll speak to Creighton about it at once."

Lilly opened her mouth to reply, but she must've realized the implication behind Alberta's words—she really had no right to live in this house any longer. She closed her mouth with a snap, turned on her heel, and marched back to the door. She threw it open so hard it banged into the wall, making the rest of them flinch.

Instinctively, Frank turned back to Sarah. He was out of his depth here and needed some guidance on how to handle these high-strung rich people. Fortunately, she understood his predicament.

"Katya lost her baby this afternoon," she explained.

Frank winced at the rush of memories. "Is she . . . ?"

"She's all right," Sarah assured him. "But that's why everyone is upset."

"And let's not forget my fiancé has been arrested for a murder he didn't commit, too," Alberta reminded them sarcastically.

Two murders, Frank thought, but he didn't correct her.

"Did he confess?" Sarah asked.

"Not yet," he replied.

"*Not yet?*" Alberta echoed. "Why not? Didn't you have time to beat him thoroughly enough?"

The accusation stung, but Frank refused to react. "He admitted he went to Snowberger's apartment yesterday to ask him to give him his job back. The doorman saw him. He also admitted Snowberger refused."

"That doesn't mean Lewis killed him!" Alberta argued.

"Alberta, would you leave me and Mr. Malloy alone for a moment?" Sarah asked suddenly. "I want to talk to him about Mr. Reed."

Alberta looked uncertainly at them both. "He didn't kill anyone," she repeated.

"Of course he didn't," she said to Frank's surprise. "Please, just give me a chance to talk to Mr. Malloy."

Reluctantly, but with a slight glimmer of hope, Alberta excused herself and left them alone.

"He admitted he went to see Snowberger," he reminded her when the door had closed behind Alberta, "and he's the only one who could have done it."

"I know you're sure about Lewis, but no one else is."

"No one else would be happy about my other suspect, either," he pointed out.

"I know, but if you're going to upset people anyway, we

better be sure you've got the right man. Tad had a good reason to kill Snowberger, too," she said. "And did you hear what he said to Lilly? He said he should've killed her *instead*."

Yes, he had heard that. He'd almost forgotten in all the excitement.

"He said something similar to Lilly this afternoon, too," she said, "and again to me later when I saw him by chance. I think he may be trying to confess."

"But he didn't leave the house yesterday," he reminded her.

"No one saw him leave the house, but I think I figured out how he could have done it without anyone seeing him."

"He already said there's no drainpipe outside his room."

Sarah smiled slightly. "He also said he wasn't as adventurous as Creighton, and climbing back up a drainpipe is very difficult. No, I think he got out over the rooftops."

Frank looked up, not because he expected to see anything but because he was trying to picture the outside of the Van Dyke house. "How would he get up there?"

"The Van Dykes have a rooftop garden. There are stairs leading to it right next to Tad's room."

"I saw those stairs," Frank remembered. "I thought they were for the servants to get up to their rooms on the fourth floor."

"No, the servants' stairs wouldn't be so close to the family's bedrooms," she explained, making him feel like a fool for not realizing that. "Tad could've slipped out and back in again without anyone noticing. The houses are close enough together that he could have crossed to a building with a fire escape or a ladder. I haven't looked, but I'm guessing you'll find one nearby. Mischievous boys usually manage to locate things like that early in life."

Frank thought back to what had happened in the

moment before Lilly had barged in and made her accusation against Tad. Alberta had asked Tad to vouch for Reed, and he'd acted very strangely. Frank could still see the way he'd gathered himself and stood up and insisted Lewis Reed hadn't killed Snowberger, as if he were positive he couldn't have done it.

There was only one way he could be so positive.

"I'm going to have a talk with young Mr. Van Dyke," he told her. She only nodded, but she looked relieved.

Frank remembered where Tad's room was from when he'd been up here putting Creighton under guard several days ago. He didn't bother to knock. He opened the door to find Tad slumped in a chair with Creighton down on one knee before him, as if he were proposing. The bed was unmade, and the room littered with discarded clothing and empty liquor bottles of various sizes and shapes. Tad hadn't exaggerated when he'd claimed to be drinking his father's liquor supply. He must've forbidden the maids access as well.

Creighton looked up at the intrusion and rose to his feet. "I've been trying to get him to tell me what happened between him and Lilly, but nothing he says makes sense," he explained.

"Don't worry about that. She isn't going to bring charges against him. Could I speak to your brother alone, Mr. Van Dyke?"

Creighton instinctively moved closer to Tad and put his hand on the boy's shoulder. "I think I should stay. Tad isn't himself, and he might say something—"

"Go away, Creighton," Tad said wearily. "I need to talk to Mr. Malloy. I need to make this right before Reed and Bertie get hurt any more."

"What do *they* have to do with this?" Creighton asked in

alarm. "You see," he said to Frank, "he isn't making any sense. He's had too much to drink."

"Or not enough," Tad said with a bitter smile. "Creighton, get out of here before I throw you out. I've got some business with Mr. Malloy, and I don't want you here."

"You can wait out in the hall," Frank offered. "I don't think this will take long."

Torn between Tad's wishes and his own duty to protect his brother, Creighton hesitated for a long moment before making his decision. "I'll be right outside if you need me," he told Tad. With one last warning glance at Frank, he started for the door.

Because he was looking at Frank, he didn't notice the empty bottle sitting on the floor beside Tad's chair, and he kicked it over. For a second he must have considered stopping to pick it up, but then he realized how silly it would be to right one bottle in the midst of all the chaos, and he let it lie.

The moment he was gone, however, Frank walked over and picked it up. It was a bottle of French brandy. A very fancy bottle. A bottle with real gold trim. Just the kind of brandy bottle everyone had said Gregory Van Dyke was giving Allen Snowberger as a gift on the day he died.

15

Every nerve in Frank's body crackled to life, but he knew better than to let Tad know he'd recognized the bottle. He set it down on the table beside Tad's chair. The boy didn't seem to notice.

"What did you want to talk to me about, Tad?" Frank asked, figuring he'd give the boy the opportunity to clear his conscience.

"Lewis didn't kill Snowberger," he said, managing to sound more sober than he was. "You have to let him go."

"How can you be so sure?"

Tad took a deep breath and let it out slowly. "Because . . . I know. He couldn't kill anyone."

Frank glanced around and saw a straight-backed chair nearby. He retrieved it, brought it over to face Tad, and straddled it. "When did you figure out that you could sneak out of the house by going over the roof?" he asked casually.

Tad's eyes widened in surprise. For a second, he looked as if he was going to deny it, but then his shoulders slumped in resignation. "I was about fourteen, I guess. How did you . . .? Oh, Sarah," he remembered.

"Is that how you got out yesterday without anyone seeing you?"

Tad closed his eyes. He could deny it. He could deny everything. The temptation was almost irresistible, but he managed to overcome it. When he opened his eyes again, the fear and the wariness were gone. "Yes. I didn't leave right away. Too bad I didn't, because I would've run into Lewis at Snowberger's place. If he'd seen me there, I might not have gone through with it."

"Lewis was gone by the time you arrived?"

"No. I'd waited until the doorman took someone up in the elevator, and then I went up the stairs. When I got to Snowberger's apartment, I heard him and Lewis inside arguing. He was saying terrible, insulting things about Bertie, and finally, Lewis couldn't stand it anymore and left. I hid until he'd gone, and then I went and knocked on the door."

Automatically, he picked up the glass from the table beside him, but it was empty. Frank took it gently from his fingers. "Better wait until you're finished with your story," he advised. "What happened when Snowberger let you in?"

Tad's hands curled into fists. "He opened the door right away. I think he expected that Lewis had come back for one more try. When he saw it was me, he laughed."

"Why did he laugh?"

Tad's face darkened at the memory. "He knew about me and Lilly. She told him, I guess. And he knew she'd chosen him. Maybe he thought I'd come to beg him not to marry her or something. I don't know, but he just kept laughing.

Then he turned and walked away. He left me standing there, like I didn't matter. After what he'd done, I couldn't . . . Well, I couldn't let him get away with it."

"Was that when you picked up the poker?"

Tad was staring past Frank now, remembering. "I wanted to hurt him. I didn't mean to kill him. I'd just gone there to confront him and tell him I knew what he'd done. I wanted to see him punished, but dying was too easy. So I looked around for something to hurt him with, and I saw the poker." He shuddered slightly at the memory.

"After you hit him, why didn't you just leave him there?"

Tad ran a hand over his face. "I knew he was dead, and if the police knew he was murdered, you'd try to find out who did it. I didn't want to go to prison for killing him, and I didn't want someone else to, either. I tried to think of a way he could've died that wouldn't make you try to find a killer."

Frank debated telling Tad that Snowberger hadn't been killed by the blow, but he decided not to. If the boy realized he'd hung a living man, he might not be able to bear it. Besides, who's to say Snowberger wouldn't have died as a result of the head wound anyway?

"You were very clever," Frank said instead. "You almost fooled me."

"But I didn't," he pointed out sadly. "*You* almost scared me to death, though. I was tying the sheet to the chandelier when you started knocking on the door. My heart nearly stopped in my chest."

Too bad Frank hadn't sent the doorman for the key then. He might've saved Snowberger's life and Tad's freedom.

"Now you know," Tad was saying, "so you can let poor Lewis go and arrest me."

"Are you going to confess to killing your father, too?" Frank asked mildly.

Tad's bloodshot eyes widened in surprise. "Of course not! I didn't have anything to do with that."

"Then Lewis Reed is still in trouble, because he had the best reason of all to want your father dead."

Tad shook his head. "He might have, but he didn't do it. Why do you think I went to confront Snowberger? As soon as I realized he and Lilly had been having an affair and were going to be married, I knew—Allen Snowberger killed my father!"

WHEN MALLOY WENT UPSTAIRS, SARAH WENT TO FIND Alberta. She'd gone to the back parlor, where she sat alone, rereading Lewis's letter as tears ran down her cheeks. She looked up hopefully when Sarah came in, but the hope died when she saw who it was.

"He says he's sorry for all the hurt he's caused me," she said in wonder. "As if his own suffering doesn't matter at all."

"We often find it easier to bear tragedy ourselves than to see the ones we love bearing it," Sarah said. If this was true for Lewis Reed, he must be in agony, knowing the woman he loved would have to choose between bearing an illegitimate child or marrying an accused murderer.

"He'll be cleared," she said, as if trying to convince herself. "He must be! They can't execute an innocent man."

Sarah was sure it had happened more times than she wished to know about, but that wouldn't comfort Alberta. Neither would the only alternative she had to offer.

"In order to clear Mr. Reed, Mr. Malloy will have to find the real killer," she began, feeling her way cautiously.

"He should have done that in the first place," Alberta replied angrily. "If he had, poor Lewis would be a free man."

"The real killer must be someone who had a personal

grudge against your father and Mr. Snowberger."

Alberta frowned. "Of course, that goes without saying."

"That's why Mr. Reed seems like a good suspect, even though we know he couldn't possibly have killed anyone," Sarah added. "But who else would have had a grudge against them?"

"Many people, I'm sure," Alberta said. "Men don't become rich without making some enemies. At least, that's what Father used to say."

"But how many businessmen are blown up by their enemies?" Sarah asked, hoping to lead Alberta's thinking toward a more personal motive. "Murder is usually motivated by the kind of passion we only feel for the people close to us. Who might have felt that kind of emotion for both men?"

Alberta obviously hadn't considered this before. "You mean the passion of love?"

"Or hate. Jealousy and greed, too. The things that drive people to desperation and despair."

Alberta nodded slowly. "I can see why Mr. Malloy would believe Lewis capable of murder," she admitted grudgingly. "We were certainly desperate and despairing before Father died."

"Family members are often cruel to each other. Creighton actually had to leave the house," Sarah reminded her.

"He and Father were always at loggerheads," Alberta remembered. "A father wants his son to grow up to be his own man, but when he challenges the father's authority . . ." She shook her head sadly at the memories.

"I suppose Tad was beginning to do that as well," Sarah tried.

But Alberta wouldn't concede that point. "Tad was spoiled," she said decisively. "Father got impatient with him, but they never quarreled the way he and Creighton did."

"Sometimes we don't know how deeply hurt someone is," Sarah said. "Especially boys. We don't allow them to show their true feelings the way girls do. They just keep it inside until they can't bear it anymore."

But Alberta couldn't believe it. "Family arguments can be painful, but to kill someone . . . that requires a kind of deep hatred I don't think either of us can understand, Sarah."

Sarah sighed. How could she make Alberta see? How could she prepare her for the horrible news she would hear when Malloy was finished with Tad? She was still frantically trying to figure it out when Alberta spoke.

"It's odd, but the more I think about it, the more I'm sure that the only person who hated Allen Snowberger enough to kill him was Father—and the only person who hated Father enough to kill *him* was Allen Snowberger."

"WHAT MADE YOU SO SURE SNOWBERGER KILLED YOUR father?" Frank asked Tad.

"I told you, because of Lilly. They'd been having an affair, and he wanted her for himself."

"Is that why you killed him? Because of Lilly?"

Tad looked away as the color crawled up his face. "I figured you'd think that, but I told you, I didn't intend to *kill* him. I wanted to confront him and tell him I knew he'd killed Father and tried to make it look like Creighton's anarchists did it. I wanted to see his face because I had to be certain, but then I was going to tell you. I wanted to see him arrested and charged with murder. I wanted him shamed so Lilly would never want to hear his name again." He looked up at Frank, his eyes bright with certainty. "Then she'd come to *me*."

His theory made a certain kind of sense, but Frank knew it didn't quite fit the facts. First of all and no matter what

Tad might think, Frank was fairly certain Snowberger didn't really want Lilly, not before Van Dyke's death or after. He might've been willing to sample Lilly's favors again, but according to Sarah's description, when she'd informed him they were getting married yesterday, he'd literally fled the house. This was not the reaction of a man who had killed to possess her.

And then there was the brandy bottle.

"What's this, Tad?" Frank asked casually, picking up the elaborately decorated bottle from the table where he'd set it earlier.

Tad grinned blearily. "The best brandy in the world, I'd guess."

"Where did it come from?"

"France, I think," he replied. "Look at the label."

Frank smiled. "No, I mean where did *you* get it?"

"From my father's room," he said without hesitation. "He didn't like to drink that much himself, you know. He just begrudged anybody else the really good stuff. He'd buy cheap liquor for his guests and keep the best for himself."

"Is this the kind of brandy your father bought to give Mr. Snowberger?"

Tad frowned. "Why would he give Snowberger a bottle of brandy? Especially one so expensive? He hated him."

Frank looked at the bottle again. *Now* it all made sense.

Sarah had been listening for footsteps on the stairs, and when she heard some, she slipped out of the back parlor, leaving Alberta rereading Reed's letter. Malloy was coming down, his expression grim, and for some reason he was carrying a very fancy liquor bottle. He hesitated a moment when he saw her, but only to make sure she was alone. When he saw she was, he came down the rest of the stairs. He looked very tired.

"Did he confess?" she asked him in a whisper when he was close enough.

He indicated they should go into the front parlor, and she led the way. He closed the door behind them.

Sarah waited, clutching her hands together tightly.

"He confessed to killing Snowberger," he said.

Sarah flinched. Even though she'd already been certain, hearing the bald truth of it brought the pain of how this would affect the rest of his family. "Does Creighton know yet?"

"I sent him in to let Tad tell him," he said.

Sarah couldn't blame him for that. She should probably send Alberta up as well so she wouldn't have to break the news. Then she realized what Malloy *hadn't* said. "Did he confess to killing his father as well?"

"No," Malloy said, "and I don't think he did."

"But I thought . . ." She gestured helplessly.

"That he killed them both over Lilly?" he guessed with a sad smile. "No, that would've been too simple. He didn't even intend to kill Snowberger. That was an accident."

"Hanging him was an *accident*?" she asked incredulously.

"He thought Snowberger was already dead, and he didn't want to be charged with murder, so he tried to make it look like suicide. You were right, he underestimated the police."

"If he didn't intend to kill Snowberger, why did he go to see him?"

"He was convinced Snowberger had killed his father so he could have Lilly. He wanted to confront him and get him to confess. Then he was going to turn him over to me, or at least that's what he claims. It's a good story, at least."

"Do you believe it?" she asked.

"Yes, I do."

"Then who killed Van Dyke?" she asked with a new sense of dread. "Please don't tell me you still think Lewis Reed did it!"

He sighed. "I did until I found this in Tad's room." He held up the liquor bottle.

"What does that have to do with any of this?"

"Remember Van Dyke was supposed to be taking a bottle of expensive brandy to work to give to Snowberger on the day he died?"

"Yes, you thought he was putting it in the liquor cabinet when he found the bomb and accidentally set it off."

"I think this is the bottle and that he never took it out of this house, but I need to talk to Van Dyke's valet first."

"Why? What does he—?"

"I won't know until I talk to him."

Sarah didn't understand, but she said, "I'll ring for the maid. She can fetch him."

She pulled the bell cord, and almost immediately, a maid appeared. The servants would surely know something awful was happening and would be lurking close by in hopes of overhearing something.

"I need to see Quentin," Malloy told the girl.

She nodded nervously and disappeared again.

"If Van Dyke told everyone he had a gift for Snowberger that day, why didn't he actually take it with him?" Sarah asked when the girl was gone.

Malloy shook his head. "I'm not sure yet. It's just an idea I have," he said, which explained nothing.

"Will it mean Lewis Reed is innocent?" she asked.

"If I'm right," he replied, but he didn't seem too certain.

They waited in silence for a few more minutes before someone knocked on the parlor door, and Quentin came in.

"You wanted to see me, sir?" he asked uneasily, closing the door behind him, but keeping his back to it, as if he wanted to be able to escape quickly.

"Have you ever seen this before?" he asked, holding up the bottle.

The valet's eyes widened in surprise. "That's the brandy Mr. Van Dyke bought for Mr. Snowberger."

"Did he only buy one bottle?" Malloy asked.

"Yes, sir, just the one. He wasn't fond of brandy himself, and he'd gotten it to please Mr. Snowberger especially." He was still puzzled.

"I thought you said he took it to work with him the day he died," Malloy said.

"He did . . . That is, I thought he did. He made a point of telling me he was going to, at least."

"Did you *see* him take it with him?"

"Yes, I . . ." Quentin considered for a moment. "I saw him with the box that it had come in. I thought . . . Well, I assumed the bottle was inside."

Sarah still didn't understand what all this meant. She watched Malloy set the bottle down on the nearest table, as if it were no longer important.

"Quentin, you said Mr. Van Dyke owned a lot of guns, and that he filled his own cartridges." This seemed like an odd change of subject, and Quentin apparently thought so, too. He blinked in surprise, but he didn't falter.

"Yes, he . . . he enjoyed working with his hands. He liked to stay busy."

"What kinds of things did he do?"

Quentin shrugged one shoulder. "Nothing in particular. He just tinkered down in his workshop."

"Workshop? Where is it?"

"In the basement."

Malloy stiffened slightly, and Sarah could see this was important information. "Mrs. Van Dyke said he was making her a gift for their anniversary," Malloy said.

"Yes, he was," Quentin confirmed now that he'd reminded him. "He'd never attempted anything like that before, and he was very excited about it. He'd been working down there for weeks. He called it his special surprise."

"Oh, no!" Sarah cried out as the truth suddenly became crystal clear.

Malloy and Quentin both looked at her. Quentin had no idea what he'd just told them, but Malloy did. She could see it in his eyes.

He turned back to the valet. "Quentin, can you take me down to Mr. Van Dyke's workshop?"

If the request surprised him, he was too well trained to show it. "It's locked, I'm afraid."

"Doesn't someone have a key?"

"No, Mr. Van Dyke was the only one who . . . Oh, wait, I think it was among his effects. I picked them up at the morgue the other day. I'll get it."

Malloy and Sarah waited until he was gone, and then Sarah said, "You think he was building a bomb, and that he was going to kill Snowberger with it."

"It's the only thing that really makes sense," he said. "He was used to working with gunpowder and clever enough to find out how to make a bomb. He and Snowberger had been trying to best each other for years, and Snowberger had finally succeeded in humiliating him in the only way he couldn't avenge."

"Except by killing him," Sarah said.

"But he'd have to do it in a way that wouldn't bring suspicion on himself," Malloy pointed out.

"Was he trying to implicate *Creighton* by making it look like anarchists were responsible?" she asked in horror.

"We'll never know for sure, but he did leave everything to Creighton in his will, so he must've expected his son to be around to manage his business. Maybe he figured Creighton couldn't possibly be blamed since he was completely innocent. Maybe he thought if Creighton believed anarchists had tried to murder his father, he'd give up his revolutionary ideas and come back home."

"But why did he make up that story about buying the brandy as a gift for Snowberger?" she asked.

Malloy frowned, still working out the details in his mind. "I'm guessing he planned to use it somehow to get Snowberger to open the cabinet. Since he'd rigged the bomb to go off when he pulled the wire outside in the alley, he must've intended to tell Snowberger about the brandy and leave him alone with a temptation he couldn't resist."

Sarah nodded in understanding. "And when the bomb exploded in Van Dyke's office, everyone would assume it was intended for Van Dyke, so no one would ever suspect him of planting it."

"And he'd be far enough away that he wouldn't have to worry about being injured in the explosion. A pretty clever plan," Malloy judged.

"Why didn't he actually take the brandy with him, though?"

Malloy smiled wryly. "From what I know about Van Dyke, he probably didn't want to waste good liquor, but the real reason is that he used the box the brandy came in to carry the bomb."

"Oh!" Sarah could see it clearly now. "Everyone knew he was bringing in a bottle of brandy for Snowberger, so no one would suspect he'd carried the bomb in himself. He must've been setting it when . . ."

"When it exploded accidentally," Malloy finished for her.

Sarah shook her head in wonder. "Just a few minutes ago, Alberta said the only person who hated Allen Snowberger enough to kill him was her father."

"Your father said the same thing," Malloy said.

"My *father?*" Sarah echoed in surprise. "When did you speak with my father?"

Malloy looked like he wanted to bite his tongue off. "The other day," he admitted reluctantly. He'd obviously had no intention of telling her.

"Did you question him about the case?" she asked in confusion.

"Of course not," he snapped. "He sent for me. He . . . had some information."

Now she understood. "Mother said he would speak to you if he knew something," she remembered with a smile. How amazing. Sarah would have to find out exactly how her mother managed to have so much control over her husband. Someday Sarah might need to know that secret, she thought, with a sly glance at Malloy.

She wanted to ask Malloy how he and her father had gotten along, but she couldn't possibly do it. He'd wonder why she cared. She couldn't exactly ask her father, either, but if she waited, sooner or later they'd both let her know their feelings for the other. So she'd wait.

"Did my father's information help?" she asked.

"Not much, and of course he didn't know Tad was going to kill Snowberger."

Sarah sighed. "Poor Tad."

"Creighton will hire a good lawyer. He'll probably get

off. After all, he was defending his father's honor. They'll probably say he was defending Lilly's, too."

"Lilly's?" she echoed in surprise.

"That's what they'll say," Malloy assured her. "Snowberger had seduced his stepmother to spite his father. She's just a silly female, but he was evil and deserved to die."

A discreet knock told them Quentin had returned with the key. Malloy followed him out and down the stairs, leaving Sarah to consider Lilly's fate.

Tad's trial would be a sensation. Sarah knew from experience how the newspapers loved a good scandal, and this would have everything they needed to sell thousands of papers—unfaithful wife, feuding partners, vengeance, and murder.

After Tad's trial, Lilly's reputation would be ruined. She'd never get another rich husband now, and she'd have to scrape by for the rest of her life on the stingy allowance her husband had left her. She'd be miserable.

Van Dyke had obviously intended to strip her of everything she'd considered important, but even still, it hardly seemed a harsh enough punishment for what she'd done. He'd intended to kill the man responsible for his humiliation by blowing him to bits. Lilly might be miserable and poor, but at least she'd be alive and well.

But Van Dyke hadn't intended to die himself, Sarah suddenly realized. He may have changed his will as a precaution—building a bomb was dangerous work—but he'd expected *Snowberger* would die, and he'd live on for many years. Had he planned to continue living with the woman who'd betrayed him? She'd be a constant reminder of his humiliation, even if he sent her to live in the country or even divorced her.

Could he possibly have loved her in spite of what she'd done? Did he love her too much to give her up? Van Dyke had told Lilly that he'd been making her a special gift for their anniversary. Lilly must not have realized Quentin had the key, or she would have certainly gone down to get it by now.

Except, Sarah remembered in horror, he hadn't been making anything for her at all. He'd been building a bomb to kill the person who had humiliated him. Or to kill the *people* who had humiliated him.

"No!" she screamed and ran out of the parlor, across the hall and to the stairs that led to the first floor. *"Malloy! Wait! Don't go down there!"* she cried at the top of her voice as she flew down the stairs.

A maid was waiting at the bottom, her eyes as wide as saucers at Sarah's unseemly behavior. "The basement workshop, where is it?" she demanded breathlessly.

The girl pointed wordlessly, and Sarah ran on, screaming Malloy's name.

They'd left the door standing open to the steep stairs that led downward. *"Malloy, stop! There's a bomb!"* she cried, jerking up her skirts and plunging down the steps.

She was halfway down when she saw Malloy at the bottom, looking up at her with the oddest expression on his face, and then the whole world exploded.

Epilogue

SARAH WALKED QUICKLY DOWN MULBERRY STREET, clutching her cape tightly against the cold. She'd spent the morning at the mission, and now she was trying to decide which was worse, not going to see Aggie at all or having to leave her after a visit. Both held their own special kind of pain. Lost in thought, she absently glanced at Police Headquarters as she passed, and was startled to see a familiar figure emerging from the front door.

Malloy hadn't seen her. He was too busy holding on to the railing with his uninjured hand as he descended the steep front steps. His other arm was in a sling, and he moved slowly and carefully, like a man who'd almost been blown to kingdom come. Sarah could only imagine how sore he must be from being thrown by the force of the explosion.

Without bothering to consider whether she was being too bold, Sarah crossed the street, dodging the piles of horse manure.

Malloy was still concentrating on the steps, but Tom, the doorman, recognized her from previous visits. "Good morning, Mrs. Brandt," he called cheerfully.

Malloy's head jerked up, and for a second she thought he might lose his balance, but he caught himself just in time.

"Good morning, Tom," she called back, stopping at the foot of the steps and looking up at Malloy. "And good morning to you, Detective Sergeant."

He didn't smile, but she could tell he was glad to see her just the same. "Stopping by to report a crime, Mrs. Brandt?" he deadpanned.

"I haven't seen one yet today," she teased right back. "But it's still early."

"Are you on your way to the mission?" he asked.

"No, just coming back. How's the arm doing?" she asked before he could inquire about Aggie. She didn't want to discuss Aggie on a public street.

He carefully took the remaining two steps before answering. "The doc said I was lucky it wasn't broke, but it hurts like a . . . it hurts a lot," he corrected himself.

"Sprains often take longer to heal than breaks," she told him sympathetically. "I guess your mother is making sure your cuts are doing well, too." He had several plasters visible at various places on his head and one on his face.

"She's driving me crazy," he grumbled, making Sarah smile. The old woman would be in her element tending to him.

"You're not back to work so soon, are you?" she asked.

"No, I . . ." He glanced at Tom and looked a little embarrassed. He took her elbow and directed her up the street, away from the doorman's eavesdropping and the prying eyes of the newspaper reporters stationed across the street from Police Headquarters. When they'd turned the corner onto Houston Street and were safely out of earshot, he said, "I just wanted to give Commissioner Roosevelt a full report."

"I hope he was suitably impressed that you managed to figure out what had happened," she replied.

"He would've preferred to find out the anarchists were behind it," Malloy said with a frown.

Sarah thought he was probably right. The Van Dykes would undoubtedly agree.

Malloy cleared his throat. "Quentin and I are pretty lucky you figured out the bomb was down in the cellar."

"I just wish I'd figured it out a few minutes sooner. Maybe you wouldn't have been hurt at all."

"A few seconds *later,* and Quentin would've walked through the door," he reminded her. "He would've taken the blast full in the face, exactly the way Van Dyke had planned it for Lilly." They had decided he was going to take her downstairs to show her the "surprise" gift. When the bomb exploded, killing her, everyone would assume it had been set to kill him, as the one in his office had been.

Instead, Quentin had just unlocked and opened the workshop door when they heard Sarah yelling. Malloy had walked over to the steps to see what was going on, and the valet had turned away from the door instead of stepping through it. He'd been injured, but he'd recover.

"Creighton is making sure he has the best medical care," Sarah told him. "The doctor doesn't think he'll have any permanent damage, just a few scars."

Malloy touched the plaster on his forehead. "I'll take a few scars any day."

"It was such a clever plan," Sarah marveled. "Van Dyke

would've blown up both his unfaithful wife and her lover with bombs people would have believed were meant for him."

"If he hadn't blown himself up first," Malloy reminded her. "What's going on with the rest of the Van Dykes?"

"The coroner finally released Mr. Van Dyke's body, so they're going to bury him tomorrow. They're hoping to do it before word gets out about what really happened. You were right about Creighton, too. He hired an excellent attorney, and Tad was released on bail. He also sent Lilly to their house in the country for now, but she won't be staying there long. He told her she's got to find her own lodgings because he wants her completely out of their lives."

"What about the other sets of lovers?" Malloy asked.

Sarah frowned. "Only one is going to live happily ever after, I'm afraid. Alberta and Mr. Reed are going to be married on Friday in a small, private ceremony. She asked me to stand up with her. Oh, and Creighton has asked Mr. Reed to manage the business for him, so his financial future is secure."

Malloy nodded, not really surprised. "Creighton wasn't able to convert Katya to capitalism, I guess."

"She didn't even give him a chance. During all the excitement after the explosion, she disappeared."

"But she was . . . not well," he protested.

"She was well enough to run away. Creighton went looking for her the instant he realized she was missing, but no one on the Lower East Side will tell him where she went."

"Did he check with Emma Goldman?" he asked, his voice hard when he said the woman's name.

"Apparently, she's left the city, too. Seems she didn't find midwifery very exciting, so she's gone on a lecture tour or something. Creighton hired a Pinkerton detective to find

Katya, but even if he does, I don't think she'll come back to him."

"I wonder if this will change Creighton's mind about her politics," Malloy said.

"I hope he'll at least remember his plans to make working conditions better at his father's factories."

Malloy gave her a look that warned her not to get her hopes up. They walked across the next street, dodging various vehicles and the inevitable piles on the cobblestones.

When they were safely on the sidewalk again, Malloy asked, "Did you see little Aggie today?"

"Yes, I . . ." Sarah sighed. "We have to decide what to do with her. She can't stay at the mission forever," she said, half-hoping he'd magically offer a solution.

"I was thinking," he began and then hesitated.

"What?" she prodded curiously.

"Well, she wouldn't think Brian was strange because he can't talk, would she? Since she doesn't talk either, I mean."

Sarah was so surprised, she almost bumped into a woman carrying a bundle of laundry. "No, I don't suppose she would," she agreed when she'd regained her balance.

She waited, but he didn't say anything, forcing her to prod him again. "What did you have in mind?"

He started to shrug one shoulder, then winced from the effort. She pretended not to notice. "I was thinking maybe she'd like to visit Brian sometime." He glanced down to check her reaction, then looked away again. "He'll need to get used to other kids if he's going to go to school."

Sarah could hardly believe she'd heard him correctly. "Oh, Malloy, you're going to send him to school!" she cried happily. "Which one did you choose? The one that teaches sign language?"

"Yeah, he'll start after Christmas." He glanced at her

again. "So, do you think Aggie would like to visit him? You'd have to bring her," he added, as if she might not have realized this.

Somehow she managed not to grin like a fool. "Aggie and I would be happy to visit Brian," she said. "And you," she added meaningfully.

This time when he looked down, he met her gaze squarely. And he smiled. "Good."

Author's Note

Readers often want to know where I get the ideas for my stories. Usually, they are the culmination of so many bits and pieces of information that I can never say for sure, but this book is different. The idea for *Murder on Marble Row* came from the newspaper! When I was researching the last book in the Gaslight Series, *Murder on Mulberry Bend,* I happened across a story in *The New York Times* on October 22, 1896, about a man being killed by a bomb in his office. Hamlin J. Andrus was the secretary of the Arlington Chemical Works, which his brother, John Emory Andrus, owned. He arrived at his office in Yonkers the morning of October 21, and a few minutes later, a bomb that had been planted under his writing desk exploded, killing him instantly.

The newspapers reported several theories about who might have planted the bomb. The most popular one blamed anarchists and theorized the bomb had actually been meant for John Andrus, who was a millionaire. One employee at the company claimed Hamlin Andrus had recently acquired the type of pipe used in building the bomb and theorized he'd been doing chemical experiments in his home workshop. Some thought the explosion might have been an experiment gone wrong, while others suggested Mr. Andrus had committed suicide.

As the ne'er-do-well younger brother, Hamlin Andrus had failed in several careers before his more successful brother gave him a job at Arlington. This gave rise to yet another theory, that the bomb really had been meant for John Andrus and his brother had been planting it when it accidentally exploded. Unfortunately, the case was never solved, perhaps because the real solution would have brought embarrassment to a rich and powerful family or perhaps because the police did such a poor job of investigation that the real killer could never be identified.

Whatever really happened that morning, I couldn't help seeing the parallel between what anarchists were doing in those days to draw attention to their cause and what terrorists are doing today. When I began researching the anarchists of the late nineteenth century, I naturally read about Emma Goldman, who is one of the most famous. Imagine my delight to learn that in November 1896, Miss Goldman had just returned from Vienna to the Lower East Side to work as a midwife. At that time, she actually lived in a German neighborhood on Eleventh Street with her lover, Ed Brady, and not in the tenement building with Katya and Creighton. She did find her work as a midwife unsatisfactory, however, and she soon began traveling the country and speaking for the anarchist cause.

John Emory Andrus continued to be a successful business-man after his brother's unfortunate death, and he also became a major philanthropist. His legacy, The Surdna Foundation (Andrus spelled backward), is now one of the largest charitable foundations in existence. John Andrus's son, also named Hamlin Andrus, became a football All-American from Princeton University.

I hope you enjoyed this book. If you missed the earlier books in the series, they are *Murder on Astor Place*, *Murder on St. Mark's Place*, *Murder on Gramercy Park*, *Murder on Washington Square*, and *Murder on Mulberry Bend*.

If you send me an e-mail, I will put you on my mailing list and send you a reminder when my next book, *Murder on Lenox Hill*, comes out. Contact me at: www.victoriathompson.com.

From national bestselling author

VICTORIA THOMPSON

THE GASLIGHT MYSTERIES

As a midwife in turn-of-the-century New York,
Sarah Brandt has seen pain and joy. Now she will work for
something more—a search for justice—in a cases of murder
and mystery that only she can put to rest.

MURDER ON ASTOR PLACE
0-425-16896-4

MURDER ON ST. MARK'S PLACE
0-425-17361-5

MURDER ON GRAMERCY PARK
0-425-17886-2

MURDER ON WASHINGTON SQUARE
0-425-18430-7

MURDER ON MULBERRY BEND
0-425-18910-4

"Tantalizing." —Catherine Coulter

AVAILABLE WHEREVER BOOKS ARE SOLD OR AT
WWW.PENGUIN.COM

(Ad # PC240)